I0603114

2016

"Son of Wales Award" for best new author and poet
"Excellence of Literature Award" for the outstanding achievement of
the epic autobiography *Cave Days*

2017

"Best Adventure Autobiography" for Great Britain and
Ireland King of the Castle Publishing.

"Best Adventure and Historical Award" for the outstanding novel
Gower of the Hills, King of the Castle Publishing

Al Cole Interview, CBS radio, People of Great Distinction book
interview for *Cave Days*, 2019

WHO WAS TALIATH SAREN?

KINGSLEY R. HILL

Copyright © 2021 by Kingsley Ross Hill

All rights reserved. Written permission must be secured from the publisher to use or reproduce any part of this book, except for brief quotations in critical reviews or article.

Published in Swansea Wales by King of the Castle Publishing.

ISBN 978-0-9879493-8-7 (paperback)
ISBN 978-0-9879493-9-4 (ebook)

Front Cover Artwork by Sylvia Nicholson, A Touch of Art, Victoria, BC

Unless otherwise noted, scripture quotations and verses are from the HOLY BIBLE, New Living Translation. Tyndale House Publishers, Inc. Copyright 2015

And New International Version Copyright, 1973, 1978, 1984 by International Bible Society. Used by permission of Zondervan Publishing House, all rights reserved.

To contact Kingsley Hill email at gowerofthehills@gmail.com

Book design by SpicaBookDesign, Victoria, BC

This book is dedicated to my Dad, Roger Elliot Fitzgerald Hill, who is one of Wales' great historians, and explorers.

And to my Brother, Fraser Mark Hill, who is my great friend and fellow explorer, may we walk many more miles together, and find many more artifacts that tell us many more wonderful stories of the past.

And to my Daughter Samantha, who travels with me to our sacred places near and far, and dances upon the emerald waters of lake and sea, where Dava the Butterfly flies with you and me, dancing to your wonderful music, Jade, play another song for me.

About the Author

Kingsley Ross Hill, was born near the city of Swansea, in Glamorganshire, South Wales and grew up in the village of Pennard, on the Gower Peninsula. [The word Pennard, means "village without a gate" in the Welsh language]. Kingsley, describes growing up in Pennard, and on the Gower Peninsula, as "living this most wonderful adventure, with no gates."

It is interesting that the Gower Peninsula Series, which includes the books, "Cave Days," "Gower Of The Hills," and "Nan's Nan," all give the reader, such a sense of freedom and adventure; like walking through a land without gates or fences. The authors books are full of mystery and adventure and are extremely accurate in their betrayal of the history and geography of the Gower Peninsula itself.

The author is humble about his many awards. I am pleased that he is becoming well known in his native Wales, and throughout the United Kingdom, and more recently in Canada and the United States, for his unique style of writing and poetry.

Kingsley Hill, lives with his family in Creston, British Columbia. He is also a pastor and counsellor and works in youth outreach.

Kingsley supports a number of charities and organizations through the sales of his books, and has inspired many young writers and poets in his native Wales, by giving them literary opportunities and awards. Kingsley Hill is an ex pupil of Gowerton Grammar School, in Gowerton, South Wales, and is developing into one of greatest writers of his generation.

Kingsley Ross Hill

Table of Contents

Chapter One

A Visit to Armes

My mother-in-law Helen made a cup of Rosie Lea, and we waited for my wife Gay and our daughter Melody to get home from visiting Gay's sister Pearl in Bristol. I heard a car coming up the driveway, and I stood up and looked out of the window.

"They're home," I said to Helen, who gulped down the last of her tea.

"How was your trip?" Helen said to Gay, who was carrying in a large bag of shopping. Melody followed carrying another bag, and she had a smile on her face.

"Guess what Dad?" she said. "What?" I replied, expectantly. "Did you get some cool clothes for school?" "Yes, look at these Dad, they are called Holey Jeans! They are made to look like they are worn," she said, "like on this leg there are three holes."

"I can't believe that you girls pay for holes in your jeans," Helen laughed, listening to our conversation. "I spend most of my time trying to keep my jeans new looking."

"They are cool," I said to Melody, restoring the smile to her face. "I remember when I holed my brand new Brutus Jeans by falling out of a tree, and my mother was not best pleased." Melody laughed and then showed me three tops she had bought.

"Aqua!" I said, "that is my favorite colour!" "I know Dad, that is why I bought this one. I'm going to wear my tops to school this week."

Gay now spoke after pouring herself a tea and asked Helen and I how the speed dating had gone. Gay had previously asked me to accompany her mum to a speed dating event that she would not go to on her own.

"I actually quite enjoyed it," Helen replied, "and I met some nice men, or at least they appeared nice. I liked one man in particular, and his name is Vince!"

"Well, we will have to invite him over for tea so that we can meet him," Gay replied. "Oh, he is here right now," Helen giggled looking right at me, and I burst into laughter!

"Am I missing something here?" Gay said, as she looked around the room for an elusive stranger named Vince. "Go on, you better explain yourself Vince," Helen said to me, "otherwise we won't hear the end of it." "Explain what?" both Gay and Melody said, looking at me with inquisitive looks.

…"You didn't Dad!" Melody exclaimed as she listened to my story. "You actually pretended to be someone else?" "Yes," I said, owning up to my transgression. "My name is Vince, and I am incredibly pleased to make your acquaintance." Gay now roared with laughter, and said, "I don't believe you did that; I wish I could have been there!"

"And one of the women fancied Vince," Helen said, unable to compose her straight face. "And she wanted to meet Kings after the speed dating, and even wanted his number!"

Gay now looked at me with a serious look, and said, "Helen wasn't the only one who had fun by the sound of it."

"You can't blame Dad for that Mum, you pushed him into it, and he was just trying to be authentic." Melody said, taking my side, "what else did you expect him to do?"

"Thanks Melody," I laughed, "I am glad you're in my corner!" Helen went on to share how the rest of her speed dating experience went and thanked Gay and I for persuading her to go.

After Helen left and Melody went to bed, I asked Gay how her weekend had gone with her sister Pearl.

"It was an amazing weekend, Kings! And I had such a great time connecting with my sister. We had this great conversation about our childhood, and growing up together, and I told her that I was adopted."

"Wow, that's huge! How did Pearl take it?"

"She felt hurt and disappointed that Mum and I had kept it from her all these years, but I did come away with something positive..."

"What was that?" I asked. "Pearl encouraged me to go and meet my birth mother. She thinks it will help me feel more complete, and I think she's right. I have always felt that a part of my life was missing, even before Mum told me that I was adopted. What do you think, my love?"

"Well, I think she's right. You would be able to piece that missing part of your life together if you met her, and a lot of questions that you may have in your heart might be answered."

"That's what I feel, Kings. I think it would really help me in my life if I met her, and for Melody's sake too. I don't want her finding out one day that Helen isn't her grandmother by birth. I want to be able to tell her. It's not that Helen won't always be my mum and Melody's grandmother. She always will be, no matter what I think of my birth mother."

"Yes, of course," I said. "Helen has been absolutely wonderful, and she will always be there for you and Melody, and you will be there for her."

Gay smiled. "It's been a good weekend for facing up to some things in my life, and Pearl has helped me to see a lot of things clearly that I haven't been dealing with." Gay paused for a moment. "Pearl was the one who encouraged me to come and meet you on the beach when you and Melody met at the Dragon Pool, and you were searching for me, remember?"

"Yes, I remember like it was yesterday, and you got Melody to wear the Evening Emerald necklace that I gave you."

"Yes, that's right, Kings. It's hard to believe that was only a few years ago. It feels like we have lived a lifetime together already."

"We have, and there are other lifetimes to live yet, my Princess."

"Oh, I love you so much, Kings!" Gay threw her arms around me, and I hugged her and kissed her lips.

"Kings, there's something I need to ask you."

"Yes, what is it?"

"Will you come and meet my birth mother with me? I think Mum knows where she lives, and I could not do it without you, Kings. Will you come with me?"

"Yes, of course I will. But there is something I need to tell you first."

"What is it, love?"

"Remember a few weeks ago when you were spending so much time translating Taliath's diary, and things were getting out of balance in our family life?"

"Yes, I remember, and I have put things right, haven't I?" For a moment, she looked worried.

"Yes, you have, absolutely," I replied, "but that's not why I brought it up. It's just that during that time, I went and spoke to Helen to have someone to talk to, and maybe get some advice on how I might better understand you."

"Understand me, Kings? You have always been able to understand me," she said, feeling threatened.

"Well, Helen told me about you being adopted, and I wondered why you hadn't told me. I went to visit your birth mother."

"You went to see my birth mother?!" Gay exclaimed. You went to see her without me! Why would you do that, Kingsley? It hurts me to know that you did that behind my back!" She began to cry.

"Helen only told me because she thought it might help me to understand you better."

"That's not the point, Kings, I thought that we talked about everything!"

"I thought that too, but then you didn't tell me that you were adopted; I had to hear it from Helen."

"I'm really upset, Kings! I need to go for a walk...alone!"

Gay got up from the couch and closed the door behind her. I watched her from the window as she crossed the road and walked up past the Heather Slade Café. She was probably heading for the Westcliff path. I'd give her an hour and then go and find her.

"At least I told her," I thought. And I felt like a weight had been lifted off my shoulders.

An hour went by, and I went out onto the cliffs to meet her. I found her on the clifftop overlooking Fox Hole Bay. It was a place where we would sit and watch the sunsets when we had first met.

"I knew you would come and find me here, Kings. I wanted you to come and find me, and I'm sorry I didn't tell you about my adoption. It must have hurt you when you heard it from Helen. It's an area of my life where I'm still wounded, and I didn't want you to think less of me."

"Less of you! I could never think any less of you because you were adopted! You are the most amazing woman in the world to me, and the love of my life! And I am sorry, for hurting you by going to see your birth mother without you. I didn't think that it might hurt you."

"Oh, Kings, what did I ever do to deserve you? I love you so much!"

After I had kissed her tears away, we enjoyed a wonderful conversation, and I was able to share my experience of meeting Armes, Gay's birth mother, at the commune. We walked back across the cliffs hand-in-hand to the house.

On Monday, I walked Melody to school and found myself standing in my old school yard.

⌒⌒

Suddenly, the years melted away, as I stood in front of the playground wall. It was here where my brother Fraser and I, along with our friends, Neil Herth, Christopher James, and Brien Thomas, used to kick the football against the wall. We named the game "fives," as each time a player missed hitting the wall with the ball, he clocked up a point against him. Five misses and he was out! The rest of us would carry on, and we would kick the ball in turn. Slowly, or quickly if you were playing badly, the points would add up to five, until only two players were left. The winner was the one who had the most kicks that hit the wall, which got to be quite a challenge as many kicks of the ball were taken from far distances and required a lot of power and accuracy to reach the wall.

Suddenly I was woken from my short daydream, as Melody tugged my hand and said, "Come on, Dad, it's time to find my classroom."

And as we walked through the corridors of Pennard School, those forgotten familiar halls and classrooms all seemed smaller than when I was a boy who walked these corridors with my classmates, waiting for the lunch buzzer or the end-of-school bell to sound. Then we could once again walk on the green, green grass of the playground, and watch the pretty girls skipping in their short dresses and playing their girly games – that were incomprehensible to us rough-and-ready boys.

Mother said that they were just like us, only they played with different toys. And we pretended not to like them, but I loved them, lipstick and all! And to impress Gillian Lowner, I pretended I had more muscles than I did, and I stood up tall. Come on, Kings, she would say, kick us the ball.

The end-of-the-break buzzer would sound, and I realized, yes, I was only dreaming! For Gillian already had a boyfriend, and in the school, there was that sad old teacher, and that big-nosed prefect, and the glad old headmaster – and back to the classroom I would go, until the lunch buzzer sounded, and again I'd play in the green, green playground of home.

Today the buzzer sounded, and we found Melody's classroom, and her new teacher, Mrs. Howels, sat her down in the second row.

"I used to sit here in the back row, Melody," I said, and then it was time for me to go.

"Bye, Melody, see you this afternoon."

"Bye, Dad, I love you."

"Love you too, my skate spearing girl."

For the next few weeks, we all settled back in to work and school, and Gay organized a weekend when she and I would go and visit her birth mother, Armes, at the commune in West Wales.

Helen offered to stay at the house with Samantha and Melody, but she was feeling insecure about Gay and I going.

"Try not to worry," I reassured Helen. "I'll bring Gay back safely. And remember what I said: Armes will never take your place in Gay's life."

The weekend to visit Armes arrived and Gay and I drove to the commune. Arwydd, the same woman who had previously met me at the gate, came to meet us. She bowed to us both, and then, having remembered my name, she said, "Hello, Kingsley, it's nice to see you again. Welcome back to our commune and settlement."

"Thank you, Arwydd. This is my wife Gay."

"Pleased to meet you, Gay," she said. "Armes has spoken of you and has been looking forward to you coming."

After we had bowed our heads, Arwydd walked us through the fields towards the settlement.

"I'm nervous, Kings," Gay said. "What if Armes doesn't like me and we don't get along?"

"She will like you," I reassured her. "She asked me to bring you, and I know you will like her because she reminded me of you."

Arwydd pointed out the different buildings along the way and what they were used for – most of which I remembered – and we soon arrived at the main commune area.

"Look at the stone huts," Gay whispered excitedly, "and that one has a thatched roof."

"And I wonder what those pale pink buildings are used for…?" she added.

"I don't remember," I replied. "I can't recall being told."

"This is amazing!" Gay continued. "They have built a whole little village settlement here, and everyone has bowed to us, my love. Do you think Arwydd has some special tribal status?"

"That is what I thought at first, but I think people bow to each other just to show honor and respect. Even Armes bows to other people."

Arwydd now led us to one of the large stone buildings that was in the middle of the settlement, and she rang the bell on the side of the door.

"I remember this place," I whispered, as we waited for someone to open the door. Just like before, it took some time before anyone answered. Finally, two women came to the door. They said something in the Celtic language to Arwydd, and then beckoned Gay and I to follow them along a dark corridor.

"I remember this corridor also," I said to Gay, "It's creepy. Wait till you see the statues and the faces on the wall."

Gay held my hand tightly as we followed along, and every so many yards there were candles burning on the wall, and frightening stone faces glared at us from behind the candles light.

"Oh my gosh," Gay whispered, "this is like something out of Taliath's diary."

Gay then commented on the two guides in front of us. "These women are only wearing thongs and sandals, and the thongs are very much like the leather Surth that we found in the chest."

I looked down at the women's feet, and they were both wearing ankle bracelets and toe rings, and they were bare breasted like the two women who had first led me down the corridor. Suddenly we reached a large statue that stood in the middle of the corridor, and we followed our guides around one side of it and continued on our way.

Gay looked back at the statue, just as I had done, and then said, "I think it's a statue of a temple priest; his face looks so evil, and he's got a dagger or knife in his hand."

"You have been translating too many Clan Queen books," I teased.

And Gay replied, "It's funny, Kings, I am getting nervous again. That statue had a bad energy to it – I could feel it."

One of the women now turned around and said something we could understand. "We are almost at Armes' quarters," she said, and then she continued walking. Finally, we arrived at the room with the large wooden door. "This is it," I whispered to Gay. "I remember this door."

One of the women rang a bell. Gay took some deep breaths as we waited, and I assured her that everything would be alright.

The heavy door creaked open, and Armes stood before us. She was dressed in a long silky gown with Celtic designs on the front. Her eyes were penetrating and bright, as she looked intently at Gay and I.

"Welcome," she said, bowing to us both individually, and we both lowered our heads in respect. She said something in the ancient language to the other two women, who bowed to Gay and I and then excused themselves to walk back down the corridor.

"Do come in," Armes said, "I am so glad you have come." Then she led us to the same large waiting room where I had waited before.

"I won't be long," she said, and she disappeared behind the big purple curtain. She came back with a bottle of wine and three glasses, and she lit three more candles in the room. It seemed awkward at first, as the three of us sat there amidst long periods of silence, or maybe it was just me who felt awkward in the silence. As I looked across at Gay, she gave me a smile to let me know that she was feeling alright.

Slowly, we all began to talk, and Armes asked us where we lived on the Gower Peninsula. She asked about Melody, and Gay described our daughter, with me adding a comment or two. The awkwardness turned to comfort, and Gay and I soon felt like honoured guests.

After we had finished our wine, Armes asked us if we would enjoy a Celtic bath. Gay and I looked at one another, and then we both agreed. We had never had a Celtic bath before, and we wondered what it entailed.

"There are two types of baths that we have here at the commune," Armes explained. "We have one for married or hand-fast couples, and another for single inter-ceremonial individuals."

"What do you mean by 'hand-fast' couples?" Gay asked.

"Once a year during our celebration of Lammas ["Loafmass"], which is held on August the 1st, trial marriages or partnerships are permitted at the settlement for a period of one year. If the couple is not compatible within a year and a day, then the marriage or partnership may be dissolved. Also, if a child is born here at the commune, they are usually only here until 5 years of age and then must leave."

"Why must they leave?" I asked.

"The law requires that a child must attend a school out in the general community, and we don't encourage homeschooling here at the settlement, as we just don't have the room for families, plus we are accountable to the education organizations that oversee homeschooling curriculums. We are a Celtic Commune, which is classified as an alternative living community, so we are very careful to avoid scrutiny from mainstream society. It's not that we do anything wrong or hide our beliefs in the way we live, but each member here at the settlement must abide by our own laws and cultural values.

"Thank you, that answers my question and more," I said.

"I have one more question," Gay said.

"Yes, what is it?" Armes asked.

"What is meant by 'single inter-ceremonial individuals'?"

"Everyone here at the commune is required to participate in our ceremonies. We have 32 different ceremonies that we participate in throughout the year. A lot of our ceremonies are sexual in orientation and expression, and single inter-ceremonial individuals are able to participate in certain ceremonies with different partners. Married or Lammas partner couples only participate in ceremonies with one another, unless a private ceremony is occurring in a private residence between couples. All private ceremonies must be given by permission of the residing commune Priestess or Bard."

"I'm sure you will have a lot more questions, and I'm happy to answer them as I can. Meanwhile, let me go and organize your Celtic bath. I think you will both find it relaxing and enjoyable."

Armes then left the room, which gave Gay and I some time to talk.

"What do you think so far?" I asked.

"She doesn't look like how I imagined her. She is a lot younger, and attractive. But I don't know what she's got herself into, Kings? I hope this place is not some kind of cult organization."

"Yes, to hear her talk about the commune being an 'alternative living community' and there being 32 different ceremonies that people participate in … it makes me wonder what it's all about," I said. "What is the attraction, apart from learning and living the Celtic way of life?"

"Well, that's just it, Kings. I think people are interested in how the ancient Celts lived, and they want to experience what it was like to live in their culture – just like you and I are interested in experiencing their ways. But there seems to be a focus on sensuality and sexual experience, don't you think?" Gay asked.

"And the population at the commune is mainly women," Gay continued before I could answer. "I haven't seen a male person under fifty. I have noticed there are more women than men, Kings, it got me thinking why? I don't have a problem with people being sensual and expressing their sexuality in ceremonies, and in their everyday lives, but it is rather strange that if they are a 'community', then why don't they embrace the whole family unit, as the Celts did in their culture? I mean you and I know enough about Celtic life and community by what we have studied through our translation of Taliath's diary. The Celts valued fertility, childbirth, and family life greatly! They even had celebrations and ceremonies that focused on pregnancy and birth, and men of course were a big part of that."

"You're right – just consider the Celtic Balwyn Festival," I said. "It's a festival that they celebrate here, according to their list of ceremonial practices."

"The Celts had a bold approach to sexuality," I continued. "If a woman did not conceive with her partner, she could take another lover at the Balwyn Festival. Many children must have come from these once-a-year pairings. The whole focus of this festival was on fertility, and you needed men for that!"

"And couples went to wells and river sources, where women could stimulate their fertility. Couples would make love on special spots like the phallus of the Cerne Abbas Giant in Dorset," [and I have read that this still happens to this day, in spite of the fences].

Gay laughed and said, "We must try it, my love, on the Gower."

"Anytime you like," I replied, and we laughed some more. "Anywhere where the landscape mimics the contours of a woman's body, such as the Paps of Anu in Ireland."

"Where did you learn this, Kings?"

"Dad studied their different cultural practices, and he passed on some of his knowledge to me."

"I'm impressed – you will have to tell me more."

Armes now returned to take us to our bath.

"Follow me this way," she said, and we followed her back down the long dark corridor until we came to another doorway that neither Gay nor I had previously noticed. It led outside the building to an open field. It was nice to be out in the sunlight again, as the waiting area where we had been sitting was rather dark and gloomy, even when Armes lit more candles.

As we walked across the field, there were cows and a large barn with hay bales and a tractor. This was obviously on the other side of the settlement buildings. I had not noticed any of this on our approach to the commune from the other side.

"Do you work the land for food for the commune?" I asked, wondering if they ran a small farm for food and produce.

"We do," Armes, replied. "We have milking cows and goats, several chicken pens, and as you can see in the adjacent field, we have three large greenhouses for growing vegetables all year round."

"That looks like beehives over there," Gay said, pointing.

"Yes," Armes continued, "we have several hives for honey. And we also have thirty sheep in one of the other fields, as some of our women spin the wool and make our clothes."

"I hadn't realized that the settlement had so much land," I said. "How many acres do you have in total?"

"We have twenty three acres in total, with a large pond and several old farm buildings, including the original farmhouse that was built in 1901." I kept looking around for the building that presumably we were going to have our bath in.

At the top of the field, we came to a wooden sty, and we climbed over it into the next field. "It's not much further," Armes said, "just a few hundred yards."

But there was still no building in sight. "Where were we going to have this sacred Celtic Bath – underneath the stars maybe?"

"Hush," Gay said, "or she will hear you."

"There it is," Armes, said, pointing to the middle of the field. And I was not far wrong – we were under the moon and stars! There was a circle of nine stones, about ten and a half meters in diameter, and they reminded me of the nine-stone circle, known as the 'Nine Ladies of Stanton Moor' in Derbyshire. My dad took me to see it one day, when we were metal detecting for artifacts. We found an ancient urn used for cremation, and it even had pieces of bone still inside. And the Nine Ladies of Stanton Moor surrounded the burial site, and they stood like grief-stricken mourners looking on. But back to the present time... In the middle of the circle of stones was a natural hot spring pool.

"This is amazing!" Gay said, "A hot water spring in the middle of a field!" As we arrived at the circle of stones, we could see the steam from the spring rising into the cooler air, and there was a small bench to sit on. But nothing else – did we just strip off and jump in?

"Would you like a male or female body servant?" Armes, asked.

Gay and I looked at each other, a little surprised.

"I recommend Heulyn," Armes, said. "She will attend to you both very well."

Gay still didn't know what to say, so I spoke up. "Please send Heulyn," I said. "If you recommend her, I'm sure she will provide good service for us."

"Sit down and make yourselves comfortable," Armes said, "and Heulyn will be along shortly."

"Provide good service… " Gay echoed back to me, not sarcastically, but with a concerned tone in her voice.

"Well, I didn't know what to say," I replied. "I thought it would be best to agree to whomever Armes recommended, not having had a body servant before."

"I'm sorry, Kings, I wasn't ridiculing your answer. I'm just concerned regarding what we are getting into. If this is a cult, I definitely want out!"

"I am with you on that," I said, "but for now, I think we should try and keep focused on the reason we are here. It is not to join the commune, or even to see if this is a cult-like operation. That we will find out soon enough, but we are here so that you can have the opportunity to meet your birth mother."

"Yes, thank you, Kings, but you would think she would have asked to speak to me by now, don't you think? Not just making small talk and telling us all about the commune."

"Give her a chance," I responded. "She is probably as nervous as you are, and this might be her way of opening up to you, by showing you how she lives and what her life is like here at the settlement."

"I know, Kings, thank you for trying to keep me focused. I guess I'm just really nervous. I have all these questions floating around in my head that I want to ask her. I want her to tell me about things. Like why did you leave me when I was a baby? Why did you give me away?"

"Listen, love, if this is too much, we can leave any time. But I know, and I believe you know inside, that you need to do this! If you don't, you will regret it, and the regret, and not knowing why, will keep you in a place of captivity, and that affects all of us – Samantha, Melody and I, and Helen too. We all love you, and we want you to be happy and free in your life. You have shown a lot of courage coming here to meet Armes. You have come this far, don't give up now!"

"Oh Kings, I love you so much! I don't know what I'd do without you. Thank you for encouraging me – I will stay and keep focused on what I came here to do."

"Hey, I think that must be Heulyn," I said, pointing to a figure walking toward us across the field.

"I think so," Gay said. "She is wearing a dress or a gown, and she's carrying what looks like towels and a bag of some kind."

As the figure got closer, we could see that it was a woman with long wavy hair, and she was carrying a large bag made of some sort of material, probably wool from one of the sheep, and she had towels over her shoulders.

"I am Heulyn," she said, and after putting the bag on the grass, she bowed to us both, and then placed the towels on two of the standing stones around the circle.

"I shall undress you first," she said to Gay, and she asked me to sit back on the bench. Gay was hesitant at first and she wanted to undress herself, but after looking back at me in protest, she allowed Heulyn, to remove her clothes. Seeing that Gay was nervous, Heulyn, told us some of the history of the spring.

"It was first recorded as being used for a bathing pool in the 9th century," she said, "by a Celtic Clan that had a small settlement within a mile of here, and they used the pool for bathing and ceremonial rituals."

"What is the bottom of the pool like to step on?" I asked, as Gay stood poised to walk in.

"The bottom is clay, and large flat stones have been placed close together over the clay, so it is flat and smooth to stand on. The four stones in the middle of the pool mark where the spring pushes up through the ground, so the closer you stand to the stones, the more life energy springs forth. Many of our commune members come here for healing ceremonies, which take place at certain times and seasons throughout our calendar."

Gay slowly walked towards the center of the pool, which started off with a step down into about two feet of water, and then gradually became deeper up to her waist.

"Its lovely," Gay called out. "The energy in here is fantastic! And there is a mineral substance in the water – it feels so soft on my skin. The stone feels like slate on the bottom of my feet – it's flat and smooth." And she continued walking toward the center stones.

"If you walk to the far side of the pool around the stones, there are two stone seats carved out of rock," Heulyn explained, and Gay sat down on one of the stone seats.

"This is wonderful," she called out, and she encouraged me to join her.

Heulyn soon had me undressed and I walked across the pool to join Gay. The water was surprisingly hot and swirled around my body as I sat on the other stone seat next to Gay.

"Oh, this is great!" I called out to Heulyn, who pulled a bottle out of her bag and poured its contents into the pool. Soon there was a lovely smell of lavender in the steam that rose from the center of the pool like a low cloud. The water began to have a smooth texture that was silky on the skin, and I stood behind Gay and rubbed her back.

"Oh, that's wonderful, my love!" she whispered, and she closed her eyes and enjoyed the lavender in the steam.

"Its lavender and honey oil," Heulyn called from the bank, as she undressed to join us in the pool. She carried two skin cloths on her shoulders, and as Gay and I stood up, she washed each of us with the cloths. Then she massaged our backs as we sat on our stone thrones in the bubbling water.

After finishing our massages, she walked back to the bank and then took a bottle of wine and two glasses from her bag.

"This is a raspberry and gooseberry wine that we make here at the commune," she said, walking back toward us. Gay and I sat up on our thrones, and she poured us a large glass each. It was dry and fruity. "Nice!" Gay exclaimed, which obviously pleased Heulyn. She was clearly taking great pride in being our servant.

"Don't drink too much," she warned. "It's a strong wine, and the pool is hot, and the combination can make you feel a little shaky and light-headed. You can finish the rest of the bottle when you come out of the pool."

Heulyn was certainly taking good care of us. It was

indeed a strong wine, and Gay and I both felt completely relaxed as Heulyn then requested that we come out of the pool.

As we left the pool, Heulyn was waiting for us with two large towels, and she dried both of us from neck to toe. She then gave me a woven tunic to wear, and I sat down on the bench beside the pool while she oiled Gay's body with what smelled like honey.

"This is a honey and rose oil," Heulyn explained, "which we make here at the commune, with an olive oil base. It will moisten your skin and is used for healing," she said, and as Gay put on her tunic, I breathed in the enticing aroma of her body.

As Gay sat on the bench next to me, it was now my turn, and I stood up and faced Heulyn. Heulyn removed my tunic and began oiling my back and shoulders. It felt rich and smooth, and the scent of honey and rose was strong but not overbearing.

"We use this oil in our fertility ceremonies, and as part of a new commune member's inauguration," Heulyn remarked.

Once Heulyn had finished oiling my body, she put my tunic back on, and she asked Gay and I to follow her across another field to a large stone building. It looked like an old farmhouse, and it had several smaller buildings and what looked like to be an old barn adjacent to the farmhouse.

It was, indeed, a farmhouse, Heulyn told us, "and it had been built in 1901. And then the property continued as a working farm until 1971, which was when it had been sold to the founding members of the commune. We have used it ever since," she said.

Heulyn led us upstairs to a quaint bedroom with high ceilings and classic designs on the plaster. A large oak canopy bed stood before us, and candles burned on large wooden stands around the bed. A fine see-through curtain hung down from the top of the canopy, giving the bed a more sacred and secluded feel to it. A harp with a high-back chair behind it stood in the corner, and there was a large metal wine rack that displayed several different wines. There was also a chaise lounge, and what looked to be a small walnut table with two wine glasses on it. It sat in front of a large arched window with a view across the fields.

I took Gay's hand and we sat on the chaise while Heulyn poured us the rest of the wine that we had started in the hot spring.

Heulyn pulled on a string that hung down from the canopy of the bed, and one side of the bed curtains lifted to show white sheets with their tops folded down, and an animal fur bed cover. As Gay and I sat on the chaise lounge and sipped our wine, Heulyn leaned over the bed and pulled the sheets back.

"Everything has been prepared for us," Gay whispered, as her eyes scanned the room.

"I think Armes must have organized it," I replied, and Gay began to have that wonderful blush come over her face. Before I could say anything else, Heulyn had opened another bottle of wine and offered us another glass, which we eagerly received, given that the raspberry and gooseberry wine had been excellent.

"This is some of our last year's stock of blackberry wine," Heulyn said as she filled our glasses. It is wonderful, both Gay and I exclaimed, as our dedicated servant played us Celtic music on the harp.

It was so romantic, sipping our wine and looking lustfully into each other's eyes, and Heulyn played so beautifully. Gay and I were completely relaxed and desiring one another as Heulyn stopped playing the harp and went into a side room.

"Shall we climb into bed, my love...?" Gay asked, looking excitedly into my eyes.

"Yes," I replied, "but we should wait for our body servant."

"Oh gosh," Gay whispered, "I am dripping wet in anticipation already. What do you think she is going to have us do next? She is not going to watch us, is she? You can see through these curtains. I wonder if she is going to come back into the room..."

I answered with a slow gentle kiss and said, "I don't know, my love, let's wait and see."

To our surprise, our body servant returned to the bedroom wearing only a thong, or leather 'Surth,' as Gay now calls them, and she had a small wooden box in her hand. Gay was speechless and just looked at me, not knowing what to say. Heulyn pulled out two ankle bracelets from the box, and she explained that it was the custom for a couple to wear them here at the commune.

"I won't ask you to wear anything else," she said, "I shall just show you how to fit the bracelets to your ankles. Once you have your bracelets on, then you may enter a Covenant Love Ceremony."

Heulyn kneeled in front of Gay and massaged her feet with scented oil. The oil smelled like a type of flower, but not lavender, and Gay began to relax again as our servant placed the bracelet around her ankle. Then Heulyn knelt in front of me and massaged my feet and rubbed them with oil, just as she had done with Gay, but when it came to fitting the bracelet to my ankle, she said that Gay was required to do this.

Our servant explained that when entering into a love ceremony, the woman was required to put the bracelet onto the man's ankle, and this was how she communicated to the ceremonial Priest or Priestess that this man was her chosen partner. If the woman refused to put the bracelet on the man's ankle, then this signaled to the Priest or Priestess that the woman's desire was to reject this partner and not have him participate in the ceremony with her. The man was then escorted from the room, and the woman was free to choose another partner.

Gay knelt in front of me, and with her eyes fixed on mine, she fitted the bracelet on my ankle, and we waited for further instructions.

Heulyn now asked Gay to stand up and to stand still in front of her while she removed her tunic. She then told Gay that she could enter the covenant bed. She did the same with me and I climbed into bed. Once we were both in bed, Heulyn lowered the curtain from the canopy, and then she sat and played the harp while Gay and I made love.

We had both been wonderfully stimulated by our whole experience with Heulyn. Our bath at the hot spring had been divine, and to experience Heulyn as our body servant was something that had added so much pleasure to our visit to the commune already … and there was still more to come.

Heulyn played the harp so sweetly, and Gay and I made such beautiful love, and then with the harp still playing we climaxed together, our shouts of pleasure rising higher than the music, and traveling across the still autumn fields. We lay in each other's arms trembling and glowing, until Heulyn stopped playing the harp, and the cool evening air breathed through the open window of our stone room.

"Stay as you are," Heulyn called from across the room. All was quiet for what seemed like a long time, and then the curtain of our bed was opened, and Heulyn stood at our bed-side with a basin of hot scented water. She then gently washed and dried us from our necks to our feet.

Then she climbed onto the bed and gave us both a lovely massage, from front to back, from our faces to our toes. After-ward, Heulyn had Gay climb out of bed and she dressed her in Celtic evening wear, and then she did the same for me.

Heulyn led us out of the farmhouse and back across the fields to the main settlement buildings. As Gay and I walked across the peaceful fields, we talked about the joys of the day that we would never forget, and each time we thanked Heulyn for her wonderful care of us, she would humbly turn, hold her hands together, and bow to us.

When we arrived back at Armes' living quarters, Armes had made a beautiful meal for us. The three of us sat and ate together, and Gay and I shared the pleasures of our day with Armes, who was clearly happy that we had enjoyed ourselves so much. And we told her what a wonderful body servant Heulyn had been. Then Armes shared that Heulyn had spent the last six months training to be a body servant. Gay and I had been the first couple she had served.

After supper, I left Gay and Armes so they could talk and visit alone, and I was given permission to walk back across the fields to take another look at the old farmhouse and buildings.

Old farmhouses have held an interest for me since I was a young boy, and my grandparents had told me many stories of their two farms, one where my father had grown up, and another where he worked as a farmhand in his teenage years.

My Grandma and Grandpa had owned and operated Reigate Farm in Surrey, England, which was my father's home during the years of the Second World War. My father was too young to fight in the war, so he worked on the farm with my grandparents, who raised animals and grew crops to feed the country. During the day, my grandfather worked in the home office in London, and he was accountable to Winston Churchill as a liaison with home security and the RAF Fighter Command.

I grew up hearing the stories of the squadron scrambles, as the Spitfires got quickly airborne and intercepted the German bombers coming in over the Channel. My dad played with his tin soldiers in an air raid shelter at the bottom of the garden, and one day a German pilot landed his parachute through my grandfather's greenhouse. As the story goes, my grandmother chased the German around the field with a pitchfork, until the big black bull chased the pair of them back to the farmhouse, where my grandmother made a pot of tea for them both as they licked their wounds together. When my grandfather arrived home, he was not best pleased to find my grandmother having a cuppa tea with a member of the German Luftwaffe.

My grandfather said "Hello," and the pilot said "Hiel Hitler!" And once again the German found himself being chased around the field with a pitchfork, but they only got as far as the bull.

It was a good thing that Grandma had kept the teapot warm, because then it was tea for three.

"And you've broken the bloody greenhouse, can't you see!"

"Sorry old chap, I didn't mean to drop in on you like this. But now that I'm here, I'd love a cuppa tea."

Back to our story today.

The evening fields were quiet, apart from the call of a distant wood pigeon, that seemed to announce my arrival at the farm. The farmhouse itself was typical of a turn-of-the-19th-century building.

It is important to remember that we knew very little about farming in this country until the arrival of the Saxons, who were great farmers in their own land before they came here to Britain with their fellow tribes of Angles and Jutes. That's right, I said "Jutes," not Germans crashing through the greenhouse!

In the Saxon farmhouses, which were built of wood and thatched with straw, the stalls for horses were placed on one side and the stalls for cows on the other side. The manservants slept in a hayloft over the horses and the maidservants over the cows. The master of the house and his family lived in a few rooms at one end, and for many years farmhouses were built in this simple way, with the cattle, the servants, and the farmer's family all living and sleeping in a long narrow barn or shed. As time went on, other materials began to take the place of wood in all kinds of buildings, and the oldest standing farmhouses today are of stone, flint, or rubble in a massive framework of timber.

In the old days, and in many communities here in Wales today, the material that is nearest at hand is most often used for the building of cottages, farms, manor houses, castles, and churches. And in the farmhouse here at the commune, the house is made of stone. There used to be an old stone quarry less than eight miles from here. And some of the locals in the nearby villages can recall stories from their family ancestry of building stones being transported by horse and cart to make local cottages and farmhouses. We will talk a little about the local stone designs unique to "Cardiganshire cottages" a little later.

I hope that you enjoy my little off-cuts, dear reader, to take you down some of the little paths and lanes of history, because often the main roads of today just pass them by, without us meeting or knowing our friends of yesteryear. Farm doorways are often large and strong, and frequently have little porch seats on each side. And as I stood in front of the farm here at the commune today, I could see a porch seat on each side of the large door. Armes, or one of her settlement members, had placed a large flowerpot with flowers on each of the stone seats, which are very welcoming to the visitor approaching the house. This evening, honeybees still buzzed around the fragrant flowers.

In some farms, the kitchens are of great size, with the open fireplace occupying the whole of one side. When Heulyn had escorted Gay and I into the farmhouse earlier, we had passed by the rooms, and only walked through the hallway on our way to the stairs and up to the bedroom. So, I opened the doors and had a look around. The large door to the right as one first enters the hallway from the front door leads to the kitchen. Right away, I saw a large open fireplace that occupied most of one side of the kitchen. There were several large logs of wood sitting on one side of the fireplace, ready to be burned in the hearth. There were large pots and pans hanging from hooks and chains, ready to cook hot food for the commune.

And according to Armes, only the farmhouse, and one other common room area in the whole commune, had electric power. So, this kitchen and stove would be well used. One last thing to mention about the farmhouse, is that there is a wonderful old water trough, which fills up from a natural spring and well here in the farmyard. This spring and well is obviously a great asset for a year-round supply of water, which is essential to sustain a settlement of this size.

The light was fading fast now, as I made my way back across the fields. In the distance I could see the dim light of a fire and people sitting around it. And I wondered how Gay and Armes had got on together. My earliest observation was that Armes seemed more interested in showing Gay and I around the settlement and wanting us to experience what life was like here living at the commune. Not that this was not a part of Armes disclosing herself to her daughter, but I thought Armes might have been more personable with Gay on a one-to-one basis. That is just my perception of things, though, and maybe she had spent some one-to-one quality time with Gay while I had been checking out the farmhouse.

I climbed over the wooden stye, which led me back to the field closest to the main settlement buildings. As I had seen from a distance, there were people sitting around the campfire, and they were singing songs in the ancient Celtic language. I recognized Heulyn as she was playing her harp, and the people were all dressed in brightly coloured garments that had a gold thread through the material that was illuminated by the flames of the fire. I watched from a nearby tree that I was leaning against, as they got up and danced around the fire, and I could see that they were wearing rings, necklaces and bracelets that were illuminated on their bodies, like the gold weave in their dresses. It was enchanting to watch them, and I could sense this energy of "simplicity and spiritedness" as they danced holding hands. And the gold necklaces around their throats twinkled like stars in a night sky, and I had this strong urge to go and join them.

One woman, who was aware of me standing and watching from under the tree, reached out her hands and beckoned me to come and join them. I wanted to, but I felt awkward in some way, like I didn't fit in. I would come across as self-conscious in my demeanor or in the way I was dressed. So, I called out thankyou to the woman and bowed my head, and then I continued my way to meet Gay and Armes.

Gay and Armes were standing outside one of the buildings talking when I arrived, and I was pleased to see it was just the two of them together. I so wanted Gay to have a good connection with her birthmother – it would mean so much to her.

"Hello, you two," I said. "How was your time together? I enjoyed looking at the old farmhouse."

"We have been getting on great, Kingsley," Armes, said. And Gay had a broad smile on her face, so I knew that their time had gone well. After talking with Armes for a few minutes, Gay and I retired for the evening. All the fresh air and walking had made us tired, and our bath in the hot spring had been so relaxing.

Armes had prepared a room for us near hers, which was across the hall. It was a quaint little room, and there was an old-fashioned high bed with a carved wooden headboard and bedposts. A honey-lilac oil, made at the commune, was heated in an incense burner by one of the candles that gave our only light, apart from some still moonlight that made the fields look silver from our one little window. When we looked out, the night clouds marched toward us from the distant hills like Celt warriors returning home to their clan.

We sat at our window and reminisced about our extra-ordinary day. We had learned so much. As the moon rose higher in the sky, we could see in the distant field the circle of stones where we had taken our sacred bath.

Our ancestors made stone circles to mark the movements and interactions of the sun and moon. My father said that the Celts could hear the moon and sun conversing in the night sky.

"They understood that what happens in the heavens affects us here on the earth, and they saw the moon as a focus for extraterrestrial energies," my father would say. Gay and I sometimes discussed the time between day and night, when we as humans can actually feel the earth's energy 'shift.'

This is something the Celts did not just feel; they understood its meaning in relation to the changes that the moon and sun, with their shifting lights and energies, made upon the earth and its peoples.

The Celts believed that when the moon was high, it was a good time to plant seeds; and when it was low, it was time to harvest. This is practiced by biodynamic farmers to this day.

The druids would make lunar calculations to advise people when to make a journey or when to conceive a child. My father once told me that an archeologist friend of his, while out on a dig, found the remains of a bronze-age body in a grave with a disc on its chest. The disc had seven notches on it, which may have been used to make astrological predictions.

Gay and I often go for walks at the time of the full moon, and we notice the effects of the moonlight. How it transforms the world, how strangely bright it is, and how strong the moon shadow is. And the more time we spent in the moonlight, the more I turned into a werewolf! Just joking, dear reader.

The more defined our lunar consciousness becomes, the more we become aware of the rhythms and cycles in the sky and in our bodies.

Gay was too excited to wait until morning to show me what Armes had given her. We opened a bottle of pure apple juice that had been placed at our bedside along with a block of goat cheese and biscuits. And there was a little bell that we were to ring if we needed anything. Heulyn would still be our servant in the morning, Armes had told Gay. We just had to ring the bell when we got up.

As I poured Gay a glass of juice, she showed me what Armes, had given her. It was a set of Celtic body jewelry that had belonged to Armes' grandmother. Each piece was made of pure gold, and Armes' grandmother had been given the collection by her mother, on the occasion of her annunciation ceremony, when she became of age to learn the disciplines of becoming a Priestess.

"Wow! It has been in your family for over four generations! And that's just what we know so far," I proclaimed excitedly.

"And look at these pieces, they are so beautiful!" Gay beamed as she saw my excitement, and I was so happy for her that Armes was reaching out to her.

"Look at this neck bracelet, Kings! Put it on me and see how beautiful it is."

It felt cold and heavy as I fastened it around Gays slender neck, and it was a perfect fit. She smiled at me again as she stood in front of the mirror while I fitted on her two large earrings, both of which had Celtic symbols carved on them. Next there were two arm bracelets, also with symbols on them. And as she held her arms up in front of the mirror, I delighted at the look of pride and joy on her face.

"You look like a beautiful Priestess," I said, my spirit rising to the joy I could feel emanating from her being.

"I do look good, don't I," she replied, as she swirled around in her long Celtic gown.

Her gown was a pure white, with gold flowered designs and stitching around the bottom edges, a perfect accent to her jewelry that shone on her suntanned skin.

Next, I put on her ankle bracelet and a toe ring, which she imagined were just like the ones Taliath had described in her diary.

"This ankle bracelet is gold, though, not iron like Taliath and her sisters wore to be identified with their clan," I reminded her, and I pointed out the emblems that were carved on the anklet and the toe ring.

"I want to make love in all my jewelry," she declared, as she swirled again in front of the mirror and then danced around the room. "I want to christen my jewelry."

And that is what we did. We made a celebration of our love as she lay dressed in all of her jewelry and nothing else, and then we lay spent and tangled until morning.

Chapter Two

Ring the Morning Bell

As we lay giggling and talking for what seemed like a long time, we wondered what new experiences this day would bring. We were greatly enjoying our time here at the commune, and Gay was getting to know Armes. The highlight for me had been our bath in the hot spring yesterday, and sitting at our little window together last night, looking out over the moonlit fields.

Armes had arranged to show Gay more of the commune today, and she had invited her to sit in on one of her teaching commitments. Armes was teaching a course on how to become a Bard or "file" [an Irish Poet-Seer].

"Not that I'm interested in becoming a Bard," Gay said, "but it will be interesting to hear Armes teach, and for her to have me there."

"I think it would mean a lot to her to have you there," I said, and I told Gay that I would like to go and explore more of Cardiganshire while she was spending time with Armes.

"I will come and pick you up from here around seven this evening."

"Are you sure you don't mind me staying, Kings? I'm sure Armes wouldn't mind you attending her class with me."

"Of course, I don't mind. The reason we came was for you to meet Armes, and for you to spend time with her. I will be quite happy doing some more exploring – there is so much to see here in Cardiganshire."

"So, what about this morning?" Gay asked. "We are supposed to ring the bell when we are ready to get up."

Gay giggled at the thought of Heulyn coming into our room and getting us out of bed. "I can get used to us having a servant, my love. As soon as we get home, I think I'll order one."

"I thought I was your servant," I declared with a smile.

"You are my special body servant, my love, not an ordinary servant."

"Special body servant! Ah, that comes with certain privileges, doesn't it?" And I wrestled with my beloved in bed.

"Stop it, Kings!" Gay shrieked. "We must be quiet. I can hear someone outside our room. I'm sure it's Heulyn, waiting for us to ring our bell."

"Ring it," I said.

"No, you ring it, Kings."

"Alright, here goes," and I rang our morning bell. Almost instantly there was a knock on the door, and we both called "Come in!"

Heulyn arrived pushing a wooden cart on wheels, and she served us a lovely breakfast in bed. We had bacon and eggs, and homemade bread with blackberry jam. And was it good! Almost as good as my favorite "Bacon and Eggs Day" that I had celebrated when I lived in Bacon Hole. But not quite.

There is nothing like eating bacon and eggs when you are living in a cave out in the wilds. Food always seems to taste better when one is outdoors.

Our first course was followed by a fresh fruit salad and honey yoghurt. "And the honey comes from our own bees," Heulyn said proudly. She then made us a lovely morning tea, and we sat at our window and watched the morning sun chase the shadows across the waking fields.

"Can I run you a bath?" Heulyn asked while we finished our tea, "and will you be staying at the commune for lunch?"

"A bath would be wonderful," I said, "but I won't be here at the commune for lunch, and Gay will be attending Armes' teaching session later this morning."

After we finished our bath, Gay asked if we could go and look at the stables.

"I'd like to spend some time with you, Kings, before you leave for Cardigan. I saw a building on the other side of the farmyard yesterday that I didn't have time to explore. And I think that it must have been the old horse stables."

Heulyn had washed and folded our regular clothes, and I put mine on as I would be heading to Cardigan after we had finished exploring the stables. Gay continued to wear her Celtic gown and jewelry, as she would be joining the Celts who would be attending Armes' teaching.

We thanked Heulyn, who had taken wonderful care of us again, and then we walked across the fields to the other buildings. It was another fine day as we arrived at the farmhouse, and the morning chorus of the birds was in full song.

"I think those are the stables over there," I said, pointing to a large building that had two wooden doors that were open, and a faint smell of horse manure rode on the light breeze that blew in our direction.

"It certainly smells like the stables," Gay said as we walked through the doors, and it was.

Inside we saw mangers, hay racks, corn bins, and large wooden pegs on which the saddles and harnesses were hung.

"This is an old stable," Gay commented, as she looked around at the design of the building. "How old did Heulyn say the farm was?"

"She said it was built in 1901."

Above our heads there was a hayloft, and we climbed up the wooden ladder to look around. It brought back so many wonderful memories for us as we remembered Maggie who had been like a mother to me when I was living on the cliffs and in my cave. When I injured my foot on the Worms Head, she allowed me to stay with her in her cottage in Penmaen and taught me so much about life. Maggie was someone who believed in me for who I was, not just for what I could do or achieve. She brought such love and healing into my life, and taught me how to love myself, and to receive unconditional love, and that has changed my life forever! And then there was Heather who owned the stables and riding club where Gay used to keep her horse, Blaze. And it was Heather who taught me how to ride my stallion, Great Thunder! It is strange sometimes how a place, even a hayloft where one has never been before, can remind us of somewhere else and awake our feelings and memories, and we can walk in yesterday once more.

"That was the first time I ever rode a horse," I reminisced, "and Blaze bucked me off his back, remember?"

"I remember, my love, and after that you learned to ride your wild stallion Great Thunder."

"Oh, it just seems like yesterday when Great Thunder and I rode around the Gower on our adventures. I wouldn't trade those times for anything, and I will never forget when you gave me your special saddle, before you moved away to England, and I've kept it ever since. In some ways, it helped me to hold on to my dream of finding you again one day, and I did."

Gay began to weep at my words, and she told me how much she loved me.

For the reader who may not be familiar with the different usages of farm stables, I will explain a few...

In the summer months, farm horses are unharnessed and fed with corn in the stable, and then turned out into a field for the night; but in wintertime they are generally bedded in the stable. The bedding may be of straw or sand, but in many counties in Britain where there is a lot of moorland, bracken fern is cut and stacked for winter bedding.

One of my first jobs when I moved to Devonshire to live with my grandparents was to work as a carter. The work of a carter is to see that the horses are fed, watered, and groomed. I was also required to keep the harnesses bright and clean. The old English word for stable was "hangar," a word that has been adopted for airplanes, which after making their flight, return to their "hangar" for maintenance or repairs.

Near the village of Stony Stratford, in Buckingham-shire, there is a place called Daneshangar. It is just beyond the borderline that once divided the Danelagh, or Danish district, from the English territory, so that the name seems to indicate that the Danes, who were splendid horsemen, had a "hangar" or stable here. Farm stables are generally large and well ventilated, as well as warm and comfortable. Farmers know that a horse in a nice warm stable requires less food than one in a cold or damp building.

Nailed to old stable doors you will often see horseshoes of all kinds and shapes. The hoof of a horse is really an enlarged toenail that constantly keeps growing, and if a horse were kept in a stable without moving around or working, the hoof would grow so long that he would be unable to stand. Horses and ponies that live in the wild are able to wear down their hoofs simply by travelling over the landscape as they forage for food or run with the herd. But when horses have to pull heavy loads on hard roads, their hoofs wear away more quickly, and if they don't have shoes on, they would soon become lame. To avoid this, iron shoes are fastened to the horny substance that forms the outside of the hoof, and a person who shoes horses is called a "farrier." When the Normans arrived on our shores, they attached great importance to the art of shoeing, or "farriery." Henry de Ferrers, who came to this country with the Conquerors, received his name and the manor of Tutbury in Staffordshire for his work in charge of the King's farriers.

Gay and I found seven horseshoes nailed to the inside of one of the stable doors, and it was as if they were speaking to us of the stable's bygone days. There still was the smell of horses, though faint in the air, and the horseshoes on the door and also the still air whispered of a time long ago when hardworking horses rested their tired legs and enjoyed apples and oats as they relaxed in the stable or lay on their beds of straw.

Swallow's nests sat in rows up on the beams of the stable roof, their young having already flown the nest. And we watched them darting back and forth catching their breakfasts in the morning sky, while they told their summer stories to Gay and I.

On this farm in 1901, and for many years after, horses were used for ploughing, reaping, and hauling, in spite of the invention of the "Metal Horse" – the tractor, which was to revolutionize farming practices, and not all for the good.

In this stable there were probably three breeds of horses -- the Shire and the Suffolk, which are English, and the Clydesdale, which is Scottish. All three breeds are powerful working animals and invaluable to the old farms of yesteryear.

It was time for Gay to go and hear Armes teach her class, and for me to leave the commune and do more exploring of Cardiganshire. We walked back across the fields to the main settlement buildings where I said goodbye to Gay.

"Bye, love, I will pick you up at the gate at 7:00."

"Bye, Kings, have fun exploring." And I was on my way to Cardigan.

The last time I was there, I had explored some of the cliff paths between Newport Bay and Dinas Head. But today I would go to a place that over the years has become "sacred" to me – Lower Fishguard harbor. Places that we have not seen in quite some time are like long-lost friends, and as we reconnect with them, it is the memories that we have of them that make them sacred to our souls.

I have happy memories of Lower Fishguard in each of the four seasons of the year. In the summer, my father would take us sailing and fishing on his sailboat, which he moored in the harbor. He named his boat "Wistful," meaning dreamy or nostalgic. And it was those dreams that I had come to walk with and talk with today, as the gentle winds of memory stirred. On the days when the winds blew too strong, and the sea was angry, my father and I would just sit in the boat in the harbor and dream wistful dreams. Dad would shine the brass fittings and clean the porthole windows, or sand the mahogany deck making it red like the sunset. My brother and I would catch crabs, and trade fishing tackle, and eat our Mars bars that we had bought from the post office with our shiny fifty-pence pieces that Dad had given us for pocket money.

On the days that the wind blew just enough to say good morning and how do you do, and the sea smiled by only showing the whites of its front teeth, it was a day when we could sail.

"Can we sail, Dad? Can we sail?"

"I think so, boys. Look at the sea and the sky, and feel the wind, and then you will know." Wistful is dreaming with us, you know.

And once again the tide reaches the twin keels on Wistful's hull and begins to lift her off the muddy harbor floor. My brother Fraser and I sit on her mahogany seats and dream of the adventures we will have, as my father unwraps the sails.

Bump, bump. We feel her keel hitting the sand a few times more before she lifts and there is enough water below. She is facing the wind, and like us, she is excited to go! The breeze catches her sails, and it is up with the anchor, and her polished horn blows and shouts, "My name is Wistful, you know!"

And we answer, "Yes, yes, we know, let's go!" as we gently sail out of the sheltered harbor and out into the adventures of the Emerald Irish Sea.

There are Puffins, Peregrine Falcons, Manta Rays, Dolphins, sunbathing women with tits to the wind – just a few of our friends that we can expect to meet along the way.

Lower Fishguard is not a long drive from the commune near Eglwyswrw, and I would soon be there.

It was another lovely autumn day as I parked the car beside the pub and the little stream that runs into the muddy harbor, and the smell of that lovely soft mud and the green seaweed drying upon the stones of low tide greeted my nostrils and my memories as I walked towards the harbor quay. And I wished that I had my wellington boots and a bucket so I could play in the smelly mud and lift the stones to find the little crabs to put in my bucket. Sometimes, either my brother or I would get one of our boots, or even both of them, stuck in the mud, and we couldn't move. We were not allowed on the boat or back in the car with our dirty smelly boots on, and mother would make us wash them off under the tap at the end of the quay.

Men and boys, and tomboys, were potting around boats and moorings, and a clean dog quickly became a dirty dog. As I walked along the wall of the quay, the riggings of the sailboats pinged against their masts in the fresh breeze, which began to blow as the tide, after much contemplation, decided to make its journey up the harbor once more. Herring gulls sat and watched from their high perches on masts, waiting to swoop down and catch a chip or two as people began to come out of the chip shop with their fish and chips wrapped in newspaper and to sit on the benches along the wall. Mm, chips with salt and malt vinegar, and battered cod with tartar sauce. I will have to have some myself on the way back from my walk to the end of the quay, I thought, and I'm not sharing mine with you, Mr. Seagull!

Kingsley Ross Hill

As you walk along the quay, lovely old stone houses – their dark slate roofs contrasting with their coloured windowsills and doors – stand together in timeless rows. Only their quaint little gardens change with the seasons, as they talk out loud to the passersby – rose bushes, rhododendrons, climbing vines of honeysuckle and clematis, and in the spring daffodils and tulips. Today, purple clematis and climbing roses call out and say 'hello' and I stop and then walk slowly – there's the old lady in the window, a ghost from years ago.

At the end of the quay, there are a few benches where you can sit and look out across the bay, and see the boats leaving or returning. I sat on the bench closest to the harbor mouth, and I breathed in the fresh sea air and had a conversation with yesterday. People tried not to stare, as I talked to myself, it appeared, but yesterday and I, we didn't care.

Lower Fishguard has more recent history to add to its talking walls, as in 1971 the Dylan Thomas film 'Under Milkwood,' starring Richard Burton and Elizabeth Taylor, was filmed here, as was the 1956 film 'Moby Dick,' starring Gregory Peck.

Fishguard consists of three parts: Fishguard, Goodwick, and Lower Fishguard. Goodwick is where, in the early 20th century, a new harbor and breakwater were created by the Great Western Railway, and where today ferries depart for Rosslare in Ireland. It was originally hoped that Goodwick might become a major terminal for transatlantic liners from New York. Indeed, in 1909, the luxury liner Mauretania called in, but the trade eventually went to Southampton, and Goodwick had to settle for the Irish ferry business.

The main town of Fishguard sits up on the hill between Goodwick and Lower Fishguard.

The walk and the salt air were making me hungry, so I made my way back along the quay toward the chip shop. Halfway along the quay, I noticed that the little ice-cream 'hole-in-the-wall' shop was open, and it was the same little shop that had served my brother and I our ice-cream 30 years ago.

"I'll have a walnut cone, please, with two scoops." So much for having ice cream for dessert. I will have ice cream first and then have my fish and chips. 'What do you think of that, Mr. Gull?'

'What? Ice cream and fish and chips? You lucky devil!'

'Yes, I am a lucky devil, and I'm not sharing with you Mr. Gull, not this time, so you may as well fly off.' And he did.

I sat on another bench overlooking the harbor and the spot where my dad used to moor Wistful. There was another boat there now, and it looked like a small fishing boat with some netting and floats sitting in the stern. Across the other side of the harbor was an old steel-hulled boat that I remembered very well, and it still had the same number painted on its old red and white hull. It was the AB58 fishing vessel of Lower Fishguard Harbor. 'And I'm Kingsley Hill,' I shouted. 'Remember me?'

'Yes, of course, I remember you. How's your brother – caught any mackerel lately?'

'My brother is fine, Mr. AB58, and thanks for asking. And yes, we caught some lovely mackerel back in the summer. I'm just off for some fish and chips, actually. Would you like to join me, Mr. 58?'

'I'm anchored here, my friend. Sorry, maybe another day.'

'Alright 58, goodbye now, I am on my way. And I look forward to talking to you another day.'

I ordered one large piece of haddock and medium chips. They gave quite good portions of chips if I remembered rightly.

"They do indeed," said Mr. Gull.

"Hey, I thought you had flown away?"

"No, I am here to stay, as long as there's chips I won't fly away."

"Come on, Mr. Gull, these are my chips. Now go away."

There is nothing like fresh fish and chips hotly wrapped in newspaper, with the smell of salt and malt vinegar seeping through. And I walked back up along the quay to my bench at the end, and my taste buds did a dance.

'Oh, Mr. Gull, these taste bloody marvellous! And they have given me a little tub of tartar sauce too.' And I sang a song my father used to sing. "The British, the British, the British are best! I wouldn't give two pence for anything less!"

'I will tell you something, Mr. Gull. They can't make proper fish and chips in Canada. They can't even make proper batter! And what about the Americans? They are even worse! They don't even know what a chip is! They call chips 'crisps' you know, like the ones we buy in packets.' "I knew that. I'm not stupid, you know!"

'I know, Mr. Gull, I wasn't saying that at all. It's just that the Americans and Canadians can't make proper fish and chips to save their lives!'

'Well, us seagulls know all about that. A few of us flew over there on holidays once, and the chips were so bad we refused to even raid their trash cans, as they call them. We soon flew back to the British Isles because in a seagull's life, there are some things where you just can't compromise, and one of them is having decent fish and chips.'

'So which place was worse, Mr. Gull, Canada or the USA?'

'As I said, they were both piss poor! But the worst fish and chips I ever had was in Victoria British Columbia, Shit, I had food poisoning there, and that's pretty bad for a seagull! We generally have a high tolerance for bad chips. And then there was that other place…?'

'Oh, now I remember. We got tired of flying, so we rode the rigging on one of the ferries from Victoria to Vancouver, and a gull friend that we met on the ferry invited us to a place called Richmond. And they were all bloody nuts there, and they couldn't speak proper English. There were so many of them that we thought we had taken a trip to an anthill, not somewhere in Canada, and they ate seagulls just like us, those dirty buggars! We soon flew out of there and made our way back to good old England, where people love their dogs and cats, and us seagulls are the Queen's Bird, and we are not eaten or crossbred with bats in some laboratory.'

'One thing we did like in America, though, was **Mr. Trump** and his Retrumplicans, who said that we could drink disinfectant, which helps fight off the virus Covid 19. Funny enough, it tasted like scotch! And I was feeling no pain after drinking it, but apparently humans don't fare so well. But we seagulls do – my dry cough and high fever went away pretty quickly! The only problem was once I arrived home in England, I was banned from all fish and chip shops for fourteen days, and I couldn't squawk around with my friends in Teignmouth.'

'I don't blame you Mr. Gull, I won't be going back to Richmond anytime soon. Here, can I offer you a chip? Ketchup or tartar sauce?'

'Just the salt and vinegar, please, sir and thank you.'

'You're very welcome, my feathered friend. You take care now, and I will see you next time I'm at the chip shop.'

As I finished my chips and looked out across Fishguard Bay, I wondered how Gay was doing at the commune, and how Armes' teaching was going. Hopefully, Gay and Armes were continuing to get along well and would have ample time to talk once the class was over.

Time was going by quickly now, and it was already four o'clock, so I drove to Fishguard town and looked around until it was time to pick up Gay.

Gay met me at the gate as planned, and we drove back over the mountains towards our home in Pennard. As we drove along, Gay shared with me how her day with Armes had gone.

"I feel encouraged that I've been able to make a connection with Armes," said Gay. "She will never be my mum, of course – that title will always belong to Helen – but at least I feel that a hole in my life is closing as I am getting to know my birth mother. Thank you, my love, for coming with me to the commune this weekend, I wouldn't have come without you. And we had so much fun on Friday night and all of Saturday, didn't we?"

I smiled and nodded.

Gay continued. "Some of the time when Armes was teaching the class, I could hardly concentrate. I kept thinking about our sacred bath, and then us making love in our room, and then sitting and looking out across the fields from our window. It was so romantic, my Prince!"

"I enjoyed it too, my lovely lady. I think we needed a weekend where you and I could connect, and we certainly did!" Gay held my hand and leaned on my shoulder as we crossed the lonely hills and headed for home. It was now dark outside, as we continued our conversation….

As we approached home, Gay said she had something to ask me, and for the very first time since we had been married, I felt an uneasiness in my spirit as to what she was going to ask. "What is it?" I asked.

"Armes has invited me to take the Bard training program that she is teaching, and the commitment is for me to be at the commune every second weekend from Friday evening to Sunday night. I know that it would mean a big sacrifice for you and the girls to make, and I would ask Mum to help on those weekends that I would be away. What do you think, Kings?"

"When would this start?" I asked, "and what is the duration of the training?"

"It starts next weekend, and it lasts for twelve weekends."

"It will be a sacrifice," I shared, "and I am concerned that it would be particularly hard for Melody, having you away every second weekend, especially with her having so recently started her new school. I also don't know how comfortable I feel about you being at the commune alone – it's different than us being there together…. Let me think about it, okay?"

"I can appreciate how you feel, Kings, and if it's too much, I understand, especially with you being a pastor. It does feel like the commune is a bit like a humanist settlement, as well as a Celtic community. And I know they live and teach a lot of what you don't believe to be right. And I do not believe a lot of what Armes is teaching – I just would like to have the opportunity to get to know my birth mother more. Armes and I got on well over the weekend, and she did make the effort today to make the space for just her and I to spend time together. I feel that I have missed out on knowing my birth mother and taking the Bard training would give me the chance to get to know her and give her the chance to get to know me."

"Do you think she would be willing to leave the commune on some weekends and stay with us at our home?" I asked. "She would be welcome to do that. It would be an option, and then you would still be home for Melody and me."

"I did offer for her to come to our home, Kings, but she said that she had already made the teaching commitments, which, along with her other commitments at the commune, means that she doesn't have the time to be away."

To me, that sounded like an excuse, and if I had not seen my daughter for as long as Armes had not seen Gay, I certainly would make the time to see her in whatever way I could! I kept those thoughts to myself, however, and didn't tell Gay what I was thinking.

Instead, I said, "I do know how important getting to know your birth mum is, Gay, and I do want to support you in this. Can you just give me a few days to think about it?"

"Of course, my love," she replied, "and as I said, if you don't want me to go, I won't."

I wanted to talk to Helen and ask what she thought of things, and a to make sure that she was alright with spending extra time here at the house with the girls and I, although I was sure in my heart that she would be.

We arrived home at 10 p.m., and it was a quick goodnight to Samantha and Melody, and off to bed for Gay and I, as we were tired from our full weekend.

During the week, I called Helen to tell her what Gay had asked, and I found that she was surprisingly supportive of Gay developing a relationship with Armes. She was also excited to spend more time with Melody and I on the weekends when Gay would be away. She did, however, have some concern that Gay might get caught up in spending too much time and energy on her training and get emotionally burned out, and then Melody would feel neglected again, as she had done when Gay was spending too much time working on the translation of Taliath's diary.

"What are your thoughts, Kings?" Helen asked.

"I think she has learned and grown from her experience of taking on too much, and she was willing for me to say no, if I thought it necessary. I think, under the circumstances of her wanting to get to know Armes, it would be best to give her our support; otherwise, she might regret later down the road not having taken the opportunity."

"I think that's wise, Kings," Helen said, encouraging me in what I had been thinking.

I then asked Helen if she would be able to come down on Friday, as Gay would be starting her training on the weekend.

"I thought we could all drive up in the one car," I said, "and drop Gay off at the commune. Then I'd like to take you and Melody to a Bed & Breakfast that I know, and we can spend Saturday and Sunday exploring."

"That sounds wonderful!" Helen said excitedly. "I will look forward to seeing you and Melody on Friday."

After speaking to Helen, I waited for Gay to come home from work, and then I told her that I wanted to support her in taking the training with Armes. Gay was thrilled at my words, and she threw her arms around me. "Oh, my love, thank you for understanding how much this means to me!"

"I'm happy I can support you in getting to know your birth Mum," I said. "I just don't want to see you getting burnt out."

"I know, Kings, and I have learned my lesson. I love our family so much, and I wouldn't do anything to jeopardize what I have."

"I know," I replied, and I kissed her.

On Thursday morning, I walked Melody to school, and I told her that Helen and I were going to take her to a bed-and-breakfast on the weekend, and that we were going to explore some of Cardiganshire. "If the weather is nice, we can spend some time on the beach."

Melody got excited, and she did a little jig in the playground. "Can we make a sand boat on the beach?" she asked.

"Yes, but it's too cold to swim in the sea now. Maybe we will make a huge sandcastle and then watch the tide come in around it."

"You mean the pirates, Dad?"

"Yes, the pirates on the waves."

The school bell rang, and Melody headed to her classroom.

I booked two nights at the Salutation Inn, near Eglwyswrw, where I had stayed with my brother Fraser and his wife Lynn for a weekend the previous summer. It was close to the commune where we would be dropping off Gay, and close to the beaches where we could go and explore. I had wanted to come back to the Inn one day as it had been a friendly place with great service, and this was my chance.

Soon it was Friday, and Gay had been able to take the day off work. We packed our clothes before walking Melody across the road to the bus stop at Pennard Stores. She and her friend Beverley from next door were excited, as today was the first day they were taking the school bus with the older children.

"When are we leaving for Cardiganshire, Mom and Dad?" she asked, before getting on the bus, "and is Samantha coming with us?"

"Samantha is spending time with Glynn this weekend, but I am sure we can do something with Samantha soon. We will be leaving as soon as you get home from school, Melody."

"We will meet you at the bus when you get home."

And with a big smile on her face, Melody got on the bus. She sat upstairs in the front seat and waved to Gay and I as the bus pulled away.

"Our girl is growing up…" I said, taking Gay's hand as we walked back across the road to our house. Helen would be arriving from Cardiff around the time Melody would be getting home from school, and then we would head off for our weekend.

Gay and I spent the whole day out in the garden, which was lovely. I was able to mow the lawn, and trim the tomato plants in the greenhouse, which were still producing tomatoes, even though the evenings were starting to get colder. Gay trimmed the edges of the lawn and the flowerbeds, and we went across the road to the Heather Slade Café for lunch.

I was still waiting to bump into some of my boyhood friends who still lived in the village and had families of their own. Fraser had kept me up to date as to our friends who still lived in the village, but so far, I had not seen any of them. I would have to call around at some of their homes one of these days, and maybe some of them would still be living there, or their folks would know where they were.

"We have only been back in Pennard for a couple of months," Gay reminded me, although we agreed that it seemed a lot longer with our lives being so full.

Helen arrived with her suitcase, and the three of us walked across the road to meet Melody as she got off the bus. She was all smiles when she saw us, and she danced across the road.

"It's wonderful to see her so happy," Helen commented, and we followed our dancer into the house.

Gay had made us an early tea so that we wouldn't have to stop along the way, apart from the bathroom and maybe some extra snacks. We finished our tea and loaded our suitcases into the car. Samantha was still out with her boyfriend Glynn, and they would be staying at his house over the weekend.

It was a lovely drive to Cardiganshire, and Gay and Helen sat in the back seat and talked about how things had gone with Armes. Melody and I played a game of "I spy," leaving Gay and Helen to chat, but I was sure that Melody was wondering who this Armes woman was. It would be up to Gay to tell her about her birth mother, and I would encourage her to do it soon. As we drove along, I was so impressed by Helen's acceptance and support of Gay's developing friendship with Armes. What a lovely, graceful lady Helen is, I thought. It can't be easy for her.

As I looked back at Gay and Helen through the rear-view mirror, Gays eyes caught mine, and she smiled with a look of love that always made my heart skip, and I would miss her love and touch this weekend. Gay was on her own journey in getting to know Armes, and I would support her on this journey. As Gay and Helen continued to talk, and Melody and I finished playing our game of 'I Spy,' I thought about my wonderful marriage to Gay. In so many ways it felt like we were still on our honeymoon! We were learning and growing to care for one another so deeply. We were still like teenagers in a springtime of discovery and love. Sometimes the energy between us was so electric that I could feel my desire for her flowing through my veins like a river racing its way to the sea.

We arrived at the commune, and Armes was waiting at the gate. We all got out of the car to greet Armes, and Helen and Armes embraced one another with a hug and talked about old times for several minutes while Gay, Melody and I stood by. Armes then came over and hugged Gay, and said hello to Melody, and we all talked for a few minutes before Helen, and Melody and I got back in the car. "Bye, my love. We will pick you up about 7 pm on Sunday."

"Bye, my wonderful family. Have a lovely time in Cardigan!"

"We will!"

"Who was that lady that mum was talking to?" Melody asked.

"It is the lady who mum is taking her course with," I answered, and we drove on towards the Inn.

It was 7:30 p.m. when we arrived at the Salutation Inn, and a nice lady named Innes showed us to our rooms. She recognized me from when I had stayed previously with Fraser and Lynn last autumn.

"It's a nice two-bedroom," she said, showing us around, and turning the heater on for us. "Breakfast is anytime between 8 and 10 a.m." And after a few more instructions she left us alone to settle in.

"Oh, and the bar and restaurant are open until 10 p.m." she added as she walked down the hall.

"Thank you!" Helen and I replied together as we closed the door.

Melody was thrilled to share a large room with Helen, "and it has a television on the wall!" she exclaimed excitedly. And within a few minutes she was curled up on top of the bed with a blanket and a bag of crisps.

Helen and I unpacked the suitcases and then sat down to relax.

"It's so good to see you, Kings. Would you like a glass of wine? I was able to find a nice blackberry wine in the Cardiff Market."

"I'd love one," I replied. "I have been looking forward to coming back here for some time, and now I get to share this special place with you and Melody!"

Helen poured us some wine, and we sat on the couch in front of the window that overlooked the garden and a river that ran in front of the property.

"It's lovely here!" Helen proclaimed. "Look at all the beautiful roses, and the river that's at the bottom of the property."

"It is lovely," I said, as I looked forward to some good conversation with Helen. Since marrying Gay, I had enjoyed becoming friends with Helen. She truly had the spirit of a young girl and a passion for life, which made it a pleasure to be in her presence. She was also gentle spirited and had a depth of wisdom that I had seldom experienced in other relationships. Through my conversations with Helen, I was learning to become a better husband and lover to my Gay, as she imparted such an understanding of the opposite sex to me. And as we sipped our wine in front of the window, I thought how fortunate

I was to have such a lovely, classy lady and mentor in my life. It is rare for a man to have such a splendid and informative relationship with his mother-in-law, and I told Helen what she meant to me in my life. She smiled humbly and thanked me for bringing her to the Inn to spend time with Melody and me.

After a few glasses of wine each, she pulled out some crackers and cheese that she had packed, along with some black forest cake – which was Melody's favorite.

Helen took a plate of cake to Melody and then came back and sat at the table. For a few minutes we didn't say anything. We just smiled and looked into each other's eyes which said everything we felt inside.

"I am glad that I have a son like you," she said, "and that my daughter is married to such a lovely man."

"Why thank you, Helen," I said, and I toasted our friendship. Helen also told me how she had seen Melody blossom since I had come into her life.

"I am blessed to have a daughter like her," I replied, "I always wanted a second daughter and now I have one. And it is so nice to see Samantha and Melody become so close and enjoy each other so much as sisters."

After another glass of wine and some cake, I went and checked on Melody, and she was fast asleep. I gently pulled the door closed and went back to join Helen at the table, and we talked until late.

Saturday morning arrived with a breeze that made my curtains skip, and I made Helen and Melody a lavender tea in bed.

"Tea in bed, how lovely!" they both said.

"I have never tasted lavender tea before, Dad, and it's really-good!" "Glad you like it," I said with a smile, "and it is a lovely day outside!"

"What shall we do today?" I asked my lovely ladies, although I already had somewhere in mind.

"Wherever you would like to go," Helen replied,

"And I don't have to ask you where you want to go, Melody," I continued, "you want to go to the beach!"

"Right, you are Dad, let's go to the beach!"

And I said, "Let's go to Aberystwyth, with its lovely historical town and promenade, and if the tide is out, we can go down onto the beach and make sandcastles."

"Melody and I would both enjoy that," Helen said, sipping her tea.

Melody now took the last sip of her tea, and said, "I'm hungry. What are we having for breakfast?"

"We are going down to the breakfast room in a little while," I said, "so you go and get dressed."

"Okay, Dad," she said cheerfully, "I will go and get dressed."

As Helen brought the teacups out to the kitchen, I opened the curtains for her to see a lovely, blue sky day. "Perfect for a day at Aberystwyth," I said, "and if the wind is not too cold, we can take Melody down to the beach."

I took Melody down to the breakfast room while Helen finished dressing. One of the things I appreciated about Helen was that she dressed for the occasion. Even in this fast-paced culture, she embodied a calm and stillness that seemed to create an invisible sphere of peace around her – like she could step in and out of time and use it to her advantage in whatever the circumstances.

And today, she had dressed for the occasion of breakfast. Blue heels and white nylons, and a blue dress that complimented her beautiful blue eyes. As she entered the restaurant, this powerful feminine lady lit up the room with a presence like a glorious sunrise! And it made everyone else in the room stop to behold something so lovely. And I wondered why Helen had not met a man, or even wanted to it seemed.

"How lovely you look, beautiful lady!" I exclaimed. "Yes, you look beautiful, Grandma," Melody echoed, and Helen blushed like a pink rose as I pulled out her chair and sat her at the table.

'What a blessed man I am, to have you two lovely ladies in my life;' I exclaimed to myself, 'my beautiful wife Gay, and my lovely friend and mum, Helen, and I love them both.' I celebrated in my heart as the waitress handed us our menus.

Melody and I both ordered a "full British Breakfast," which, for those of my readers who haven't yet blocked their arteries by having one, I highly recommend that you indulge yourself. Smoked sausages, baked beans, hash browns, fried tomatoes, gammon, and black pudding if you're in the mood, and of course two free-range eggs on fried bread. Bloody marvelous!

Melody and I went wild with the bangers and beans, dipping the sausages into "Dad's Brown Sauce." You don't see Dad's sauce served with breakfast too often these days; it's all H.P. Sauce nowadays.

"That's enough beans, my girl," said Helen. "Otherwise, you will be tooting all the way through Eglwyswrw."

"You mean a farting Zulu from Eglwyswrw?" Melody queried, as she roared with laughter!

And lovely refined Helen did not know where to look as several people turned and stared! After breakfast, Helen went back to her room to change, and she packed a day bag of clothes for the three of us. Then we headed off to Aberystwyth, and we managed to find parking right on the promenade at the seafront, which can be quite a challenge on Saturdays.

Helen asked me what I knew about Aberystwyth, as she had only ever been here once, many years ago, and she couldn't remember anything of its history apart from it being a university town.

"Well, it has a lovely promenade as you can see. It goes all along the seafront, and there is a pier with a coffee shop and a restaurant, and also an amusement arcade for the kids. But that's not what you're interested in, is it?"

"No," she replied, "although I love the promenade and being able to look out to sea."

"Aberystwyth is the largest town in the borough of Cardigan," I stated. "The name 'Cardigan' is an anglicized pronunciation of Ceredigion, the Welsh name for the county of Cardiganshire. Although Cardigan is close to the Welsh woolen trade, the woolen garment called a 'cardigan' does not get its name from the town, but from the seventh Earl of Cardigan, who led 'the Charge of the Light Brigade' and wore that type of sweater beneath his uniform to keep him warm."

"Tell us more about Aberystwyth," Melody said, taking Helens and my hand and walking between us.

"Aberystwyth is really at the 'heart' of Wales, right between North and South – a capital in all but name," I stated.

"And it is a university town and a seaside resort. What I like about Aberystwyth is that it has a feeling of being cut off from the outside world by the mountains. As you can see, it has a backdrop of steep green hills, a wide sweep of a bay, and stately Edwardian guest houses that follow the curving Promenade."

"And what I like," added Helen, "is that you can feel the age of the buildings, and if you listen carefully, you can hear them calling out their stories from the past."

Melody held our hands tightly and made us stand still and listen. "Can you hear what they are saying, Melody?" Helen asked.

"They are talking about a battle that once happened at a castle," replied Melody, "and there was a man that ruled the town from his home in the castle."

Helen and I looked across at one another and nodded our heads in agreement.

"What I like about old buildings," I said, "is that they are able to have different conversations with different people."

Melody looked down at the ground, pondering what I had said. "You mean like they say what they want to say to each person? Which makes what they say always interesting because there are so many different stories to hear?"

"Well done Melody!" both Helen and I said together.

"That is exactly what it means," I added. "Each of us hears what they say in a unique way, so the old buildings are having multiple conversations with people as they walk along the promenade."

Melody's face beamed at our affirming words.

"Look, Dad, there's a castle up on the rocks!" she exclaimed. "I bet that is the oldest building of all."

"I think you're right," I said, and then I asked, "Who would like to hear what the castle is saying to me?" "I do!" both Helen and Melody said together.

"Alright, but it's only fair that I tell both of you that I already know some of what the castle has said to other people through its history, so it is kind of repeating to me what it has already said."

"You mean like someone who tells the same story over and over again, like the old lady who used to live across the road from us in Cardiff, Dad?"

"Yeah, that's right, but the castle has something very interesting to say to all of us, and we can learn so much from history."

Melody waited for me to say more…

"Are you ready to hear what the castle is saying? Are you listening, Melody?"

"I'm listening," Helen said excitedly.

"And I am too," echoed Melody.

"Okay, Mr. Castle, what do you have to say?" I asked aloud, and then I launched into a bit if history…

"Aberystwyth Castle was built in 1277, by Edward the First, to protect the settlement that stood at its feet. The castle changed hands many times before a man named Owain Glyndwr made it his base in the year 1404. Two centuries later, in 1637, a mint was set up in the great hall to produce coins made of silver from the local mines."

"There were silver mines around here, Dad?"

"Yes, there certainly was, but I don't know if any silver is still mined here today.…The coins were used to pay Charles the 1st' soldiers during the Civil War," I continued, "when Oliver Cromwell had control of the London Mint."

"Civil War! See, I told you, Dad, that the castle whispered to me that there were battles, and that a man ruled. And he must have been Owain Glyndwr. See, Dad, I didn't know anything about the history of the castle, and I heard the old houses telling me about what had happened there."

"You are right, my girl. That is the wonderful thing about the past. If we listen, it still speaks."

"This is quite a lesson!" Helen said. "Now who wants to have an ice cream at the pier?"

We all raised our hands and headed across the road to the pier.

"The pier at Aberystwyth today is short," I said, "but it once protruded out into the sea for 900 feet. Then in 1938, it was swept off its legs by a storm."

We walked to the little café and ice cream shop at the side of the pier, and we each ordered a large ice cream.

Melody wanted to go down onto the beach and build a sand boat, but the waves were almost reaching the sea wall already, so we decided to walk around the town and do some shopping instead. Helen took Melody around to the clothing stores, while I went into the hobby shop to see if they had anything that I could add to my model railway.

It was rather a letdown when I went inside. They only had boxed train sets, and very few individual trucks or locomotives, or other model railway gear. Nothing classic or rare, or made in Britain – only the 'Made in China' rubbish. I prided myself on having a collection that was all made in Great Britain, although I did have a few coal trucks that were made in Italy.

After the girls had finished their shopping, we had a pub lunch in the town. When we came out of the pub, the weather had turned bad, with wind and rain driving in from the sea, so we headed back to the inn for an early evening. Melody watched a movie while Helen and I talked in the living room.

We sat in front of the window and enjoyed some blackberry wine and a good conversation. I was able to talk to Helen about some thoughts that were on my heart, and although she was nervous at first, she listened.

"I don't understand why you don't want to have someone special in your life?" I inquired. "You are such a lovely lady and have so much to offer someone."

"I did give things a try, Kings," she replied, "when I went out on some dates I met at speed dating, but I didn't really connect with anyone, and there are so many predators out there, who would take advantage of a woman like me."

"I am not belittling what you are saying, Helen, but there are also some good God-fearing men out there too, who are looking for a special lady like you."

"Thanks, Kings, and I know that you are trying to encourage me, but I am a big girl, and I know what I want in a man."

"What do you want?" I smiled.

"I want a relationship like you and Gay have, full of passion and adventure!"

"There is no reason why you can't find someone who is adventurous and passionate," I replied, and we finished our wine.

On Sunday, the weather had turned warm again and we were able to take Melody down to the beach where we built a sand boat and waited for the tide to come in. We had lunch in the town in the afternoon and went to the museum and a local art gallery where Helen bought an original oil painting by a local Cardiganshire artist. It was a picture of a family building sandcastles on Aberystwyth Beach.

"It will remind me of our lovely weekend here," Helen shared, and we spent the afternoon exploring. We drove to a place called Devils Bridge. "I have heard about this place," I said to Helen and Melody as we drove along, "but I have never been there."

"Does the Devil live there?" Melody asked with a mischievous smile.

"I hope not," I replied, "I don't want to see him anytime soon," and both the girls laughed. "Grandpa told me about a legend derived from the Devils Bridge," I continued, and we pulled up at the side of the road close to the bridge. "Come on," I said, "let's go and explore." As we reached the bridge, we were fascinated to see that there are two other bridges built below this one. The middle one was built in the eighteenth century, and the lowest one was built in medieval times.

"Tell us about the legend, Dad," Melody asked.

We all stood and stared over the high ravine, as I told the story.

"An old woman's cow had strayed across the ravine, and she could not get the cow to come back. A monk appeared and offered to build a bridge if she promised to give him the first living creature that crossed it. The old woman promised that she would, and the bridge was built, and he beckoned to her to cross. However, the crafty old woman had spotted his cloven hoof, so she called her black dog, and threw a crust of bread across the bridge. The dog ran after it, and she told the devil he could keep the dog, while the cow crossed back from the other side and came back to the woman."

"So, the old woman, out-smarted the devil!" Melody exclaimed. "Yes, that is right," I replied, as Helen continued to stare down at the ravine below.

"The reason for the popularity of the bridge," I explained, "is not because of the bridge, but because of the magnificent waterfalls by which the river goes down to join the Rheidol in its wooded ravine."

It was time to go and pick up Gay from the commune, and I wondered how things had gone with Armes.

We arrived at the commune right at 7:00 as planned, and I could see Gay and Armes waiting at the gate.

After a quick hello to Armes, and a hug and kiss from Gay, Melody and I went for a walk along the road, leaving Helen to talk with Armes and Gay.

Only three weeks ago, I could never have anticipated this happening -- Gay, Helen and Armes, all talking together!

"Come on, you Zulu from Eglwyswrw," I said to Melody. "Let's walk back to Mum and Grandma."

"There is that lady again. I can tell Mum really likes her," Melody commented.

It seemed she was decerning the importance of Armes in relation to her mother's life, and ultimately her own, and I felt uncomfortable not telling Melody who Armes was. She obviously knew that Armes was someone significant, I thought, as Melody waited for me to add to her statement. All I could muster up was "she is teaching Mum about the ancient Celtic people."

"You mean the people whose chest we found?"

"Yes, that's right," I replied.

On the drive home, neither Gay nor Helen mentioned anything about Armes, other than Gay telling us about what she had learned about becoming a bard and a priestess. And there was no tension in the air between Helen and Gay, and I pondered again of how supportive and gracious Helen was towards Gay in supporting her efforts to get to know her birthmother.

'It can't be easy for Helen having Armes coming back into Gay's life,' I thought. I would talk to Gay tonight, when she and I were alone, and find out how her time with Armes had worked out and encourage Gay to tell Melody who Armes really is.

It was almost 10 o'clock when we arrived home in Pennard, and Samantha was home after having spent the weekend with her boyfriend Glynn. Melody raced into Samantha's room, excited to spend time with her big sister. This gave Helen and Gay time to talk, and as I made a pot of tea, Gay shared with Helen regarding how things had gone with Armes. From what I heard of the conversation; things had gone well. Armes had made time outside of her teaching to give Gay some one-on-one time with her. Gay and Helen both seemed comfortable talking about things. This made me feel good, as potentially this situation could have been awkward for all of us.

Samantha spent time with Melody, and Helen stayed in her room for the night as it was too late to be driving home to Cardiff.

Chapter Three

The Hero and the Phantom

On Monday morning, Gay and I walked with Melody across the road to catch the school bus.

"Bye Melody, have a good day at school."

"Bye Mum, bye Dad, see you tonight."

Gay then got a lift with Helen into Cardiff.

"Bye, my love, see you tonight."

"Bye, Kings, see you tonight."

"Bye Helen."

"Bye Kings."

It was study and preparation day for me, so I could work from home as I prepared tomorrow's lesson for my youth group. Just before eleven, Dad rang, and he told me that we were getting behind in our translation of the diary. He asked if Gay and I were still interested in the three of us working on it together. I assured him that we were and tried to explain how busy we had been over the last several weeks.

"Are you free one evening this week to go metal detecting?" he asked. After checking our schedule, I invited him and Mary over for supper on Wednesday evening, and said that we could go detecting after supper.

Dad and Mary arrived around four on Wednesday, and I picked up a takeout from the village to give Gay a break from cooking. After tea, we all went detecting, including Mary, who usually stayed at home.

"I thought I better come this time – I don't want to miss finding another treasure chest," she joked. "And besides, it's a beautiful evening for a walk."

We drove to Southgate Village and then walked across the golf course to the castle. Finding the chest, or should I say, Nan's Nan finding the chest, near the castle had given us renewed enthusiasm to keep trying our skills in the area, although we had not found anything near Pennard castle with our metal detectors for quite some time.

"Maybe today we will," Dad said, always full of optimism. We turned on our machines and walked in a line about ten feet apart. Melody helped Gay with her detector, taking turns in digging up pop cans and a couple of old pennies, which were like finding gold for Melody! Dad found an old bottle which he said was worth some money. "Look, it's an old Coca Cola bottle, the ones that were made long before the twist tops, and it's got the writing indentation in the glass, which makes it even older." Dad had been collecting bottles now for a few years, but I wasn't particularly interested in them. I would much rather find some ancient Roman coins, or a sword or helmet, but I found nothing this evening, only a rusty old bicycle chain and a modern hair clip.

"I wish I'd stayed at home," Mary said. "I could have finished my book."

"Okay, time to call it an evening," Dad called out, and we headed back to the car. At least it was a nice walk, I thought, and Gay and I held hands as we walked along.

When we got back to the house, Dad and Mary wanted an updated tour of the house, as we had still been unpacking boxes the last time he and Mary were here. Dad was thrilled to see my model railway room, and the set-up I had made of a Cross Country Line, with farms and buildings and even a few terraced houses that had been built from kits. "Samantha and Melody have helped me a fair bit with the buildings," I said to Dad.

When we reached the room that Gay had been working on, however, both Dad and Mary were stunned!

"I have never seen anything like this, Kings!" Dad said, with a look of bewilderment on his face. "She has made the room into an ancient temple – look at the detail! There is,an altar and candles, and look Mary – she has the items from the chest all laid out as if they are waiting to be used. Look at that fearsome looking ram's head, and that evil looking dagger in front of it!"

Fortunately, Gay was still downstairs with Melody; otherwise, she would have been quite taken aback by Dad's reaction to her room.

"Where is she getting this information from, to set up a temple like this?" asked Dad. "What has she been reading or studying? Taliath's diary hasn't described anything like this yet – at least from what I have translated, it hasn't!"

As Gay was still downstairs, I thought it best to tell Dad about Gay and I visiting the commune. I didn't want him to find out from anyone else – he would likely feel hurt and wonder why I had not asked him to come and visit the commune, as he had such a great interest in the Celtic culture and way of life.

I would leave it to Gay to tell him and Mary about Armes in her own time, if indeed she wanted to.

Dad was pleased when I told him about Gay and I visiting the commune, and as I had thought, he wanted to come and experience it for himself. I did not tell him, however, that Gay was spending every second weekend there and training to become a bard and priestess. I would also leave that part for Gay to tell. She would be excited about it, and he would be impressed!

Before we ended our evening, Dad shared with Gay and I where he was at in the translation of the diary. "Taliath is talking about a ghost or phantom horse that has been connected to her family lineage for over six hundred years!"

This interested Gay and I, and we asked questions about the horse.

"It fights in clan battles, and tramples its enemies to death," Dad said, "but it only fights for one clan, which is Taliath's clan. And they have kept a record of the events and whereabouts of this phantom mare for over six hundred years."

"What else does Taliath say about the horse in relation to her clan and family?" I asked.

"I'm still translating more about the horse, Kings, but Taliath does say that the mare kills enemy warriors during clan battles with other clans. And sometimes the horse joins the clan's hunting expeditions and fights off wild animals. She also records that during times of peace, the mare attaches itself to protecting the wellbeing of an individual clan member."

"Is there any particular social status of the individuals that are protected by the horse?" Gay asked.

"It would appear that they are leaders or highly esteemed members of the clan, like the Clan Queen's family, rather than a common clan member," Dad replied. "This phantom animal protected Taliath, and her grandmother before her, and the list goes on, even recording names through all these generations of Taliath's family lineage!" Dad exclaimed, obviously excited. And then he said something that related to our experience with Nan's Nan, and I wondered how Gay would react...

"Taliath records that the mare communicates events of the past to her clan, by leading them to buried artifacts, and she even digs them up with her hoofs. Maybe that is what happened with Nan's Nan leading you to find the chest," Dad said, with a half-joking smirk on his face.

Dad was not there to see Nan's Nan digging in the sand like she knew it was there, I thought. And it was not amusing for Gay either, as she gave me a nervous look, and then excused herself from the room.

"I hope it was not something I said," Dad shared, surprised by Gays reaction to his words.

"I'm sorry, Dad," I said on Gay's behalf. "It's nothing personal. Gay is afraid of Nan's Nan. Not that the mare would harm her in any way. She is afraid of the connection that she has with the horse and does not understand what the connection means."

"I would encourage you to delve deeper into this connection that she has with the horse, Kings. There is more here than meets the eye."

"Yeah, I sense that too, Dad."

"What has Gay said to you about her connection with Nan's Nan, Kings?"

"She did say something, but it's quite a mouthful and not easy to understand."

"Go ahead, Kings, try and explain."

"She told me that she had been having vivid dreams about Nan's Nan, in relation to events of her past. I asked her what the events were, half expecting her to shut down the conversation, but she didn't. She appeared nervous at my question, and she could not quite describe what the events were, but she tried to tell me how she felt."

"I don't know if the events are from my past or from the future," she told me. "If they happened in the past, I don't remember them. I see myself with Nan's Nan as a young girl, and I recall people that I met while roaming around the countryside riding on her back. But in my present reality, I had never met Nan's Nan until last summer, when you brought her to me with Melody riding on her back."

"And then in other dreams, I see myself with her as a grown woman as I am now," she told me, "and I recognize certain places where she leads me in the present, but I also recognize these places from my past. I can see, for example, what Pennard Castle looks like today – a ruin, right? I can see it in its present form like everyone else can. But I also remember how it was in the past and I have memories attached to it! But my dreams don't connect to any specific event in my life that makes any sense."

As Dad listened, I continued. "She also went on to say, 'I am afraid of Nan's Nan, because we both recognize each other in reality, in the present time as well as in my dreams. When I see her in the physical realm, like I did when she led us to the chest, I have this awareness that she knows we are together in my dreams. It is not just a feeling or a hunch. It's a 'knowing' that I have no doubt about, and It scares me, because I don't know what it means.'

"My word, Kings! She has a puzzle going on in her mind – that is quite bizarre! What on earth were you able to say back to her?"

"I had no real answer, Dad, other than saying, 'Thanks for telling me, and Nan's Nan will bring you no harm. Remember how she protected us from the storm before leading us to the chest?' And I told her that when you are meant to understand things, you will; and sometimes we just sense and know something, and we don't understand why."

"Well done, Kings, you will make a good psychologist yet!" Dad said, and we both laughed!

"But how did the horse protect you from the storm, then?"

"It was uncanny, Dad. Nan's Nan blocked the doorway to the castle room so we couldn't get out. I was ready to push her out of the way, or give her a gentle boot, as she was so stubborn, but Gay said, 'Wait, she is trying to tell us something!' And she was! Within ten minutes, the thunder and lightning were right over our heads. And she even formed a half circle around us with the other horses, as Gay, Melody and I faced the castle wall while the lightning flashed, and the thunder rumbled. She knew the storm was coming back!"

"Well, I'm a believer, Kings! That is what the Monkeys sang, wasn't it? Or was it 'Last Train to Clarksville'?"

"Both, Dad, I think. Anyway, you have heard it from the horse's mouth, so to speak." And we both laughed again.

"Now, as far as Gay's dreams are concerned," said Dad, "I'm not an expert on dreams, but from what you have told me, I have a strong sense her dreams mean that her present life has a connection to the past – given the number of specific events that have happened – and that they will have great influence on her future. Though at present, they are not understood, and thus she finds them confusing. I do know an expert on dreams, should Gay want to delve any further, and this person would likely be able to help her interpret their meaning."

"Thanks, Dad, I will see how things go."

Gay finally returned to the room, and dad apologized for anything he might have said that had offended her.

"I'm sorry, Dad," she replied. "I have been having some rather strange dreams lately, and they are related to Nan's Nan, the mare that led us to find the chest. And I am also very tired these last few weeks, as I have been taking a course."

"Not to worry," Dad said, "and there is nothing to apologize for. I will let you and Kings know what else comes up in the translation of the diary, and I understand that you are both busy so you can't spend much time translating. I will carry on, and as I said, I will let you know if I find anything more that is particularly interesting or relevant to the horse or artifacts."

Gay and I walked Dad and Mary to their car, and then called it a night.

⌒

One Sunday evening, when Helen, Melody and I were driving home from a day at Caswell Beach, there was a backup of cars in Pennard lanes.

"It's probably a minor accident," Helen said, as we came to a complete stop. We waited for what seemed like a long time, but there was still no movement in the traffic.

"I'm going to find out what's holding up the traffic," I said, stepping out of the car. Helen and Melody followed me out. As we walked along to the front of the line, other people were getting out of their cars, and a few people were walking back to their cars, having already checked things out.

"Poor animal," we heard one woman say, and a man commented on how a car had hit a horse and damaged the front end.

"Hit a horse!" Melody repeated after hearing the man's words. "I hope it's not one of our horses, Dad," she said, holding onto my hand tightly, and Helen took Melody's other hand as we approached a crowd of people who were standing around in the road. Suddenly, Melody's concerned voice broke the silence, as she let go of Helen's and my hands, and raced to the side of a horse that appeared to have been killed by a car.

"Dad!" she cried, bursting into tears. "It's Nan's Nan! It's Nan's Nan! She has been hit by a car!" Helen and I quickly ran to her side, as she knelt and held Nan's head in her hands and sobbed.

"What are you all staring at?" she shouted. "Get some help! Don't just stand there!"

But it was too late – Nan was dead!

"Can you do something, Dad?" she pleaded.

I put my hand on the horse's belly, and I listened and felt for breath at her nose and mouth. But she had stopped breathing. Helen's eyes were full of tears, and there was nothing we could do.

"Who hit the horse?" a policeman asked, as he arrived on the scene.

"It was just standing in the middle of the road when I came around the corner," said the driver.

"You were driving too fast," said a woman who had been riding her bike.

"The horse was protecting some other horses that were in the road in front of her," she said to the policeman. "And there was a little foal right in the middle of the road, and that horse walked right in front of the car to protect the foal!"

Helen and I continued to look at one another, as Melody continued to sob and rub Nan's head. There was nothing we could do, and we felt totally helpless!

"Come on, Princess," I said. "There is nothing we can do, sweetheart."

"We can't just leave her here like this, Dad. She's a hero! She saved the little foal's life! You heard the lady!"

"Come on," the policeman said. "You have to leave the horse now, so we can get the traffic moving again."

"It's my horse, and she is a hero," Melody shouted!

I didn't know what to say, and how to comfort Melody, so I shouted: "This is Nan's Nan. She is the great leader of the Gower horses, and she just saved the life of a young foal by standing in front of the car to protect the foal! She's a hero!"

Helen looked at me and smiled, and Melody took my hand while the policeman escorted us out of the way. And two elderly ladies clapped their hands, not for what I had said, I told Melody, but for the hero lying in the road. Nan's Nan, who had laid down her life for another.

Helen consoled Melody while we sat in the car until the traffic started moving again through the lanes. As the cars passed slowly by, we noticed someone had covered Nan's head with their coat, and we drove on through the village to home. Helen stayed and helped me to comfort Melody, until Gay arrived home from her training at the commune.

Seeing that Melody was upset, Gay asked her what had happened. "Nan's Nan is dead," Melody told her, shedding fresh tears. "She was hit by a car, Mum, protecting a young foal that was in the road."

Gay looked at me, and I replied, "Yes, she stood between the foal and an oncoming car, to save the foal's life."

Gay seemed strangely unemotional at Melody's and my words, and if I was not mistaken, she had a look of relief on her face… Melody took her mother's reaction – or should I say 'non-reaction' particularly hard.

"Why aren't you upset, Mum?" she asked. "It is Nan's Nan who died, not just any horse! Nan's Nan was the first horse I ever rode, remember, when Dad put me on her back!"

"Yes, I remember," Gay said, with an unconvincing voice and expression.

"What's wrong, Mum?" Melody asked. "Don't you care about what happened? You don't care, do you!" Melody said angrily, and she went upstairs to Samantha's room.

"Aren't you going to say anything to her?" Gay asked me.

"No," I replied. "I have said what she needed me to say, and she is right, my love, in thinking you don't care. She just needed you to say something in support of how she was feeling."

"I know," Gay said. "I know, and I don't expect either of you to understand."

"Understand what?" I asked.

"Oh, never mind. I can't talk about it now. I am sorry, my love, I will explain it to you one day."

"But Melody needs you to explain right now," I said. "Or at least go upstairs and try to comfort her."

After I had finished speaking, Gay went upstairs to talk to Melody, but left me wondering why she was not able to share with me what was going on in her life to cause her to act this way. Was this training at the commune with Armes changing the way she thought and reacted to things? Was it having a negative influence on her life in a way that I did not understand?

We were going to have to talk about this, I vowed to myself, because it was beginning to have a negative effect on our relationship, and our family life. Helen could see it too, and although she remained supportive of Gay taking her training at the commune with Armes, she was becoming concerned about her mental and emotional wellbeing as well.

Gay called to me from upstairs to come to Melody's room. I was pleased to see Gay hugging and comforting Melody, as they both lay on Melody's bed, and Melody asked if I would tell her a story about Nan's Nan.

"You have known her for a long time, haven't you, Dad?"

"Yes," I replied, "and I would be happy to share some of the special times I have had with her."

Gay went to have a bath, and I told Melody about some of my precious memories of Nan, who was a special horse, and Melody listened carefully.

"What made Nan so special?" Melody asked.

"I first found out how special she was when I was nine years old. It was Sports Day at Pennard School, and I was in the one hundred metre sprint. For my age group, I was the fastest runner in the school.

"Is that why you run with the horses, Dad?"

"Yes, that's right," I said, as Melody gently smiled and dreamed of being there with me.

"Although I was the fastest runner for my age group, I was not always able to compete, because I suffered from asthma," I said. "And if I had an asthma attack on gym day, which was on Fridays, or on Sports Day, then I was not able to take part. So, when I didn't have bad asthma, I really looked forward to competing and running my best against the other boys in my class. There were three other boys in my class that were fast runners too, and one of them, whose name was Donn Luces, was almost as fast as I was, and sometimes we were so close as we approached the finish line that I had to run with all my heart to beat him. But I always managed to win, and he was jealous of me being able to beat him."

"Donn Luces." Melody said, laughing. "Just like the pirate of Port Eynon!"

"That's right," I said. "He had the same sounding name as the pirate, and in fact he behaved like a pirate!"

Melody roared with laughter, and Gay could hear us from the bathtub. "What are you two laughing about?" she shouted.

"Pirates," Melody called back, and I continued.

"As I said, they had sports day at Pennard School. It was held on the last day of school before the summer holidays, and it was a big day for us kids because our parents came to the school on sports day to cheer their children along.

During this particular year, Donn Luces started threatening me a week before sports day. He told me that if I ran in the one-hundred or two-hundred-metre races, he would beat me up. He had beaten me up a few times before during the school year – once when a girl he liked preferred me over him, and another time when I scored against him three times in a football game when he was the goalie. He would punch and kick, and sometimes hit me with a stick, so I got nervous when he threatened to beat me up for competing against him on sports day.

For a whole week, he threatened to punch me in the face and break my nose. Sports day finally arrived, and I told him that I was not going to pull out of the race, even if he did try to beat me up. My dad had told me that I needed to teach him a lesson and run the fastest race I could and beat him by a long lead.

Anyway, about half an hour before the start of the race, some of the wild horses came into the school grounds. It was not uncommon for the horses to wander into the school field throughout the school year, but they had never come onto the field on sports day before. So, the headmaster, Mr. Evans, and the caretaker, Mr. Jones, tried chasing the horses off the field. But one of them – and it was Nan's Nan, the leader – ran back onto the field. Donn Luces tried to scare her by waving his hands in front of her face, but Nan's Nan chased him around the field and bit him on the arm.

'That horse is your friend!' Luces shouted at me, and he started pushing me around the school field. When Nan saw what he was doing, she charged him and knocked him flat on his face, and everybody laughed. He was so embarrassed and upset that his parents had to take him home, and he didn't get to compete on sports day."

"What happened to Nan, Dad? Did she get in trouble?"

"Mr. Evans, the headmaster, and some of the parents chased her out of the school grounds."

"And what happened to you on Sports Day? Did you win the one-hundred-metre race?"

"Yes! I won the one-hundred and the two-hundred-metre races, and I came in second in the three-hundred metres. And I only came in second in the three-hundred because I was tired from the first two races."

"Wow, you were fast, Dad, and I am glad Nan bit the pirate." We both laughed.

"It sounds like I'm missing all the fun," Gay said, coming back into the room in her pyjamas.

"You did, Mum, you missed the story of how Nan's Nan bit Donn Luces on the arm and protected Dad on sports day."

∽

Nothing more was heard or said about Nan's Nan for several weeks, until Helen, Melody and I went for a walk to Pennard Castle.

We played a game of hide-and-seek in the castle grounds like we always did, and it was Melody's turn to hide. She almost always hid in the castle room, and Helen and I pretended that we didn't notice. Slowly we would walk around the castle walls and out of the main castle gate. Sometimes Melody would hide in the tall ferns that grew outside the castle near the dunes, but today Helen had caught a glimpse of Melody's pink jacket going into the castle room.

Helen and I called out, "We are coming to find you, Melody. Where are you?" And we walked quietly towards the room.

As we entered the castle room, we were not prepared for what we were about to see. There was Melody, kneeling beside a horse that looked exactly like Nan's Nan!

"It can't be," Helen whispered to me in disbelief.

"Look, Grandma, it's Nan! She has come back to us! Look, Dad, it's her! She has the same white socks above her hooves, and the white line down her face, and her pink nose. And when she walks, she still has the limp in her left hind leg."

"What do you think?" Helen asked me again. "It looks exactly like her – maybe she was not dead after all?"

"She was dead alright," I replied. "I checked her for any respiration or breath, and she had none. She was dead."

As Helen and I conversed, Melody looked at us strangely as if to say why can't you just believe what your eyes are seeing?

"Can you stand her up, again, Melody?" I asked. "I want to see how she walks on that lame leg of hers..."

"Stand up, Nan," she called out, standing up herself.

And Nan's Nan stood up. "Come on, girl, walk," Melody said, "so Dad and Grandma will know that it's you."

The horse stood up, and then walked just as I had seen her do countless times before, and there was no doubt that it was Nan's Nan – her limp, her facial features, and those piercing bloodshot eyes that looked at you like no other horse.

"It's Nan's Nan!" I proclaimed. "I am sorry for doubting you, Melody. You knew it was her right away." Melody had grown wise beyond her years, but she did not need to know how or why Nan's Nan was alive again. It was only us adults who needed to reason things out in order to see.

As we walked back across the golf course, Melody skipped along in front of us, celebrating her joy in knowing that Nan's

Nan was alive. Helen and I walked along in silent wonder, which was both exciting and haunting at the same time.

Our experience with Nan's Nan, however, was not over yet! As we approached the pine woods at the side of the golf course on the path from Pobbles Beach, we spotted Nan's Nan galloping toward us, and then passing us along the path. I could hardly believe my eyes as I could see right through her body!

"She is see-through!" Melody shouted. "I can see the trees and the grass through her, Dad!"

"I have never seen anything like it," Helen said, holding my arm tightly. "That is a phantom horse!"

"It's still Nan's Nan," Melody said in a bewildered voice, as if she was trying to convince herself of what we had just seen. Melody then took my other arm and the three of us walked in a kind of somber silence until we reached the car.

I locked the doors and started the engine.

"We are all in agreement as to what we have just seen, right?" I said.

Melody was first to answer. "Yes, Dad, we saw the ghost of Nan's Nan."

"It was a phantom horse," Helen said. "I never thought I would ever see anything like that! And you are right, Melody, it did look exactly like Nan's Nan, and we could see right through it!"

"You're quiet, Kings," Helen said, as we drove along. "What are you thinking?"

"I saw a ghost girl once, but I have never seen a ghost horse!"

"Should I tell Mum?" Melody asked as we neared home.

I looked across at Helen, who gave me a gentle smile.

"I don't think anyone who hasn't seen the horse for themselves would be able to understand," I said, "and considering that Mum is actually scared of Nan's Nan, it might be a good idea not to mention it."

"But we saw a ghost horse, Dad! Nan's Nan is alive again. And you said that we should not keep secrets from each other."

"You're right, Melody, we should not keep secrets from Mum, but I think we should be careful in what we say to Mum, because she does come across as being afraid of Nan."

"What do you think, Grandma?" Melody asked.

"I think your dad is right. We need to be careful and pick the right time to tell Mum what we saw."

"Like read what sort of mood she is in, you mean?"

"Yes, that is exactly what I mean."

When we arrived back at the house, Helen, drove home to Cardiff, as she had a hair appointment in the morning, and Melody and I waited for Gay to come home from the commune.

Melody and I agreed that we would not say anything to Gay until she had eaten and settled in for the evening.

Gay said she had enjoyed her weekend at the commune, and she shared with us some of the things she was learning.

"I will be finishing my training soon," she said, and she asked me if I would come to her initiation ceremony for becoming a bard and priestess.

"I would love to," I replied, and I kissed her on her lips.

"Mm, I have sure missed your kisses this weekend, my love," she said.

Once Gay had finished having something to eat, and changed into her nightgown, Melody could not wait any longer to tell her mum about what we had seen.

Gay became uncomfortable, and then angry with Melody, as Melody tried to tell her about Nan's Nan and what we had seen happen to the horse.

"I don't want to hear any more about it," she said to Melody.

And then Gay looked across at me with a look of frustration on her face. "Nan's Nan is dead, she was hit by a car, and that is all there is to it! And I wish you would stop encouraging her to talk about phantom horses, Kings – she is going to be talking about it at school."

"It's hard to ask her to stop talking about something that is true," I replied. "What she shared with you is true. We did see Nan's Nan at Pennard castle, and then we saw what looked like her in the form of a phantom horse galloping past us on the path from Pobbles! And if you don't believe us, call your mum – she was there, and she will tell you exactly what we saw! I thought you of all people would believe your own family when we tell you something like this! What is wrong? Why are you afraid? You must have some idea why…? Don't you trust me anymore as someone you can confide in?"

"I am sorry, Kings," she replied, bursting into tears. "I know I have hurt your feelings, and Melody's too. I do believe you – I'm just really scared of that horse, but I can't talk about it right now."

"It's okay," I assured her. "Just go up and tell Melody that you believe her. She has been biting her lip and wondering if it's okay to tell you, because we don't know how you are going to react whenever we talk about Nan."

When Gay had finished apologizing to Melody, I suggested that we do something special as a family on the weekend.

"That is a great idea, my love," she responded. "Why don't we take Melody to Rhossili Beach and see if we can walk out on the Worms Head."

"A great idea," I said. "I will check and see if the tides are right for crossing the shipway out to the Worm."

So that was the plan. We would spend some family time together and have some bonding time while we re-explored Rhossili Beach.

I was not any closer to understanding what was going on with Gay, however, in relation to why she was afraid of Nan's Nan. Maybe next weekend she would open up and let me into her world again. I sure missed the intimacy that this horse issue seemed to be taking away from us.

⁓

The week went by quickly, and it was soon Saturday morning again. Gay packed one of her wonderful picnics, and some warm clothes in case it got cold, and we were off to Rhossili for the day.

After parking our car, we walked out across the cliff path towards the "Worm," which beckoned us from a distance like a mysterious monster coming out of the sea. Gay and Melody held onto my arms as we walked along the cliffs, and I wondered what wonderful adventure would befall us as we ventured out onto the Worms Head.

We checked in at the Coastguard station to make sure our tidal information was correct. At low water, the rocks called 'the shipway' that connect the Worm to the mainland are exposed and one can walk across them. From where we stood at the Coastguard station, there was a great view of the narrow stretch of rocks that the Worm is named after. The Worm juts far out into the sea in the form of a serpent that has three heads – the inner, middle and outer heads. And during certain times of the tide, the Worm can be heard breathing and sneezing and blowing into the sea like a waking monster. The girls held onto my arms tightly as I recited one of my poems that I had written about the outer head of the Worm, as it breathed and spat through its blow hole into the wild air of Rhossili Bay.

Today, the sea mists had gone to play elsewhere, and we were able to see the whole of Carmarthen Bay; and Lundy Island sparkled like a jewel in the crown of a faraway sea as we looked across to the coast of Devon and Somerset.

As we left the Coastguard station, the man warned us of the fast-flowing tides. "You don't want to spend the night on the Worm," he said.

"Little did he know that I had already spent a night out on the Worm," I said to Melody. "And it wasn't when the serpent was sleeping either; it was when it was awake and hissing and blowing in a thunderstorm. And there was torrential rain, and winds so strong that I had to hold on tight to the creature's back, so I was not blown into the foaming black sea with its white snarling teeth that ate into the iron rocks like popcorn!"

"Like popcorn!" repeated Melody, laughing and shouting across the bay at the seagulls, as she clung to my arm even tighter.

"I will never forget when you first told me about that night when you twisted your ankle on the Worm," Gay said. "I hope we don't get stuck out there today."

We climbed down the steep worn path to the start of the shipway rocks. "Make sure your shoelaces are tied tightly I said, and keep one hand free while we are crossing over the sharp rocks – in case you lose your balance."

"How far is it from here to the outer head and back?" Melody asked.

"Nearly three miles."

"Three miles?" Gay and Melody queried together.

"I agree it does not look like it would be three miles, but the distance is deceptive, and it also takes longer when you have to navigate a path across the rocks."

We all made it across the rocks safely, and we then climbed up to the inner head. The first thing that attracted our attention on the inner head was the soft spongy turf.

"Look Mum, I'm bouncing!" Melody shouted, and we all jumped around on the grass.

"It was here," I shared, "where I spent the night in the storm all those years ago, when I sprained my ankle and then was cut off by the tide. The wind was so strong that I held on tightly to the long grass as the wind blew across the head." Gay and Melody held on to some clumps of grass as they tried to imagine what it had been like.

Slowly we followed the inner head to the low neck and then on toward the Devil's Bridge. To reach the middle head, one must cross the Devil's Bridge, and we walked across in single file. First, I crossed, while Melody followed, and Gay encouraged Melody from behind.

"Dad, I'm scared!" Melody called. "Don't look down," I said. "Keep your eyes on your footing and come toward me. You're not going to fall."

"Listen to Dad, Melody," Gay called out, and she followed quickly behind.

"It's not so bad on a day like this," I said. "But it is when the wind is blowing so strongly that it feels It feels like it's going to blow you off the bridge into the heaving sea."

Once we were safely onto the middle head, we sat down for a snack. The view from anywhere on the Worm is spectacular, but there are some places that really take your breath away, like when you are standing on the Devil's Bridge and looking back across the golden sweep of Rhossili Beach, with the purple heathered downs above. When the tide is in, and the white crests of the waves ride like horses up the beach, it makes you feel like you are standing over them and riding on the wind up to the dunes. My Grandfather used to call the Devil's Bridge "Gods Balcony," as he and I would look out across the bay. And it really is one of the most wonderful places on God's earth. There is a great sense of wilderness and adventure, as one is surrounded by such wondrous natural beauty and the seabirds perform their dances to the music of the winds, as they fly over the wild crashing waves below.

Once we finished our snack, we made our way out to the outer head, and I showed Gay and Melody a game that I had played with my father when I was a boy. If you know what you are doing, it can be great fun, but one must always be careful when exploring near the edge of the high cliffs.

Underneath the turf of the outer head, there are innumerable little holes in the rock that connect with the large blow hole in the north side of the head.

I took Gay and Melody to an area that I had memorized on the turf, and we stood in a circle holding hands.

"What are we doing?" Gay asked, smiling. "Yes, what game are we going to play, Dad?" Melody asked. "Not ring around the roses, I hope. That's boring!"

""No, we are not playing that," I assured them. "We are going to play, Listen for the Monster!"

"Listen for the monster?" repeated Melody, and she and Gay laughed.

"Yes, that's right, on the count of three I want us to listen…. "

Suddenly, there were little blasts of air coming up through the turf, and eerie moaning and whistling noises filled the air.

Melody screamed "I can hear the monster!" And a blast of wind blew Gay's hat right off her head. Gay ran shrieking after her hat, and then once she had retrieved it, we formed another circle holding hands at the same spot. This time, a small whistling wind blew up my trouser leg, followed by more eerie moaning and whistling sounds.

Suddenly, I threw my hands up into the air and pretended to be a monster, while both girls ran away shrieking! We played for almost half an hour, and then, as we continued to the top of the outer head, the girls agreed that they had never had so much fun.

We left our backpacks on the grass while I attached a climbing harness and rope around our waists. And we climbed down the face of the outer head. As we descended the cliffside, the wind blew gently against us. The head stands about 175 feet above sea level, and on a clear day like today, the view is glorious! We could see Rhossili Bay in the near foreground, with the islet of Burry Holms at the far end of the bay. And we could see the whole coastline of Carmarthen Bay with Pembrey Sands,

Pendine Sands, Saundersfoot, Tenby, and then with our view fading, Caldy Island with St. Govan's Head showing dimly beyond. And we could just make out Lundy Island standing out against the skyline in the southwest.

"This is fantastic!" The girls said, waking me from my daydream as I skipped across the waves in my mind and traveled back to the Worm from Lundy Island.

"Okay, who is our timekeeper?" I asked. Melody put her hand up and read out the time. "It's time to climb back up the cliff and make our way back to the inner head," I said. I clipped us back into our climbing harnesses, and up we went. A few times I gave Melody a push from behind, but she was doing well as she scaled back up the cliffside, and Gay followed behind me.

We were soon back on top of the outer head, and after the climb, one couldn't help but feel that they had made a connection with the mysterious Rock at the End of the World!

"We conquered the Worm!" Melody shouted out upon the wind. And Gay and I both called out together: "Nice to make your acquaintance, Mr. Worm!"

On the way back to the inner head, we skirted the northern edge of the headland, and we saw many unique views of Rhossili Bay – that were enhanced by the ever-changing lights and shadows playing on the Rhossili Downs, and the soft ethereal effects produced by the drifting mists on its heights.

Today, the mauve of the heather seemed to be illuminated through the mist, as if being carried to the Beacon of Rhossili Downs, where nature would start her painting of the day, mixing the mauve with the yellow of the gorse flower, and the lush greens of the hillsides. The colours contrasted with the grey rocks as the low clouds both deepened and lightened the grey as they moved across the singing fields that waved their hands under the blue sky in worship of the sun.

Safely back on the mainland, we climbed the steep path up to the clifftop and then made our way back to the carpark. Close to the carpark and just out on the cliff is one of the most beautiful views of Rhossili Bay. The bay runs almost due north for a distance of three miles, and today we watched a series of waves breaking in parallel lines for as far as the eye could see, and it was a sight that one can never grow tired of watching.

There are certain places that stoke the wildfire in each of us, and they reach inside our human soul and caress us, whether we invite them in or not. This is one of those places!

When we reached the car, we drove into the village and had our picnic lunch on the green.

"Thank you, my love, you have packed my favorites," I said, my mouth watering.

Gay had packed Cornish pasties, crab sandwiches, Welsh cakes, and bird's custard pudding on sponge cake and strawberries for dessert. Gay laughed as noises of pleasure from Melody and I filled the fresh sea air, while gulls squawked and circled with hopes of tasting a sandwich.

After we had finished eating, or as Melody more appropriately called it, "wolfed our picnic down," Melody went to visit the three ponies and a foal that were playing on the green. This gave Gay and I some time to talk, and my hopes for our time together became fruitful, as Gay opened up to me again.

"I want to tell you what has been going on in my heart, Kings, and I hope you will forgive me for having been so distant and preoccupied in my relationship with you."

"Of course, I forgive you. I just don't understand why

you haven't held me in your confidence like you have always done in the past."

"I am really struggling, Kings," she said, bursting into tears. "I need to find out who my real father is, and Armes won't talk to me about him. It feels like there is a whole piece of my life that is still missing. I thought that if I got to know my birth mother, that hole in my life would be filled, but it's not!"

"As I get to know Armes, I am aware that I have a father somewhere who I have never met, and even three sisters!"

"Sisters?" I choked. You have sisters other than Pearl?"

"Yes, Kings, and I yearn to know them!"

"Come on, don't cry," I said, holding her in my arms.

Melody looked across at us, and she seemed to sense that her mum needed my undivided attention, so she continued visiting with the ponies.

Gay was able to calm her emotions and she continued sharing her heart.

"The whole reason I went to the commune and the reason I'm taking the bard training is so I can get to know my birth mother, and it's just not happening! Armes is hiding something from me, I know it! When she and I are together and there is no one else around, I can feel this 'big secret' that she is hiding from me."

"Do you think maybe she is just afraid to tell you what it is because she is just getting to know you as her daughter, and she doesn't want to complicate these first steps you're taking in getting to know each other? I am not saying that keeping something from you is right, but it just might be her own insecurity that is keeping her from telling you, and you can feel her discomfort and hesitation around it."

"I think you're probably right, Kings, but it's just so hard knowing that there is something so important she is not telling me, especially when I know so little about my family of origin. I have a right to know, don't I, Kings?"

"Yes, of course you do," and I leaned over to hug her.

"As I said, when she and I are together, I know she wants to tell me something, but for some reason she won't. It is probably as you have just said, Kings – she might think that if she tells me, it will turn me away from her. I just don't know what to do, my love. What do you think?"

"Would you like me to talk to her? She seems comfortable around me."

"She is, Kings. She has told me how much she likes you, and how fortunate I am to have you. And I am Kings! I am so blessed to have you in my life and for you to be my husband. Thank you for listening to me, and I am sorry I didn't tell you sooner how I was feeling. You and Melody have already sacrificed a lot in allowing me to be away at the commune so much, and I thought that it would just be too much to unload all this on you guys."

"It's not too much, and I will support you in any way I can. That is what we agreed to when we married. If we don't come to one another for support, then we are both missing out on the love and support we were meant to have in our relationship."

Gay took my hand and said, "I love you, Kings. Thank you for listening."

Melody looked over at us again, and she could see that Gay was now smiling, so she came running over. "Is everything alright now, Mum?"

"Yes, everything is alright now, Melody," Gay replied. "Mum just needed to talk to Dad about something."

Once we had finished our picnic on the green, we walked back to the carpark on the cliffs.

"I want you to see the sunset," I said to Gay and Melody. "We can sit and watch it from one of the benches that overlooks the bay."

As we looked back at the Worm from the cliff, it was mysteriously shrouded in mist, lying peaceful like a sleeping serpent in a tranquil sea of purple and yellow haze.

Other times when I have looked out at the Worms Head from the cliffs, it has stood out in the waves like a noble knight, with its majestic outer head holding out against the thunderous advance of the waves rolling in from the open Atlantic. One can hear the strange, tormented hissing and booming from its Blowhole that shoots high into the air.

Today the Worm was asleep, but as we looked out at its haunting form, we knew that it could stir and wake at any time, and then hiss and boom across the bay.

We had enjoyed a wonderful day, and it was time for us to head home.

Chapter Four

Dunlins and Dunes

On Sunday we had a lovely family day enjoying our home in Pennard. Samantha and Melody played games on the lawn, and Gay and I worked in the garden and enjoyed the autumn flowers that were still in bloom – including the purple clematis that my Grandma and Grandpa had planted beside the wooden trellis at the back door of the house. On one side they had planted clematis, and on the other side, honeysuckle. The vines had grown thick and strong over the trellis, and today the sweet smell of honeysuckle rode upon the breeze and danced with my memories. How blessed I am to live in my Grandma and Grandpa's old house, surrounded by wonderful memories – and making new ones with my own family in this sacred place!

In the evening, Helen came over for tea, as she had been visiting a friend in the village, and after tea we played board games until late.

Soon it was Monday morning again, and Melody caught the bus to school, while Gay parked her car at her friend's house in Swansea and made her regular commute to Cardiff by train.

I was still working only part-time at the church, though I was up to a four-day week this month – which still gave me Mondays off, and today I had arranged to meet Helen in Swansea for lunch so that we could talk and catch up. I had sure missed her over the last few weeks, as circumstances had not allowed us to spend our usual time together.

Helen caught the train down from Cardiff, and I met her at the coffee shop in the Swansea market. There are several coffee shops and eateries in the market, but we met in the one in the middle of the market where I often like to sit with my fellow countrymen and watch the world go by. The world that I know and love so well, that is. I know that there are other wonderful places, and I have been to some of them, but I am happy here in my world of Swansea and Gower Land.

"Good morning, lovely lady, how you light up this grey morning like the first bluebells of spring!"

"Good morning, handsome man, how you light up this grey day with new wonders and adventures!"

"Two coffees please, and a couple of Welsh cakes," I said to the waitress.

As our conversation began to flow, I shared with Helen the progress I was making with Gay.

"That's great," Helen replied, "I know you were concerned about how she has been so preoccupied lately."

"And how are things going at the commune and with Armes?" she asked.

"Gay seems to be doing well in her training to become a bard," I replied, "but she wants Armes to tell her about her father."

"And how is that going?"

"Not too well, I'm afraid. Gay feels that Armes is keeping something from her, and she wants to ask her what it is, but she is hesitant to ask. Getting to know Armes has brought up a lot of feelings for her in wanting to find her dad."

I wasn't sure if I should mention Gay's other sisters to Helen in case she didn't know. Besides, I didn't know if I even believed what Armes was saying. Anyway, I decided not to mention anything else unless Helen brought it up.

"As for finding her dad… that may be difficult," Helen replied, with a look of concern on her face.

"How difficult?" I asked. "And would you mind telling me what you know? I would certainly appreciate it, as it would help me in supporting Gay."

"I will tell you all I know, Kings, but it's very little."

"Thank you!" I said.

"When I met Armes and Gay at the commune, Gay's real father was not in the picture at all. Armes was in a relationship with another man at the commune, as I think I already told you."

"Yes, you did, but nothing about Gay's biological father."

"I know nothing about him, Kings. Only that Armes is Gay's birthmother, and Armes gave Gay to my husband John and I to bring up, and of course we have always treated her as our own from that time onwards."

"When John and I inquired about Gay's father, Armes would never tell us anything about him, so we assumed that he was abusive, or that something traumatic had happened. You could talk to Armes about anything, except for Gay's father."

"How about Gay's birth certificate?" Helen asked. "Armes showed you that when you first visited her at the commune, didn't she?"

"Yes, she did, but it only had Armes' name on it, and her surname is Saren. But there was no recording of any father on the certificate."

"That is strange, Kings. I did not think you could have a birth certificate registered without the father's name. Maybe Armes didn't know who the father was?"

"That's what I was thinking," I said. "Maybe she just doesn't know." "Well, she must have some idea, Kings."

"Yeah, you would think so."

"Sorry I can't help you, Kings."

"That's okay and thank you for trying."

It was great to see Helen, and to share with her what had been going on with Gay.

Before Helen returned to Cardiff, we made plans for her to come and stay at the house the next weekend. Gay would be away at the commune doing her training, so we thought we would take Melody for an adventure on the Gower.

"I want to see that phantom horse again," Helen said. "I can't believe that such a thing exists!"

"Neither can I! We will try and find Nan's Nan again and find out more about her."

"Bye Helen, have a good day, lovely lady, and see you on Friday evening."

"Bye, Kings, see you then."

☙

The week seemed to go by slowly, until Thursday, when I took my youth group hiking into the hills. We had a rip-roaring good time and cooked steaks on a fire that we had made, and then we went rock climbing in the evening and climbed the face of the Three cliffs Rock. Gosh, I love my job! Working with the youth and helping them build faith into their lives is so rewarding. Working with teens and youth was something I thought was going to be difficult. It has its challenges, of course, but once you earn their trust, they treat you like one of them. And that's how they make me feel – "like one of the boys, with some extra wisdom and life experience."

On Friday morning, Gay packed for her weekend at the commune and took her car to work, while I walked Melody across to Pennard Stores to catch the school bus.

"Bye, Dad, I love you!"

"I love you too, Melody! See you when you get home from school. Don't forget that Grandma is coming over tonight, and we are going to look for Nan's Nan tomorrow."

"Nan's Nan, the Spirit Horse! Cool!"

As Melody climbed onto the bus, I felt glad that she was not afraid of Nan's Nan. Whatever that horse is or isn't, I was looking forward to finding out more about it.

When Helen arrived in the evening, we relaxed and had a games night indoors. The evenings were drawing in quickly now, and by 6:00 p.m. it was almost completely dark outside as autumn's shadows grew tall. Samantha and Melody made a fire in the sitting room fireplace, and we sat with our tea and hot chocolate, and the biscuits that Helen had brought from the market.

The seasons of the year have their own unique rhythm, and I was looking forward to the slower and reflective days of the golden fall, as summer's days ride away upon the gentle winds, with only their memories whispering between the falling leaves. In the garden, the leaves on the silver birch were turning to yellows and browns, and the helicopter seeds were swirling to the ground as gallant October rode through the sycamores. Meanwhile, the young collar doves that were born in the spring sat and cooed on the telephone wires between the sleepy lamp posts, as their bright new feathers glistened in the late afternoon sun. Rabbits hopped and skipped on the lawn, not yet afraid of humankind, and the owl returned to hoot in the nearby pines.

Samantha placed another log on the orange chattering fire that shone a golden light on our faces as we told our stories within the listening walls of this sacred room. And I reminisced about my Grandma and Grandpa's tales, as I told a few of my own, and tonight all my memories of happy days gone by, dwelled here together with new ones we were making, and I was surrounded by love, and I thanked God for my happy home.

Saturday morning arrived on a breeze, that blew gently upon my face from the open bedroom window, and I looked forward to the adventures of the new day.

As I stood in the shower, I could hear that Melody was up, and her feet ran around the wooden landing like an excited bird, and the smell of frying bacon woke up the whole herd.

Samantha stirred and cooked, and eggs smiled and popped as they were shaken onto crispy toast, and marmalade and marmite waited upon the table ready to wrestle with our tastebuds.

"More bacon Dad?"

"Oh, yes please!" Helen dressed and the world stood still, and Melody and I ate enough bacon to make a horse ill. "Look, Dad, there's a songbird on the windowsill!"

After breakfast, Samantha and Glynn went to spend the day in Swansea, which included a walk from the Slip Bridge to the Mumbles, along the bay.

"Bye, Dad and Helen and Melody, have a lovely day."

"You too, my love, have fun walking across the bay, and say hi to the Mumbles, and tell him I will see him another day."

Helen, Melody and I drove to the village and parked on Bendrick Drive. And we walked along the path beside the golf course towards Pobbles, and then cut across the dunes to the castle.

There were no horses within the castle grounds, and we peered through the crumbling windows to the valley below.

"There they are!" shouted Melody, already excited. "There are nine horses in the valley!"

"And that brown one looks like it might be Nan's Nan," Helen said, with a rather subdued kind of smile.

"Let's go and see, Dad!" Melody said. "Let's run down the sandy path, and I will race you and Grandma to the bottom. First one to put their hand in the river wins!"

"You're on," I said, looking at Helen, who gave me a nod.

"On your mark, get set, go!" And off we went bolting down the sandy path like rabbits out of Mr. McGregor's garden. Melody fell flat on her face, and got up spitting sand and laughing, which gave Helen and I a chance to catch up and pass her. Helen then stopped to take off her shoes and I was in the lead! I reached the banks of the Pennard Pill and dipped my hands in, and I was followed by Melody and Helen pulling each other back and forth at the bottom of the slope to claim second place.

Well, we were all wide awake now, and as we approached the herd, I think we all wondered if what we had seen the other day would still be real. Not that what we had seen wasn't real, but rather it was hard to believe, especially as time had gone by. Would we see the same wonderous thing again? Or would Nan's Nan turn out to be just an ordinary horse today?

"That is Nan," Helen said, pointing to the old brown mare with the white line coming down her forehead and just falling short of her nose.

"It is definitely her," both Melody and I affirmed, as we walked right up to her and started patting her on the head. Melody had brought an apple to feed her, and Nan ate right out of her hand.

"She is not a spirit horse now," Melody said, as Nan happily crunched the apple and made a juicy mess all over Melody's hand. Once she had finished eating the apple, she walked off to join the other horses, and I watched the limp in her hind leg.

The three of us stood watching from a distance, and everything looked ordinary. A herd of horses grazing in the Three Cliffs Valley.

All of a sudden Nan's physical form seemed to change.

"Is this real? Are we imagining this?" I said questioning my senses. What had we just seen? I pondered for a few moments. All three of us had seen Nan's Nan change from her normal physical form to a see-through phantom and back again!

"Wait a minute, look!" Helen called out. "I can see through her again!"

Melody and I immediately turned our eyes back to the mare, who was standing up as if startled, and she appeared to have changed to what looked like an illuminous fog, though retaining her form and colour. Suddenly, she turned away from the other horses and began to gallop like a young horse, and we could see right through her body.

"Oh, my gosh!" Helen exclaimed, looking at me with a wonderous look that I had only seen once before, and that was last week when we had seen Nan's Nan galloping past us large as life.

"She did it again," Melody said, quite unperturbed. "She can transform into a spirit horse any time she likes!"

"What do we do now?" I asked. "Who do we tell, and who would believe us?"

"We certainly can't tell the authorities," Helen said. "They will only come and take her away and she will not be safe with them."

"You're right," I said, "Either that or they will laugh at us and think we're crazy. And besides, this is our discovery! Our secret! And there must be a reason that Nan's Nan has shown us that she can transform herself."

"Grandpa Roger would believe us," Melody said, "and he might be able to tell us what this all means."

"You are right, Melody, well said! Grandpa Roger will believe us, and he will keep things a secret, so people don't come bothering Nan and the other horses."

"So that is what we will do," I said. "I will speak to Grandpa on Monday when I go over and visit him and Mary."

The car ride home was loud with silent contemplation.

⌢⌣

Sunday was another lovely autumn day, and I did as I had promised to do – take Helen and Melody to somewhere where they had never been before on the Gower Peninsula. The significance of yesterday began to get crowded out of our minds as we focused on the new adventure of the day. But as we drove along towards our destination, a few haunting thoughts would come and go in my mind. Oh well, maybe Dad would throw some light on things when I visited him tomorrow.

We arrived at the little hamlet of Nicholaston and we found the path that led out across the Burrows. We each carried a backpack containing our lunches and snacks, and of course plenty of water. Even in the cooler days of the fall, it was thirsty work rambling across the Burrows and walking through the deep sand of the dunes.

"Where are we going on this mystery tour?" Helen asked.

"I am going to take you to watch the Dunlins," I replied.

"Dunlins! What are dunlins?" Melody exclaimed.

"It sounds like a type of bird," Helen said, although the look on her face seemed puzzled.

"Wait and see," I said, "and there is lots more to see along the way."

To our right was the beautiful Crawly Woods. We made our way along the deep sandy path through the Burrows, as it slowly began to descend toward the beach.

"My feet are heavy," Melody said, giving me a tired but cheerful look. "Will we be there soon?"

"Yes, the sea is right in front of you."

Before the dunes shake hands with the beach, there are a few places where one should stop and take in the view of the delicate greens of the grasses, the greenish-blue sea, the blue sky, and the variegated foliage of the woods. And as you come out onto the beach and look to the right, the headland of Oxwich Point calls out to you to follow the path west. And to the left, the magnificent view of the western side of the Great Tor and Little Tor call you to walk to the east.

"Which way?" Melody asked, looking back and forth at the beckoning headlands.

"Which one is calling the loudest to you?" I asked.

Melody pointed right, in the direction of Oxwich Point.

"Well done! We are turning right," I said, and we held hands as we walked across the yellow sands. Helen and I took off our shoes and socks and we walked in the gentle waves, while Melody followed the tideline ahead of us and collected shells.

As one continues to walk westwards, the cliffs completely disappear, and they are replaced by burrows and marshes that extend inland for several furlongs. From here to Oxwich Point, and especially inland to the marshes, Is a bird watcher's paradise. Along the shore, we saw gulls of many types, and wading birds, and a Kestrel and a Harrier flew over the marsh grasses hunting for their prey.

"Alright, it's time to tell you what a Dunlin is," I said, "and Helen is right, it is a bird, and they fly in a group of hundreds!"

No sooner had the words left my mouth when Melody shouted, "There!"

And there they were! What a marvelous sight! A hundred or more birds flying in close formation and traveling at a terrific speed, with perfect leadership and under complete control. All wheeling and turning as one bird, a flash of silver as they turned. In view one moment, a complete disappearance the next, and just as suddenly a reappearance – missing the water by a hair's breadth one second, a hundred feet in the air the next, and then a dive down at a steep angle to make a perfect landing – all still in close formation. It was enough to make any squadron leader jealous, and the magnificent Red Arrows Aerobatics Team look like first-time pilots.

We all stood silent as we watched them, with Melody's occasional "Wow!" breaking the otherwise windy and tranquil wave-breaking chorus.

"So, they are Dunlins," Helen exclaimed. "What an amazing bird, to fly in such perfect coordination and control! Thanks Kings, for showing us."

"Yes, thanks Dad, they are amazing."

On the beach, we enjoyed our lovely picnic that Helen had made, and then Helen and I joined Melody in collecting shells along the tidelines, as we headed back toward the path and up through the Burrows to the car.

Helen stayed until Gay got home from the commune, and then headed home to Cardiff. It had been a wonderful weekend.

Chapter Five

Lock the Doors!

On Monday evening, I went over to visit Dad and Mary in Swansea as planned, and I told them about our experiences in seeing Nan's Nan change into a spirit horse.

"You are joking, aren't you, boy?" Mary said, seemingly quite amused.

"I wish I was," I replied. "The horse can transform from a normal physical form to having an illuminated see-through body. You can see the plants and trees on the other side of her!"

"You are not joking are you, Kings." Dad said, seeing the concern on my face.

"No, I'm not."

"Well, sit yourself down, boy," Mary said, "and tell us more about this horse over a cuppa tea."

After sharing everything we had seen, Dad said what I thought he would say: "I must come and see this phantom horse for myself. And you said that Helen, the librarian, saw it too?"

"Yes Dad, we all saw it."

"Well, if the librarian saw it, it must be true. She is not one for making up stories, is she, Mary?"

  Kingsley Ross Hill

"No, if Helen saw it, then it must be true. Not that your Dad and I don't believe you, Kings. Seeing a ghost horse is quite a statement, and hard for anyone to come to terms with – even your Dad, and he's seen UFO's!"

I finished having tea with Dad and Mary, and we arranged a time on Thursday evening to go and visit Nan's Nan in the valley.

The rest of the week would not go by quick enough, until finally it was Thursday. I really wanted Dad to see what we had seen, not that any of us doubted in any way what we had seen, but Dad was such an authority on the supernatural, and if he could see Nan's Nan transform into a spirit horse, then he could probably make sense of some things that we couldn't. Anyway, I hoped that Nan's Nan was still in the valley.

We had a quick tea at our house, and Melody and I went with Dad in his car to the village. Gay was still not in the least bit interested in finding out anything more about the horse, and Dad thought it very strange. We parked in the village and walked across the golf course to the castle. We looked over into the valley and there was no sign of any of the horses. Just when I needed them to be there, they were gone, I spoke aloud, feeling frustrated. We crossed back over to the beach path and decided to see if the herd had moved over to the hills and dunes above Pobbles beach. They had not, and there was no sign of them anywhere.

"Oh well, not to worry," Dad said, "we will try again tomorrow."

On Friday, however, the horses were in the valley, and Helen was able to join us on the search.

"Let's just pretend we are minding our own business and walk past them first," Dad said, "and then when they are used to us being near them, we can approach them and see what happens."

As we walked down one of the sandy slopes beside the castle, a few of the horses lifted their heads to see who was approaching them, and the others continued to graze on the lush marsh grass that grows around the Pennard Pill. Once we reached the foot of the slope and then started to walk towards them, almost all the horses lifted their heads and seemed wary of our presence.

"Let's give them a wide berth and walk right past them," Dad said, "and have you spotted Nan's Nan yet?"

"She is right there," Melody said, pointing. "She just looks like an ordinary horse right now."

"It's Nan's Nan alright," Helen said, as we walked right past them.

"Keep walking," Dad said to Melody. "Don't stop because we don't want to scare them off."

We walked about fifty feet past the herd, and then we stopped to observe. Nan's Nan was in her physical form, and there did not appear to be anything unusual about her presence or behaviour. She continued to graze with the other horses while keeping a wary eye on us to make sure we did not come too close. There were three foals with the herd that had been born in the spring, and the younger mares appeared to be very protective, watching our every move.

Dad looked across at me with a look of expectation, as

if to say, 'well I am here, and I don't see anything unusual happening.'

"We will just have to wait and watch," I said to everyone.

"Maybe there has to be a specific event to trigger the transformation?" Helen suggested.

"That's a good point," I said. Let's keep observing for another ten minutes, and then walk closer to the herd and see what she does." I reminded Melody that we would have to be careful as we approached the herd, as sometimes the mares will charge towards you to ward you off, and even bite you if they feel particularly threatened.

"Okay, let's start walking toward them," I said. "Walk slowly and be ready to back off if they become aggressive."

They allowed us to walk almost right up to them, and Melody was about to pull an apple out of her pocket to feed one of the mares, when Nan's Nan's coat suddenly became illuminous!

"There is something happening!" Dad said excitedly! "Look at her coat, it is shining, and she looks fluorescent!"

And as we all set our eyes upon her, she suddenly came up on her hind legs and neighed loudly with her front hooves in the air.

"I thought she was an old horse," Melody whispered to me as she held my arm tightly. "An old horse can't rear up on its hind legs like that!"

Suddenly, Nan's Nan lowered her front hooves to the ground and began to gallop around us in a circle. Helen held onto my other arm while Dad watched in amazement as we could now see that Nan's Nan had transformed from her physical form to what Dad called, a "phantom appearance."

The horse continued to gallop around us, closing its circle tighter and tighter as if rounding us up like a herd of sheep.

"It's going to trample us!" Melody cried, clinging to me now and expecting me to do something.

"What are we going to do?" Helen shouted at the other side of me, her calm demeanor having given way to a frightened expression that I had never seen on her face before.

"Should I be afraid?" I thought, as the creature got closer and closer.

"Okay, everyone, stand back-to-back and form a circle!" Dad shouted, looking as white as a sheet! And just when we thought we were going to be trampled, the animal vanished before our very eyes. A few sparkling lights appeared in the shape of a horse, lingered for a few seconds in the air, and then were gone!

"My gosh!" Dad shouted, "Let's get out of here now! Everyone back to the car!"

Helen's eyes met mine with a look of both astonishment and relief, and Melody said, "Are we alright now, Dad? Has the phantom horse gone?"

"Yes," I replied, trying to convince myself that we were safe and could now walk back across the golf course to the car. As we walked along, I could feel both Helen's and Melody's hands trembling, and my eyes scanned the hills and dunes fearing that the phantom might return.

Dad is not a man whom I would call 'bold of heart'. He is rather fearful of ghosts and the spirit world, and I recalled an occasion when he paid my brother and I to go into the old Romeo Vickers Building in Swansea and take photographs in the boardroom. The original building had been bombed out and destroyed during the Second World War, after which the Vickers Building had been built on top of the old site, and it was said to be haunted. Dad, who had done work in the building, had heard strange noises and had felt the presence of a spirit or two brush past him in the corridors. And in some of the rooms where he would be working, he would feel the room suddenly get very cold.

"Especially in the boardroom," he said, "the room would get ice cold, making the hairs on my arms stand up!" Dad gave my brother Fraser and me a five-pound note and two king-size Mars bars each to take his infrared camera into the boardroom and take photos at different angles around the conference table. My brother and I remember feeling a cold presence in the room, but we never saw anything other than each other's nervous and sometimes frightened faces. We did what we had to do for our money and the Mars bars and then got the heck out. Dad would always ask us if we had felt or seen anything, and then he would pay us our money while we wolfed down our Mars bars in the car.

Dad had his own photo lab at home, and he processed his own photographs from the negatives. One day, he showed us the images of what he said were spirit beings sitting around the table where we had taken the photos. I think I had nightmares for a fortnight after that, as I imagined who those creepy dead people were inside those outlines in the picture.

But today was different. We were scurrying away from what looked like a ghost horse, and it was not just my brother and I getting spooked; it was the four of us, including my father, and I was a grown-up now, and I could buy as many Mars bars as I wanted to…. We made it safely back to the car, and Dad locked the doors. Nothing much was said on our way back to the house, other than Dad saying: "Well, that's that, we have a ghost horse on our hands." He recommended that we not go back looking for the horse alone, but if indeed we did go back to take another look, that we go in numbers. Personally, I was quite happy to let sleeping horses lie, so to speak, and to not get too close to her again, whatever she might be.

When we arrived back at the house, Helen and Melody went inside, and Dad and I sat in the car to debrief.

"I don't know what to tell you, Kings? Other than even though it seemed like a close call, if the creature wanted to harm us it could have…"

I nodded.

Dad continued. "My first thoughts are that it's from another dimension, and that it is visiting us here for a reason. My questions are: what is it doing here and what does it want? It must be here because there is something here in this dimension that it wants or needs."

"Yes, Dad, but this is Nan's Nan. I have known her since I was a boy, and there are many witnesses of that – friends and peers over the years have known her as Nan's Nan. It was less than two years ago when I put Melody on her back and led her across the beach with a rope."

"Yes, I understand that, Kings, but the Nan's Nan you knew was hit by a car and killed a few weeks ago. This is something different, Kings! As we saw earlier," he continued, "this horse can transform itself into something from another dimension! We are dealing with a phantom horse here, and until we can learn more about it, and why it's here, we would be wise to leave it well alone."

After our conversation, Dad headed home to Swansea, and I went into the house to catch up with Helen and Melody.

Melody seemed to have brushed things off and was playing a game with Samantha in her room, while Helen was having a cup of tea with Gay. I joined them for a cup of tea, and each time Helen tried to speak of what had happened, Gay immediately changed the subject to something else. How strange…

"I don't know why Gay is so determined not to talk about Nan's Nan," Helen said, as I walked her out to her car.

"I don't know either," I said.

Helen looked at me with a smile. "I am so looking forward to seeing you this week, Kings, on your day off. We are overdue for some conversation time together."

'We are," I agreed, and I gave her a hug.

"Will you be coming up to Cardiff, lovely man? Or would you like me to come down to Pennard?"

"I will come up to Cardiff on Wednesday. I would like to look around the market and have one of those wonderful cinnamon buns at the bakery."

Helen smiled, and then headed home to Cardiff.

As Gay and I retired for the evening, she thanked me again for allowing her to be away at the commune every second weekend. "I know that it is a sacrifice for you and Melody," she said, "and I will be graduating as a Celtic Priestess soon."

"I will look forward to coming to your inauguration," I said proudly. "And I know Dad will be proud of you too!"

"Thank you love," she smiled, "I could not do it without your support."

As Gay fell asleep in my arms, I thought about our relationship.

I felt as close to her as I could be, I pondered, considering that she is away every second weekend at the commune, and she does seem to be acting very strange around any association with Nan's Nan. Anyway, Gay and I had enjoyed a nice time sitting and talking in front of the fire tonight, and as always, our lovemaking was spectacular!

About two in the morning, the phone rang. Fortunately, we don't have a phone in the bedroom, and it didn't wake Gay, or anyone else in the house. I raced down the hall, fearing it was bad news from somewhere. Good, it was not a Canadian number, so it wasn't one of my boys calling me. It was Dad's and Mary's number!

"Dad, what are you calling at this hour for? Are you and Mary alright?"

"Yes, we are fine, but you will never believe what I have found out."

"What, Dad?"

"I have been doing more translating of Taliath's Diary and this is what she says..."

"The horse is understood by the people of our clan as being both physical and spiritual in form. A phantom mare that is able to transform its appearance from a physical animal being, to a spirit horse."

"It's just like what we saw tonight, Kings! I believe it is the same creature recorded here in the diary in the year 970 AD. And as I translated earlier, Taliath records that the phantom mare has an attachment not only to its specific clan, but also to one family lineage within the clan. And furthermore, from this family lineage, the horse identifies with one individual person. This person is always a woman and is descended from one family with the family name being "Saren.""

When I heard the name, I almost fell off my chair!

Saren was Gay's maiden name. It was time for me to tell Dad about my experience when I first went to the commune and talked to Armes alone.

"Armes told me that Gay's real birth name is "Taliath Saren.""

"You're joking, Kings!"

"No, I am not, Dad! I wish I were! Gay's birth name is Taliath Saren!"

At my words, Dad was silent on the other end of the phone, and I imagined him sitting back in his chair and taking off his glasses as he always did when pondering something.

"I am astounded, Kings. Astounded…!"

"Me too, Dad. This is crazy!"

"I don't understand things yet, but the fact that her maiden name is also Saren, is going to reveal a lot of things, Kings, I can tell you that!"

"Do you think she is connected to the family lineage that the horse identifies with, Dad?"

"It is hard to say at this point with any certainty, but I would not be in the least surprised if she is, it is too much of a coincidence."

At Dad's word's, shivers ran up my spine, as I remembered how uneasy Gay had been when Nan's Nan had led us to the chest and was digging in the sand. She felt like the horse knew her in some way from a time in the past, and yet to my knowledge Gay had only met Nan's Nan once before that. And that had been down on the beach when I had brought Melody to her, riding on Nan's back. And then there were the vivid and confusing dreams she had had about the horse in relation to past and future events.

I said goodbye to Dad on the phone and went back to bed.

I don't know what all this means, I pondered, but there is definitely something very mysterious afoot. I would just have to wait and see what happened next.

I will try and persuade Gay to come and see this phantom horse for herself, I decided. Maybe then she will understand something of her connection with the creature. And I will gain some understanding of why she is so resistant and afraid every time Melody and I try to have a conversation with her about the horse.

Wednesday was my day off and I drove up to Cardiff to spend time with Helen as planned. Gay wanted me to keep encouraging Helen to try and meet someone, and to take her out and about a bit when I could. It seemed she wasn't really interested in meeting anyone, I thought, and I was not going to push her. Helen was a wonderful conversationist, and well read in her understanding of history and geography, which I enjoyed no end, and I looked forward to what was becoming our weekly conversation time. Helen had told me that she had read over three thousand books, and it was not because she worked as a librarian, though that did give her the perks of discovering the best books.

It was wonderful to have a friend like Helen, and to have her wisdom and experience watching over our family.

As I crossed the Jersey Marine Bridge, I began to get excited. It would not be long now, and I would be with my lovely friend Helen. We were going to meet in our favorite coffee shop upstairs in the market. And a coffee and cinnamon bun would be the order of the day.

I parked my car near the train station and walked to the market to meet Helen. She was already sitting at our favorite table that overlooks the ground floor of the market, with the wonderful sound of the exuberance and energy of the new day and its people rising to meet us. The taste of coffee and cinnamon buns warmed our tummies. Helens big blue eyes looked at me with the freshness and excitement of a young girl, as we began our conversation.

We talked about the family, and Gays strange behavior around the spirit horse, and it remained a mystery why she seemed so afraid of the strange creature. I shared with Helen, what dad had most recently translated in the diary, and his call in the early hours of the morning.

It was time to talk about Helen now, and I asked her why she was closer to Gay than she was to Pearl, though Pearl being her biological daughter.

"Pearl is the daughter of my body," Helen explained, "but Gay is the daughter of my spirit. Even though I did not give birth to Gay, our hearts have always walked together, and I have a love and affection for her that transcends far beyond the physical. I don't understand it, but it is quite lovely, and it embraces my soul."

"You don't have to understand it," I replied, "it is what it is, and it is a blessing to celebrate." And we ordered a latte each, and another cinnamon bun to share.

"It is a good job that I work out and teach my yoga class," Helen laughed, as I said cheers, and we supped on our latte's.

"I love my Pearl, dearly," Helen continued, "but Gay has always rocked my world!"

"Mine too, I declared!" And we toasted Gay.

Chapter Six

Change is in the Air

The autumn began to grow old now, and the flowers in the garden all but vanished into the new seasons hold. We spent time in the evenings playing games in front of the fire, and I managed to connect with some of my boyhood friends that I had grown up with, and Gay and I enjoyed getting to know them and their families. It was wonderful living in Pennard again, and especially in the old house that already felt like home.

Gay continued her training at the commune and would soon be graduating. A part of me was excited that she would soon be home every weekend, but another part of me wanted things to stay the way they were, with Helen and I being able to spend every second weekend together and continue our wonderful conversations. I looked forward to our next adventures exploring more of Wales. During the weeks that Helen did not come down on the weekend, I drove or caught the train to Cardiff on one of my days off. It is time that you met someone, I continued to tell her. 'But I don't need to,' she would say, 'I have all the fun I need hanging out with you, Kings.' Maybe if I was out of the picture, then she would miss the companionship, I thought, and would try to meet someone. Oh well, things would work out the way they were meant to, and in their good time, I concluded, and besides, Gay will be graduating soon now, and Helen and I won't be able to hang out as much.

On the weekends when Gay was at home, we went metal detecting with Dad. Things seemed to have calmed down now regarding Gay not feeling afraid of her connection with Nan's Nan, and she had not had any more dreams about the phantom animal for quite some time. Dad and Melody and I tried not talk about the horse around her, and I am sure that was a factor.

There was one thing that both Dad and I had noticed however, and that was that Gay had completely lost interest in doing any more translating of Taliath's diary. And she never wanted to talk about how the translating was going or answer our questions as to why she was not interested anymore.

Melody found it hard to come to terms with the fact that her mother did not want to study the artifacts we had found in the chest anymore. This had been something they had enjoyed doing together, trying on some of the items of clothing and studying what they were used for. At the same time, Gay had been enjoying imparting her understanding of the Celtic culture and history to Melody, who was developing a keen interest herself. But suddenly, that connection she had with her mother, completely stopped.

Gay said another strange thing to Dad and me. Every time that we mentioned something new that we had translated in the diary, she would say "yes I know all about that," dismiss it as nothing significant, and carry on with her previous stream of thought. In Dad's word's, Gay had gone from being the most excited of the three of us about the translating, to not caring about it at all. And I must say, I agreed with him. I had witnessed a night and day difference since Helen, Melody, and I had reported seeing Nan's Nan as a phantom horse.

"This is a very strange reaction, Kings," Dad would say, "and what I find haunting about it is that maybe she does know and understand what is written in the diary."

I, however, was not ready to hear this, and I tried to dismiss Dad's words as farfetched. But I wrestled inside with an underlying gut feeling that what Dad had said might be true. Melody had also come to me one night and told me that Gay had told her a bedtime story about one of the candlesticks that we had found in the chest. "It was not an ordinary story, Dad," she said. And when I asked her what she meant about it not being an ordinary story, she answered, "It sounded real when Mum was telling it, Dad, and I could feel in my heart that it was not made up."

What was I to think? Dad had said what he said, and now Melody had told me this…? I could not get my head around it, or did I even want to?

This bothered me for some time, and I decided to talk to Helen about it.

⌒

I drove up to Cardiff and met Helen at our coffee shop in the market.

"I don't know what to tell you, Kings. She is acting so strange. There is no question in my mind that she has some sort of connection with that horse, but what that connection is, is a mystery to me."

Helen sipped her tea, and her big blue eyes revealed that she was deep in thought. Suddenly Helen jumped back in her chair and looked startled.

"What is it I replied?!"

"There is something else, Kings, come to think of it. I have just remembered something that could be very significant. I don't know why I didn't remember this before."

"Please," I pressed, pouring her another cup of tea. "Please go on."

"Alright I will. Do you remember when I told you that Armes gave Gay to my husband John and I to bring up, when we were living at the commune?"

"Yes, I remember. 'A strange adoption,' you called it."

"Yes, you remember. Not that you would forget something like that."

"Well, once John and I realized the responsibility we had in bringing up Gay, we left the commune with her and moved to Pennard, as I told you before."

"Yes, I remember that."

"So, we lived in Pennard, and only went back to the commune once every couple of months to check in with Armes, to see how she was doing without Gay. To be honest, John and I were afraid that she was going to change her mind and want her back. But happily, for us, she didn't."

"Then after about two years, Pearl was born, and we stopped going back to see Armes altogether. Then one day, John and I decided to take the girls for a holiday in Pembrokeshire. We camped in a little campsite at a place called Brynberian.

Try saying that after three classes of wine. Anyway, it was not far from Newport Bay where we could take the girls down to the beach. Well, on our way back to the campsite from the beach, we took a wrong road and got lost. We drove around for an hour trying to find our way back while Gay and Pearl were sleeping in the back seat.

Finally, we pulled over to the side of the road. We thought we would make a phone call from somebody's house or ask for directions back to the campsite.

While we were pulled over deciding what we were going to do, Gay opened her eyes in her car seat, and her little voice said, "Mum. I know where we are."

"John and I almost fainted! Up until then, Gay had hardly been able to put a few sentences together with the familiar words we had taught her, let alone been able to reason in her little mind the situation we were in, being lost. But that little girl spoke with authority, and she had figured out the situation. She was only about three and a half years old. And there is more!" "Yes, carry on."

"Gay pointed her hand out of the window and said, "This way, Mum." What did we have to lose, we were lost anyway so we continued on the road we were on, and as we were driving, Gay would say, "I remember here," and "I remember there," pointing at buildings as we were driving along. First, we thought that she was making up a game, and so we tried not to take things seriously, until she said something that could not be a coincidence. She said, "Over there's a farm. It's got a red door and funny roof and Aylwen milks cows."

"Sure enough, as we turned the corner, there was a farmhouse with a red door and a thatched roof. And Gay began to get excited! She said people's names and pointed at the farmhouse. The names were Celtic Welsh names, and I can remember only a few, but she said 'Aylwen and Afon live here, and Eurneid lives there' as she pointed to another house across the courtyard. It wasn't that she was just saying names. It was the way she was saying them, and how excited she was about them, like she had an emotional attachment to them."

"I said to John, 'Park the car, and let's go and knock on the door.'

John agreed, and said "yes, we were going to ask for directions back to the campsite anyway."

John lifted Gay out of her car seat, and I carried Pearl in my arms, and we walked across the courtyard to the door. Gay raced ahead of us, seemingly familiar with her surroundings. 'Come see the swing,' she said, and she pulled my hand to walk around the back of the farmhouse. I handed Pearl to John, and I followed Gay to the back of the house. There was a swing set with two swings on it."

"Push me, Mum," Gay said. "Aylwen won't mind. The swing isn't green anymore."

"John knocked on the door with Pearl, while I stayed in the back yard with Gay. She jumped up onto the swing and I couldn't stop her. 'There, Afon's pigeons,' she said, pointing to a single pigeon that had just landed on the farmhouse roof.

As I was trying to get Gay to come off the swing, John and another gentleman were walking towards us. I, of course, assumed that it was the person who lived in the farmhouse, but I was not ready for what happened next! Seeing the man walking towards us, Gay's face grew into a big smile.

'Afon!' she called, and she jumped off the swing and ran full pelt into this stranger's arms! Luckily, he caught her, and Gay kept saying his name 'Afon, Afon, Afon' over and over again and tried to hug him. The man was quite taken back and looked at John and I very strangely."

'My name is Afon,' the man said, 'but I don't know you, do I?' he choked out, looking intently into my eyes? 'No, I don't think so.' I replied. I was shocked just like he was, but not embarrassed. Gay knew this man, I was certain of that, and John was just speechless. 'Come on,' Gay said, pulling on the man's hands, 'let's go see Aylwen.'

'You had better come in,' Afon said, and John and I followed the man into the farmhouse. The man's wife was called Aylwen, and Gay ran and jumped into her arms. The woman laughed as Gay tried to hug her, and then gave John and I the strangest look. It was a look which said, 'I don't understand what all this is about, but what a wonderful little girl you have.'"

"The couple were kind to us, and I can only imagine how they must have felt with Gay bursting into their lives like that. But they made us a cup of tea and gave us a tour around the house. There is so much that happened that day, Kings, and I don't think I will ever understand it, but Gay knew her way around that house like she had lived there all her life! Or should I say during a whole other life, given that she was not yet four!"

"John asked the man about the other name that Gay had mentioned, and the couple told us that they had lived in the house for almost forty years, but there was a name carved in the wood of an old cupboard down in the basement, and it was the same name as Gay had mentioned to my husband John and me. Before we left, the man took us back around to the swing set at the back of the house and pointed out another name that had been carved onto one of the wooden seats."

"What did it say?" I stuttered out to Helen, hardly believing what I was hearing?

"It did not mean anything at the time, but it does now," she replied. "It said, Taliath Saren!" And I spat out my tea, almost choking!

"And there is one more thing, Kings. When the man was pointing out the name on the swing, I noticed some of the paint had come off the metal frame, and the paint underneath the blue was green, just like Gay had said. I hope all that helps, Kings."

"Helps? ! I need a bloody stiff drink! I'm surprised the pigeon didn't fly down and introduce himself! No, don't tell me that it did!"

"No, not quite, Kings. The man and his wife did wonder why there were always pigeons around the property."

"Thanks Helen, that's about all I can cope with right now.

"You alright Kings?"

"Yes, just feeling overwhelmed with everything. Would you like to accompany me for lunch and a bottle of wine on Bute St.?" I said changing the subject.

Helen laughed, and we walked down to the seafront arm in arm. "I will have a bottle of your best red," I said to the waitress, "and fish and chips please."

"You had better bring two bottles of wine," Helen added, and we both laughed.

After lunch. we booked a taxi back to Helen's house as we were both feeling rather tipsy, and we danced in the doorway of the restaurant until our ride arrived. I visited with Helen until the wine wore off. I had a lot to muss over, in what Helen had told me about Gay having recognized that farmhouse and those people. And the name Taliath Saren, that was carved into the wooden seat of the swing, that really stunned me!

Helen made me a snack for my journey home to Pennard, and I was on my way. "See you soon, my lovely man," she said. "See you soon lovely lady," I replied.

That was a shocking and haunting conversation, I thought, as I drove along the motorway towards Swansea. Gay was picking up Melody from school today, so I was able to take my time driving through the country lanes from Swansea out to my beloved Pennard.

As I thought about my day with Helen, and everything I had learned about Gay from when she was a little girl, it had been such an amazing revelation of things! But I was not any closer to finding out what was going on with her and her connection with Nan's Nan. What could I do next? The only thing I could think of was to go and talk to Armes. Maybe she would have some insight as to what was happening.

For now, I would just take Dad's advice and observe things closely, and when I had the opportunity, I would drive out to the commune and talk to Armes.

Chapter Seven

That Fateful Day in November

Over the next few weeks nothing more was seen, and little was talked about in relation to the phantom horse Nan's Nan. That was until that "fateful day" in late November!

Melody and I had finally persuaded Gay to come and spend time with the horses in the Three Cliffs Valley. It was a Sunday afternoon and Gay packed one of her famous picnics for tea, and we were on our way. Melody brought some apples and carrots to feed the horses. We wanted to get close to some of the foals that had been born in the spring. Melody and I had watched some of the mares giving birth, and we had named some of the foals. Melody was excited to show her mother two of the little stallions that had been born. One we named "Dancing Cloud," because of the low clouds that hung over Cefn Bryn on the morning that he was born. And the other we named "Water Dancer," because he skipped and played in the Killy Willy stream shortly after standing up for the first time on his long wobbly legs. No matter how many times I watch a foal being born, it never ceases to amaze me how quick they can stand up on their spindly legs and skip around their mother.

When we arrived at the valley, the horses were nowhere to be seen, and Melody was disappointed. To tell the truth, so was I. After all the work to get Gay to come with us and the herd was not there. We had only seen them two days ago, I reminded Melody, and I said they were probably having a walk on the beach.

"Let's sit and have our picnic," Gay said. "I'm sure they will be along soon." Gay laid out our blanket upon the marsh grass and we sat at the river's edge and enjoyed our picnic. The late afternoon sun was warm for November, and we dipped our feet into the water as the Killy Willy stream sang us a song, tumbling its way to the waiting sea.

"What is that noise?" Gay asked, as Melody and I lifted our heads to listen.

"It's just the wind," I said, as we got back to eating Gay's wonderful sandwiches and Welsh cakes.

"Now I hear something," Melody said, standing up and gazing up the hill to Pennard Castle.

Suddenly, I could hear neighing too, and then I saw a herd of horses coming down one of the sandy slopes beside the castle. "Look, Nan's Nan is with them," Melody shouted excitedly, and we counted nine horses coming down the path.

"They are probably coming for a drink," Gay said, "and they usually like to spend the night sheltered in the valley away from the sea winds that can blow strong up on the hill tops."

We packed away our food and rolled up the blanket. Melody held up an apple and several of the horses started walking over towards us. Most of the horses knew Melody and

I quite well from all the times we had visited them over the spring and summer.

"Look, Mum, there's Dancing Cloud," Melody said, pointing out the one white sock that the young stallion had on his front left foot.

"Look how much he has grown, Melody," I said, "and there is Nan's Nan behind him."

"Have you ever ridden a wild horse, Mum?" Melody asked, smiling across at me as she had heard the story many times of how I had tamed and ridden Great Thunder when he was wild and fierce.

"No, I haven't," Gay answered, "but I helped Dad to learn to ride on my horse Blaze when we were teenagers. No one dared to ride a wild stallion like your Dad did!"

I smiled and puffed up with pride at Gays words. And then Melody reminded us that she too had ridden a wild horse, when she rode on Nan's Nan's back when she was only eight years old.

"Yes, we remember that," both Gay and I said together.

Melody smiled and then said, "Mum, why don't you ride on Nan's Nan right now? She is here with us, and she hasn't changed into a ghost horse yet."

Gay looked back and forth at Melody and I, and then gave us a nervous smile.

"Come on, Mum," Melody pressed. "Show us that you are not afraid of Nan's Nan."

While Melody was speaking, a strange dark mist began to move in from the sea, and it traveled up the valley to where we were standing with the horses. Within minutes, the horses, and Pennard Castle up on the hill, were cloaked in the cold dark mist. It got thicker and thicker like fog, and I shivered in the cold. Melody and I looked at one another as if to say, 'What the dickens is going on?' Gay however, seemed quite unperturbed, and to our surprise, she said, "Yes, alright. Give me one of your apples, Melody, so she will come close, and I can mount onto her back." Nan's Nan walked out from the fog and stood in front of Gay.

Melody and I watched in anticipation as Gay fed Nan's Nan the apple and then climbed onto her back as if she had been riding her regularly. She had not ridden in years as far as I knew, but then Gay had always been a good rider.

"Is Mum showing off?" Melody whispered in a quiet and surprised voice.

"I don't think so," I whispered back. "Well, maybe just a little bit."

"Stop whispering, you two," Gay called out from on top of Nan's Nan's back. "It's rude to whisper."

Suddenly we could see the grass and trees through Nan's Nan's body, and she glowed with a fluorescent light. Gay's countenance changed too, and she glowed with an orange and yellow light! Melody and I looked at each other in utter astonishment as Gay appeared to change into a spirit form, and then galloped off on Nan's Nan's back, disappearing into the fog.

Suddenly, out of nowhere, came a wind that whistled and swirled around us, and Melody held onto my hand tightly. I remained silent, trying to be brave for Melody, but inside fear gripped me hard. What was happening? I could hardly believe my eyes!

"You're trembling, Dad," Melody said, giving me a troubled look.

Then the strange and deliberate wind blew the fog away from the horses, and we could see the herd standing in front of us again, but Gay and Nan's Nan were nowhere to be seen.

The haunting fog still hung thick and cool on the hill above us, cloaking the walls of the castle like a man wearing a black overcoat. Melody and I climbed up the steep sandy path towards the castle hoping we would find Gay. What else could we do, I thought? It all seemed like a dream as we trudged our way up the hill through the deep sand, and I hoped that when we reached the castle, this bad dream would come to an end.

When we arrived, the strange wind continued to blow, but gentler now, and holes appeared in the fog that looked like time passages, as Melody and I peered through them and could see parts of the castles crumbling walls. Faces appeared and seemed to stare back at us from these yesterday windows, and voices whispered above the heavy silence in the air.

Suddenly, out of the dark shrouding fog, reappeared the phantom horse and its rider in a yellow orange glow. Was it Gay? Was it real? All our senses shouted "Yes! It's real!" And we watched as they galloped away and disappeared over a distant hill.

"This has got to be a dream!" I shouted, unable to control my emotions anymore. And I pinched myself to make sure I was awake! Alas, I was! This was no dream, and I stood numb and shaking.

Melody broke the haunting silence by crying out loud, and shouting "Mum, mum, come back! Oh Dad," she cried, "Mum is a ghost! What can we do? Did you hear me, Dad? I'm afraid!"

I felt helpless as she cried and cried and would not let me console her. Finally, I was able to speak between her sobs.

"Melody, listen to me! Listen! Stop crying for a minute so that you can hear me. Mum is not a ghost. Mum hugs you and kisses you and holds you in her arms. Ghosts can't do that because they don't have flesh and blood."

"But I saw right through Mum. Mum was see-through like Nan's Nan."

"Melody, I know there is something happening with Mum that you don't understand. And I don't understand it either. Do you remember when you first rode on Nan's Nan's back down on the beach?"

"Yes, I remember."

"Okay, well Nan's Nan was not a ghost then, right? You could pat her and feed her apples and carrots, right?"

"Right,"

"Do you know what I think?"

"No, Dad, I don't. I just don't want my mum to be a ghost!"

"She is not a ghost. I think your mum and Nan's Nan may have special powers. They can transform themselves from their physical appearance to a spiritual appearance, so they look like ghosts."

"But it frightens me, Dad. My friend's mothers aren't like that, you can't see through their bodies."

"I know, darling, I know. But I need you to trust me until we find out what is going on."

"You won't vanish like Mum did, will you, Dad? I don't want to lose you too!"

"No, I won't. I promise I won't leave you Melody, and Mum will come back, I'm sure. I think she might have gone for a ride on Nan's Nan just to show us that she's not scared of her." But in my heart of hearts an eerie, sinking feeling was coming over me.

"But Mum is scared of Nan's Nan – you know that Dad. So why would she go for a ride on a horse that she is afraid of?"

"I don't know, sweetheart. We did ask her to ride the horse, didn't we? And she did not seem afraid of Nan's Nan then. She just jumped on her back and galloped away."

"Will Mum be waiting for us at the car, Dad?"

"I don't know, Melody, but I hope so. I think she will either be in the car waiting for us, or she will meet us at home. And then she can explain what the heck is going on!"

"She better," Dad, otherwise I don't know what I'm going to do!"

"Just wait and see, Melody, everything will be alright. Now carry the blanket and I will carry the picnic basket. Come on, let's walk back to the car."

As we walked back across the golf course, Melody's eyes scanned the hills and the ditches for signs of her mother, and her normally peaceful looking countenance had given way to an expression of fear and traumatization, which only enhanced my own dread of what we had just witnessed. And I felt angry! And I wanted an explanation as soon as we found Gay.

Maybe she and Armes were practicing some crazy Celtic magic at the commune, and maybe this transformation from the physical to the spiritual and being see-through, was all connected to what Gay has learned in her Bard training. I should never have agreed to her going to the commune and spending time with that crazy woman Armes! Our lives were wonderful before she came on the scene. This is all so crazy! I said to myself. And I felt like I was lying through my teeth to

Melody. I didn't know what to say to her about her mother. I felt traumatized too after what we had just seen, and as far as I was concerned, Nan's Nan and Gay had turned into ghosts or phantom-like beings. Tell me, anybody, how can you explain what Melody and I had just seen?!!!

"Gay! You better have a damn good explanation for all this, that is all I can say! Now, where the heck are you?"

"Dad, stop shouting. You're scaring me!"

"I'm sorry, Melody, I'm upset that all this crazy stuff has happened to us."

"It's okay, Dad. Let's just find Mum, okay?"

"I'm trying, sweetheart, I'm trying."

We reached the car and there was no sign of Gay or the horse. We sat and waited in the car until darkness fell and still there was no sign of Gay.

"Come on Melody," I said still upset, "let's drive home."

Melody was quiet and still in shock as we drove through the village.

We arrived at the house, and Melody grabbed my arm as we walked up the driveway to the front door. As I opened the door, Melody continued to cling to my arm, and she would not let go as we looked around the room for a ghost or something. We were both spooked and didn't know what to expect. I wanted my wife back and Melody wanted her mother. We searched each room as if looking for a clue … or something? What a horrible feeling to experience this kind of fear in one's own home.

"What do we do now, Dad? Mum's not here."

"We just wait for Mum to come home, that's all we can do."

Samantha was out, so we turned on the TV to try and take our minds off things. It didn't work, we were both afraid!

"Have you ever seen a spirit, Dad? Like what we saw Mum turn into?"

"Yes, but I don't want to talk about it now. Let's just wait for Mum to come home."

An hour went by, and then two, and the big hand on the grandfather clock got louder and louder. We turned the TV off and sat in silence, as if in some way our silent shouting fears would help Gay come home. They didn't, and another hour went by and then two more.

"Shall we call the police, Dad?" Melody said, breaking our painful silence.

"Those are my thoughts exactly, sweetheart, but hard as it is, I think we should wait a bit longer."

"Let's call Grandma and tell her what has happened. Maybe Mum is at Grandma's, Dad?"

"I don't think so, sweetie. I am sure she would come home to us first."

I called Helen and tried to explain what had happened. After a long silence, as she tried to get her head around what I was saying, she said she would leave Cardiff right away and be here as soon as she could.

"What did Grandma say, Dad? Is she coming over?"

"Yes, she will be here as soon as she can."

"Then do we need to call the police?"

"Let's just wait to see what Helen says, and maybe by the time she gets here, Mum will have come home."

"I hope so, Dad, I really miss her." Melody burst into tears, and again I asked myself: Is this really happening?

Every fifteen minutes seemed like two hours as Melody and I sat and waited, and the clock struck the hour chimes again.

"Don't cry, Melody, I know that we don't know what is going on with Mum, but things will be alright somehow."

And I prayed to God and asked him to give us his peace. I also called Samantha, who was out with her boyfriend and asked her to come home.

Finally, Helen's car pulled up the driveway and Melody raced to the door. I made a pot of tea as Melody cried in Helen's arms, and we sat around the table and told Helen about everything that had happened.

Fortunately, Helen believed us, having seen Nan's Nan change into a spirit horse herself, but she struggled with the idea that Gay had transformed the same way to.

"I am so glad you believe us," I said, as I threw my arms around her and hugged her tightly. "Melody and I were thinking of calling the police, but I don't think they would believe our story if we told them."

"No, I don't think they would either!" Helen exclaimed, "and a person has to be missing for at least twenty-four hours before they will start looking for them."

"Yes, I think you are right," I replied. "Let's just wait and see if she comes home tonight, and then if she is not back by the morning, we can call the police and report her missing. I don't know what we can say to the police though – they would laugh at our phantom horse story. They would think we were crazy."

Melody spoke up and said, "We can just say that we saw Mum get on a horse and gallop away into the distance. That is true, isn't it? We don't have to say she was on a ghost horse, or that she turned into a ghost herself."

"Well said, Melody! You are exactly right! We can just say that Mum got on one of the wild horses and rode off and we have not seen her since."

Melody smiled at my words of affirmation that she was being helpful, and now that Helen was here with us, I felt that somehow, we would get through this nightmare. Helen reassured us that she would stay until Gay came home and stay the night if necessary.

The hours continued to go by, and Helen made us a snack as we continued to wait, but no one felt like eating.

We tried to pass the time by making ourselves feel busy. Helen got Melody to help clean the kitchen while I stared out the window. There was no use going back to the castle or the valley to look for Gay as it was dark outside. We waited up until Samantha came home at 11:30, and after telling her more about what had happened, we all retired for the night, and I felt mentally and emotionally exhausted as my head hit the pillow. I prayed I would wake up and find out that this had all been a bad dream.

Chapter Eight

The Nightmare!

Morning came, and as I awoke from my restless sleep, I reached out to find no Gay lying next to me. My nightmare was not over yet – it was not just a bad dream, it was definitely real!

As I stumbled down the stairs still half asleep, I could hear someone in the kitchen. Helen was up and had cooked us breakfast. Samantha and Melody were still sleeping, which gave Helen and I some time to talk and discuss what to do next.

"You need to contact the police," she said, having checked around the house for any signs of Gay. She had not left a note or anything, and there were no messages on our cell phones. "I'm so worried, Kings. This is so unlike Gay to not get in touch with any of us. I fear something terrible has happened!" Helen broke down and cried.

"She would never disappear from our lives without telling us. She is so happy right now having found you again after all those years. Do you think something might have happened at the commune with Armes?"

"I don't know," I replied, "all I know is I want her to come home!"

"I know you do," Helen said, taking my hand and squeezing it. "I just don't know what to do, Kings. She would never just leave us, and especially you, and Melody and Samantha – you three are her world!"

"I don't know what to do either," I replied. "I can't think of any reason why she would not want to come home to us. Unless she has been influenced in some way by Armes, and what was she involved with at the commune? And as far as going to the police, what am I going to say? She turned into a ghost and galloped off on a phantom horse?! They would have me locked up if I tried to tell them what really happened."

"Just tell them what we decided last night – that Gay went riding on one of the wild horses and galloped off into the fog, and we have not seen her since. That is what happened, wasn't it?"

"Yes, but both her and Nan's Nan were fluorescent and see-through. You do believe me, don't you, Helen? I really need you to believe me, and Melody can confirm what we saw."

"Of course, I believe you, Kings. I have seen that horse change myself, exactly as you describe. But you and Melody are going to have to say something that makes sense to the police. Otherwise, they will be suspicious and think that you are hiding something."

"Yes, you're right."

Samantha and Melody arrived at the table, and I told them that we had still heard nothing from Gay. Samantha looked at me with a worried and confused look, and Melody – well, her spirit just sank. She had gone to sleep believing that her mother would be home by the time she woke up, and she began to cry.

Both Helen and Samantha tried to console her as I got up from the table and walked around. What should I do? What could I do?

I decided to call Dad and Mary and ask them to come over as soon as they could. Meanwhile, I headed off to the police station.

~

When I arrived, I spoke to the clerk at the front desk. "I would like to report a missing person," I said, in a sad and subdued voice, as the reality of the situation sank in at the sound of my own words.

"Would you like to sit down, and can I get you a cup of tea?" the kind lady said, obviously seeing my distress.

"Yes, please," I replied, and she escorted me into a small office where I sat down.

"Constable Dixon will be along to see you shortly," she said, "and he will take a statement. And how long has this person been missing?" the lady asked, "and is the person a relation?"

"Yes, she is my wife, and she did not come home last night."

"I see. Well, please wait here and Constable Dixon will be along shortly."

The clerk returned with a cup of tea, and I sat and waited for the constable to arrive.

How did I ever get to this place in my life? I pondered, as

I sipped my tea. I was a happily married man, I thought, with a beautiful wife and family. And here I am waiting to make a missing person's report on my wife! What had happened to her? Who would believe my story if I told them? Dad and Mary maybe, and Melody was there, of course. At least Helen believes me, even though she was not there.

It seemed I had been waiting forever and a day, until finally the constable arrived.

"Mr. Hill," he said, "I hear you want to file a missing person's report."

"That's right, Sir, I mean Constable Dixon."

"Would you like to tell me who is missing and the circumstances around it? And once we have finished speaking, there is a statement form here for you to fill out."

"Thank you," I replied, nervously.

"It all started yesterday afternoon, when my wife Gay and I, and our daughter Melody, went for a picnic at Three Cliffs Valley," I stuttered feeling anxious.

"Yes, go on, tell me what happened."

"We went to the valley for a picnic, so we could visit the wild horses. My daughter and I wanted to show my wife one of the horses that we had become quite friendly with, a mare that is known locally as Nan's Nan. Melody wanted to show her Mum the horse because it had become a special horse to her."

"A special horse for your daughter, you mean, not your wife?"

"Yes, that's right, constable. My daughter Melody had enjoyed riding the horse a few times last summer, and for some reason she felt that her mum was afraid of the horse, and she wanted her mum to make friends with it."

"You're a horse family, are you?"

"Yes, we all like horses, and especially the wild horses on the Gower."

"So, you went to see the horses, and what happened then?"

"Well, my daughter asked her mother to prove that she wasn't afraid of Nan's Nan, and to ride her."

"The horse is a mare, right?"

"Yes, that's right, and she is an old horse who has been around since I was a teen. Anyway, Gay mounted the horse and galloped off, and we have not seen her since. And that was yesterday afternoon."

"Do you know what time exactly?"

"Not exactly, but around 2 o'clock, I think."

"Now, as you're making a statement, Mr. Hill, I do have to ask you some personal questions about your relationship with your wife, okay?"

"Yes, that is fine."

"First question then: Have you and your wife been having any marital problems recently? Or had you had an argument about anything that might have made her feel like she didn't want to come home?"

"No, we have always enjoyed a good marriage, and if we ever had a disagreement about something, we always talked it through".

"Has she ever stayed away or not come home before?"

"No, never. She would always phone or tell us if she was going somewhere or was going to be late."

"So not coming home last night is out of character for her then."

"Yes, it is. That is why I feel that there is something wrong, that something must have happened to her."

"Now normally, Mr. Hill, your wife has not been absent long enough for us to file a missing person report through our constabulary, but as you have explained, this is very much out of character, so we will start our inquiries immediately."

"Thank you, constable. Thank you very much."

"That's alright, Mr. Hill, we will try and help you find her. Before you leave the station, could you please write out on the form the statement you just gave me, and leave it at the desk on your way out."

"Yes, I will."

I filled out the form, trying not to contradict anything I had said to the constable, and then headed home.

When I got home, Dad and Mary had arrived, and they suggested that we all take a walk down to the valley and up to the castle, to look for any traces of Gay. Melody felt that Gay might have had an accident and fallen off the horse when she had galloped away. We all agreed to go, even if it only meant putting Melody's mind at rest that her mother had not fallen off the horse and was not lying injured somewhere.

I did not think that we would find any clues of Gay's disappearance. But I went along with the others, of course, and who knows? – maybe we would find something. The horrible underlying feeling or sense that I had, was that if Gay wanted to come home, she would have done so by now. But I forced myself to try and think positive. And I needed to keep a positive attitude for my family.

We all squeezed into Dad's car and headed off to start our search. As Dad drove through the windy lanes of Pennard

Village, it all still seemed like a bad dream, and I felt numb. Seeing my family sitting around me in the car, and listening to their conversations, seemed to be the only reality that told me this thing was real! Gay was missing, and she had not come home last night. Not even a phone call to tell us where she was. And we had no idea what had happened.

We parked the car on Bendrick Drive and walked our usual way to Pennard Castle via the golf course path. Dad and I walked several yards in front of the others, and he asked me if there were any problems Gay might have been having, and was everything alright in our relationship?

"She seemed alright, Dad, as far as I know. She was continuing her training at the commune and that was going well. And things were going really well between us as far as I could tell. I did tell her that I was feeling a little distant from her as she had been spending so much time with Armes at the commune."

"Did you contact Armes yet to see if she had gone there?" Dad asked.

"Yes, I called late last night and she wasn't there. Besides, her car is still at home. If she was going any distance, she would have taken her car, don't you think?"

"Yes Kings, it's all rather strange I'm afraid, this is so out of her character, isn't it?"

"Yes, Dad, I am very worried. I have such an uneasy feeling about things."

"Try and keep positive, Old Son, it's only been one night. And Mary and I will help you all we can."

"Thanks Dad, I sure appreciate you being here."

We looked around the castle grounds first, and Mary asked what Gay was wearing. Melody described her mother's clothing, and we walked across the golf course in the direction where she and Nan's Nan had galloped off into the fog. Dad now pulled out his binoculars and scanned the distant hills for any signs of a horse and rider, but to no avail. I described the mysterious dark fog to Dad, and he thought it strange and unusual.

"You generally only have fog at the castle during the summer months, when the sun burns hot and then meets the cooler morning air," said Dad. "And you get the sea mists in the autumn and winter months."

"I know, Dad, that is what makes it strange. And it was a dark fog, almost like smoke in colour, not like the mists we usually get coming in from the sea and up through the valley."

The girls concentrated on looking for items of clothing, and footprints in the sand.

"There are hoof marks in the sand," Samantha shouted, having knelt in one of the sandy patches beside the castle.

"There are lots of hoof prints," Helen answered, "at least three or four different ones."

"There are too many horses roaming around to pick out any individual ones," I said. "Let's walk down the path beside the castle to the valley and look down there."

As we walked down the sandy path, it was like looking for a needle in a haystack. What were we looking for anyway? Items of clothing, or Gay lying in a ditch somewhere? And I felt angry that we were in this situation, and I wanted to shout, "Gay, where the heck are you? Don't you care about your family! Where have you disappeared to?"

Instead, I comforted Melody, who was now in tears after calling out her mother's name on the wind for the last twenty minutes.

"There is no one in the valley," Dad said. "We had better get back to the house in case she phones."

Mary had called the hospital before we left this morning, and there had not been anyone admitted who fitted Gay's description.

"Where has she gone?" Helen whispered, as she tried to hold onto her composure. By the time we got back to the car, I had three crying girls in my arms. Samantha had joined in the chorus, and Dad and Mary helped me to calm them down.

When we arrived home, there was a message on the answering machine from the police station. They wanted us to call them as soon as we heard anything from Gay. If she had not returned by tomorrow evening, we were to contact them so they could upgrade their search.

"Upgrade their search," I said angrily. "They should be doing everything they can to find her now!"

Dad reminded me that it was still only the second day that she had been missing, and that the police have their protocol as to what they regard is a priority missing-person search.

"It's not that they don't think looking for Gay is important, Kings," Mary said. "It's that they don't think she has been missing long enough to warrant a full-scale search."

At Mary's word's I began to calm down. I guess all we can do now is wait, I said to myself. Maybe she will walk through that door at any moment. And I stood again in front of the window watching the driveway.

"Come on Kings, sit down," Mary said, "I will make us a cup of tea. Standing staring out of the window is not going to help anything."

Dad and Mary stayed until 10 p.m. and then headed

home to Swansea. Helen stayed another night, and then waited until I made my phone call to the police to see what they would say. They said that they would start an active investigation now that it had been over 48 hours, and for us to call them if we heard anything. Meanwhile, they would come over to the house and talk to me further tomorrow afternoon.

"I will head back to Cardiff and pack some clothes," Helen said, "and I will come back as soon as I can."

Suddenly it was just Samantha, Melody and I again in the house, and we tried to support one another by saying positive things and trying to remain cheerful. And I was so glad that Helen would be coming back – I needed her support so much.

By 3:00 in the afternoon, Helen had arrived back from Cardiff, and she said she could stay for as long as we needed her. Meanwhile we had heard nothing from Gay, and all we could do was keep waiting.

Every night we went for a walk in the valley and searched for any signs of Gay but alas we found nothing. The herd remained in the Three Cliff's Valley, but Nan's Nan was nowhere to be seen.

One night, Samantha and Melody retired to their rooms early, which gave Helen and I time to talk.

"I will stay with you for as long as you need me, Kings," she said again, holding my hand and looking at me with her caring eyes. "I want to be there for you and the girls in any way I can."

At her words, I wept in her arms. It had been so hard to stay strong, and I felt I could always be myself with Helen. She rubbed my back and tried to encourage me.

"She is not coming home," I wept. "I can feel it in my soul. She is still alive, but she has gone somewhere far away. Otherwise, she would have come back by now."

"I believe you are right, that she has gone somewhere, Kings, knowing Gay as I do, but why doesn't she call and let us know where she is?"

I sat up on the couch for as long as I could keep my eyes open, watching the front door and waiting for the phone to ring. Once or twice, I thought I heard it ring, 'but it was just in my head,' Helen said, and I headed off to bed.

"Try and get some sleep, Kings, and I will be in the other room if you need anything."

"Thanks Helen, and good night."

I was up with the sound of the seagulls and climbed into the shower. After my shower, I made breakfast. It was going to be another dark day in our family unless Gay walked through the door. But I had no idea just how bad it was going to get!

Helen said she would come with me to Melody's school to talk to the teachers and headmaster. Melody had not felt up to going to school for the last six days, but we needed to let the school know what was going on. And then at 1:00 this afternoon, the police were coming to the house to interview me again. I told Dad and Mary I would call them with an update after talking with the police again.

Melody's headmaster Mr. Evans was incredibly support-ive, and he said Melody could take her time coming back to join her class, and that he would also contact the school counselor, Mrs. Pretty, and book some appointments for Melody to come and see her. The hardest part of the visit with Mr. Evans was telling him that Gay was missing. Not sick or away visiting family but missing! And I will never forget the confused look Mr. Evans gave me, as if to say, 'well, you must have some idea where your wife is?' But I didn't, and thank God Helen was there to support me. I felt like running out of that headmaster's room like a frightened schoolboy!

We also got to talk to Mrs. Howel, the teacher Melody had most of her classes with. Mrs. Howel was kind, but she also struggled to understand how I could not know anything about Gay's whereabouts.

Not that it was any of her business, I was tempted to say, feeling frustrated. But Helen gave me a look, as if to say, 'Just don't say anything, Kings. She is struggling to understand things herself.' And Helen was right – Mrs. Howel was trying to be supportive, and it was not her fault if she was confused and shocked at the fact that Gay had disappeared.

"I will be praying for you all," she said, and Helen and I left the school and returned to the house.

As 1:00 drew near, I became more nervous.

"Try and relax, Kings," Helen said. "You haven't done anything wrong."

"I know," I said. "I just feel very uncomfortable with them asking me more questions. I have already given them a written statement of what happened, and a verbal account of the situation. What more do these people want?"

"Try and calm down, Kings, they have to make their inquiries. Remember, you have not done anything wrong, and you have nothing to hide."

"I know," I replied. "But the questions they asked me made me feel like a suspect and that it's my fault that it happened."

"It's not," Helen said again, and she took my hand and gently rubbed it with her fingers.

Once I felt calm again, Helen and I talked to Melody, who was alone in her room. "We spoke to your teacher, Mrs. Howel," I said, "and she is looking forward to you going back to your class when you're ready, Melody. And we also spoke to your headmaster, Mr. Evans."

"I don't want to go back to school!" Melody retorted. "I will never be ready to go back to school, not until my mum comes home!"

I sat next to Melody on her bed and just hugged her. There was nothing I could say or do, other than reminding her how much I loved her.

"Alright, Dad," she said, after hugging me for ten minutes. "I will go back to school tomorrow, but I really don't want to go. I feel sad."

"Mr. Evans has arranged for you to see Mrs. Pretty, the school counselor," Helen said, as she entered the bedroom.

"I like Mrs. Pretty," Melody answered, as Helen and I gave each other a look of relief.

After our conversation with Melody and an early lunch, Helen and I sat and waited for the police to arrive while Melody went across the road to the store. Samantha had left the house early for university and would not be home until about 4:00.

As I watched the clock, each five minutes seemed like an hour. "Oh, I wish they would hurry up and get it over with!" I said.

I looked at Helen. "Thank you for your love and support, my dear Helen. I don't know what I would do without you." She gave me a loving smile and rubbed my arm.

Finally, a police car came up the driveway. I walked to the window, and I saw two bluebottles getting out of the car. One looked like the same constable that had taken my statement down at the station, and the other was a policewoman, also in uniform but carrying a small case.

"I will get the door," Helen said.

"I wish you wouldn't," I said, forcing a smile.

"You behave," she said, looking back at me as she opened the door.

"Hello," Helen said, "please come in and sit down."

The bluebottles sat on the couch and Helen, and I sat on two separated chairs facing them.

"Well, Mr. Hill," Constable Dixon said, "I assume you have not heard anything from your wife, otherwise you would have contacted us."

"No, nothing," I replied. "Nothing yet."

"We just need to eliminate you from our inquiries, Mr. Hill," he went on to say, "and this is Constable Mason who is part of the investigation. Would you mind showing us around the property."

Reluctantly, I showed them around the house going room to room. I wondered what on earth they were looking for.

After answering several questions, Constable Mason asked me to come down to the police station to do a swab of my **DNA**, and to take my fingerprints.

"Fingerprints!" I protested. "Now wait a minute here! Fingerprints are for suspects, not for grieving husbands. What the heck is the matter with you people? Why are you not out looking for my wife instead of interrogating me?"

"We are not interrogating you, Mr. Hill. As we previously mentioned, we just want to eliminate you from our inquiries."

"You people are treating me like a suspect!" I continued. Helen gave me a look of concern but said nothing.

"And who are you?" the policewoman asked Helen.

"I am Gay's mother."

"Nice to meet you, and I'm sorry it's under such difficult circumstances."

I got my jacket and accompanied them to the police station.

Constable Mason took a swab from my cheek, and then told me that she was going to take my fingerprints. She opened a tin of ink cloth, very much like what the kids use to make stamp pictures on paper. Only we were not making pictures.

The constable now took my thumb and pushed it into the ink, and then rolled it over from side to side on a paper form. She then did the same thing with my index finger. And I felt like giving her two fingers, but I didn't.

"Sorry, Mr. Hill," Constable Dixon said, "this is one of the things that we must do. And as I said, this does not mean that you are a suspect. We just need to rule you out of our inquiries for our database."

Database, my arse! No, I didn't say that. "It's alright" I said, "it just feels intrusive and unnecessary."

"You just let us do our work, Mr. Hill, and let us know if you hear anything from your wife."

"I will," I said, and I left.

"You did well," Helen said, after telling her of my ordeal. "If they had taken my fingerprints and a swab, I would have been pretty upset too."

Time went slowly by, and still there was nothing from Gay to let us know whether she was alive or dead. But in my heart, I still felt that she was alive somewhere. Maybe I was in denial? I don't know. I only know that my life had become dark, and I was waiting for some light to shine through.

We did get one call from the police, stating that they were going to search Three Cliffs Woods, and the neighboring fields and farms, for any clues.

"It feels like they have done nothing," I said to Helen, "like they don't care. Otherwise, they would have started a search much sooner."

"They probably have been searching," Helen answered, "only we have not seen what they have been doing behind the scenes."

As the weeks, and months continued to go by, we were still in the dark as to what had happened to Gay. The police search had given no clues, and according to the investigator in charge, they had no suspects in any foul play. "That is good news in some ways," Helen said, trying to encourage me that Gay was still alive, but my season of darkness continued.

In a small village like Pennard, everyone knows everyone else's business, and I found this particularly hard. People meant well, but every time they saw Helen or I, they asked if we had heard anything about Gay. "No, not yet," we would say, and they would ask the same thing the next day. It got to the point where I didn't even want to go across the road to Pennard Stores to get groceries. I would rather stay inside where people did not ask questions. But people still did, as my own family asked questions, sometimes of themselves, as they tried to come to terms with what had happened.

Helen suggested that the four of us go away on weekends and spend time to ourselves, and that is what we did. Samantha joined us on the weekends that she was not busy with her university studies. I also called my sons Jonathan and Benjamin in Canada, and we cancelled their trip to visit me. I did not want them to see me like this. They were understanding regarding my decision, and I re-booked their tickets to come out in the spring of the New Year. Hopefully, my life would be a lot more settled by then.

Spending the weekends away, and exploring different parts of Wales, was great therapy for our family. Helen, Melody, Samantha and I began our journey of healing. There were still tough days, and some experiences were very hard to go through, but somehow, we managed to get through them.

One Monday morning, after being away for the weekend in West Wales, the school counselor Mrs. Pretty called, and she wanted to see me quite urgently. I arranged to go and see her at the school the following day.

"What do you think she wants?" Helen asked.

"I don't know," I replied. "Obviously, something to do with Melody."

I parked the car and proceeded to Mrs. Pretty's office.

"Good morning, Mr. Hill."

"Good morning, Mrs. Pretty. Please call me Kingsley."

"Alright, Kingsley. I would like to talk to you about Melody. This must be no surprise."

"It depends what you mean by no surprise," I replied.

"Melody is drawing pictures of phantoms and ghosts in her art class. And she draws pictures of fierce looking horses with the rider being her mother."

"Well, it is an art class, is it not, Mrs. Pretty?"

"Yes, Kingsley, but please let me finish. She is also telling the other children that her missing mother can change into a ghost and can come back and forth. Have you considered taking Melody to see a specialist? If you haven't, I really would suggest that you do."

"You are the school counselor, Mrs. Pretty. Does she really need to see anybody else? I think that by drawing these pictures, Melody is trying to keep her mother alive in her heart. And as far as her seeing a specialist is concerned, this is the first time I have heard of her drawing phantoms and calling her mother a ghost."

"I think you are right, Mr. Hill, Melody is trying to keep her mother alive in her heart, but I think she needs to see someone who specializes in loss and grief counselling."

"Very well, Mrs. Pretty, I will try and find a grief counselor – can you recommend anyone?"

"Yes, there is Dr. Morgan in the village. She is very good, and I can give you her contact information."

"Thank you, Mrs. Pretty."

I managed to get Melody an appointment the following week with Dr. Morgan, and after seeing Melody four times, she concluded what I had known from the beginning, that Melody was drawing her mother as a ghost who was able to come back and forth in and out of her life, as a way for her to keep her mother alive.

"This is common," Mrs. Morgan said, "especially as there has not been any closure for Melody. There is no body to bury, and for Melody to mourn normally, it is not possible because her mother is still missing."

At Dr. Morgan's word's, my heart tore for Melody, and I realized for the first time that I too had not been able to properly grieve Gay's loss. I also carried the hope in my heart that Gay was still alive somewhere and would come back into our lives one day.

After Melody finished her fifth session with Dr. Morgan, I asked Dr. Morgan if she would be willing to see me for a couple of sessions. She said she did a minimum of four sessions, and I could start the following week. I found her a great help.

At home, Helen was supportive, and she encouraged me to make my counselling a priority. Things were not improving with Melody, however, at least as far as Mrs. Pretty was concerned. Melody was still drawing her phantoms and apparently upsetting the class. So, I went in to have another talk with Mrs. Pretty.

"I will get right to the point, Mr. Hill. Melody talks about you and her having seen her mother ride away on a phantom horse. Of course, I am trying to explain to her that this is not true, and I think it would be good, Mr. Hill, if you could come to Melody's next art class and explain to her that seeing her mother turn into a ghost is not true and is only her imagination."

"Sorry, Mrs. Pretty, I can't do that."

"Why on earth not, Mr. Hill? You want to help your daughter, don't you?"

"Yes, of course, but I cannot tell her that what she saw with her own eyes is not true."

"I beg your pardon, Sir, did I hear you right?"

"Yes, and there is no pardon, you heard right! Melody saw what she did, and I am not telling her otherwise."

"Why, Mr. Hill, why?"

"Because I saw it too, Mrs. Pretty."

"Have you seen a psychiatrist, Mr. Hill?"

"No, have you?"

"Mr. Hill, I do not think you're grasping the seriousness of the situation, and how it is affecting your daughter. And if I can not have your cooperation in helping Melody, then I shall have to inform Social Services."

"You do that, Mrs. Pretty, you do that!" And I walked off.

When Melody came home from school, I explained to her what could happen to our family if Mrs. Pretty called Social Services. "They could try and take you away from me, Princess."

"That will never happen, Dad. I will just lie to my teachers and tell them that I was just making the ghost part up."

"Good girl, Melody. I hate to ask you to lie, but some people just cannot understand, and Mrs. Pretty is one of those people."

"I know, Dad, I will just tell her that I made it up. Mum will not be upset with me, will she, Dad, if I lie? You and mum always taught me to tell the truth no matter what."

"No, she would not be upset with you, Melody. She would be proud that you're wise enough to understand and to tell Mrs. Pretty what she needs to hear."

"And I will do it too, I will tell Mrs. Pretty that we talked about it and concluded that our minds were playing tricks on us because of the trauma."

"Dad, there is one thing that makes me sad every day," she said.

"What is that, Princess?"

"I am sorry that I made Mum ride Nan's Nan. If I had not told her that she was scared to ride the horse, Mum would still be here. It's my fault that mum disappeared, Dad, it's my fault." And she burst out crying and ran into my arms.

"No Princess, no, it was never your fault! You must not blame yourself. Mum wanted to ride that horse, and I wanted her to ride it too. And if mum was here, she would tell you the same thing. It is not your fault, Melody – Mum wanted to ride, otherwise she would not have got on that horse."

"I miss her, Dad, I miss her so much! Do you think she will come home one day?"

"I miss her too, sweetheart. And I want to believe in my heart that she will come home one day. But until that day, Mum would want you to try hard at your schoolwork and be patient with people who don't understand what you understand."

"Like Mrs. Pretty."

"Yes, like Mrs. Pretty, and some of your friends. It's not that they don't want to believe you, Melody, they just cannot understand. And people are afraid of what they don't understand."

"Like my friend Beverly who is afraid of ghosts."

"Yes, just like your friend Beverly. So next time you have art class, draw something that is not scary for Beverly or your teacher."

"Like pirates and a treasure chest, you mean."

"Maybe just the treasure chest, sweetheart, or how about drawing one of the big sandcastles or sand boats that we made on the beach with Grandma."

"And Mum, Dad, we can't forget Mum – she makes great designs on the sandcastles."

"Yes, she did… I mean she does."

Gosh, I hate this! I said to myself. Not knowing whether she is alive or dead. I was doing my best to let go of Gay and continue on with my life but watching Melody struggle too made it harder. Will we ever be able to continue with our lives with this 'not knowing' hanging over our heads? And I felt anger towards Gay for leaving us.

The following morning. I drove Melody to school instead of her catching the bus.

"Well, Melody, you better get to class. That battle-axe, Mrs. Pretty, won't like you being late."

"Battle-axe, he-he Dad, you're so funny. If I am late, my teacher won't be looking pretty. Get it, Dad, get it? She won't be looking pretty!"

"Ha ha, Princess, I get it, and it's very funny, now off you go to class."

"Love you, Dad, meet me from the bus."

"Love you too, Princess, see you this afternoon."

Life Goes On?

The next several months continued to be the most difficult season of my life, as I tried to make sense of all that had happened, and I seemed to be left with the same questions I had asked myself during those first few weeks of Gays disappearance. Why had this happened? Why would Gay leave her husband and her daughters? If she loved us, why did she leave? And if she was still alive then why has she not contacted us? Gay would never just vanish from our lives for no reason. Was there no end to this? No conclusion, only confusion! I was coming to a place in my life where I wished she would be found, even dead. At least then we could have some closure and be able to move on. And I felt guilty for feeling like this, what kind of person was I, to wish my wife dead.

One weekend, Helen phoned Dad and told him how much I was struggling and feeling sorry for myself and trying to make sense of things that I could not possibly understand.

Kingsley Ross Hill

Dad took me out for lunch and shared a few things with me.

"It's time you stopped blaming yourself for Gay's disappearance, Old Son," he said. "It is not your fault! You are not responsible for what she did, and you cannot bring her back either. Sometimes, things just do not make sense in this life. And yes, you have been dealt a raw deal in losing your wife, but what is left of your life is good, Son. You still have a wonderful family that loves you! Your daughter Samantha lives with you. Your boys are coming out from Canada to visit you again in the spring. Plus, you have Helen to help you with Melody and Samantha who are both growing up fast. And Mary and I love you and are here for you in any way we can. You own Grandma and Grandpa's sacred family home here in Pennard. You still have a wonderful life ahead of you, Kings! And one day you will meet someone else who you can share your life with."

"I know Dad, I know that I still have a wonderful life. But there is one thing that really haunts me. Who was Taliath Saren? Who was this woman that I knew as Gay Tripp? Who is the one that I fell in love with as a teenager, and then lost for twenty years, and then found again on Pobbles Beach? I have loved and lost her twice, Dad, and her real name is Taliath Saren, and she vanished on the back of a phantom horse! She vanished into thin air! Who was she? Who was Taliath Saren?"

"We don't know who she is, Son, but you have to let this go. Otherwise, you are going to lose the wonderful life that you still have. Much of life is like a puzzle, and pieces go missing, or they don't fit where you think they should go… but you must keep going. Sometimes you find those missing pieces and they all fit together again, and they make a wonderful picture. And sometimes those missing pieces don't come back, and another picture is made with the pieces that are left. Both are masterpieces – but you have to hang this new picture on the wall and appreciate it and nurture it; otherwise, you will lose what you have now."

"Yes, Dad, I understand, and I know you're absolutely right; it's just so hard sometimes."

"Keep going, Kings. Enjoy and celebrate what you have in your life and stop looking back at the past. Your picture has not finished being painted yet. Let go, Kings, and move on; otherwise, you will lose sight of the future." I reflected on Dad's words for a few minutes.

"Now listen to me, Old Son, I know what I am talking about. You need to have a funeral, or a memorial service, for Gay, so that you and the girls can move on with your lives. And if I were you, I would start looking for someone to share your life with, you have a lot to offer the right person. Now you forget about this Taliath Saren, or whoever she is. You have been given a wonderful life, and it would be a crime not to live it!"

"Thanks, Dad! Your words have spoken to my heart. They are just what I needed to hear."

"Take them to heart, Son, and keep them there."

"I will, Dad, I will. Thank you for speaking the truth to me."

"Oh, and another thing, Kings, before you leave. How about if you and I resume translating the diary? It is a fantastic story of how the Celtic clans lived, and it might tell us where some more artifacts are hidden."

"I would like that, Dad, but I am not ready to re-start the translation yet because it is a constant reminder of my life with Gay. I hope you understand. But I would still like to go detecting."

"Yes Kings, I understand, and when you are ready, we can resume."

"I have sure missed our adventures and metal detecting, and I know Melody and Samantha have too."

"We will go again soon, Kings. Now you go home to your family and start having some fun in your life."

I said goodbye to Dad, and I returned home to the girls.

After meeting Melody at the bus stop, Helen and I took Melody into Swansea to get a Joe's Ice Cream, and for a walk along Swansea Bay.

"I take it that you had a good visit with your father," Helen said, "you look like a weight has been lifted off your shoulders."

"Yes, I had a good chat with Dad, or should I say, he had a good chat with me, and it was exactly what I needed to hear. Thank you for encouraging me to talk to him, Helen," I said.

"That's quite alright," she said, "that is what being part of a family means, that we all help one another."

"I hope I can meet someone like you, one day," I said to Helen, and she smiled at my words.

"Thank you for thinking so highly of me, Kings!"

"It is true," I said, "you have so many wonderful qualities, and I feel that through my friendship with you, God has shown me what to look for when I am ready to meet someone again."

"That is another conversation that I want to have with you, Kings, over a cinnamon bun of course It is high time that you found someone to share your life with. You and I can't hang around like this forever, people are going to talk." And both Helen and I roared with laughter at her words. Melody turned around from collecting shells, and said, what are you laughing at?"

"I was just telling your Dad that he needs to get out and meet someone, and not spend so much time with me."

"That is not something to laugh at," Melody exclaimed, "but it is true. You should try and make some friends Dad."

"Well said Melody, someone has got to tell Dad to start living his life again," Helen said. "I am glad that you told him."

When we got home from Swansea Bay, Samantha was home from her studies, and she had made a lovely fire in the living room.

"I would like everyone to sit down," I said. "I have something important to say."

When everyone was seated, I said: "I think we need to have a memorial service for Gay to celebrate her life."

At my words, all the girls shed tears, and all agreed that it would be a good idea, even Melody. As hard as it was to accept that we were saying goodbye to Gay, everyone seemed to understand that we needed to do this so we could move on in our lives as a family. And I thanked God in my heart for his grace, that had given Melody a sense of peace in her heart to face the reality of saying goodbye to her mother. He had also given me his grace and strength to continue on in my life after my loss, and the support of my wonderful family around me.

The wind blew strongly, and a fog blowing in from the sea shrouded the church and tombstones, as we stood around the stone we had erected for Gay. It read, In loving memory of Gay Nightingale Tripp. A wonderful wife, mother, sister and daughter, gone with God to walk on a distant shore. You are missed and loved, and always in our hearts.

Gay's stone was placed close to my great friend, Maggie Davies. Today surrounded by my family and friends I felt that Maggie was with me. It was as if a life had ended, not so much for Gay, who still lived and spoke within each of our hearts, but for me as I stared at an empty grave. It seemed that such a large part of me had lived and had died with Gay, and another life was beginning as I felt the stirring of life again within my heart.

People placed flowers and spoke of their memories of Gay in front of the stone, and Samantha and Melody both read a poem they had written. I had once thought that my life had ended with Gay's disappearance, but just as there was no body underneath her stone, I was not there with the dead either, but alive! And I took in some deep breaths of the cool sea air and listened to the seagull squawking up on the church tower, who seemed to sing, you're alive, you're alive!

Helen and Mary had brought sandwiches, tea and coffee, and it was served inside the old church, where people stood and talked. After overhearing too many conversations about what might have happened to Gay, and people coming up to me and saying, 'sorry for your loss' and 'how are you doing,' I decided to leave the gathering behind inside the church and come outside into the mist. Samantha, seeing me leave came out after me, and we walked together around the churchyard. Tombstones floated like islands upon the heavy mist, and Samantha asked, "are you alright Dad?"

"Yes," I replied, "I just needed to come outside. Come and walk with me a while."

"Alright Dad, I will."

Close to the churchyard wall, and standing above the other stones, is the white marble statue of a lifeboat man which stands in memory of the three lost men of the Port-Eynon lifeboat crew, that drowned in January 1916.

"I have always looked at this statue from a historic perspective," I told Samantha, as we stopped and looked at the white marble stone. "But today I think of the families of those lost men," I wept, "who never saw their loved ones again. Lost at sea and abandoned to the deep. I feel a kindred spirit of grief for those families left behind," I said to Samantha, who now wept with me, and shared in the last tears of my grief.

"They have one comfort that I do not," I continued to say. "At least they knew what happened to their loved ones. I do not know what happened to my Gay."

"I know Dad," Samantha replied, "but everything is going to be alright! You are going to leave this church today and live the life that is still ahead of you, and I love you! You are such a wonderful part of my life. Having you for my dad has made my life so special!"

"Thank you, my sweetheart," I said, now weeping uncontrollably, "thank you for being here with me."

After Samantha dried my eyes with her handkerchief, we headed back inside the church to join the others. Helen and Melody had saved Samantha and I a plate of sandwiches and some cake, and I tried to celebrate the life of my Gay, as I saw her through the people who talked and shared with me, what she had meant to their lives, and for a little while more, my Gay was with me again.

"A toast," I said, "to a wonderful woman, and to a life that touched us all, I give you, Gay Nightingale Tripp. The song of our hearts! Cheers!"

Chapter Ten

Cloud Nine!

Over two years had passed now since Gay's disappearance, and although we had had a memorial service for Gay, and had put a stone up for her in the churchyard, I still had not taken Dad's or the girls advice, and started to date again. I was feeling desperate for companionship though. I had spent the last two years waiting for Gay to come home, but she never did.

Helen and the girls had continued to be a wonderful support for me, and my boys had visited three times from Canada. But my soul hungered for intimacy again, and the girls could see my loneliness.

It is interesting sometimes when a name or face comes into our mind or heart. There is no reason why you would be thinking about that name or face, it is just there printed on the pages of your mind.

I had been seeing a face in my mind's eye for two weeks now, and I wondered what it meant? It was a face of a woman that I had had an attraction to, when I had taken Helen on that speed dating event, almost three years ago. I tried to recall the evening, and then I remembered her name, Ffion, yes it was Ffion, and we had both felt a strong connection to each other.

I decided to talk to Helen about what she remembered of that evening.

"Why do you ask?" she said surprised. "If I remember rightly there was a woman that fancied you something awful, Kings," she laughed, "and you wanted to get out of the pub before she came looking for you."

"That's right," I laughed, "her name was Ffion."

"Why are you thinking about her, Kings?"

"I don't know," I replied, "for some reason I keep seeing her face in my mind's eye, and it has been going on for two weeks now."

"Maybe you are meant to contact her, Kings, or maybe she is going to come into your life in some way or another."

"I don't know," I replied, "I think I'm just lonely, Helen."

"You are lonely, Kings, and I have been meaning to talk to you again about this. It is time you gave yourself permission to have a life again."

"What do you mean?"

"You know exactly what I mean, you are lonely for companionship, Kings, and you need to get on with your life! Your Dad and I, and the girls have tried to tell you this. You cannot spend the rest of your life waiting for Gay, you know she is gone, Kings, and she is not coming back."

I began to weep at Helens words, for I knew she was right. "It's just that you and the girls would find it…"

"Hard if you meet someone, is that what you were going to say?"

"Yes, what would you and Samantha and Melody think, if I had someone new in my life?"

"Oh Kings, you lovely man, do you think you need to have our permission to have a life? Well, I've got news for you, Kings, so listen up, I know what I am talking about! You have had our permission for a long time now. Life is too short to wait any longer, and to go on sacrificing your heart to try and protect our feelings. I want you to be happy, Kings, you deserve it, and you need someone in your life who can love comfort you in this crazy world; someone you can love again and build a life with. And have you taken a good look at your daughters lately, and your boys while they were here? They are growing up, and are big people now, and I know they want you to be happy."

"I know," I said, "I know!"

"Oh, my lovely man, if I was only younger and wasn't your mother-in-law!"

"That would put the cat among the pigeons," I answered with a smile.

"If I did what I wanted to do with you, young man, we would put the pigeons among the cats!" I laughed hysterically now, and Helen began to roar too.

"Oh, my lovely man, go and live your life. And maybe you are meant to try and find that Ffion lady who keeps popping into your mind."

"Yes, maybe I am," I replied.

"Do you remember going around to all those tables, Helen, and every five minutes the bell rang and you had to go and meet someone else at another table?"

"Yes, I remember," Helen laughed, "only it was you men who went around the tables, and us women sat at the same table all evening."

"Yes, I remember now, and just when you had broken the ice with someone and started to talk with them, the bell would ring and off you went."

"Did you ever get an email from Ffion?" Helen asked. "We got emailed all our matches with their contact information."

"I don't know," I replied, "I never looked because I was married at the time and went by the name of Vince."

Helen roared with laughter, and said, "Oh, gosh I remember that, and you came just to give me emotional support, Kings, I will never forget you doing that for me."

After my conversation with Helen, I went home and checked my old emails from almost three years ago, and sure enough, I found Ffion's emails and I read them.

Dear Vince

I received your email information a few days after we met at speed dating. I am so glad that you ticked my box as someone you would be interested in meeting. I did stay behind in the pub after the event was finished, in hope we could talk some more, as I felt we had a real connection. I will give you my phone number once we meet rather than just contacting me via email, as I don't check my email very often. Feel free to contact me anytime, I would love to hear back from you.

Sincerely Ffion.

Hello Vince.

A week has gone by since speed dating and I have not heard anything back from you. Please let me know if you are still interested in learning more about me, and maybe we could meet somewhere for a drink. Somewhere where there are no bells to end a conversation, he-he. Anyway, I would enjoy hearing back from you. Hope you are doing well.

Sincerely Ffion.

Hi Vince.

It has been a month now and I have not heard anything back from you, I can only assume that you are not interested in us getting to know each other. Anyway, I hope that you are doing well and enjoying the nice weather we have been having. I did meet up with a man named Paul and went on a few dates with him, but there was not any chemistry there. Oh well, bye for now.

Ffion.

After reading Ffion's emails, I felt hesitant in contacting her, as it had been almost three years since she emailed me. She has probably long forgotten meeting me by now, I mussed. Maybe she is happy in a relationship with someone, but as I remembered Helens words encouraging me to get on with my life and meet someone, I thought I would give things a try and email her back. I don't believe in coincidence, I told myself, and there must be a reason that she has come into my mind after all this time.

Well here goes.

Dear Ffion.

I do not know if you still remember me, I am Vince Kingsley, and we met at speed dating a long time ago now. For some reason you have been in my thoughts lately and I thought I would contact you.

Before I say anything more, I need to explain why I did not email you back after first meeting you.

When I came to speed dating, I went with my mother-in-law Helen, who I believe I introduced you to at the time. Helen was not comfortable going on her own, so I came with her. At the time I was also married, so it would have been wrong of me to pursue a relationship with anyone I met at the event. Please forgive me for not emailing you back immediately and explaining this to you.

The reason I am contacting you now, is because I am on my own and am seeking to meet someone special. You may of course have met someone by now and be in a happy relationship, and if you are, congratulations, and I hope you are doing well. I do still remember talking to you and feeling a connection with you when we talked, even though it was such a long time ago. If by chance that you are still single, and are not in any serious relationship, I would like to have the opportunity to meet you again and see where things go.

I will say bye for now, and maybe I will hear back from you. If not, I wish you all the best, and again, I am sorry that I did not get back to you when I should have and explained things.

Sincerely Kingsley, which of course, you knew me as Vince. I must say I feel a bit like a double agent writing like this, having used two names he-he, and I can assure you I am not 007, or working for the KGB, I am a man from South Wales, and my first name is Kingsley. Anyway, if I have not frightened you off and made you run for the hills, I would enjoy hearing back from you.

Kingsley.

A week went by, and I received an email back from Ffion.

Dear Kingsley,

Thank you for your email, it is so nice to hear from you after all this time. I loved your humour by the way, and no, I don't believe you work for the KGB, and I didn't run for the hills. It is rather interesting that you said you do not believe in coincidence! I don't either, and what I find rather intriguing, is that about a week ago, you came into my thoughts very strongly, and I didn't know why I should be thinking about you after all this time, and here we are emailing each other. I am still single and hoping to meet someone. It sure has been a long time since we did that speed dating event. I am assuming that you still live near Swansea. I think you told me you did, if I remember rightly. Would you like to meet for a drink some time? I will give you my phone number, and of course you have my email, so feel free to contact me and we can arrange a time to meet. I will look forward to seeing you again, Kingsley, and bye for now.

Ffion.

Wow! I am glad I took the risk I thought and went with my instinct to contact her. I called Ffion the same day I received her email, and we arranged to meet at the Pilot Pub in Mumbles the following Friday. Helen was excited for me, but I felt a bit hesitant in telling the girls.

Friday evening came, and the girls could see that I was up to something. "Where are you going, Dad?" both Samantha and Melody asked.

"How do you know I am going somewhere?" I asked.

"You do not usually take this long in the bathroom," Samantha said, "and you have styled your hair, what is her name?!"

"Get out of here," I said laughing, "it is hard to keep a secret around here."

"Yes, who is she, Dad?" Melody teased, and said, "don't forget to bring her home so I can give her the look over, I'm very protective over my Dad, you know."

"I know," I said laughing, "now let me finish getting dressed please."

As I put on my best jeans and favorite black sweater, I felt happy that both my girls seemed supportive of me going out on a date. I had felt that Samantha would be, but I was not sure about Melody, as we have never really had any closure as to what happened to Gay. But I need not have been concerned, Melody was ok with me going out on a date, and that gave me the extra tonic I needed to get out there and start making a life for myself.

Ffion lived in an area called Cline Meadows, close to where I used to work on a golf course in my early teens. It was a nice area, and not far from where we were meeting in Mumbles.

We were meeting at the pub at 7:00 p.m., so I left our house in Pennard at 6:30.

"Bye girls see you later tonight, and no boyfriends staying over, that is the rule and don't forget."

"Alright Dad, you run a tight ship around here, we won't forget the rules, and have a nice time and don't do anything we wouldn't do."

"I won't," I called out from the car, and I was on my way.

I parked on the seafront, and walked along the promenade until I reached the Pilot Pub. When I opened the door, it was heaving with people, and it seemed every table was taken. It is a Friday night, I thought, what did I expect, Mumbles was usually busy on Friday's and Saturday's. Suddenly, I heard my name being called, and it was Ffion, calling me from a table at the back of the pub.

"I am glad you found a table," I said, "it's busy here tonight."

"I thought it would be," she said, "so a came a bit early to get a table."

Ffion looked much the same as I remembered, maybe even nicer, I thought, looking at her lovely long hair and her big blue eyes, and I sat at the table.

"How long before the bell rings?" I joked, and I wasn't going to answer to Vince. Ffion laughed, and then looked at me more intently.

"It sure has been a long time," she said, and she stood up to give me a hug.

"Yes, it has been," I replied, standing up to receive her hug.

"I am glad we can do this," I said, "as I mentioned on my email, you have been in my thoughts for some reason for a few weeks now. Thank you for meeting me, Ffion, I will say it again, I don't believe in coincidences, I knew I had to see you again."

After ordering our drinks and some food, we sat and talked for over two hours. And it was obvious that we had a lot in common, and we felt a strong attraction towards one another. I shared with her about my interest in history and finding artifacts with my metal detector, and she seemed interested, especially about the metal detecting. "I will have to take you with me some time," I said.

Ffion went on to share that she had been married once but did not have any children. "Not recently," she said, "that was almost ten years ago since I was married."

"Do you mind me asking what happened?" I said. "And please tell me if you do, and we don't need to talk about it."

"I always wanted a large family," she said, "but I was not able to have children, and that was a real problem for my husband at the time. I was willing to adopt, but he was insistent on us having our own children."

As I listened to Ffion share about her past, I wondered what she would think when I told her I had four children, including my boys in Canada. I need not of had any concern.

"That is wonderful," she replied, "I hope I can meet them one day."

"You will," I said, feeling more and more comfortable as the evening went on. Finally, the conversation came to talking about my past relationship, and I thought if anything would scare her off, it would be knowing that my wife disappeared and has never been found.

But to my relief, Ffion seemed genuinely supportive, and said, "I cannot imagine how hard that would be," and she took my hand and caressed my fingers, her lovely blue eyes were full of compassion. It was so nice to feel her touch, I thought, and I held her hand in mine as we sat in silent conversation, as our hearts spoke to one another saying what words could not.

"I like your silence," she said, "and being in the warmth of your presence."

I smiled and looked into her eyes, and said, "I am so enjoying being with you tonight."

It began to get late, and we both shared that we did not want the evening to end!

"Can I see you again soon?" I asked.

"Yes," she replied, caressing my hand again, "I have had a lovely evening, Kingsley, and I would love to see you again."

We finished our drinks and then I walked her along the promenade to her car.

I saw Ffion four more times over the next few weeks, and we continued to grow in our fondness of one another. It was time I asked her over to the house for tea, I thought, and introduced her to Helen and the girls. And after we had gone for a nice walk one evening, I asked her.

"Would you like to come over to my house and have supper next week?" I asked.

"I am only busy on Tuesday next week," she said, "otherwise any evening would work."

"How about Wednesday," I replied, "my girls are usually home mid-week with their studies, and I can introduce you to them. Also, Helen my ex-mother-in-law comes over on a

Wednesday to help me with the meals and to clean the house, would it be alright if she is there too? I don't want to scare you off by meeting everyone at once."

"That would be fine," Ffion smiled, "family is important to me, and I would like to meet your girls. And your boys are in Canada, you said?"

"Yes, they are, and they are wonderful boys. I will be seeing them in the spring when they have some time off studies."

Ffion hugged me and gave me a gentle kiss on the cheek before getting into her car. For a moment I was stuck for words, and felt I was floating. How lovely to be kissed and smell perfume again.

"Okay, great," I said, "I will call you early next week, and give you directions to our house in Pennard." And I walked just short of a skip along the promenade, and I named my walk, the Cloud Nine Mile.

∾

When I arrived home in Pennard it was almost midnight, but the girls were waiting up as usual to see how my date went.

"Hey Dad, how was it?" they both said, as I came through the door.

"It was great," I said, "we are getting on so well, and we have a lot in common. Ffion is also interested in history and thought that my metal detecting for artifacts was really cool!"

"And…?"

"And what?" I replied, trying to keep a straight face.

"You know," Samantha said, beginning to laugh, "did you kiss each other tonight?"

"Oh yes," I replied, "she is quite lovely."

"Quite lovely," Melody echoed, "your face is beaming, Dad! So when are you bringing her home for us to meet her?"

"I have asked her to come for tea next Wednesday, I hope you can both be home."

"We will be here," they both said, "we wouldn't miss meeting her Dad."

"Look at the time," I said, looking at the clock, "it's time you girls were in bed, and thank you so much for waiting up for me, and giving me you're support." They both smiled and then hugged me and headed off to bed.

⤵

Once the girls were settled in their rooms, I sat in the living room and thought of my time with Ffion. She has not got any children, I thought, which might make things easier as I have 4 of my own. My friend, Karen, in Canada had told me that people who don't have children of their own can be quite demanding and selfish with their time, because they don't understand the demands and commitments of family life. I am sure that is true with some people, I pondered, but not all. Karen had had some negative experiences dating men who didn't have children of their own, but I think that you have to give people a chance. That is my motto anyway, we are all different, and some people who don't have children of their own make wonderful step-mums and dads. I think if there was one thing I am learning from my dates with Ffion, it is how much I have missed the friendship and companionship of a woman, and I looked forward to seeing her again on Wednesday. And seeing my girls happy and supportive of me meeting someone is wonderful! I feel now that I have the freedom to make a life with someone. And Helen, well, I know she wants me to be happy, but it cannot be easy for her, when she sees me developing a relationship with someone else, having lost her own daughter. Oh well, I would invite her to come on Wednesday, and see how things go.

I thought about Ffion all week, and once or twice I did the Cloud Nine Skip, and I almost picked up the phone a few times to ring her. I will ring her on Sunday, I thought, and ask her how her weekend is going. She phoned me on Friday, however, and told me how much she was looking forward to Wednesday.

"I am so glad you called," I said, "I have thought about you a lot since Tuesday, and I'm looking forward to Wednesday too. My girls are also looking forward to meeting you."

We talked for about an hour, and Ffion told me about the dance glass she was teaching in Swansea.

"You will have to come dancing," she said, and I agreed that I would go with her one day.

～

The weekend went by quickly, and on Sunday evening I phoned Helen to make sure she would be coming over to see the girls and I on Wednesday and help me with the housework.

"How was your date last week?" she asked.

"It went well," I said, "and I have asked her over for tea on Wednesday, so you and the girls can meet her."

"You did?" Helen said, her voice sounding excited! "Yes," I replied, "we are getting on well, and I think you will like her."

"What are you going to make for tea?" Helen asked, "and would you like some help making something? I am at the house anyway."

"Oh yes please," I said, "I have no idea what to make, I was going to order something in but that is expensive."

"Let me help you, she said, and we can decide what to make on Wednesday morning when I come over."

"Thanks Helen," I replied, and it felt so good to have Helen's support.

Chapter Eleven

Come On Wednesday

Wednesday finally arrived, and after the girls left for school, I waited for Helen to arrive from Cardiff. Helen was going to help me make a special tea for Ffion, and I was already getting excited!

She arrived right on time at 10 a.m., and we walked across to Pennard Stores to get our groceries.

"How about we make a nice lamb dinner," Helen said enthusiastically.

"Ffion does not have any food allergies does she or is a vegetarian?"

"No," I replied, "she says she enjoys everything except liver and onions."

"Liver and onions Mm, well we will not be making that, so you need not worry."

Hellen picked out five lovely pieces of Welsh lamb, and we bought yams, potatoes and carrots. "Oh, and we can't forget some nice fresh buns and some garlic butter," she said, handing me the produce, and I put them in our basket.

"I so appreciate this Helen," I said. "I really had no idea what I was going to make."

"I am happy to help, Kings," she smiled, "and I am excited to meet Ffion." I knew she was sincere. As we walked back across the road to the house, I thought how blessed I am, to have Helen in my life. She has been such a strength and rock of stability for the girls and I over these last three years, and even before that, her kindness and grace had blessed our lives immensely.

"So how are you feeling about this evening?" she asked, as we peeled the potatoes and carrots together.

"Oh, a bit nervous," I pondered out loud. "I keep thinking about that lyric from one of Rod Stewart's songs- I'll try and love again."

"Everything is going to go well," Helen said, sensing what I was feeling in my heart. "It is not like this is the first time you are meeting her, but I can appreciate that you feel a bit nervous bringing her home to meet the girls and me. Remember, you are a wonderful man, Kings, and any woman that you would choose for a partner, is very fortunate indeed."

"Thanks Helen."

"I mean it, Kings, it is true, you are a truly lovely man!"

"I have brought a blackberry pie and some ice-cream for dessert," Helen continued. "And the pie is the last of the summer blackberries that I picked with my friend June, and she made a lovely pastry on all the pies. Did you tell me what Ffion does for work, Kings, I can't remember?"

"No, I don't think I told you. She teaches dancing at a studio in Swansea."

"Oh, does she? What type of dancing?"

"She teaches ballroom dancing and freestyle."

"Oh, how exciting! I have always wanted to learn ballroom dancing!"

"Well maybe this is your chance, Helen, and it might be a way for you to meet someone special." "Yes, it just might be," Helen said with an excited tone in her voice, "I will have to talk to Ffion and see what she thinks."

After peeling the vegetables, there was not anything more to do with the food until early evening, so Helen did her weekly cleaning of the house, and I prepared my next lesson for my youth group.

Samantha and Melody were both home by 4:00 and started getting dressed for the evening.

"Wow! You girls look lovely," I said, as I watched them both putting on their makeup in front of the mirror.

"Having fun Dad?" Samantha said laughing, as she put on some eye shadow.

"Yes, I mean no, I just need to use the bathroom, but I can use the one downstairs."

"A good idea," Helen said, "and you should start getting ready soon."

"She's not the Queen, girls," I said, as I went downstairs to shower.

"I think she is," Samantha shouted, "otherwise you wouldn't be acting so nervous." "I'm not nervous," I shouted back, and Helen gave me her knowing look and laughed.

Who am I trying to kid, I said to myself as I stood in the shower and felt the hot water on my back, I am nervous, I haven't had a lady over to meet my family in a hundred years! Then I heard Helens words echoing in my heart, 'you will do just fine, Kings, just relax and be yourself.' Alright, I said to me, myself, and I, and I began to relax. Everyone is excited for me, I told myself, and I am sure they will like Ffion, she is a lovely lady, and so real and down to earth.

Samantha helped me to pick out a nice shirt, and Helen had ironed my best black trousers, and Melody went across the road to the store and bought some nice table flowers. And I can only describe what I felt in my heart, as a wonderful 'healing' which was to continue throughout the evening.

Helen and the girls had everything hot and ready to be brought out to the table, before the doorbell rang, and I escorted Ffion into the dining room to meet everyone.

"What lovely dresses," Ffion said to the girls. She shook Helen's hand, and Helen gave her a hug.

"You look lovely," I said to Ffion, as both the girls winked at me and gave me the thumbs up.

"Thank you," Ffion said, in answer to my compliment, and she did look lovely. She wore a velvet burgundy dress with white stockings and black heels.

"What is the scent you're wearing, Ffion?" Helen asked.

"It is called Wild Honey," she replied, "and I like it because it is pronounced, but not too strong." Helen now gave me a wink, and whispered, "well done Kings, she has got some class."

"Wine anyone? Helen, Ffion?"

"Yes, I will have some red wine," Ffion answered, and Helen had the same.

"What about you girls?" I asked Samantha and Melody.

"I will have white please Dad," Samantha said, "and I will have white too, but just a tiny bit!" Melody replied.

Helen and Samantha made the rest of us sit down while they went into the kitchen and then brought out the food.

"Oh, lamb," Ffion said, "one of my all-time favorites, and I love roast potatoes," and we were off to a great start!

After we had passed the food around the table, and poured the gravy, I gave thanks for the food and our conversations started. I had already told the girls how I had first met Ffion, even though it had been over three years ago since we had first met at the speed dating. Helen of course, knew. And we all listened to Ffion tell the story again, only from her prospective, and the quiet conclusion around the table was that Ffion and I were meant to meet.

And as the evening went on, the conversation flowed. Helen and the girls were impressed. And Ffion talked with Helen about ballroom dancing and gave Helen an invite to come and join her group at the next session which was happening next week. The girls talked to Ffion about free dance, which she also taught at a different night of the week.

"You girls should come out," she said, "and it's a nice way to meet people."

"I will bring my boyfriend, Glynn," Samantha said. Melody was interested in going also.

As I listened to the conversations around the table, I became aware of how outgoing Ffion was. I was more of an introvert, but we might complement each other nicely. I also became aware of something within myself, as I listened to my family around the table. I felt such healing and wholeness, and a freedom to be myself, and express myself again with another woman, who sat at my table and fellowshipped with my family. It is nothing less than a wonderful thing, I thought, for anyone who has lost someone, or gone through a divorce, or breakup, and to be able to feel healing and wholeness again, after going through the great heartache and pain of loss and find yourself alive again!

When you go through a divorce or the death of your partner, or the disappearance of the one you love, you feel like half of you has died. Even your friends and kin try to adjust to what has become a half and no longer a whole, but oh, to find and feel that rebirth, it is so wonderful!

After we had finished Helens wonderful blackberry pie and ice-cream, Helen and the girls retired to the living room, and I took Ffion for a walk along Westcliff in the light of what was almost a full moon.

We walked and talked hand in hand, until we reached the end of the paved road, and we walked away along the clifftops towards Pobbles.

We shared so much together, and there was an awareness we both felt like we had been especially prepared for one another, and to meet at this specific season of our lives. We experienced a wonderful closeness that was familiar yet fresh and new. A 'knowing' that we were meant to be together engulfed us like a warm glove, and we did not let go of one another's hand until we returned to the house, and I walked Ffion to her car.

Samantha and Melody had gone to bed, but Helen was still up sitting in the living room.

"Ffion is lovely," Helen said, "and although I have only met her this once, I have such a strong sense that she is the woman for you, Kings!"

"I feel that too," I replied, and I shared the connection Ffion and I had experienced on our walk with Helen. "That is wonderful, Kings, I am so happy for you!"

⌒

Over the next few months, Ffion and I saw each other at least two or three times a week, and Helen and the girls started to get to know her slowly. Helen joined Ffion's ballroom dancing class and they became good friends. The girls also enjoyed me bringing her home on the weekends for tea, and they both grew to like her. Dad and Mary also thought Ffion was wonderful, and Dad and I took her metal detecting. 'I would hang on to this one,' Dad said, 'she is a keeper, and I can see how much she loves your girls.' "Yes Dad, she is amazing!" And I thanked God for bringing Ffion into our lives.

Chapter Twelve

Aberystwyth and the Devils Bridge

The coming weekend was Ffion's birthday, and I invited Helen and the girls to come to the Salutation Inn to celebrate with us for the weekend.

Helen was unable to come as she had made previous plans to go and visit Pearl in Bristol, and Samantha had been asked to go to a music festival with her boyfriend Glynn, but Melody was able to join us, and was looking forward to another adventure in West Wales.

"Do you remember the Devils Bridge, Dad, when you told Grandma and I about the legend of the crafty old woman and the devil?"

"Yes, I remember, why do you ask?"

"Well, we should take Ffion there, and tell her the story," she said. "A good idea," I replied, "how about you tell her the story, and you can even add something to it, that is how legends come about, when people make up their own stories, or add a twist to something that has already been said."

Melody took the day off school on Friday, and after Samantha left to meet her boyfriend Glynn, Melody and I went to pick up Ffion for her special weekend.

I had managed to book the same two rooms that Melody and I had stayed in when we had gone to the Salutation Inn a previous time with Helen, but they were only available on the Friday night. We would spend the whole day in West Wales on Saturday, and that would give us time to celebrate Ffion's birthday. Melody was excited to have a room of her own this time. The Salutation Inn was becoming a family heritage for us, I thought, as we drove over the Preseli Mountains to Eglwyswrw.

We arrived at the inn just after lunch, and once we had unpacked our suitcases in our rooms, we decided to go into Aberystwyth as Ffion and Melody wanted to do some shopping, and I wanted to call in at the hobby shop to see if they had got any new model railway accessories in. If the weather held we would be able to go down to the beach which Melody was looking forward to.

We managed to get a parking spot down on the seafront, and the girls headed off to do some shopping. "We will meet back here at the car in two hours," I said, and I headed off to the hobby shop.

"Unfortunately, we have not got any more model railway stuff in," the man said. "There is not the demand these days for model railway. Everyone seems to be buying remote- control cars or radio-controlled airplanes."

"Not everyone," I said, and I left the shop feeling disappointed.

As I came out of the hobby shop and back onto the street, I seemed to be drawn to an old jewelry store that stood on the corner of a row of houses. There in the window was the most beautiful Sapphire ring! It was in the shape of a heart, and it was set in an old-fashioned gold design from my grandmother's era. It immediately reminded me of Ffion's blue eyes, and the rare qualities of her person. And I had to buy it!

Never did I think that I would one day be buying Ffion a ring! Yet here I was standing at the counter and looking at this beautiful ring, and it was the most natural thing in the world for me to buy it for her.

"That is for someone very special, I can see that" said the lady behind the counter.

"What can you see?" I queried. "I can see that you care for this person very deeply, but she's not your wife yet, is she?"

"No, she's not, and you're right, I do care for her very deeply."

"I did not mean to pry in any way, Sir," she said. "It's just that you have this excited look on your face – well, you don't see that expression very often these days when a man looks at a ring. It obviously talks to you about her."

"It does indeed, madam, and what of its vintage and history?"

"It was made in the late 1800's, and it is made of the finest genuine sapphire and high-quality gold."

I held it and rolled it in my fingers, and it had a good energy. "And what of its personal history?" I asked.

"Its personal history is most interesting," the woman replied. "It was found on Aberystwyth Beach by someone swimming in the sea in 1950. The person who found it was a lady who kept it in her home until last year when she brought it into my store. She said she had found it when she was a girl of about eight years old. Why she didn't wear it or sell it sooner, I do not know."

"I will take it please," I said, "and would you have a nice box to go with It?"

"I will find you one," she said, and she disappeared up the stairs at the back of the store.

She returned with a purple velvet box and some tissue paper, and then she put the box with the ring in a little white cotton bag.

"Thank you, Sir. I am glad it went to you, and I'm sure your lovely lady will enjoy it very much."

"Thank you," I said, and I closed the door.

It was interesting how she had been able to read me, I thought, and that she had commented on my expression. I felt excited about giving it to Ffion. I would give it to her tonight once Melody was asleep and we could enjoy some private time together.

After looking in a few more shops, I met Ffion and Melody back at the seafront, and we went to the pub for lunch. Unfortunately the cool wind began to pick up so the beach would have to wait for another day.

"Oh, it's nice not to be cooking or making sandwiches," Ffion said, as we ordered our food. Ffion had bought Melody a nice autumn jacket that she could wear for school, and a new leather satchel to replace her old one which had become rather tatty over the last few years. "Look, Dad," Melody said proudly, and she put on her jacket and swirled around.

"That looks very nice young lady," I said, and Ffion turned to me and smiled, knowing how much I appreciated her buying the jacket and satchel. I was still only working as a part-time pastor, so I did not earn very much. But God always provided for our family, and that included nice clothes for the girls.

"What did you do while we were shopping?" Ffion asked.

"I went to the hobby shop, but they did not have much of a selection of model railway gear. Still, it was nice to walk around the old part of town."

By the time we finished lunch, the weather had turned cloudy and there was rain coming in from the sea.

"Why don't we go back to the inn and relax," Ffion suggested. "It's such a nice place, we may as well go back and enjoy it."

We all agreed, and Melody was excited to be able to go back to her room and watch television or a movie. We didn't watch TV at home, so this was a real treat for her.

☙

In the evening, we all played a game of Mouse Trap and ordered food from the kitchen to eat in our rooms. Once we had eaten, Melody chose a movie to watch, while Ffion and I sat on the couch in front of the window and enjoyed a bottle of wine.

"I have something for you, lovely lady," I said, not wanting to wait any longer before giving her my gift. The ring was to tell her that I loved her, and it symbolized the covenant of my love that she would always have, no matter what the future held.

"I will be right back," I said. "Close your eyes, and don't open them until I say so."

"Alright," she said, with a rather shy look, and a pink blush on her cheeks.

"Now hold your hand out," I said, coming back into the room, "and keep your eyes closed."

She held out her hand and smiled in anticipation, and I gently kissed her on the cheek as I put the small box into her hand.

For a few moments, she rolled the little box in her hands feeling the velvet, and she lifted it up to her nose and sniffed it.

"You can open your eyes now," I said.

"I don't want to open my eyes, Kings, in case this is a dream that I have to wake up from. I wonder what it could be?"

"It's okay, lovely lady. It is not a dream, so you can open your eyes and it will still be there."

She looked up at me with her exquisite blue eyes and then opened the box.

"Oh, Kings, it's beautiful! I have never seen such a beautiful design, and I love the shape of the stone. And it's a Sapphire! How did you know that sapphires are my favorite stone?"

"I didn't," I said, "but it matches your eyes and the colour of a blue sky day, which I always celebrate when I am with you."

"Oh, Kings, I have loved you forever, it seems, only I just hadn't met you yet, and now you are giving me everything that I dreamed my life could one day have – a wonderful man who really loves and appreciates me for who I am. And when you and I and Samantha and Melody are together, I can experience what it's like to have a family, something I have never had before."

"I am happy for you," I replied. "Loving you is something very wonderful in my life, and the ring is my covenant to you – that no matter what the seasons of this life bring to us, I will always love you, Ffion."

Ffion wept as I spoke and as I put the ring on her finger – it was the perfect fit.

"You even got my size right," she said, and she gently kissed me on my lips. "Thank you, Kings, I love you. And I cannot wait to enjoy our evening together. And now I have something to give you, Kings. Wait here and close your eyes, and no peeking…"

"Okay, I won't peek."

Ffion left the room for what felt like a long time, and I heard her rummaging in the suitcase in our room.

Suddenly she re-appeared and put a small package into my hand.

"I hope you like it," she whispered, kissing my lips again. I bought it last week in Swansea, and I was waiting for the right time to give it to you. And that time is now. You can open your eyes if you want…"

I opened my eyes and then opened the small packet.

"No way," I said to myself, "it can't be! Oh my gosh it is!"

It was a man's gold ring – with the Welsh Dragon on it!

"I hope you like it, Kings. I had to buy it for you. I saw it in Samuels Jewelers, and it was like it was speaking to me! It is my gift to you, to remind you that I will always love you for what you have given to me. I know that what we share now, and will share in the future, is something that I will celebrate all my life. I have fallen deeply in love with you, and I am so excited to see where we go from here, just like on the day we decided to start this journey together when you emailed me after all that time, and when you first invited me over for tea and to meet your family. I think that I fell in love with you that evening when we walked along the clifftops together in the light of the moon. It was so romantic. Your love is something so precious in my life. And I want this ring to remind you of how I feel, every time you look at it."

"Thank you," I whispered, kissing her again, and seeing the love sparkling in her eyes.

"I will go and check on Melody and be right back," I said.

"Would you like another glass of wine, Kings?" Ffion asked.

"Yes, please."

Melody had fallen asleep already. Perfect timing, Princess, I thought, as I kissed her forehead and tucked her in with her blanket. She smiled, half asleep, and said, "Love you, Dad."

"I love you too," I whispered giving her another kiss. And I felt like the richest man in the world. I can't give her back her mother, I thought, but I can give her all my love.

Ffion and I sat at the window and looked out over the lovely garden and the river that wound its way past the inn. And after we had finished our wine, I took her hand and led her to our bedroom, where she pulled the ribbon from her hair. And for what seemed like a wonderful lifetime, we just stood and stared at one another, beholding our wonderful love.

"You see me," I said, "and I can feel you looking into my soul."

"Yes, I am with you," she echoed. "It's beautiful, Kings." And we fell deeper and deeper into our love.

"I've missed you," we whispered at the same time, and we laughed. Then we tried to say something else, and again our words came out at the same time.

"It's no use speaking," I said, and I gently pulled her towards me, and slowly and tenderly I kissed her mouth, until she moaned excitedly.

"We better check on Melody again," I said, which I did, while Ffion changed out of her clothes..

Melody was fast asleep now, and I gently pulled the door closed and went back to sit on the couch.

"I like your nightgown," I said to Ffion as she came back out of the bedroom, and her face glowed with a pink blush.

"I bought it for the next time I would see you," she whispered, giving me a wet kiss on my cheek, and I could not wait to kiss and taste her mouth again as I enjoyed the fragrant scent on her slender neck.

"Come with me, lovely lady," I said, standing up from the couch and reaching out my hand.

She took my hand and gently smiled as I led her back to our bedroom. She stood facing the window in the dim candle-light as I lifted her nightgown up over her shoulders, and then slowly, pulled down her panties.

"Oh Kings," she moaned, stepping out of them.

"Let me light another candle," I said. "I want to see your lovely eyes."

Ffion undressed me, and we stood together in the candle-light, kissing and caressing, and looking into each other's eyes.

"Oh, I've missed you, Kings," she whispered, landing another kiss on my lips, and then gently swirling her tongue around mine.

My loins throbbed with desire as I tasted her scent.

"I'm wet for you, my darling man," she whispered, almost in a moan, and I gently pushed her onto the bed. Now we kissed and rolled, and pushed and pulled, and Ffion sat on top of me. I kissed her full, pale breasts and teased her nipples with my teeth as she began to moan louder. She fixed her exquisite blue eyes on mine as my manhood pushed against her waiting womanhood trying to find my way inside her.

Suddenly, she adjusted her body and I slid deep inside her. "Oh…" we both moaned, and we kissed as she rode me like a wild mare across the Gower. "I'm coming, I'm coming!" we both called out together, and I fell into her beautiful eyes as I exploded inside her and she watched me with her soul. "I love you, Kings…." "I love you too." And we made love until Eglwyswrw fell asleep counting sheep.

We lay spent like a bottle of champaign, and I felt the pounding of her heart against my side.

"Good night, my love, blow out the candle, and we will burn again tomorrow."

"Good night, my love."

∽

Saturday arrived with a smile and a promise, and we looked forward to another lovely day together.

Good morning my love, good morning to you, we whispered, and we sang with the birds that were already singing about their hopes for the day. And we made love again, before Melody woke up and marched with the new day into our room.

As Ffion took a shower, I went and woke up Melody.

"Let's get Ffion with a pillow fight," I whispered. "She's taking a shower, so let's get her when she comes out."

"I know what we can do, Dad! When she gets out of the shower, I will call her into my bedroom, and you can hide in the closet. Then when I say 'now', you jump out of the closet, and we will both attack her with our pillows. Quick Dad, the shower has stopped – run and get your pillow and hide in the closet."

"Ffion, Ffion," Melody called, "come quickly, I need you!"

"What is it, are you alright?" Ffion shouted, as she came running into the room with just her bra and undies and a towel around her head.

"Now!" Melody shouted, and before Ffion could say, 'now what?', I jumped out of the closet with my pillow and Melody picked up hers from her bed and we began pillowing Ffion. She shrieked and laughed as Melody, and I let her have it!

Then Ffion managed to grab the other pillow from Melody's bed, and we ran from room to room chasing and hitting each other with the pillows. Melody laughed so much that she fell over, fortunately onto Ffion's and my bed, and we continued to jump and chase and sling pillows until we were completely tired out.

"I surrender!" Ffion shouted, giving Melody a final whack with her pillow.

Well, we had a whole day's fun and we had not even had breakfast yet. I quickly showered, while the girls got dressed, and then we headed down to the guest room for breakfast.

"Good morning!" said Innes, the Inn's owner. "Are you having a nice time?"

"We are, thank you," we replied, and I whispered to Melody not to mention the pillow fight, although I'm sure Innes would not have minded us having one. We had not broken any windows or furniture.

For breakfast, Melody and I had a full British Breakfast, and I traded one of my bangers for her fried tomatoes. If you eat too many sausages, you will go "bang," I said.

"Is that why they call them 'bangers', Dad?"

"I think so, sweetie, only you have to eat about ten of them before you pop."

Melody laughed. "What happens if you only eat four?" she asked.

"I think you're alright if you don't eat any more than four or five."

"I'm alright then," she said, and she continued to wolf down her last two.

"Where are you putting it all?" Ffion asked. "I can see why your dad calls you a Zulu from Eglwyswrw – you certainly eat like one."

Melody erupted with laughter again, and then it was all eyes on Ffion's breakfast.

Ffion had ordered a country cereal with yoghurt, and a blueberry scone with a large dollop of Devonshire cream and homemade strawberry jam.

"Keep your eyes off my breakfast, you two," she said, as I poured her a cup of tea.

"Thank you, lovely man, you're a gentleman and a scholar."

"Dad, you're a gentleman and a scholar!" exclaimed Melody, laughing. "And you're a banana in pajamas!" I responded.

As we waited for Ffion to finish her fabulous scone, we smelled the lovely flowers that Innes had put on our table.

"They are all wildflowers from our garden," she said, as she cleared away Melody's and my plates. And I lifted the vase for Ffion to smell the lovely rose that stood like a queen with her crown of pink petals adorning over the other flowers in the vase.

"Oh, such a lovely fragrance!" she spoke.

"I trust you have had a nice stay," Innes said, "I wish we weren't so booked up or you could have stayed longer."

"It's been wonderful," both Ffion and I said, as Innes refilled the teapot "and thank you very much for the wonderful service. We hope to be back again soon."

At our words, I realized that the Salutation Inn had already become a special place for Ffion and me, and I looked forward to bringing her here again and staying longer, sometime later in the year.

We finished our tea and then went back to our room to pack.

"Do we have to leave today?" Melody asked.

"We are leaving the inn today," I replied, "but we still have the whole day to spend in West Wales."

"We will come again another time," Ffion added. We packed our suitcases into the car and left to start our day.

"Where are we going?" Melody asked in a rather quiet, expectant voice. "I'm having such a fun weekend, Dad and … I mean Ffion."

Ffion looked across at me and smiled.

"Your dad and I thought we would make today an extra special day for you," Ffion replied. "We thought we would take you to Newport Beach." "A special day for me?" Melody echoed. "It is your birthday Ffion, not mine."

"I am having a wonderful birthday just being with you and your dad," Ffion replied.

"Newport Beach is a beautiful beach with lots of sand," I said, "and I have already checked the time of the tides, and we can build sandcastles before the tide comes in."

"Hurray, hurray!" Melody shouted. "We couldn't build castles yesterday in Aberystwyth because the tide was too high and the weather turned bad, but we can build them today! And we can have fish and chips for lunch and bring them down to the beach to celebrate Ffion's birthday," I added, almost as excited as Melody.

When we arrived at the beach, the tide was almost fully out.

"Look how big the beach is!" Melody shouted. "We have lots of time to build a sandcastle, and we could build a whole village and try to fight off the pirate waves."

"That sounds like a great idea!" I exclaimed.

As I listened to Melodys excitement, it was like she and I were back in time, a time when she was eight or nine, when we built sandcastles and boats on Port Eynon Beach. And I was reminded of the first time I met Melody, when she was playing with some other children near the Dragon Pool on Pobbles Beach. We emptied the whole Dragon Pool that day using beach pales, and it was through spending time with Melody on the beach, that I found out that her mother was my long- lost love, Gay. Today it was as if Melody wanted to go back to those sandcastle building days of yesterday when she and her mum and I used to play.

Kingsley Ross Hill

Happy as I was to build castles with her today, I felt her heart longing for the past in what she had missed, in her mother going away. Dr. Morgan the counselor had told me, that it was all part of Melodys grieving and healing, going back to where she left off in her life before her world was torn away. She had to go back to the past and stay for a while, before opening the door to the present and future, Dr. Morgan did say. And as I watched Melody play, I realized that I too had gone back to play, before opening the door to Ffion and a new day. Hurray for yesterday, and hurray for today, is the song I am waiting to hear Melody sing one day! And until then on the beach and in the waves, we will play, and shake hands again with yesterday.

There is a little general store and beach shop right on the seafront, and we bought Melody a bucket and spade, and some flags to put on top of the sandcastles.

"We are going to build a great village!" she exclaimed, as we walked down onto the sand. The sun shone down upon us like a warm kiss from the clear sky, and the refreshing breath of autumn breathed gently in the wind, giving our souls the awareness of change. Our wonderful summer was coming to an end, but we would bottle up our memories as in corked wine bottles and bring them out and drink them on those cold winter days when the sunshine hides his face, and the grey clouds win the race. Until spring and summer arrive again in a smiling warm haze, and the newborn foals skip and dance in the valley beneath Pennard Castle who laughs with the running children that tumble down his golden slopes again.

"Look, Dad, the beach pail is shaped like a castle!"

"Bring it here and let me have a look... You're right, it is! Look, Ffion!"

"Yes, I can see that it is, Melody. We are going to make some great castles with this! I put Ffion's deckchair down on the sand, and she sat and observed the beach.

"You both start making the sandcastles," she said. "I'm going to read my book until the tide has come in about halfway, and then I will help you finish the village."

"A good plan," I said. "Now bring your bucket and spade, Melody, and we will start building right here."

When the tide is out at Newport Bay, there is a wonderful feeling from the wide expanse – a barrenness of sand and sea hemmed in by the rolling hills, and the haunting headland of Dinas Head that stands like a guardian of the sands, defying the thundering surf that crashes relentlessly onto its iron rocks. And the seabirds ride the kite-flying winds and one's soul sings hymns and other things.

"Come on, Dad! Stop daydreaming!"

"Alright, but dreaming makes the world go round!"

"No, it doesn't. Don't be silly! Love makes the world go round."

"Who told you that?"

"You did, of course!"

"In that case, you're right, my Princess. Love does make the world go round, and I love you!"

"I love you too, Dad, so that means you and I make the world go round, right? Right!"

"Now you fill this pail up with sand, and I will dig a trench around where our village is going to be, and that will give us a first line of defense against the pirate waves," I said as I started digging.

"Come on, Dad, you have to make the trench deeper than that!" "The sand is hard, and I only have my hands to dig with. Tell you what. Why don't I help you with building the sandcastles first, and then I will use the spade to dig the trench, because we have lots of time before the waves reach us."

"Look, Dad, what do you think of this castle?"

"That is great, Princess! Don't forget to put the flag on top so people can see that it's our village."

In about an hour, we had made a village of ten castles, each one flying the Welsh Dragon of Wales.

"We will defeat the English, won't we, Dad?"

"Of course we will, and the Irish and Scots too!"

Melody grinned from ear to ear. "And pirates!" she exclaimed.

"And the pirates," I echoed.

"Who wants an ice cream?" Ffion asked, having walked over to the shop and bought us a tub each.

"Me, please!" we both replied, and Ffion inspected our village.

"This looks like a real Welsh village," she said. "Any sign of the Irish and Scots? They will be invading with the incoming waves."

"No sign of them yet," Melody said in her Long John Silver accent.

"What about the English?"

"Oh, they had a hole in their boat and they have sunk to the bottom already," I replied, and Melody roared with a pirate laugh.

"What about the French, Dad?" she asked.

"Oh, they did not make it out of the harbor," I replied. "They forgot their French bread and wine, and they had to go back for it, and Lord Nelson was waiting outside the harbor and fired his cannons and sank their ship."

"I never did like that Napoleon Bona-fart," Ffion stated. "He was a silly little man, and he was at sea so long that he had bad breath and tripped over his own beard."

Melody laughed and laughed, and then she ordered Ffion and I to dig the trench.

"I smell an act of piracy," Ffion said, looking at Melody, who in turn looked at me with suspicious eyes.

"Come on, everyone, we are on the same side," I said. "Let's get this trench dug to protect our village before the pirates arrive."

"Let me see," Ffion said, making her hands into a pair of binoculars. "Is it half-tide yet?"

"Yes, it is!" Melody shouted.

"It's close enough," Ffion replied. "Let's get this trench built!" And with the three of us working, we soon had our village and trench ready to fight against the pirate waves.

We still had a while to wait before the wild waves and Captain Yellow Beard reached our village, so we all took our shoes and socks off, and walked down to meet the sea. And we held hands and jumped over the incoming breakers, and I was a happy man, as wild and free as the crashing waves; and as Ffion looked into my eyes, I saw her love and joy.

The waves began to climb the beach now, and we raced each other back to our village of castles and waited for the pirates to arrive. Slowly at first, the waves surrounded our village, having been tamed by our deep trench, but then they began crashing into our castles, and the walls slowly crumbled into the sea. Melody paddled into the waves and put the flags back on top of the retreating castles, until one by one, they surrendered to Captain Yellow Beard.

I held my Ffion tightly around her waist and kissed her neck until we watched the last of our castles fall. And I knew, in those few moments when I held her, that she felt my strength and protection wrap around her, and that she could hear my commitment to our love singing loudly upon the sea winds. And as I felt her gently rub and caress my fingers, her heart cried out, "I will always love you!"

And it was time for fish and chips.

We sat and ate in the little garden at the chip shop, and Melody made friends with two other girls that were sitting and eating at the picnic tables.

"Would you like to come and hang out on the beach, with us?" they asked.

"See you later Dad and Ffion, I am off to hang out with some friends."

Ffion and I took our deckchairs back to the beach and relaxed, while Melody hung out with her new friends.

"Am I right in making this observation," I asked Ffion, "it seems to me that Melody acts like she is a lot younger, when she is hanging out with you and me, and then when she is with other teens her own age, it's like she switches on to their wavelength, almost like another level of maturity?"

"I know what you mean, Kings, but it Is safe for her to be that young girl when she is with us. And then when she is with her friends, or meets other people her own age she needs to act like them to fit in. Remember most kids have not gone through the trauma that Melody has. I don't think you need to be concerned, Kings, she is very bright, and mature when she wants to be, well beyond her years."

"Thanks Ffion, your insight is important to me, and Melody is already comfortable with you."

"I am happy about that," Ffion replied, "and it is the same with Samantha, we get on so well together. And Helen, what a lovely gracious lady, I feel like I have a second mum in her."

"Well, you are part of the family, my love, and we all love you!"

Ffion and I spent the rest of the afternoon relaxing and paddling in the waves, while Melody played a game of beach volleyball with her new mates.

As the sun began westering in the sky, and the evening shadows started their march across the happy bay, It was time to make our way home.

"Come on Melody," I shouted, "it is time to go!" She said goodbye to her friends, and then ran across the beach to catch up with Ffion and me.

"You sure make friends easily," Ffion commented to Melody.

"It is just a knack us teenagers have," Melody replied.

"Like a teenage code?" I asked.

"Yes Dad," Melody laughed, "us teenagers have our own code, didn't you when you were my age?"

"Yes, I believe I did, Melody, a code for parents, a code for teachers, and even a code between my close inner circle of friends, that excluded people that I didn't know well or didn't like."

"Mmm, Dad," Melody said, "that was good!" Ffion smiled at me, in agreement with Melody, and the three of us walked and then raced up the beach to the car!

"I had so much fun, Dad! Did you see us in the waves?"

"Yes, I did. I thought you were going to swim to Ireland, and that I might have to come and rescue you there. Come on, let's go home and see what your sister has been up to."

"Can you stay over?" Melody asked Ffion.

"Yes, I think so," she replied, "it's only Saturday today, and I needn't be home until tomorrow night."

"That's great," Melody replied, "maybe we can have a games night tonight."

"Where are we going Dad, this isn't the way is it?"

"No," I replied, "I thought we would show Ffion the Devils Bridge."

"Oh yes Dad, I almost forgot, let's show Ffion the bridge and tell her about the legend of the crafty old woman!"

"Crafty old woman?" Ffion repeated back.

"Yes, crafty old woman," I replied, "Melody is going to tell you the legend of how the bridge got its name."

"Plus, I am going to add to the story," Melody interjected.

We parked the car on the side of the road and walked onto the bridge. There were several people already on the bridge looking down at the deep ravine below.

"Wow! This is high," Ffion said, her voice full of wonder. "And there are two other bridges below us!"

"Yes," I replied, "the middle bridge right below us was built in the eighteenth century, and the bottom one in medieval times."

"So, tell me about the legend Melody," Ffion asked.

"Okay, it goes like this. An old woman's cow had strayed across the ravine, and she could not get it back. A strange monk suddenly appeared , and offered to build a bridge if she promised to give him the first living creature that crossed it. The woman agreed, and the bridge was built, and he beckoned to her to cross. However, the crafty old woman had spotted his cloven hoof, so she called her black dog, and threw a crust across. He ran after it, and she told the devil he could keep the dog."

"What are you going to add to it?" I asked Melody.

"I would have asked the devil to cross it first and say that I need to know that the bridge is safe before I allow anything of mine to cross it. And the devil crossed the bridge, thinking to himself that he would get the woman's cow. But all he got was himself, because he was the first living thing to cross the bridge!"

"Well done, Melody," I said, "I think what you have added makes the woman come across as more 'crafty'. And how about what I said," I continued, "it makes the woman 'come across', as in come across the bridge, get the pun? 'Come across'?"

"Oh Dad," Melody laughed, as did Ffion, "that is so lame!"

"Lame, get it!" Ffion added, "the woman couldn't walk across the bridge because she was lame."

"He He," both Melody and I laughed.

"And I will add to the legend," I said. "And the devil realizing he had been out witted by the old woman, became so mad that he threw himself off the bridge, and that is how the bridge got its name."

"Very good, Dad," both Ffion and Melody said, "now let's get the devil out of here before the woman comes back with her dog!" And we did.

Chapter Thirteen

Glorious Devon

The girls studied hard for their exams over the next few months, and Christmas came and went.

It would soon be the Easter Holiday's. Helen suggested that we all take a holiday, 'and make sure that you invite, Ffion,' she said with a twinkle in her eye.

"She showed me the lovely ring you bought her in Aberystwyth. So, when are you going to ask her to marry you, Kings? I know that is what she is waiting for."

"Soon Helen," I replied, "I have just been thinking of when to ask her."

It was now the weekend before Easter, and Ffion was coming over for tea on Saturday night. Helen was also staying for the weekend as she would be visiting her friend June in the village.

As we were sitting at the table having tea on Saturday evening, I asked the girls if they would like to go to Devonshire for the Easter Holidays.

"We can catch the train from Swansea, and stay in Torquay close to the seafront," I said, feeling excited! It was a unanimous decision and Helen, and Ffion were as excited as Samantha and Melody, well almost, as Samantha shouted hurray and Melody did her Zulu from Eglyswrw dance around the table. "We are a bit excited, aren't we," Helen exclaimed with a giggle.

"Yes, just a little bit," Samantha said, and then laughed.

On Monday morning I phoned my friends Rob and Donna who own the Patricia Hotel in Torquay, and I was able to book three rooms for Friday, Saturday and Sunday night, and we would travel home on the morning of Easter Monday. 'It is a reward for studying so hard and doing so well on your exams,' Helen said to the girls, but we all knew that it was so much more than that. This was the first complete family holiday that Ffion would join us on, and I felt so excited about introducing every-one to Devonshire, where I had lived with my Grandparents for almost six years in my late teens and early twenties, and it became a sacred place to me.

On Good Friday morning we left the house early to catch our train at 8:30 a.m. from Swansea. We would have one change at Temple Meads station in Bristol, and then straight on to Torquay.

As we stood on the platform and waited for our train to arrive, my mind and heart became flooded with wonderful memories from my boyhood, as I remembered the journeys that my brother Fraser and I took with our grandparents to Devonshire every summer for a month. Grandma would travel down from Devon by train, and pick us up at Swansea station, and then travel back with us to Exeter or Dawlish, where my grandfather met the train, and then would drive us to their cottage.

The trains were far more exciting then, back in the 1970s and 80s, when the Electric Diesels ruled the lines. 'They had so much more character than the modern trains of today,' I thought as we watched several trains arrive and then depart that all looked much the same. The old diesels were noisy and smelly, but they had personality, and my brother and I knew some of them just by sound, as we watched then rumble through Star Cross, Dawlish Warren, Dawlish town, and Teignmouth on their way to Torquay, Paignton and Penzance. At Paignton they still have the Old Steam Railway running between Paignton and Dartmouth, and I looked forward to taking Ffion and the girls for a day trip on the Steam Train to Dartmouth and to explore the historic maritime town. There is a wonderful little restaurant on one of the little cobblestone streets that makes the most wonderful crab sandwiches, and I felt hungry already, as our trains arrival was announced over the intercom. "Platform three," Melody shouted! "Yes, I know," Helen answered, "we are standing on it!" Good I thought, I won't have to lug these suitcases around anymore.

Our train whistled up the platform, and as the carriages got slower and slower, we all grabbed hold of our suitcases ready to board as soon as it came to a stop.

"You must wait for the passengers to get off first," the porter said to Samantha and Melody who were poised at the door to jump on.

"Let's try and sit in one carriage," I said, as the last of the passengers stepped off the train, and Samantha and Melody jumped on. I carried Helen's suitcase and mine, while Ffion jumped on with hers and followed the girls. It was a good job the girls had jumped on quickly and saved us some seats, because the train was full.

Across on the other platform was the express train that runs between Swansea and Cardiff, the same train that Gay used to take for work. Gay seemed to only cross my mind occasionally now, and I no longer looked for her face in the crowd or through the windows of the morning express. I had my Ffion to look at now, and life was good!

We sat in our comfortable bucket seats, and the station master blew his whistle and raised his flag, and our train began to pull away along the platform. Ffion's eyes met mine and she smiled, and our first family holiday together was underway.

Our carriage gently rocked over the sleepers, as the grey brick buildings passed by, and it was as if it was yesterday once more, as much as it was today, as our happy family rolled away. Signals and bridges flashed by now, and rows of semi-detached houses waved, as they stood in line like grey haired old men waiting for the pub to open.

When one is on a train there is a notable feeling of excitement that one is going somewhere, even if only to the next little town, but we were on our way to Bristol and then on to the next train that would take us to glorious Devon!

Samantha and Melody talked and laughed as only excited girls can do, and us adults were equally excited on the inside, as we dreamed of the fun and adventure that awaited us.

Towns and villages between farms and fields raced by as we picked up speed and caught up with our dreams that were as high as the church steeples that welcomed us to each new grey town. Look, there is Mrs. Morgan with her knickers down! And there is old Mr. Williams who always wears a frown! We flew past town to town. Neath, Port Talbot, Bridgend, and Cardiff all greeted us westbound, and then said goodbye like old friends, as we raced along towards the Severn Tunnel. The Severn Tunnel was always a milestone on our journey when my brother and I were boys, and it was again today, as suddenly our carriage became dark, and the damp grey walls of the tunnel flashed by here and there, reminding us that we were now under the sea. Ffion took my hand and I kissed her in the dim light of our carriage, that gave us the feeling of solitude, before we would burst forth into the light again. The girl's conversation stopped in the dark, at least for a few minutes, as they pondered how we could be travelling under the sea. Helen who had put down her book, sighed, and said, 'it has been such a long time since I traveled past Newport, and Castle-Nedd and then through the Severn Tunnel that makes you feel like you're in bed.'

Suddenly, as quick as it had become dark, we burst into the light again, and we would soon be arriving at Bristol Temple Meads.

We arrived on time, and it was a twenty-minute wait until we made our connection to our west country train.

"Who wants a cupper- tea?" Helen said as we lugged our suitcases up the stairs and over the walk bridge to platform four. "Me please," we all said, as I thought of a nice ice-bun and a hot cupper-tea. Samantha and Melody sat with the suitcases on the platform, as Helen and Ffion and I went to the café. Bring us back a hot chocolate and a Chelsea bun, the girls called out, and we will keep an eye on the suitcases. 'Keep an eye on the boys more like it,' Helen laughed, and we ordered our tea. It had been a good journey so far, I thought, as I sank my teeth into an ice-bun and supped on my hot tea, almost too hot to drink.

"Ah," Helen sighed, "nice and hot. There is one thing I cannot take, and that is lukewarm tea." Ffion nodded her head and agreed, only she ordered a latte. Ten minutes had gone already, and I ordered two hot chocolates and a pair of Chelsea buns for the girls, and we walked back to the platform.

"About time, Dad," Samantha said, "I hope you have not eaten my bun." Melody looked inside the bag to make sure there was two, there was, and all was well in the world.

"How long before Torquay?" the girls asked.

"About two hours," I replied, "if we have no delays."

"The train Is now arriving at the station," said the man's voice on the intercom, and a fresh wave of excitement, shouted out as the whistle blew, and the carriages passed us quickly on the platform. "Come on," Samantha said, "let's try and sit in the same carriage again," and she and Melody chased the train which still had not stopped along the platform.

"Come on!" they shouted as the train finally came to a stop, and they waited for the passengers to get off. We caught up with the girls as they stepped onto the train, and we all managed to sit together again.

"Well done girls," Ffion and Helen said, as we sat down.

"Welcome aboard," the conductor said. "Ladies and gentlemen please have your tickets ready, and make sure you have your luggage stored in the luggage compartments as we have a full train today and people need to sit down."

"The carriages are all full," Ffion said, "and we are

fortunate that we can all sit together." After what seemed like a long time, the whistle blew, and we were on our way again.

Memories were coming into my mind and heart now, like the rolling waves of the sea, and I was doing something with Ffion that I had never done with Gay. I was taking her to Devonshire and going to show her the sacred places of my late teen years when I lived with my Grandma and Grandpa in their cottage in Dawlish.

We arrived at Starcross, where Grandma and Grandpa had their farm, and where my Dad grew up. To our left was the beautiful estuary of the River Exe that runs between Starcross, and Exmouth on the other side of the estuary, where Grandma and Grandpa used to take my brother Fraser and I for holidays.

"Are you alright, Kings?" Ffion said, "You seem miles away."

"Yes," I replied, "I am just taking a walk with yesterday, and you can join me if you like."

"I would love to, Kings," she said, "I love getting to know all about you," and I shared with her about my life here in Devonshire with Grandma and Grandpa.

We passed the little village of Cockwood, where my Grandfather shepherded the local church, and then we whistled towards Dawlish Warren, and Dawlish town, where the red sandy beach and seawall spoke loudly to my heart as it flashed by as quick as my memories could travel.

The girls were getting excited now as there was only another two stops, and we would be in Torquay. "It will be too cold to swim in the sea yet," I said to Samantha and Melody who were exchanging stories of their swimming adventures on the Gower Peninsula. Helen was looking forward to visiting the clothing boutiques in Torquay and checking out the local entertainment, while Ffion and I, looked forward to spending time together and celebrating our love.

"This is the last stop before Torquay," I said, as we reached Teignmouth, one of my favorite little seaside towns, and I was looking forward to taking Ffion there, and catching the little ferry across the River Teign to Shaldon. There are some wonderful tea shops, where we can have a Devonshire tea, with scones and real Devonshire cream and a dollop of strawberry jam. Gosh, my mouth is watering already!

The train stopped outside the Grand Hotel in Torquay, and we wheeled our luggage through the park to Belgrave Road and on to the Patricia Hotel.

I rang the bell in the Hotel reception area, and my friend Rob soon came to meet us.

"Hello Kingsley," he said, giving me a hug. "You have brought the family with you I see," and I introduced everyone to Rob. In the middle of our introduction's, Rob's wife Donna arrived, and once we were all introduced, Donna showed us to our rooms. Helen and the girls shared a two- bedroom suite on the 3rd floor, and Ffion and I shared a room across the hall on the same floor. "It looks out over the road and shops," Donna said, opening the curtains for us, and Ffion said that 'it would be nice to sit and look out from the window in the evening when we get home from our day.'

"I will look forward to it," I smiled, "it will be quite romantic."

Leaving Ffion to unpack her suitcase, I went back down-stairs to talk to Rob.

I had stayed at the hotel at different times over a number of years, during my holidays in the west country, and had become friends with Rob and Donna, who are the most amazing hosts, and treat every guest like they are someone special. 'It is a rare thing these days to experience people taking such wonderful care and pride in their service to others and making them feel like they have a home away from home each time they come and stay at the Patricia,' I would often say, and Rob and Donna would humbly reply and say, 'It is what we love to do, Kingsley.'

Two years ago, there was a bad storm in Torquay, and the roof of the Patricia was severely damaged over the common room, and Rob had to close it down for repairs.

"Come and see the room, Kingsley," he said excitedly! "It has been completely redone, and it is so nice to have the common room up and running again for our guests."

Rob pointed out the plaster work on the ceiling, which looked like art to me, with the lovely ceiling sculptures and classic antique wallpaper. He had new pictures on the walls and a pool table, and an old turntable record player, with a great collection of LPs. "Wow! This is great Rob," I said, "You have done an amazing job!"

Another thing I enjoy about Rob and Donna's service, is the great British Breakfasts, and the Rock-n Roll music playing on the radio every morning. Add Rob's great sense of humor, and he and Donna's food, and you have a great start to the day!

It was only four in the afternoon, when we arrived, and once the girls had finished unpacking their clothes and getting settled into their rooms, we headed to the town and seafront to check things out. Helen and the girls seemed happy going from shop to shop along one of the main streets, while I took Ffion down to the promenade.

The seafront was busy with the Easter weekend holiday makers, and we walked hand in hand looking at the boats in the harbor. There were several sail boats birthed at the front, and one reminded me of Dad's boat which he named Wistful. I went over to have a closer look, and it was a mahogany all through, twenty-seven-footer, single mast, with an inboard Briggs and Stratton engine. It was a Dragonfly series alright, and a sister boat to Dads Wistful.

Ffion and I continued to walk along the seafront heading west towards Paignton, and about halfway along the promenade is a big Ferris Wheel. "I do not like heights," I said to Ffion, but she loved Ferris Wheels and persuaded me to go on with her.

"Only for you," I said, as the attendant made sure we were buckled in and the seat bar locked. The wheel moved slowly, and the view from the top was fantastic! "I am glad I came," I said, and I pointed out the various sites across the bay.

"Torquay, Paignton, and Brixham, are all part of what is known as the English Riviera," I explained, and pointed out the distant headland of Brixham, which looked like a long grey rock contrasting with the orange sky of the late afternoon sun, that had begun westering on the horizon. Every so often the wheel would stop for about thirty seconds for people to take photographs, and Ffion kissed me every time the wheel stopped, and what could I say to that? Nothing, other than, I like playing this game, please continue!

After we had finished our ride on the Ferris Wheel, we walked the whole length of the seafront until we came to a park on the clifftop, and we sat on a bench and looked out across the sea again.

"I'm enjoying myself already," Ffion said, and she thanked me for bringing her to Devonshire. "I especially like spending time with your family," she said, "and doing things together."

"You are part of my family now," I replied, looking into her lovely expressive eyes and giving her a long tender kiss.

"I am," she replied, coming up for air, and I kissed her again.

"I want to get as much kissing in now," I laughed, "before we catch up with the others and they tell us to get a room."

"We better not stop to talk then," Ffion laughed, and kissed me long and deep, "and besides we already have a room," she teased tickling my neck with her tongue.

As we were walking back along the seafront to meet Helen and the girl's we heard our names being called from the Ferris Wheel.

"Dad, Ffion," Samantha and Melody called. "Come on the Ferris Wheel with us!" I looked up to see them on the wheel and Helen was up there too. "We have already been on," I shouted, "we will meet you back at the hotel."

It is quite a walk back up the hill to the hotel from the seafront, and we were glad to put our feet up in the common room while we waited for the girls. After a short visit with Rob and Donna, Helen and the girls arrived back.

"How about we go out for tea tonight," Helen suggested, and it was a unanimous yes. Rob and Donna recommended the

Bull and Bush pub which was just a few hundred yards up the hill from the hotel. "They do a good supper in there," Rob said, "and that is no Bull!" We all laughed and headed up the hill to the pub.

It was music trivia night in the pub, and 'Helen and I were a team as we were the oldest' Melody announced, and Ffion and the girls joined sides to form our other team. Helen and I won hands down, as the music trivia was from the sixties and seventies era, and we even won free drinks and appetizers which we shared with Ffion and the girls. "You better share with Ffion, Dad," Samantha joked, "otherwise she is not going to be happy."

After a fun evening at the pub, we headed back to the Patricia for the night.

In the morning Ffion and I ordered Rob and Donna's famous full British Breakfast, with Rock n Roll playing on the radio as always, and as I sat with Ffion and looked around the room, I felt again, that I was at my home away from home. Soon Helen and the girls arrived in the dining room, and Rob joined two of the tables so we could all sit together, and he talked and joked with us between serving the other guests.

"It is good to see you again, Kings," Rob said again, "and welcome all of you to the Patricia."

After breakfast we decided to spend the day in Dawlish, and if we had time, I thought, we could walk along the sea wall to Dawlish Warren and have dinner in the pub there, before coming back to the hotel for the night.

As we walked down the hill to the seafront, the new day was waking up all around us, and I think the seagulls were as excited as we were, as they flew down from the chimney tops and picked up what they could find from the pavement, as passerby's dropped parts of their breakfasts as they hurried off to work.

The girls ran ahead to the bus terminus that was right in front of the harbour.

"Look out for the #2- Dawlish Warren," I shouted, "and save a seat for us." We arrived at the bus stop a few minutes after the girls, and the #2 was due in five minutes.

"I love double decker's," Samantha said, as the #2 pulled up. "We do not have many double decker buses in Canada," she continued, "apart from the tourist buses in downtown Victoria in the summertime."

We all climbed upstairs and sat at the front of the bus. As we pulled away my memories were back, and I sat and reminisced about the years that I had lived with my grandparents. Dawlish was our hometown, and I knew it well, and the years melted away as we got closer and closer, passing little towns and villages along the way, each one seemed to have a sweet memory attached to it, as my wonderful heritage called my name out loud. To share the land of my teenage years with Ffion and my family was going to be wonderful!

"We are almost at Teignmouth," I exclaimed, as our bus climbed down the steep hill into Shaldon, and then on over the bridge across the Teign Estuary into Teignmouth town. Teignmouth was where my Grandfather took Grandma and I out for special dinners, as we celebrated birthdays, and anniversaries throughout the year, and sometimes we just came here for a Sunday drive or to walk around the quaint little town.

"Do we get off here?" Melody asked. "This looks like such a lovely town to explore."

"No, not yet" I replied, "Dawlish is the next town from here."

Dawlish is famous for its Black Swans that live in the little stream that runs through the center of the town. It has little benches to sit and shops to explore on each side of the stream. There is also a lovely green where people can go and sit and have a picnic, and 'I thought we would do that today,' I said to Ffion, who was now almost as excited as I was to see my beloved little town.

The sign read Welcome to Dawlish, and we got off the bus.

We walked along beside the stream, and there was one of the Black Swans sitting on its nest.

"Another few weeks and it will have signets," I said excitedly, as Samantha and Melody took photos with their phones.

"How many black swans are there?" Samantha asked.

"I believe there are always about four adult pairs," I replied, "and then it depends on how many of the signets survive. I can remember one spring when my Grandma and I were feeding the ducks, and two seagulls swooped down and carried off two of the signets. My grandmother and I were very upset."

Helen and the girls had found a giftshop and went inside, and I took Ffion to sit at the edge of the stream, and we watched the ducks dipping and squabbling over some bread that someone had thrown into the stream. Ffion leaned back upon my breast as I gently caressed her hand.

"I am having a wonderful time already," she whispered, turning her head and giving me a kiss.

"I am too," I echoed, looking into her beautiful blue eyes. And we just sat and caressed each other's hands in silent conversation, as the spring sang its joyous chorus all around us. I watched a pair of robins collecting little feathers and sticks for their nests. And I was doing the same, I pondered, not so much building a nest; that was already built in our home in Pennard, but I was building a life, and I knew in my heart that the woman beside me was who I wanted to be my wife. 'I must ask her soon,' I thought, as the little robins flew off together. I can't wait to love Ffion in all kinds of weather, through the spring showers and in the summer heather. I want us to spend our lives together.

Helen and the girls were walking across the green, and I shouted out to them, letting them know that Ffion and I were here by the stream.

"What did you buy?" I said to the girls who were each carrying a shiny white bag.

"Clothes, Dad," they said, and they showed Ffion and I what they had bought.

"What shall we do for lunch?" Helen asked.

"There is a sandwich shop open on the high street."

"Why don't we have our lunch on the green," the girls asked, "then we can watch the swans and the ducks."

"A good idea," we all agreed, and I went with Helen to buy our sandwiches.

"Thank you for bringing me to this lovely place," Helen said, as we walked across the green.

"I am so glad that you came with us," I replied, and I told Helen that no matter what the future holds, that she would always be part of my family.

"I know that Kings," she replied, "but it is so nice to hear you say it. I had a sad moment while the girls were buying their clothes."

"What made you sad?" I asked, feeling concerned.

"Oh, it was just one of the shops," she replied. "It was called Gay's Creamery. It just made me think of her, you know."

"Yes, of course it would," I said, putting my arm around her. "I had forgotten that shop was here. It has been here since I lived in Dawlish with my Grandparents back in the eighties, and they make their own fudge and pastries. I still think of her too," I said, "and I think we will think of her all our lives. She will always live in our hearts." Helen smiled and kissed me on the cheek.

"Thank you, Kings, for always hearing my heart. You will always be part of my life too."

"What sort of sandwich would you like, Kings?" Helen asked.

"I will have a shrimp and tomato baguette and Samantha and Ffion will have the same, and I forget what Melody asked for…"

"I remember," Helen replied, "she wants an egg salad sandwich, and I will have the same."

We sat and had lunch on the green and watched the Black Swan guard his nest. The swan reminded me of Helen, always watching over and protecting our family. And every time another swan got too close, it would open its mouth and hiss, and move its head back and forth like it was going to strike out at the intruder. I did not tell Helen that she reminded me of a swan, however, as that might ruffle her feathers.

"Who would like to walk along the Dawlish Wall to Dawlish Warren?" I asked, as we finished up our sandwiches.

"I am in," Helen said, being the first to speak, "I need some exercise after that big sandwich."

"Me too," everyone else said, and we walked to the bottom

of the town to where the stream meets the sea. On our way to the seafront, we saw two more pairs of black swans and several different species of duck, and I pointed out to Ffion some of the old houses with the thatched roofs.

"This is such a charming place," she said, "I can see why you like it so much, Kings."

Once we were on the sea wall we walked eastwards towards the Warren.

"Why do they call it the Warren?" Melody asked.

"Because a giant rabbit lives there," I replied, as I tried to keep a serious face.

"Giant rabbit!" Melody repeated and laughed.

"Good try, Dad," Samantha said, joining the conversation.

As we walked along the wall, I pointed out the Red Sandstone Rock that the cliffs are made of, and we did see some wild rabbits sitting in the afternoon sun.

"Look there are rabbits Dad, you were right," Samantha said.

"But I don't see the giant one," Ffion laughed as I climbed up upon the railway wall.

"What are you doing, Kings?" Helen asked.

"I used to climb up on this wall when I was a boy," I replied, "and wave to the trains as they raced by. And the engine drivers always blew their horns and waved. I can hear a train coming now," I said, as the rails began to make a ringing sound. Suddenly the express train from London Paddington to Penzance came whistling around the corner, and I waved my arms at the driver, who in turn blew the trains horn and waved.

"They still wave at you!" Samantha exclaimed, and I climbed down from the wall having talked with my memories.

It was the girls turn now to climb up on the wall, and I held onto Samantha's hand, and Helen held onto Melody's, as another train came along in the opposite direction, and the engine driver beeped his horn as the girls waved excitedly.

About three quarters of the way along the seawall to the Warren, one comes to a spectacular looking Red Rock, called the Langstone Rock, and it shines a rich colour of red in the afternoon sun. As the rest of the girls rested on one of the benches looking out across Dawlish Bay, I took Samantha up on top of the Langstone Rock to show her the view. It is a rather steep climb up a winding path to get to the top of the rock, but it is well worth it as the view is spectacular.

As a boy the Langstone Rock was a place of refuge, where I would come and reminisce after a long day at work, or to have some quiet time away from the busy town center where I could come and meditate on life.

"I can remember coming here and dreaming about what my life would be like one day when I had my own family," I shared with Samantha, as we sat near the edge of the clifftop. "And here I am, with my lovely daughter and family."

"I am glad that you dreamed of having a family when you were a boy, Dad," she said. "And I get to be part of that family you hoped and dreamed of," she smiled.

"You are," I smiled, "and I am so blessed to have you for a daughter."

From where we sat on the clifftop, we could see Exmouth, in the distance. "It is on the other side of the River Exe estuary," I pointed out to Samantha, and in the forefront, we could see the Dawlish Warren sports and entertainment park.

"Is that where we are going?" Samantha asked.

"Yes," I replied. "Let's climb down and join the others."

When we arrived at Dawlish Warren, we all had a ride on the bumper cars. Samantha and Melody were a team, and Ffion and I were the other, while Helen watched from behind the barrier.

"The bumper cars are fun," Ffion said, as we sat side by side in our car, and chased and bumped into the girls, who screamed and laughed every time we bumped them, before being swept away and bumped by the crowed of other drivers who spun around the circuit in one banging and crashing direction.

After we had finished riding the bumper cars, I took Helen on the two-seater Go-Carts that were fast and furious, and Helen almost brought up her lunch as we spun around the racetrack like it was the Grand Prix, and it was as far as I was concerned, as I tussled with another go-cart for the lead as we took the final corner. Ffion and the girls shouted from the side stands, as Helen and I took the checkered flag!

"I can't move," Helen said, as she sat there in a daze. "Oh Kings, I'm too old for this!"

"No, you're not!" I said, giving her a winner's kiss, and we climbed out of the Go-Cart and wobbled back across the racetrack to the victory shouts of the girls.

"That is enough craziness for one day," Helen exclaimed. "I need a whole bottle of wine after that victory, she laughed, and we all headed off to the Ship and Anchor Pub for a late lunch and early supper.

It was fish-n-chips all around, and while Helen sipped her victor's wine, Ffion and I ordered a pint of Devonshire cider each, and the girls had a Shandy.

"The chips are good." I said, as I asked for some extra tartar sauce. "And the halibut is great too," we all said, and ate as much as we could, barely leaving room for chocolate fudge and ice cream.

It was 8:00 p.m. before we left the pub, and the next bus to Teignmouth was not for another hour, and then we had to catch the Torquay bus from Teignmouth, the schedule at the bus stop said.

"Let's walk back over the railway bridge to the train station," I said, "and see if there is a train coming soon."

"There is one in ten minutes," Helen said, and we all gave out a sigh of relief as we didn't want to wait another hour for the bus.

"The train is a lot quicker too," I reminded everyone, "and we don't have to change trains, it goes right through to Torquay."

"I'm glad we were able to get the train," Ffion said, as she lay back on my shoulders and the train pulled away.

"That was a wonderful day!" Everyone exclaimed as we climbed up the hill to the Patricia.

"See you all at breakfast in the morning," I said, and we headed off to our rooms for the night. Ffion and I sat at our window for a while and looked out over the busy street before retiring from our fun filled day.

Easter Sunday arrived, and while Ffion took a shower and got ready for the day, I went down to the dining room to talk to Rob. "Would you like a cup of tea while you're waiting for the others?" he asked.

"Yes," I replied. "Good morning Rob."

"Good morning Kings, what do you have on the agenda today then?"

"I thought I would take the girls on a boat ride to Dartmouth," I replied. "It looks like a blue-sky day, and none of them have been to Dartmouth before."

"A good choice, Kings, it will be lovely out on the water today."

As I waited for the others to arrive, I meditated about what this Easter Sunday meant to me.

Easter has always represented 'New Life' to me. In my grandparent's garden, now part of my family home in Pennard, grows an ancient Purple Iris. After blooming beautifully for almost three months in the summertime, it dies off in late autumn, and its lovely purple and sweet-scented petals fade and turn to a dull brown before falling from the stem, and eventually, disappears altogether.

The Iris seems dead, and its fragrant blossoms become only a memory.

My grandmother taught me about God through the old purple Iris. She said that "the bulb of the plant was very much like the life of Jesus, God's Son. While Jesus was on the earth his life was a blossom of blessings, healing and saving many lives. And then he died on the cross, being put to death by evil men. But after laying in a tomb for three days, he rose again to life!"

My grandmother and I stood over the lifeless Iris, and talked of the summer days now gone, when we had enjoyed its beautiful purple flower, and smelt its lovely fragrance with the butterflies and bees, it was now a memory, and its life seemed gone. It seemed sad to say goodbye to something so beautiful.

But my grandmother would always cheer my heart by saying, "it isn't goodbye, King, it is, see you again in the Spring!"

She explained how sad Jesus' disciples felt and all those who loved him, when he died on the cross. "They did not understand that he was dying for them, so that they might have life in believing in him, and that he would rise again on the third day, death being unable to hold him. Don't be sad about the Iris, King," she would say, "God has built life inside its bulb, so though it seems dead to us now, it will burst forth into new life again in the spring! You have that same life in you, King, if you are willing to trust Jesus in what he has done for you."

Over the last few years, since my precious flower Gay disappeared from my life, I have often thought of the lesson my grandmother taught me from the old purple Iris.

I am like that Iris that bloomed and danced in spring, and when my Gay left, my petals fell off and I lost my scent of life. But just as the Iris bulb lay dormant in the ground, I was not dead. A season of my life has come and gone, and now I am to bloom again. I feel the joy of life reborn within me, as winter has gone and spring has come again. Thank you, God, for helping me to understand. Today is Easter Sunday, and I am alive again, hurray, hurray, hurray!

The girls arrived in the dining room now, and we all sat down for breakfast. Music played in the background and the food was good as always.

The boat to Dartmouth leaves right from the Torquay seafront, and we all walked down the hill to the quay.

"You would not think it was Sunday," I said, as shopkeepers brought out their newspaper and magazine stands, and sale signs from the clothing shops appeared out onto the street.

"Some of the shops keep the sabbath," Helen said, as we walked past Warren's Pastry shop that was closed.

"I can do without a Cornish Pasty for one day," I said, "and appreciate having my pasty even more on the other days."

As we queued up to board the boat, the sea looked calm over the English Riviera, and we sat on some seats outside the cabin which had a better view. The captain and his first mate were both tour guides, and they pointed out the various beaches and landmarks along the way, one which included the birthplace of Agatha Christie, and another the Singer family estate, where the inventors of the Singer sewing machine had lived. We passed lovely beaches and coves, and rocks that were bird sanctuary islands of interesting shapes and sizes coming out of the sea. We called in at the historic town of Brixham, with its bright coloured houses overlooking the sea, and its fishing and crabbing boats moored along the harbor front. My big surprise for Melody was the Pirate Ship moored in the harbour with people dressed as real pirates! We went for a quick tour of the famed vessel, with its skull and cross bones flag proudly flapping in the wind. On board Melody bought a pirate hat and sword and threatened to use it if we did not take her for an ice cream. I, however, was looking forward to my favorite crab sandwiches and a pint of Old Speckled Hen beer when we arrived at Dartmouth. "Stop talking about food, Dad," Melody said, "you are making us all hungry."

When we pulled into Dartmouth, I pointed out the Britannia Royal Naval College up on the hill, which was where Prince Philip attended and met the future Queen Elizabeth II.

There is so much to say about Dartmouth, but that would require a chapter of its own. So, I shall move on with my story, and save the town of Dartmouth, and the Paignton Steam Railway for another day.

I did have my crab sandwiches however, and a pint of Speckled Hen, and the girls loved Dartmouth so much that they did not want to leave. And we rode the Steam Train to Paignton and caught the bus back to Torquay. We were happily exhausted and rested the rest of the night.

The next morning, after our favorite breakfast with our favorite hosts we and grabbed our bags, and travelled home by train to Swansea, where Dad picked us up from the station. What a wonderful holiday, we all exclaimed! And we vowed to come back again soon and do some more exploring.

Chapter Fourteen

Find Me a White Scarf

Ffion and I had been seeing each other for over a year now, and I wondered what I was waiting for? I had grown to love her deeply, and I knew that she loved me. Samantha and Melody also thought the world of her, and she loved those girls like they were her own. "When are you going to marry Ffion?" Helen asked me. She had become good friends with Ffion, who had told Helen of her longing to be my wife. 'I will ask her to come to West Wales with us on a getaway,' I thought. 'It has been a while since we had had a family weekend away. And I would ask her to marry me then.'

One evening when Ffion had come over for tea, and we were all siting in the living room, I decided to ask everyone if they would like to go away for a weekend.

"How about we go to West Wales for a couple days and stay at the Salutation Inn?" I asked.

"Oh, yes please, yes please!" Ffion and Melody shouted in excitement.

"Can we stay in the same room as we did last time?" Melody asked.

"I will book the same room if it is available," I replied, "and maybe Samantha can come with us too if she's not busy with her boyfriend."

What better place to ask Ffion to marry me than at the Salutation Inn, I thought? I felt it was going to be our special place from the very first time we visited there. And for me, that first visit was the time I realized that I had fallen in love with Ffion.

On Friday morning, I phoned to make the arrangements, and we could leave right after Melody finished school.

After walking Melody to the bus in the morning, I phoned Innes at the Inn, and our room was available. I booked it for tonight and Saturday night, and we would enjoy a full day exploring on the Sunday before coming home in the evening. Samantha, unfortunately, had already made plans for the weekend, but she didn't seem too disappointed that she wouldn't be able to come.

"Boyfriends will do that," Ffion said with a smile. "I know because I have one of my own," she joked. 'Little do you know, lovely lady,' I whispered to myself, 'that this weekend I am going to ask you to marry me.'

After booking our rooms, I drove into Swansea to buy Ffion a ring. We still had the rings we had given to each other in the Cardiff market, which were like promise rings. But this weekend was going to be even more special. I would ask her to marry me on Saturday, and then enjoy a romantic night, after Melody had gone to sleep.

Once I arrived in Swansea, I went into the Swansea Market and visited my friend David Tucker at his jewelry sales and repair booth, and he had the perfect ring for Ffion!

It was a beautiful pear-shaped ruby, on yellow gold, and with a classic Celtic design on the band. The ring came in a lovely blue velvet box, and I could not wait to give it to Ffion on Saturday and ask her to marry me.

David knew of Gay's disappearance, and he wished Ffion and I all the best.

Just before I left the market, a strong impression seemed to stir in my heart and mind, and I pictured Melody's face as Ffion, and I were exchanging our rings. Melody's face looked sad. She was our ring bearer, and I could see that she wanted a ring of her own to celebrate with us! So, before I reached the market doors, I turned around and went back to David's booth.

"Do you have any rings for a teenage girl?" I asked. "Melody is turning fifteen in a few months, and she is going to be the ring bearer at our wedding."

"I have three rings that would be suitable for Melody," he said, and he put them on the counter for me to look at. One was a beautiful pearl mounted on a classic gold band, and another was a small sapphire in the design of a flower. It would have been perfect if it had been a ruby to match Ffions ring. The third ring was a small cluster of diamonds mounted on a very thin band. Too ordinary for my Melody, I thought, and I asked Dave if he had anything else.

"I don't think so…," he said, kneeling and looking in one of his storage drawers.

He pulled out two more little velvet boxes, the same blue colour that held Ffions ring. I opened the first one and it was a ruby! It was in the design of a flower and stem, mounted slightly curved on top of a yellow gold band.

"This is a modern style ring," Dave said, "but it has an older classic design."

"I like it," I said, "and it would match Ffion's Ruby engagement ring."

"I will give it to you for my cost," he said. "I have had it for a long time. It must have been waiting for you, Kings."

"Indeed, it was, Dave, and thank you very much."

It felt complete now, and I looked forward to giving Melody her ring on Saturday too.

When I arrived home from Swansea, Helen and Ffion were already at the house. Helen was staying at the house over the weekend as she was visiting her friend June in the village. She had also packed our suitcases and had tea all ready for when Melody got home.

"We will leave right after tea," I said, "and we will eat as soon as the Zulu from Eglwyswrw comes home."

Helen laughed at my words, and she said, "I haven't heard you call her that for a long time, Kings."

"You look lovely," I said to Ffion, who was wearing a classy looking blue and white dress with white heels.

At my words, Ffion looked into my eyes, and a blush grew upon her face. It was as if she could feel what was going on in my heart, and I could not wait to hold her in my arms and ask her to marry me. I want to thrill her heart and see the joy glowing on her lovely face.

I had told Melody that I would meet her at the bus stop, so I walked across the road and waited outside Pennard Stores for the bus to arrive.

"Hello, you Zulu from Eglwyswrw. Grandma has already made tea for us, so I'll race you across the road."

"Dad, you look so excited!" And she had read my heart as usual.

"You're right, sweetheart, I am excited. I have you and Ffion and Samantha in my life, and we live in our wonderful house in Pennard. And we are going to the Salutation Inn as soon as we have finished our tea!"

"Is Samantha coming ?"

"No, she has made plans with her boyfriend."

"You mean Glynn, Dad?"

"Yes, Glynn. See what happens when you have a boyfriend, Melody? You miss out on going to the Salutation Inn."

"Not true, Dad. You and Mum told me that love makes the world go round! And Glynn makes Sam's world go round."

"He does, does he? Well, I don't want your world to go round too quickly Melody."

"Oh Dad, I'm fourteen! And I want my world to spin!"

"Okay, come on then. I will race you across the road!"

Melody grabbed my hand, and we ran across the road to our house. As she was grabbing my hand, I knew something had shifted in her heart. The heaviness that had cloaked her countenance so often since her mother's disappearance, had gone, and my happy girl was back. And as I studied her more closely, I could see that she had grown from a girl to a young lady. Maybe a big part of her sadness had been connected to mine. I was excited about life again! The past had rung the doorbell and then gone away! For I was no longer there to answer the door to sadness, but rather I was walking into the future that was bright and cheerful and my whole family could feel it.

We sat and finished our tea, and Helen left to visit her friend in the village.

"As soon as you have changed your clothes, we can leave," I said to Melody, "and we can leave the dishes until we get back. Maybe they will do themselves." Melody and Ffion laughed, and on our way out I left a note for Samantha, who was madly in love with her boyfriend Glynn again and would not be home till later tonight.

Melody sat in the back seat with her suitcase, and Ffion, dressed to the nines, sat next to me. Her lovely scent filled the car and made promises of a wonderful night to come.

It was a cool evening as we drove through the village, but there was no rain in sight, and the forecast was fair for the whole weekend. One must take the weather forecast, shall we say, not too seriously, when you live in South Wales. It can sunshine and hail and blow a gale, all in one lift of the sail. But Ffion had packed some warm winter clothes, and rain or shine we would all be fine. For me and these girls of mine, let it shine, let it shine, shine, shine.

We arrived at the Inn in good time, and Innes, remembering us from our last visit, was thrilled to see us again. She took our breakfast orders and gave us the key to our room. 'See you all between 8 a.m. and 10 and have a good night.'

"We will Innes, and thanks for saving our special room."

"Glad that you like them and see you in the morning."

Melody went right to her room and put the movie channel on, which gave Ffion and I the evening to ourselves, which was just what we needed.

Our room had a nice electric fireplace, and we sat at our table for two in front of the window. In the spring and summer months, one can look out over the garden and the river that flows past the bottom of the property line. There are picnic benches where you can eat or sit and watch the sunset. This time of year, it was dark, of course, but we opened the windows to hear the river as it sang its November song.

Ffion had brought some beeswax candles and she put one in the middle of our small table and opened a bottle of wine. 'Ruby Red' it was called. And I thought to myself: What an appropriate name! – as I would be giving her a ruby red ring tomorrow. We talked and sipped our wine, and we both agreed that it had been far too long since we had spent a weekend away. Our eyes danced and played games over our glasses of wine, and I felt so close to Ffion as our conversation excited my heart.

"I have missed you, Kings," she whispered, pushing a wet kiss upon my cheek.

"I have missed you too," I echoed, "like the sweet summer rain."

Ffion excused herself to the bathroom and I went to check on Melody. She was fast asleep already, and I kissed her gently and turned off the TV.

Ffion had run the bath and she asked me to undress her.

With my heart beating fast and my body trembling with excitement as she fixed her exquisite blue eyes on mine, I took off her earrings, and I removed the sticks holding her hair, which was high in a bun with a few of her auburn curls rippling down her face -my favorite style. I pulled my fingers through her curls until her full head of hair fell, almost covering her face. As I took off her sweater and undid the buttons on her shirt, her sparkling eyes watched me with desire from behind the veil of her curls, and her red lipstick spoke boldly in the flickering light of the candle.

After taking off her bra, I took another sip of wine and then held it up to Ffion's mouth so she could take a sip. Kneeling in front of her waist, I undid the button of her skirt, and she stepped out of it, exposing her tiny panties. Her legs quivered and she quietly moaned as I lowered her panties down to her painted toes.

Ffion turned off the taps of our bath and poured in some oil, which scented the whole bathroom with its fragrance. "It smells like wild strawberries," I said, as she slowly undressed me, and kissed me from my neck to my toes, and my manhood stood to attention like the captain of the guard, and we stepped into the piping hot bath.

Ffion laid back against my chest as I gently caressed her nipples with my fingers. "Oh, Kings," she moaned. I kissed the side of her cheek as she turned her head to meet my tongue, and we wrestled and darted in and out of each other's mouths with love and lusting tongues. Ffion stood up and pulled me to my feet, and we dried each other's bodies just enough, so we didn't leave a trail of water from the bathroom to the bed. And we rolled and crashed and banged, and it wasn't an earthquake, just two people raptured in love.

After we had stopped the world, we sat in our glow in front of the window and finished our wine. And we talked and laughed and kissed and giggled and fell into sleep's embrace.

Melody knocked on the door and it was 8:30 a.m., and we all got dressed to be in the dining room for 9:00. "Good morning," Innes said, "your table is ready." And she led us to the far table in front of the window. It was the same table that we had the last time we were here. And we could see the fast-flowing river, who's song we had fallen asleep to. The willow tree danced in the strong breeze, and the rolling clouds mirrored their reflections upon the fields as they held hands with the wind and raced off to start their November day. And Ffion, Melody and I shouted, 'Hurray, hurray, we will catch you up later in the day.' And we saw a cat that wasn't a stray – "he lives here," Innes said, "and his name is Smokie, and he's the same colour as an Eglwyswrw Day."

After one of Innes's wonderful breakfasts, we joined the clouds and headed off to start our day.

We drove to Aberystwyth and walked along the promenade. The tide was out and there were people flying kites on the beach. We counted six different types of kites, and Melody wanted to fly one. On my last visit to Aberystwyth, I had found a hobby shop not far from the pier, and I had seen a kite in the window.

"Let's go and see if we can find the hobby shop," I said to Melody, who became instantly excited at my words. The three of us held hands and walked back along the promenade to the pier.

"I don't see the hobby shop," Ffion said, as we looked at the different storefronts.

"It's just up one of the side roads across from the pier, if I remember right?" We walked up the road in line with the pier and found the store.

"Look, Dad," Melody shouted, "there is a kite in the window."

"By Jove, it looks like the same one I saw in the window last year," I replied.

"It's probably the display model," Ffion said, as we opened the door and went inside.

"Good morning," said a large smiling man, what can I help you with today?"

"The kite in the window, can we have a look at it?"

"That is my best-selling kite – it's called a box kite, and you need a moderate to strong wind to fly that one."

"Yes," I replied, "we have just come from the seafront, and there is quite a strong wind off the sea."

"Lovely," the man said, "then a box kite will do you very well."

"Can we have the one in the window?" Melody asked. "I like the colours of that one."

"I can't get you that one," the man said, "because it's my display model and I would have to move a lot of stuff that's in the way, but I will see if I have another red and white one in the back."

And the man disappeared for some time. As we waited, I looked around at the model railway trucks and locomotives that were displayed in a glass case in front of the till.

"Gosh, I love trains," I said to Ffion, who had been trying to get my attention to show me another kite on the far wall. "Sorry, love, I was miles away playing trains."

Melody laughed, and then said: "Do you want a train set for Christmas, Dad?"

"Oh, yes please!"

The man now returned with a large oblong box. "This is the box kite model," he said. "It is the last one and I don't know what colour it is? I will just open the box and find out…."

"You are in luck – it's red and white!" "Yes!" Melody shouted. "Can we buy it, Dad?"

I looked across at Ffion, who was smiling. "Yes, sweetheart, and you can help me set it up."

"We timed that right!" Ffion said as we left the store. "We got the last one!" When we got back to the seafront, the wind was blowing stronger, and we needed to find somewhere sheltered where we could set up the kite.

"It's too windy to set it up on the beach," Ffion said. "The instructions will blow away!"

"Maybe we will blow away!" Melody said laughing.

"Then who would fly our kite?" I teased.

"We would be kites, if we blew away, and then we wouldn't need to fly one," said Melody.

"Very funny, girl! Now come on, let's find somewhere where we can organize the kite."

About halfway back along the promenade was a lookout booth with wooden benches. "Let's set it up in there!" Melody called out, racing ahead of us and carrying the box.

"I love these family times," Ffion said, taking my hand and snatching a kiss from me while Melody was not looking.

"You naughty lady," I said, "just you wait till I get you back to our room."

"Oh, I can't wait, Kings!" and she kissed me again.

"Come on, you two," Melody shouted, having reached the booth, and now she was opening the box.

"Lie the sticks and the material out on the bench," I said, "and give Ffion the instructions."

It seemed strange to me now for Melody to be calling Ffion by her first name, and I looked forward to her calling her 'Mum' after Ffion and I got married. It just emphasizes how I feel about Ffion, I thought to myself. I want her to be my wife and for Melody to have a mother again.

"Come on, Dad!" Melody shouted, waking me up from my daydream. Fortunately, my dad had taught me how to build box kites and I didn't need the instructions, so I soon had the kite set up to fly. The only difference between this kite and the ones that Dad made was where you used to have to glue the wooden frame, this one had plastic clips that held the wood into the box shape, and the material was already custom cut with ties to attach to the clips. Within fifteen minutes, we were all ready to join the string to the front swivel of the kite and head down to the sand. "You have done this before," Ffion remarked, looking rather impressed.

We climbed down the stone steps onto the beach and the wind blew strong and cool.

"Have you ever flown a kite before, Melody?"

"No, Dad, I haven't."

"You have not flown a kite before? That is a crime!" Melody giggled and brought me the kite. "Now you hold the handle of the string, and let the string out as you feel the kite pulling up into the air. You move the string holder back and forth like this…" And I demonstrated how to move one's wrists back and forth so that the kite pulled the string off easily. "The most important thing to remember, Melody, is to hold onto the string quite firmly, and do not let it go – otherwise, the wind will take the kite way out to sea."

"Can you see which way the wind is blowing?" I asked Melody. "See how everyone else is standing? They are standing with their backs to the wind, and their kites are lifting in front of them. The more string you let out, the higher the kite goes into the air."

"What's my job?" Ffion asked, not wanting to be left out

of the fun. "You can attach the string to the front of the kite," I said. "You attach it to the swivel, which twists around and around with the angle of the kite, so it doesn't tangle." Ffion attached the string, and we were ready to fly.

"Let some string out as I showed you, Melody," and I walked down the beach with the wind blowing behind me. Turning around and holding the back of the kite, I shouted, "Okay, Melody! I am going to lift the kite into the air now and let it go, so you hold the string tightly, because it's going to pull quite hard as I let it go."

I let the kite go, and off it went!

"Wow, Dad! I can feel it pulling!"

"That's it, move your hand from side to side and let the wind take it, but don't let go of the string!"

Higher and higher it went, until it was as high as the other kites, and our kite danced back and forth with its colours flying proudly.

"Dad, look at that, wow! Look how high it is!"

"Well done Melody," Ffion shouted. Ffion and Melody took turns flying the kite, and as I watched them, memories of my kite-flying days flew across the wild and windy pages of my mind. I remembered a birthday when my mother took me for a drive in the car right in the middle of my birthday party! Why had she taken me away in the middle of my party? I thought. We had only driven a short distance when she turned the car around and headed back to our house. She must have forgotten something, I thought.

Then as we arrived back at the house, my mum said, "Look, Kings, look in the sky!" And there was a box kite high in the air with a big tail attached to it, and it read "Happy

Birthday Kings!" As I followed the string from the kite back down to the ground, I saw my father standing behind the birch tree in our front garden. "That is why he wasn't at the party, Mum, he is flying the kite!" Another memory I had, was when my dad and I spent a whole day building a kite. It was a box kite like the one we were flying today, but it had no clips or pre-cut material. We made the whole thing from scratch in my dad's workshop. We glued the balsawood, and cut the design from a cloth, and we even painted the material with our names on it and drew an eagle on the side with wings so that it looked like a real bird. This kite was my pride and joy, and Dad took me over to Pennard Castle to fly it over the Three Cliff Valley below.

There was a strong wind that day and the gusts were even stronger. As I was letting the string out slowly and watching the kite look like a real eagle, a strong gust of wind pulled the string out of my hand, and I watched our beautiful kite climb higher and higher until it was almost out of sight, and it disappeared over the woods and fields miles away. And as I wept, my dad said, "Don't worry, old son, we can build another one."

"Not like that one," I said, still sobbing. And I was right, we never did build another one quite like that one!

"Dad, Dad!" Melody shouted, having let go of the string!

Out of my daydream I did run, charging across the sand and trying to catch the string handle that was dragging along the beach faster than I could run. "Run, Dad, run!" I heard Ffion and Melody shouting! And I ran past people and dogs, and finally the string handle got caught on a piece of wood that was sticking out of the sand! Just in time before it went into the cold sea! "Have you got it, have you got it?" Melody shouted.

"Yes!" I shouted back proudly, still puffing from my

sprint. "That was fortunate – we almost lost it!" I exclaimed out loud to myself. "Had the wind pulled the kite just a little further, it would have gone out to sea."

Well, that was enough exercise for one morning, and we went to a pub for lunch. While we were eating, Ffion noticed a poster on the wall. The local theatre was advertising a play, and it was "Romeo and Juliet."

"It's playing at the theatre just up the road, and there is a performance at 2:00 p.m. tomorrow," Ffion said. "Shall we go?"

We all agreed that it would be fun to go, and Melody was particularly excited because she had never been to a pantomime before, only her Christmas and Easter plays at school, which she always took part in.

As we were finishing our meal, I thought about all the kites we had seen flying on the beach, and how we almost lost ours out over the sea – and suddenly I had a wonderful idea!

'Why don't I ask Ffion to marry me via a kite!' I thought. 'I can buy the materials in the town, and make a tail for the kite, and write "Will you marry me?" on it. And I imagined Ffion's face as she saw my proposal in the sky.

Yes, what a great idea!

And I will ask Melody to help me… She needs to be a part of this, and she will love it! She loves the idea of fun surprises. I don't want to ask Ffion to marry me and then tell Melody after the fact – she would not be happy about that, I thought. Especially after what had happened with her mother.

Gay took off without saying a word to her and lived a mystery behind our backs for God knows how long…? And that secret has bred a certain amount of insecurity and suspicion of people in Melody's heart.

As Ffion and Melody finished their dessert, I wondered how I could put my plan into action?

I know. I will ask the girls if they want to go window shopping after we leave the pub. We can walk around the shops and get some ideas for Christmas, and maybe buy a few gifts.

The girls liked my idea and we headed off to the shops, and while Ffion was looking in a shoe shop, I told Melody that I had something to show her in a shop across the road. This was perfect! Whenever you get Ffion into a shoe shop, you have bought yourself at least half an hour to forty-five minutes to go and do something else before she has finished. There was a price to be paid for all those sexy shoes, and today I was benefiting from it.

"Come on, Melody," I said, "let's go! I have something to show you across the road."

"Bye Ffion, we are just across the road, and we will meet you back here."

Ffion gave me a smile and carried on with her shoe inspecting.

"What is it, Dad?" Melody asked, as she took my arm, and we crossed the road. "What is it, Dad? Tell me."

"There is something I want to ask you, Sweetheart, something I need your help with…"

"Okay, Dad," she said excitedly, "what is it?"

For a moment I hesitated "Come on, Dad, out with it! That's what you say to me when I have something on my heart that I need to tell you about."

"Okay, here goes!"

"What would you think if I ask Ffion to marry me?"

"Really, Dad, really? Wow! I mean that would be great! I know that she loves you, and for sure she'll say yes!"

"She will? Are you sure?"

"Yes, Dad, I wasn't born yesterday, you know."

"No, you were born the day before."

Melody slapped my arm and laughed.

"How do you know she will say yes?" I asked.

"Oh come on, Dad! I have seen you too together when you think I'm not looking. Holding hands and kissing. And the way you look at each other in public, it's disgusting!" she said, laughing. "Anyone can see that you love each other. So, let's face it, Dad, you're busted!"

"Oh no!" I said with a smile, "and I thought I was doing such a good job of hiding it!"

"No, no, Dad. I am almost fifteen, you know. I know things."

"You do, do you? You have grown up almost overnight, my girl. Okay, Melody, I am busted! And I am relieved that's over!"

"Wait, Dad there's more!"

"No, no, I can't take it. Don't tell me anymore! Are you a spy or something? Who are you working for?"

"I am the spy who loves you, Dad. And I have heard you guys talking and making noises in your room."

"No, no more please. Have mercy!"

"Sorry, Dad, I told you, you're busted!"

"And how do you feel about me marrying Ffion so soon after your mother, ah, ah, um…"

"Go ahead, it's alright to say it, Dad … after mum left us."

"Yes, sweetheart, that is what I was trying to say. It's just that my heart still hurts."

"I know, Dad, it's okay. Everything is going to be alright, and I love you, Dad."

"Thank you, sweetheart, you are such an amazing young lady!"

"I feel good about it, Dad. I would like Ffion to become my Mum. She is really beautiful, and everyone we meet thinks you two are together and make a lovely couple!"

"They do, don't they. Thank you, sweetheart, and yes, Ffion is beautiful, and I do love her very much."

"I love her too, Dad."

"Now there is something I need your help with… What do you think about me putting a message on the kite – saying, 'Will you marry me Ffion?' We can go into a store and buy a white scarf or a piece of fabric, and write the message on it, and then attach it to the kite like a tail, and then go and fly the kite down on the beach where Ffion will see it."

"That is an awesome idea, Dad! She would never guess that you would do something like that!"

"Great! I'm so happy you like the idea, and we can do it together!"

"Are we going to do it today, Dad?"

"Yes! Because it might be raining tomorrow, or there might not be enough wind to fly the kite."

"That's great, Dad! Today is perfect!"

"Okay, Melody, you go back to the shoe store and keep Ffion occupied. Get her to try some more shoes on, or you try some on yourself, and I will go and find a white scarf and get some red paint from the hobby shop so we can write on it.

"Okay, Dad, this is so exciting! Wait Dad! Wait! What about a ring? You have to give her a ring and kneel on the beach, and then point up to the kite. I will fly the kite, Dad, and I won't let go of it this time!"

"I love your idea about kneeling on the sand, Melody, that will be so romantic. And guess what!"

"What, Dad?"

"I bought a ring already, and I have it back at the Inn. I will go and get the ring, and it won't take too long. After you and Mum, I mean soon-to-be Mum, leave the shoe shop, can you tell Ffion that I asked if you girls could pick up a picnic, because we are going back to the beach. I will meet you on the beach in about an hour."

"Okay, Dad, I will do it. Meet you at the beach."

As Melody raced back to the shoe shop, I felt thrilled that she was so supportive and even excited about having Ffion as a mother. And she was excited to be part of my proposal too. And I prayed and thanked God for having Melody in my life. Now help me find a white scarf and some red paint.

I went first to a charity shop, which was just down the road, and they had a few scarves but not the right colour. And the only other material they had was an old orange curtain. That was no good, so I started looking in the windows of the clothing stores, but no one seemed to have one. I will never make it back to the beach in an hour, I thought. And then I found one! There was a white scarf on a mannequin in the window of a men's store.

"You can't have that one, sir, it is our display model."

"Please sir," I said to the man, "I'm going to ask a woman to marry me down on the beach in an hour, and I need a white scarf."

"Sorry, sir, but you cannot have this one."

'Who is this idiot?' I thought. 'I am popping the question down on the beach in an hour and I need that scarf!'

Just then another man walked up and joined the conversation. He must have been the manager because he told the man off.

"Did you not hear what the customer said!" he exclaimed. "He is getting married in an hour, and he needs the white scarf in the window! Now go and get it for the man!"

"Thank you, Sir," I said. "I really need it."

"So, you are going to pop the question, are you Sir, down on the beach...?"

"Yes, Sir, I am."

"Well, congratulations! It's good to see romance is still alive these days!" It was a silk scarf and quite expensive, but it was also soft and luxurious, and how often does one get married? A few times, I guess, in my case.

"Thank you, Sir, and good day to you, Sir."

"Good luck in your marriage, Sir, that is if she says yes!" And we both laughed.

As I walked over to the hobby shop, I held out the scarf and looked again at its length. It's long enough and wide enough for the words to fit on, I said to myself, and not too heavy for the kite.

I arrived at the hobby shop just in time, as he was about to close. "Do you have any red model paint?" I asked, "And I better take a brush too." "Red model paint, Sir, and a brush."

"Yes please."

"Here we are, Sir, some red paint and a brush. Doing some modeling, are you Sir?"

"Yes," I replied, not having any time for a conversation.

I checked my watch and I only had 15 minutes to get back to the Salutation Inn and get the ring. I was going to be late getting back to the beach, but I was sure they would wait until I arrived.

When I arrived back at the Inn, I took a quick look at the ring. The ruby sparkled in the afternoon light coming in from the window. And I felt so glad that I had bought a ring for Melody too. She so deserves it, I thought, and I want her to feel special. Melody's ring sparkled in its blue box as I held it up to the window. What a special day it was going to be for the three of us!

I picked up the rings in their little velvet boxes and carefully zipped them into my jacket. Then I drove back to the beach. Thank heavens there was a parking spot on the promenade – I was 20 minutes late.

I looked down across the beach and I could see them in the distance. I recognized Melody's yellow coat, and Ffion's long auburn hair. I quickly climbed down the steps onto the beach and ran excitedly towards them.

"Where have you been?" Ffion asked. "We saved you some lunch."

"Good! I am hungry, my lovely lady."

Melody looked at me with her famous mischievous expression and said, "Hi Dad." I quickly wolfed down my picnic, and then I said to Ffion, "I need you to go for a walk, lovely lady, while I talk to Melody for a few minutes. Why don't you walk along the beach towards the pier, and we will catch you up in a little while?"

Ffion smiled, her eyes giving me a searching look, and then she started walking.

"Quick, Dad," Melody whispered. "Did you get the scarf and the paint?"

"Yes," I said with a smile, "let's just wait until she is a bit further up the beach."

I pulled out the scarf from underneath my jacket, and the paint and brush from my pockets.

"The scarf is perfect, Dad!" Melody exclaimed, "and the red paint will really show up well on the white."

"Can you paint the words?" I asked, "And I will attach the scarf to the kite." Melody was thrilled that I had asked her to do the lettering on the scarf, and she got right to work. The paint dried almost instantly as it sank into the silk and the wind helped it to dry.

"That looks great," I said. "I just need to figure out how I am going to attach the scarf to the kite – I forgot to get a safety pin or something to hold it on with."

"How about this?" Melody said, taking off the broach that was on her velvet shirt.

"That is your best broach – we better not lose it," I said, "but it will be perfect to connect the scarf to the fabric on the kite."

I pierced two holes using the pin of the broach in one end of the scarf, while Melody continued to paint on the letters. I then pushed the pin of the broach through the material of the kite. It was a tight fit, and it took a bit of persuasion to lock the pin back on the broach, but it worked! The scarf was now tightly attached to the kite.

With a box kite, there is no difference in the shape of the kite from one end to the other, so it is a good design to put a message tail on, as it does not dart erratically back and forth like the acrobatic kites do, but rather moves in a slow deliberate movement.

Ffion looked back at us a few times as she walked along the beach, but she was too far away to see what we were doing.

"I'm finished!" Melody announced excitedly, and I praised her for her excellent work. The letters were well sized, and big enough to read without them being crammed too close together.

"How did the broach work, Dad?" Melody asked.

"I think it will hold," I replied. "And how is the paint – is it dry yet?"

"It's a bit sticky but it's not runny."

"Okay, great! Let's get the kite in the air before Ffion turns around` and starts walking back. Do you remember how we did it this morning? You hold the string and stand with your back to the wind, and I will stand in front of you and lift the kite into the wind, so it does not touch the sand."

"Yes, Dad, I remember."

"Good. Now don't forget to hold the string handle firmly. And twist your hand back and forth as the wind pulls the string off the holder – until the kite has reached its altitude. Okay, Melody, let's go!"

The kite climbed quickly into the wind, and the tail flowed beautifully. "Look, Dad, I can read it easily. Can you see it?"

"Yes, well done, Melody! It's perfect! You keep the kite at that same height and don't let out any more string. And I will go and get Ffion

"Try and stop her looking up, Dad, until you get back."

"I will," I shouted, already having started to walk away.

Then I ran and caught up with Ffion.

"What are you two up to?" she asked, giving me an inquisitive look.

"Oh nothing, you will have to wait and see – it's a surprise. Now hold your hands over your eyes, and no peeking!"

"Okay, but you will have to put your arm around my waist as we walk. Otherwise, I won't be able to walk in a straight line."

I put my arm around her waist, and we walked back towards Melody.

"Can I open my eyes yet?" Ffion asked.

"No, not until we get back to where Melody is on the beach."

"What are you guys up to?" she repeated, "I know you guys are up to something."

"You will see soon enough." I said. "Now keep your hands over your eyes and no peeking, or you will spoil the surprise!" As we walked towards Melody, the kite flew proudly in the sky, and the writing was plain for all to see. Several people on the beach stopped and pointed to the kite, and I felt inside my pocket to make sure the rings were still there.

Finally, we arrived back to where Melody was standing, and I could feel my heart pounding inside my chest.

"Okay, you can open your eyes now!"

Ffion looked at Melody, who was smiling, and then she looked back at me with a look of wonder. "What is it?" she pondered. Then she looked up and saw the kite, and she read my proposal out loud: "Marry me Ffion." And I almost melted as she looked at me with those big blue eyes, as tears of love and joy rolled down her face. And I knelt upon the sand and said: "Will you marry me, Ffion? I love you so much, and I want you to be my wife."

"Oh, yes! Yes, Kingsley! It is what my heart wants more than anything! Of course, I will marry you!"

And I stood up and held her in my arms and kissed her.

Then Melody called out, "I love you too, and I want you to be my mother!" The few people on the beach clapped as they heard the response.

Both Ffion and I beckoned Melody to join us, and the three of us hugged and kissed and hugged some more, and Melody let go of the kite.

We watched as it climbed higher and higher into the air, and then it sailed out across the bay, slowly disappearing into the distance.

"What does that mean?" I asked, even though I knew.

"It means forever!" Melody proclaimed. "Kingsley and Ffion, forever after!"

"Now I have something for you both," I said. "Let's go and sit on the rocks at the top of the beach." And the girls each took one of my hands and we ran up the beach to the rocks.

"Congratulations!" exclaimed Sylvia and Charlee the seagulls, as they flew and dipped their wings over our heads.

And I said, "Why, thank you! You two are the first to know."

When we reached the rocks, I told Ffion and Melody to sit down. And I told them both to hold out one of their hands. "You must keep your eyes closed until I tell you to open them," I instructed. And I put a little ring box in each of their hands. "Okay, you can open your eyes now!"

"I got one too!" Melody called out loud.

Ffion gently rolled the box around in her hands with her eyes fixed on mine. And then she opened the box.

"It's a ruby!" she said with a smile. "I have always wanted a ruby, Kings! And to get one for my engagement ring – oh, it's beautiful!"

Ffion stood up and kissed me, and more tears of love and joy rolled down her face, and I placed the ring on her finger.

"It fits perfectly, darling! I love it!" And she kissed me again.

"Now it's your turn," both Ffion and I said to Melody, who had been patiently waiting and watching Ffion open her present.

"I love the blue velvet box, Dad."

"Go on, Princess, open it."

"Oh Dad! It's beautiful! Is it a ruby too?"

"Yes," I said, and I slid the ring onto her finger. "Only the best for my girls!"

"Thanks, Dad! And it fits perfectly, just like Mum's." And she jumped up into my arms with a big hug.

"Two beautiful girls!" I exclaimed. "I am so blessed!"

"Let's celebrate with an ice cream on the pier!" said Ffion.

"A great idea!" I said. "I'm going to have a Nicker-Bocker-Glory!»

Melody roared with laughter, thinking I was talking about "knickers."

"No," I said, 'not knickers-Nicker'! It's the name of a real ice cream!"

"It's true!" Ffion said, backing me up. "I have had one myself."

"Well, I am having a ninety-nine," said Melody. "That's a vanilla ice cream with two chocolate flakes sticking out of the top."

"What are you having?" I asked Ffion.

"Mmm, now let me see. I think I will have a ninety-nine too, as I can't have a Knickers-Bocker-Glory!"

Melody and I roared with laughter, and when we had all got our ice creams, we sat on the pier and looked out across Cardigan Bay.

On our way back to the Inn, we decided to buy some food and eat in our special rooms to celebrate. That way, Melody could watch a show after tea, and Ffion and I could celebrate our engagement with a romantic evening. And we made nachos for tea, along with cooked prawns and dipping sauce. And of course, a bottle of French champagne.

After tea, Melody raced off to spend time in her room and watch a movie, while Ffion and I sat at our little table in front of the window. Most of the leaves had fallen from the trees now as the November winds carried summer's leaves over hill and stream, and we watched the yellow leaves of a silver birch dance and swirl around a tree, and they told their summer stories to Ffion and me as we drank a glass of our champagne.

"Oh Ffion, my darling, I can't get close enough to you," I whispered without a word.

"Come, come and dance with my soul," she replied as her blue eyes beckoned me to come inside. And I opened the door and we danced. "I am so happy," she whispered, with happy tears in her eyes, and I gently kissed her. I poured us another glass of champagne and we moved to the comfortable couch. I ran my fingers through her long soft hair and cupped her face in my hands. And our hearts uttered what words could not say.

Ffion rubbed the hair on my arm and caressed my fingers, telling me oh such wonderful things – that made my heart sing.

There was such a peacefulness and maturity in Ffions love, and she was able to embrace all of me. Our deep and meaningful conversations, that were both intellectual and fun loving, were a doorway to intimacy for us, along with our touch and words of affirmation – we spoke the same language.

This evening, we enjoyed a wonderful conversation about the Preseli Hills, and the peoples that once lived there, and where the artifacts and the remains of their cultures had been found. Ffion has such a keen interest in the history of Wales, and its peoples and customs.

And we agreed to go and explore the Preseli Hills one day soon and see what we could find.

After we had finished our champaign, Ffion asked if I fancied a bath.

"Does that include you in it, lovely lady?" I asked with a smile, and she blushed as she stood up to go and run our bath.

"There is a bottle of blackberry wine on the counter," she called from the bathroom. "Could you please open it, Kings, and then give me about ten minutes…?" I poured myself a glass and sat again at our little table in front of the window. Another thing I like about Ffion, I thought, is that she is so rarely hurried or stressed. Her gentleness and humility, speaks loudly amongst a restless boisterous crowd, and she is also robed in kindness.

I had surely found a priceless treasure, and she had agreed to become my wife, and a mother to Melody! What a wonderful day! And I rejoiced as I tasted the rich texture of the wine.

"Almost ready," Ffion called out, and can you please bring in the wine…"

I carried the wine and glasses and tapped the bathroom door with my foot, opening it slightly.

"Enter, my darling," she called, and she was already soaking in the bubbles. She had lit four candles, one in each corner of the room, and there on the little glass table beside the bath was a card with my name on it.

"Shall I open it now?" I asked.

"Come and lie in the bath with me, and open it later," she said.

I handed her a glass filled with wine. And I climbed into the tub.

Tonight, I lay back upon Ffion, whose soft breasts were like cushions, and we held hands amongst the bubbles, and she kissed my cheeks softly.

"It's been a wonderful day," she exclaimed. "Let's toast to our engagement!" And we held our glasses high and tapped them together. "To a wonderful happy marriage and a long life together! Cheers! And thank you God for this wonderful blessing of one another!" And I turned to meet her kiss.

It was so magic to just hold hands and caress each other, and to listen to the bubbles and the beating of Ffion's heart, that, like mine, beat faster as we talked about such precious things. We talked about our wedding, and where we wanted to have it. And when she asked me what I wanted for my wedding gift, I told her I already had it. "You are all I want, my lovely lady." And tears filled her eyes.

"And what do you want for a wedding gift?" I asked.

"I want you to make love to me out in the wild, in your cave and on the beaches, and up in the sand dunes amongst the long grasses as we listen to the roaring surf and wait for the kiss of the sunset that promises that our tomorrows will be spent in one another's arms."

As she spoke, I could feel her heart beating faster, and I began to get excited too. "I cannot wait to take you to all my sacred places and make love to you, my Ffion. I want to swim with you in the rock pools, and kiss you in the sea, and make the mermaids jealous!"

"Let us go to bed," she whispered in my ear, "and play in each other's souls."

I climbed out of the bath first and held a towel out for Ffion. She stepped onto the mat, and I dried her from her toes to the top of her neck, as she made sounds of pleasure.

"I love it when you dry my body, Kings. You dry between each of my toes, and I love how you are both gentle and deliberate, touching and exploring my sacred places. You take me to where I have only dreamed of going before. Oh, Kingsley, come on, my darling, let's go to bed..."

By the time we reached the bed, I was intoxicated by Ffion's love and dripping with excitement. And we walked and squawked through our Garden of Eden and dreamed as far away as the Galapagos Islands.

Chapter Fifteen

Romeo and Juliet

Sunday the sabbath arrived, and we were woken by a knock on our door. Melody was already dressed and excited to go and watch the play in Aberystwyth.

"Why don't you go and see Innes," I suggested, "and see if we can have our table in front of the window, and Ffion and I will start getting ready."

"Alright," Melody said cheerfully, see you and mum there, I mean Ffion," and she headed off to the dining room.

"It's so nice to be called Mum," Ffion said with a smile. "This is what I always wanted – a loving family of my own. Thank you, my love for giving this to me."

"It is God's gift to us," I replied.

Ffion and I were soon dressed, and we made our way to the dining room. When we arrived, Melody was sitting at our favorite table in front of the window.

"Good morning," Innes said as we passed by. "As you can see, Melody has already reserved your table. I will be over in a few minutes with the menus."

"Thank you, Innes," I said, and Melody called us over to sit down.

"Well done, Melody, you got us our favorite table."

Innes and her cooks made us a wonderful breakfast of eggs on English muffins, smothered with Innes's secret cheese sauce, along with bacon, smoked sausage, fried tomatoes and beans, and then a fruit salad, and homemade scones with Devonshire cream and raspberry jam.

"I wish I had another stomach, Dad," Melody said, as she and I kept our eyes on Ffion's scone. Ffion and I had champaign and orange juice, while Melody had Innes's homemade garden smoothie.

"Thank you, Innes," we all said, having eaten far too much.

"I am happy you enjoyed it," she said, "and have you enjoyed your stay?"

"Very much," Melody replied, speaking for all of us.

"It's time to return to our room and pack our clothes," Ffion said, "and make our way to Aberystwyth. Then we can arrive at the theatre early and get some of the better seats close to the front of the stage."

We soon had our suitcases in the car, and we were on our way.

Aberystwyth can be a busy town on weekends, even well into the autumn months. We drove along the seafront trying to find parking, as the sideroads in the town were all full. Finally, we parked in the town car park – at least now we wouldn't get a ticket.

When we reached the theatre, we were over an hour early for the play, but the lady at the ticket booth allowed us to buy our tickets and go inside.

"We are the first ones here!" Melody said in a quiet voice as she looked around the large, darkened room, and we sat about four rows back from center stage. "There is a great old smell of wood and curtains," Ffion remarked, "and the old seats look like they were made of oak."

"Look at that lovely old velvet curtain," I said to Melody. "It almost reaches the roof of the theatre and it comes all the way down to the stage."

"I can hear voices," Melody whispered. "Can you hear them, Dad?"

"Yes, I can. They are the voices of the cast, practicing their lines behind the curtain."

Suddenly, some brighter lights came on, and slowly the seats began to fill up around us, and we began to get more excited.

"What is Romeo and Juliet about?" Melody asked.

"What!" I replied rather loudly. "You don't know what Romeo and Juliet is about?"

"Well, I know it was written by William Shakespeare. My teacher taught me that."

"I won't tell you too much about it, Melody – otherwise it will spoil the play. I will tell you that it's about two people whose love was very powerful."

"Like yours and Ffion's."

"Yes, that's right," I said, and Ffion looked over at us with a pink blush growing on her face.

The theatre was almost full now, and it seemed to be taking a long time for the curtain to rise. Finally, the lights dimmed, and the curtain lifted, and everyone began to clap.

"Welcome to Romeo and Juliet!" a man exclaimed as he stood on the stage, and then he disappeared behind the curtain.

For the next hour and a half, Melody's eyes were glued to the stage, and she seldom turned her head to speak to Ffion and me. That is, until it came to the part when Juliet woke up to find Romeo dead, and she did not want to live without him, so she stabbed herself. Melody looked across at me with tears in her eyes, and then back at the cast.

At the same time, Ffion whispered in my ear, and then looked at me with her big blue eyes, and said, "I love you so much, Kingsley, that I wouldn't want to live without you either."

And as I looked into her eyes, I could feel her love for me in my heart, and I knew her words were true. And the way we looked at each other was more powerful than the play; and I felt the cast would stop at any moment. But thankfully they didn't, and our love remained a secret. Even Melody did not see our souls dance as she remained enthralled in the play.

After the play, we walked back down to the carpark, and it began to rain quite heavily.

"We timed that right," Ffion said as we got into the car. With the rain coming in from the sea and the light beginning to fade, we decided to slowly make our way home to Pennard.

"That was a wonderful play!" Melody exclaimed. "Thank you, Mum and Dad."

Melody turned to Ffion. "Can I call you Mum even before the wedding?" she asked.

"Yes, you may," Ffion replied with a big smile, "and when we get home, I want you and Samantha to help me with planning my wedding."

"Really, Mum?"

"Yes, of course!" And listening to their conversation made me excited too.

On our way home, the rain became torrential, so we decided to stop for tea until the worst of the weather had passed. And we still made it home in good time, even with the weather. "Well, that was a wonderful weekend!" I said to the girls, and they both agreed with happy smiles.

When we arrived at the house, Samantha was home with her boyfriend Glynn, and they had made a nice fire, so we all sat and talked until it was time for bed. And I went to bed even more excited because Samantha was so happy about Ffion's and my engagement.

 ⁓

Over the next few weeks, all the girls were busy planning the wedding. Samantha, Melody and Helen, would all be Bridesmaids. Ffion asked Dad if he would give her away, as her own father had passed away a few years ago. Ffion's mother, Beryl, helped Ffion choose her bridesmaid colours, and Samantha and Melody helped her choose the style of the dresses. Ffion would wear a traditional white wedding dress, and I could not wait to see her in it and walking barefoot along the beach. When I had first started dating Ffion, I could not have imagined her agreeing to be married on a beach, but once I shared with her the significance of what my cave and Pobbles beach meant to me, she eagerly agreed to do so. Mary, and my brother Fraser's wife Lynn, had offered to decorate our house and plan the reception there, as we did not want to waste money on renting a hall. Our home was certainly big enough, and Ffion and I thought it extra special to have our reception at my Grandma and Grandpa's old house.

"In a way, they will be there with us," she said, "celebrating our special day."

"They will," I replied. "I often feel them with me in and around this house."

Dad and Fraser, along with my sons Jonathan and Benjamin, would all be a combination of my Best Men and Groomsmen. I just had to ask my friend and colleague David Griffiths if he would marry us down on the beach.

David and his wife Jackie were good sports, and David agreed to marry us outside our Family Cave. I think he had visions of wild horse adventures again, as he had experienced at Gay's and my wedding. We would have to wait and see. Our family cave is a very sacred and mysterious place, but I did not anticipate any horse guests this time.

It was decided that we would get married in the early Spring, towards the end of March, when the skylarks begin their beautiful spring songs, and the cuckoo bird makes his journey from afar, to return to the Gower Peninsula and announce the new season with his special call: cuckoo – cuckoo – cuckoo. Maybe we will invite him to the wedding. The skylarks will come anyway; they don't need an invitation.

And I phoned my boys Jonathan and Benjamin, who were excited to come. They would not come for Christmas now, but only for the wedding, as they could not take too much time away from their studies. They were both happy for Ffion and me, especially as they had been worried about me since Gay's disappearance. And as they were now coming out in the Spring, they could stay longer, about six weeks. March the 29th would be our special day – somewhere between the roar of the high tide and April showers. No matter what the day, rain or shine, along with the bluebells and the wild dune flowers it would be a wonderful day!

As the winds of November blew, the last of Autumn's leaves did their farewell dance, and the trees were bare again. It had now been almost four years since Gay had left us. Anniversaries and birthdays came and went. And memories of that first painful Christmas, and an Easter that seemed to have no resurrection, faded away. Sadness blew its cold winds over us only occasionally. And this year, as Christmas approached us, and birthdays and Gay's and my wedding anniversary came and went, sadness joined sorrow and went to live far away.

A POEM FOR FFION

My sorrow has turned to gladness,
as my down cast soul has learned
the dance of Joy again,
and a flower has burst forth in my garden,
and her name is Ffion.
Her love gently fell on my dry parched land,
bringing a chorus of sweet summer rain.

The memories that we have made together,
and the promises of our future are
mixed in your raindrops like
the sweet water caught
in the petals of the fragrant rose,
and I sit underneath the breeze blown lilac and
taste your love.
The season of singing has come,
and the cooing of a dove is heard in my valley,
and her song is just for me.
Like the crocus and the daffodil from
my sleeping bed,
I rise at the sound of your voice.
You call to my heart and say, wake up my darling,
wake up,
Spring is here again!
Hold me, and kiss me, and thrill my heart again.
The long dreary winter has gone.
Hurray-hurray, for Kingsley and Ffion, hurray!

©Kingsley Ross Hill

The lights of Christmas began to shine along the village streets, and Christmas trees in windows flashed and sparkled with the promises of the season. For me, the promises were connected to the Bethlehem Babe, the birth of the Lord Jesus Christ. And a wonderful promise in God's word that spoke to me about God's plans.

"For I know the plans I have for you, declares the Lord. Plans to prosper you and not to harm you; plans to give you a future and a hope." – *Jeremiah 29 vs 11*

And that is how I felt this Christmas. Yes, I had lost my Gay, twice! But my God still had a great plan for my life. He was giving me Ffion for my wife and making us a family again. And I felt so thankful.

Such Peace and Joy had returned to my heart. And Ffion was such a big part of it already. She was not just a Maggie May, who filled my time, as Rod Stewart once sang about. Ffion was here to stay as my wife and companion, and she was going to be such a wonderful mother and a blessing to all our lives.

~

December was going by so quickly, and it was soon Christmas Eve. Samantha and Melody had joined a carol singing group and were singing carols around the village. Ffion and Helen and I, waited excitedly for them to come to our door, and they did.

They sang O *Come All Ye Faithful*, *We Three Kings*, and one of my favorites – *Do You Hear What I Hear?* As I listened to my daughters singing, my faith, which seemed to have weakened since Gay's disappearance, became renewed again, and I wept with joy as hope and peace filled my heart.

~

On Christmas Day, Dad and Mary along with Fraser and Lynn, came over for Christmas Dinner, and we sat and reminisced around a crackling fire in our living room. And it was as if all our Christmases were mingled together tonight, with our memories and stories that traveled around our cozy room like a warm blanket. And it only seemed like yesterday, which was now yesteryear, when Fraser and I sat around the fireplace with our beloved Grandma and Grandpa and Mum and Dad, who always made our Christmas so special. And tonight, was special again!

Helen and Mary, along with the girls, created a wonderful turkey dinner with Ffion's special stuffing, the recipe having been handed down to her from her great-grandmother. There were roast potatoes, yams, and Mary's amazing gravy. There were steamed carrots, peas, and Brussel sprouts. And round the table there was silence. Wonderful gob-smacking silence, which said 'Oh, this food is so good!' So, we talked with smiles and sparkling eyes, and I ate until I hurt.

Ffion wore a beautiful blue dress with my favorite white stockings that clung to her shapely legs, and her blue heels matched her dress and her beautiful eyes that danced with mine in the candlelight. The girls giggled, and I wriggled, while we waited for Mary to bring in the trifle. Fruit in jelly, and Bird's custard, and real whipped Devonshire cream, with sprinkled chocolate and cinnamon.

After the trifle, came my grandmother's famous steamed pudding, with melted caramel toffee, and I screamed some more! 'Later, later!' Ffion's eyes said, and you can scream some more and more!

Fraser and I ate so much that we could hardly move from the table to the settee in front of the fire. And we all sat and played games and sang songs, and Dad played the organ. And Peace and Joy filled our home, and we celebrated until the clock struck 12:00. Then Dad and Mary, and Fraser and Lynn, left for their homes in Swansea. 'What a wonderful Christmas,' we all agreed.

As I climbed into bed, I felt something down by my feet. "What is it? I wonder," I said to Ffion – who would only give me a smile. It was a square box covered in brown paper and tied with a string bow. "Open it," she whispered, still wearing her smile.

I pulled loose the bow and undid the brown paper and found a wooden box with a lid. I gazed at Ffion's face, which was now a pink blush. "I wonder what it is..." I said again. "Open the lid, my love," she said, "and you will see."

So, I did, and it was a beautiful gold ring, with three small rubies – "one for each year we have been together," Ffion said, blushing. "And all the years of our future together," I echoed back, and I kissed her.

Before we went to sleep, we talked to my boys in Canada, and they thanked us for the gifts we had sent them. And they reminded us of how excited they were to be coming out for our wedding in the spring.

Over the holidays, we were all able to enjoy some wonderful family time together, and we were soon into the new year. Time seemed to be going by so quickly, and it would not be long before our wedding in March. As the days and weeks continued to go by, Ffion and I talked a lot about our family, and the home we would share together here in Pennard. And we made exciting plans for the future. One of them included Ffion selling her house in Swansea and paying off the mortgage on our home in Pennard. We could both retire at a young age, although I wanted to continue to do my work in youth outreach, at least part time. As for Ffion, she was looking forward to being a mum and a housewife.

"Loving all of you is what I want to do," she said. "it is what brings me the most joy in my life."

As I watched Ffion with the girls, she was wonderful, a natural as far as being a mother is concerned. I believe that being a wife and mother is one of the most under underestimated and underappreciated ministries there is! Wives and mothers are wonderful, and vital in the health and wellbeing of the family. I know, because I have had to be both mum and dad for my children. Our God created abilities and roles for men and women which are uniquely different and need to be appreciated and celebrated for what they are. Children need both their mother and father whenever possible, and as in my upbringing, Grandparents who can step in and help whenever a family is at a deficit, lacking a mother or father's love and protection. Well done mums and dads, and grandparents, you are so irreplaceable!

⌒

It was a mild winter on the Gower Peninsula, and throughout West Glamorganshire. We had our usual winds and rain, and the mists coming in from the sea, but no heavy snow fell, and there were not many days when the temperature dropped below zero. Then in late February, spring began to sing its song.

The wedding plans were all made, and we waited for our special day to arrive.

On the weekend before the wedding, Ffion and I drove up to London to pick up my boys from Gatwick. Ffion said that she felt a bit nervous, and I reassured her that both Jonathan and Benjamin would love and accept her. "Don't be nervous, my lovely lady," I said. "They will think the world of you!"

And they did.

"I did not realize how beautiful you are," Jonathan proclaimed. "You look even lovelier than in your photos."

I smiled as I heard my son talk. He is a true romantic like me. Benjamin echoed his brother's words, and Ffion blushed like a rose.

"I told you," I said, and Ffion smiled happily.

We drove as far as the other side of the Severn bridge, and then stopped in Newport for a stretch of our legs and something to eat. Ffion had packed sandwiches, and we sat at a picnic bench. As the boys talked and got acquainted with Ffion, I looked forward to showing them around the Gower again. The Gower Peninsula is such a unique and wonderful place. It always has something new to discover, and even the sacred places that you do know, give you the wonder and excitement as if you are discovering them for the first time. Tis the Gower boy! She has many secrets! Yes Sir, I know! There is no place like her, boy! Yes Sir, I know! Well done boy, you are a Gower Boy through and through! Thank you, Sir!

"There are many adventures ahead of us," I said, as we got back into the car and drove the remainder of the way to Swansea. Apart from saying how strange it was driving on the left side of the road, the boys sat quietly in the back seat and tried to get some rest. It is always a long haul flying in from Canada and being cooped up with so little leg room.

"Like sardines in a can," Jonathan said, and we all agreed that comfort was not on the priority list when the planes were designed. "It's better than taking a ship that would take weeks to get here," Benjamin said.

"You're right there, Son," I replied. "Flying unfortunately is the only way to get here. But you guys are safely here now, and that is what matters."

"That is right," Ffion said, "And I'm so glad that you're here."

Finally, we arrived in Abertawe, which is the Welsh name for Swansea, and then it was only a short drive out to our home in Pennard. As we arrived at the house and the boys unpacked their suitcases, I felt such a great joy and sense of satisfaction in having my whole family safe under my roof, and I thanked God for providing and caring for us in such a wonderful way.

∾

It was soon the day before the wedding, and the boys wanted to do something special for me. "An old man's stag," they called it.

"Old man?! I'm only in my fifties, I'll have you know!"

"Where can we go?" Jonathan asked.

"I want to go to one of the pubs that you told us stories about, when you were a boy," said Benjamin. "In that case, let's go to the Plough and Harrow," I suggested. "I have been going there since I was 14."

"Fourteen!" Ben echoed. "You have to be 19 in Canada, before you can go into a pub and have a drink. How did you get into the pub when you were fourteen?"

In Wales, you can legally drink at 16. I always looked a bit older than I was, because I was able to grow a mustache at fourteen, and the owner of the pub knew the two older boys who I used to go with. We played pool and darts every Friday night. And if the police ever came in to check if anyone was underage, we had an escape plan…"

"An escape plan, Dad?"

"Yes, an escape plan."

"Okay, Dad, let's hear it."

"At the back of the pub, around the corner from the bar, was a back door that opened onto a farmer's field. And whenever the police came, Mr. Bailey behind the bar would point behind his head, which was our queue to run and disappear out the back door. The only problem was that in this field was a ferocious bull that would chase us with his horns across the field.

And one night, a few of my underage friends came with me to the Plough and Harrow, and the police came in right in the middle of a game of pool. Mr. Bailey immediately pointed his finger over his shoulder for us to get out, and the four of us playing pool rushed to the back door and into the field. The bull was not best pleased to see the four of us sprinting across his field, and he gave chase. And those horns were big! He was grunting and snorting behind us, and my friend Martin fell down right in front of him. Fortunately, the bull kept chasing the other three of us, so Martin was able to get up and escape. As we turned around to see if the bull was gaining on us, we could see that Martin had fallen head-first into a cow patty, and his face was covered in shit! The three of us were laughing so hard that we were peeing our pants. The bull was gaining on us, and we only had about **20** yards before we reached the barbed wire fence at the end of the field.

I can remember running like heck and hearing the bull's thundering hooves behind me, and my friend Vincent, shouted

"Split up!" So, my two friends branched out into a different direction, and I kept going straight. Unfortunately for me, the bull followed right behind me.

I could hear my friends laughing, and I turned around only to see the bull right behind me. The fence was coming up quickly, and I braced myself, ready to jump and climb over the barbed wire. My friends were shouting 'Run, run, run, he's right behind you.'

And he was! I could feel his breath on my neck, and all of a sudden, he lifted me up with his horns and threw me over the fence into someone's garden.

My friends were killing themselves laughing, and meanwhile I had two holes in my new jeans and a sore arse."

Jonathan and Benjamin howled with laughter, and they said together, "Let's go to the Plough and Harrow tonight!" So that's what we did.

I pushed on the old heavy door, and we were inside. Going back to the Plough and Harrow was like going back in time, and nothing had changed. Old men sat at the oak tables, some of whom had grown older while I had been away. And I pointed out to my boys that the man sitting at the little table in the back of the pub was old John Wheel. John had been old when I was a teenager, and there he was wearing his old green Mackintosh and Wellington boots. Old John never learned to drive and never got married, and he walked everywhere. Sometimes on a Friday or Saturday night, I would be riding my motorcycle along the narrow lanes heading for home, and I would see this tall head and shoulders above the hedgerow. Many times, I was startled, thinking it was a ghost; but it always turned out to be Old John. He lived with his three brothers and his mother on a farm.

"How old is he now, Dad?" my son Jonathan asked.

"He must be well into his nineties," I answered.

"He's ninety- nine," the man behind the bar said, having heard our conversation. "And what can I get you boy's?" "Three pints of scrumpy cider," I said, and the man laughed. My boys were taking me out to the pub for an 'Old Man Stag,' they called it. Little did they know that after one pint of scrumpy, they would barely be able to stand up, it was so strong! I would be driving them home, that was certain, and I laughed to myself as the barmaid brought us over our drinks.

"This tastes great!" Both the boys exclaimed as they drank it down quite quickly. And we were soon all laughing and telling stories.

"Another pint?" the barmaid asked.

"Yes," I replied laughing, "but just bring us a half pint each."

When it came time to use the toilet, the three of us staggered across the wooden floor like sailors on a heaving ship. We managed to relieve ourselves without falling over and we made it back to our table.

"Can we go out into the bull field?" Benjamin asked. "I want us to be chased by the bull, just like you were when you were a teenager."

"You must take a bull very seriously," I replied. "He can crush you with his hooves or stab you with his horns if he catches you! Anyway, I don't know if there are still bulls in the back field."

"Let's go and check," Jonathan said. I paid for our drinks, and we all walked towards the back door of the pub. To my surprise, it opened, and we could see that there were cows in the field. Suddenly, Jonathan let go of the door, which he was holding open with one hand. It slammed shut, and we were locked out of the pub and standing in the field. And instantly I had a feeling that this narrative wasn't going to end well.

"Oh no!" I shouted. There was no way back into the pub without climbing over a barbed wire fence at the bottom of the field. I tried to keep calm as the boys said, "What are we going to do, Dad?"

"We will have to cross the field and climb over the fence on the far side," I replied calmly. But inside I wondered how the heck we were going to get out of this mess, and if there was a bull in the field, we would be in real doo-doo.

As we looked around, we did not see a bull, but lots of inquisitive cows started to follow us.

"Shit, dad, we're done for!"

"No, we are not, they are cows, not bulls. They may follow us, but they won't charge."

"Let's walk fast and straight," I said, "and keep going until we reach the far fence. As we walked, my eyes scanned the herd for a bull, but thank gosh these creatures all had udders.

"Dash it! I stepped in cow shit!" Ben protested, and I tried not to laugh.

"Me too!" Jonathan shouted in disgust. "Look at my new running shoes!"

I could not hold back any longer and I roared with laughter. Not for long, however, as I tripped over a hump and fell, unfortunately putting my hand in a heap of cow poo as I fell.

"Shit!" I shouted. And the boys roared with laughter.

Finally, we made it to the far fence, and it was as I thought – still barbed wire. This was going to be a quiet riot!

Or a loud one if we get caught on the barbs! To get back to the pub, we had to climb over a five-foot barbed wire fence, into someone's garden, and then get back on the road. We were all in deep manure, as my old headmaster Mr. Emlyn Evens used to say!

Now climbing a five-foot barbed wire fence is no easy feat. Add the challenge of having drunk one and a half pints of scrumpy cider, which has an alcohol content between 12 and 17 percent proof, and the fact that you are climbing into a stranger's backyard, the unexpected can happen. Or should I say from my past experiences in climbing over barbed wire fences, that the expected will happen. And as I stood with my sons facing this angry looking fence, I felt all my fifty some years of age saying to me, "I don't think this is going to work out too well." But I carried on nonetheless, it was my stag, after all. And I was supposed to get in some sort of pickle, was I not?

"Anyway, let's go for it!" I said to the boys, who were still looking around for a bull.

Ben was first to climb, and with his football playing physique, he managed to navigate between catching his jeans on the barbs and the swinging movements of the fence, which reacted mercilessly to his movements. "I'm over!" he shouted proudly.

"Quiet!" I whispered loudly, "or the owners of the house will hear us in their back garden."

Suddenly there was a cantankerous cow right behind us! Up until now, the cows had stayed a distance away.

"Get away!" I said, having picked up a stick from the field, and I waved it in front of her nose. Ben laughed from the safety of the other side of the fence.

Jonathan was next up, and he too had the strength of an athlete but the build of a rugby player. So, his extra muscle weight might be a factor, I thought quietly. And I wondered how on earth I was going to make it over? The cantankerous cow had plucked up her courage again, only this time she had brought two of her friends with her to stand right behind us. They blew through their noses and mooed loudly. Again, I waved my arms, but they stood fast and wouldn't move. "Come on Jonathan, I said, you better get a move on!"

With one more look at those intimidating barbs, and a look over his shoulder at me and the cows behind, he jumped up and grabbed the wire. The fence writhed back and forth as he climbed, and he shouted, "My jeans are caught!"

And they were! He could not move forward or back, and I tried to reach the barbs where he was caught, and loosen his jeans, but he was caught fast, and I was at full stretch. The aggressive cow now pushed against my back, and I was afraid she would step on my foot.

"Off with you, you mad cow!" I shouted. Ben was now peeing himself with laughter, and I expected someone to come out of the house at any moment.

"Keep your balance," I called up to Jonathan, "and try and free the barbs one at a time," which he did. Finally, he reached the top of the fence and leaped to the ground.

Suddenly a light flicked on in the house. "Quick, get down and be quiet!" I said, and I began to rehearse what I was going to say if someone came out: "Sorry Sir, we got chased by a bull--...Sorry Ma'am, but we got locked out of the pub, so I thought we would do a break-and-entry into your garden."

"Come on, Dad!" the boys shouted, "Someone is coming!"

This was not funny anymore! And I took a jump up onto the fence, my hand missing one of the barbs by an inch. And just when I thought I had made a good start, I felt my trouser leg get caught by a barb.

"Come on, come on!" the boys shouted.

"Alright! Alright! I have got my leg stuck." Slowly I twisted and turned my leg to try and get free, but once I got free of one barb, I was caught on another.

Finally, I pulled free, tearing my nice trousers that Ffion had recently bought me. At least they aren't my dress pants, I said under my breath, as I climbed to the top of the swaying fence.

"Jump, Dad, jump!"

And I jumped into the garden.

"Come on," I said, "let's get out of here."

We bolted like rabbits around the side of the house and into the front garden, only to meet the owner of the house, who had come out to see what all the noise was about.

"Hey! What's your game!" He shouted angrily. "What are you doing on my property?"

The boys and I sprinted past him, and we did not look back until we were halfway down the street.

"I called the police!" the man shouted.

"Quickly," I said, "let's get back to the pub and get the car"

We reached the car, jumped in, and headed for home. Then as we caught our breath, we all began to laugh.

"That was a rush, Dad! That was great!" Jonathan said. "We got to live out one of your adventures with you. Just like one of the stories you told us."

"What did you think, Ben?" I asked, seeing that he was still looking nervous.

"I thought that man was going to run after us, Dad, and I didn't want to get caught. And do you think he called the police?"

"Maybe," I replied. "We were running around his garden. But we didn't do anything wrong."

"That's right," Jonathan said. "We were just running away from the cows in case one of them was a bull. Right, Dad?"

"Yes, that's right, and that's no bull!" Ben laughed, and we arrived home having had a wonderful adventure.

As we opened the front door, we could see that Ffion and the girls were sitting in the living room.

"Let's quickly go and change and throw our clothes in the washing machine. We smell like cow shit."

The boys and I laughed our way down the hall, and we threw our clothes into the machine.

"What are you boys laughing about?" Ffion and Samantha called out.

"Oh, nothing," we shouted back. "We got a bit wet."

"Then how come it's not raining?" Melody called out. She knew better and could smell a rat.

After putting on some clean clothes, we joined the girls in the living room.

"Did you boys have fun?" Melody asked.

"Yes, we had a great time," Jonathan and Ben answered. "Dad took us to the Plough and Harrow, the pub he used to go to when he was a teenager."

Ffion gave me a knowing smile, and we sat and had hot chocolate in front of the fire.

Chapter Sixteen

An Unexpected Guest

The day of the wedding arrived, and the gentle winds of memory stirred, as I thought of Gay's and my wedding that was not so long ago. Time had helped to heal my broken heart, and I had a new love now. My beautiful Ffion, with her eyes of blue and a love so true. My daughters were here too, and my sons! What more could I want? I was so blessed. And I thanked God for his goodness to me and his many blessings upon my life.

Pastor David and his wife Jackie arrived at the house, and Ffion and the girls would travel to the beach with him, including Helen and Ffion's mother Beryl. The boys and I would go with Dad, and Jackie, Mary and Pearl, who had come down from Bristol, would stay at the house and prepare for the reception.

It was a cool but sunny day, as Dad parked the car at the Southgate car park, and we walked along West Cliff towards Pobbles Beach. Dad walked and talked with the boys, and I walked closely behind them, and I could hear their conversation. Dad and Mary would be taking the boys to Stonehenge, and metal detecting on the Salisbury Plain, while Ffion and I were away on our honeymoon. Samantha was going to spend time with Melody and take care of the house. The boys sounded so excited as they walked along in their smart looking suits.

The skylarks hovered and sang the sweetest songs above us in the March sky, as they were invited to the wedding too. The cool wind blew on an emerald sea that crashed below the clifftops. And the headlands of the Three Cliffs and the Great Tor, and Oxwich Point in the distance, all stood proud like best men at a wedding. And of course, they were.

When we arrived at the beach, David and the girls were already standing at the cave. Ffion's lovely gown danced in the sea breeze, and her bare feet with her painted toes stood out against the yellow sand of Pobbles Beach. A white flowered veil covered her lovely face, and I imagined the glow of her pink blush. Helen and Samantha held the train of her dress, and Melody held the rings on a turquoise pillow which was the same colour as the bridesmaid dresses that Pearl had so delicately designed. Dad, Fraser, and my boys stood to my left, and Ffion and her mum and the girls to my right.

The tide roared in the distance, making its way further in after contemplating the low tide. "Come on," I said, "you're invited," and at my words the waves seemed to heave more quickly up the beach.

David now called the wedding to order, and the seagulls squawked above. I looked across at Ffion, wanting to look into her exquisite blue eyes. But I would have to wait until I could lift her veil, and our hearts would put up our sails.

David began to conduct the ceremony, and he shared with us about the goodness of God. "God works all things together for the good for those who love him and are called to his purposes," David reminded us.

My life is a witness to that, I thought, as I listened to St. Paul's words. That promise in God's Word was one that I had taken great strength and encouragement from, during those first hard and painful months when Gay had first gone missing. And today, as David read those words from the Bible, my own heart testified that they were true! God had worked all things out for the good in my life, even though at the time of Gay's disappearance, I thought nothing good could come out of this heartbreaking mess. But I was wrong, and God was right! He did as only He can do, and that is make something good out of something that seemed so bad and hopeless. And as I looked at Ffion and my family standing around me today, my heart praised God again! My faith had been renewed! Thank you, God, for restoring my life.

As pastor David continued to conduct the ceremony, and as Ffion and I were saying our vows, David suddenly stopped talking in mid-sentence. A strong presence was around us.

"I can smell a horse," Ffion whispered nervously and began to look around.

I could smell it too, and I felt a powerful presence standing next to me on my right.

David looked at me with fear and confusion. What is going on? he asked me through his eyes. The guests began to talk among themselves as the wedding came to a halt. And Ffion looked at me as if to say, 'Do something!'

It was time for me to speak.

"Don't worry, everyone! The wedding will resume momentarily. My last Best Man has just arrived. You cannot see him, but there is nothing to fear. He is a horse, and he has come to my wedding."

David looked at me as if I was a madman.

But not my Samantha and Melody. "Look, Dad!" they shouted together. "There are hoofprints in the sand right next to you!"

And there were! And the smell of horse grew stronger.

"It's Great Thunder!" I proclaimed excitedly! Look at his footprints leading back to the sea!"

Samantha and Melody quickly followed the footprints down to the waves. "They are coming out of the sea!" they shouted back.

"I know it is Great Thunder," I said to Ffion. "He has come to celebrate our special day with us."

Ffion took my hand and spoke with her lovely eyes. "I'm glad he's come, my lovely man." And our wedding was now complete.

"Can everyone please take their places," David shouted.

And Samantha and Melody came running back up the beach and stood next to Ffion and me. Ffion and I continued to repeat our vows after David, and when he said, "Kingsley, you may now kiss your bride," there was a loud neighing, and then the hooves that had stood next to us began galloping down the sand to the sea.

People watched in amazement as an invisible horse splashed back into the sea.

"Thank you for coming, Thunder!" I shouted.

"Please come and visit again soon and thank you for coming to our wedding!" Ffion shouted. People did not know what to say or think, and even Dad and the boys looked nervous. But it didn't matter – I didn't care what anyone else thought. "It's my wedding, and I'll neigh if I want to. You would neigh too if it happened to you!"

When I came up for air, after kissing my bride, both Jonathan and Benjamin came over to Ffion and admired her lovely dress.

"You look beautiful!" we all exclaimed. And my eyes adored my gorgeous, classy wife.

"I love you, my darling," I whispered, and the love radiating from her face almost melted me.

"I love you, Kings, my lovely handsome man," she said, smiling.

It was time to head back to our house for the reception. And as we walked along the cliff path, Dad said to me, "Was your stallion an invited guest, or did he just crash the wedding?"

"Oh, invited, Dad, always invited, and my best man."

Mary, Pearl, and David's wife Jackie had done a beautiful job of decorating the house and getting the food prepared for the reception. And it was wonderful to celebrate our special day in Grandma and Grandpa's old house, now our sacred home.

For our honeymoon, I took Ffion to our special place, the Salutation Inn, in West Wales. Samantha and Melody took care of the house as planned, while Dad and Mary took the boys to Stonehenge and explored the Salisbury Plain. I would hear about their adventures when we got back, and we would find out if they found any artifacts metal detecting.

Meanwhile Ffion and I began our Honeymoon.

As we walked around Aberystwyth, I was so proud to have such a beautiful woman on my arm. Ffion is only two years my junior, and she looks like a model in early fifties. A healthy and mainly vegetarian diet, with lots of walking and yoga, was the secret to her youthful physique, she said. I would have to incorporate some of her lifestyle, with fewer trips to the bakery, I thought. Then again, I do love my Cornish pasties and Chelsea buns, and a nice cold beer on the weekends. And besides, I do a lot of rambling and hiking, and I swim almost every day. So why change a good thing? How's that for justification!

We spent three lovely days at the Inn, and Innes made sure our room had fresh flowers each day. And she brought a beautiful breakfast and champagne to our room each morning.

In the evenings, our favorite table overlooking the garden and river was always reserved until we arrived for our tea. Innes had only heard about our marriage when I phoned her to book our room, but she had gone out of her way to make our stay special. What service and class!

I had surprised Ffion by renting a caravan in Cardiganshire for the remainder of our time. It was at the same caravan site that my mother and father had taken my brother and I to each spring for many years as we were growing up. "And the caravan that we had owned was still at the site," I pointed out to Ffion, "only it was owned by someone else now." From what I understand, all the caravans are still privately owned, and some are rented out annually. Ffion and I had a nice modern one with a modern kitchen, a large bedroom, and a living room that looked out across the Preseli Hills. At the back of the caravan was a large area of woodland, and the chorus of the birds played sweet and loud as we sat and relaxed in our living room. We usually went out to a pub or restaurant for tea, as we explored the little towns and villages in the area. For breakfast and lunch, we either ate at the caravan or made a picnic for our day as we went out exploring. It soon felt like a home away from home, as we looked out onto the ancient hills or sat on our comfortable couch with a hot tea or a glass of wine enjoying our conversations.

As the night clouds came and drew the curtains of each day, we sat and told stories in front of the electric fire – that looked almost real. Then we entered our bedroom of dreams and enjoyed our romantic nights.

One evening, we were sitting in front of the window watching a sunset that God had painted behind the Preseli Hills, and I shared with Ffion how I had felt right after our wedding.

"I felt a 'oneness', I said, a 'completeness'. And when I hold your hand and look into your eyes, I feel that the part of me that was missing, has been returned, and now I am whole."

Ffion wept at my words and told me that she had been searching for me all her life, and that she too was now complete.

How beautiful, I thought, to give oneself to another, and to find that something within yourself that was missing, has now been returned.

"You search and search," Ffion added, "and you don't know exactly what you are searching for until you find it. All you know on your journey is that something is missing, and that you must find it, because that special something, makes you whole."

Then I talked about a priest friend of mine, who taught me many things when I was learning to be a pastor and counselor. And he helped me to understand the meaning of what he called "Adam's rib" in the Bible.

Genesis 2 vs 21:

So, the Lord God caused the man to fall into a deep sleep; and while he was sleeping, he took one of the man's ribs and closed up the place with flesh.

"God took one rib from Adam and made one woman for him from that rib," I continued. "For years, women have been offended when they were identified as having come from the rib of a man. But this is not what the Bible teaches. The woman is so much more! It was only the woman's body that was fashioned from the rib. Her spirit and soul were already complete before her body was ever made!"

Gay would not let herself believe that Eve was made out of a rib taken from Adam's body, and that this was a good thing. She did not understand the significance of the 'rib' in relation to the 'oneness' that God intended for a man and woman to experience with one another.

"It is not a negative thing, or a put down for women," I explained. "In fact, when things are understood in the right context, what God did in fashioning a woman from a man's rib, is an exaltation of womankind."

"Go on, Kings, please share some more," Fion said, as she listened intently.

"No matter how great a building looks from the outside, without the hidden beams or ribs holding it up, it would collapse onto the ground," I said. "And the same is true for a man. Why did God take a rib out of a man and then fashion a woman? Because he was not complete without her! A part of the man was missing! It was not that the man missed the physical rib that was taken out of him. He was not complete without Eve. He was incomplete without Eve's spirit and soul as his companion and partner. The world sees a man's tough exterior, and the prideful façade he often puts on like a garment of clothing," I continued. "But his wife is the hidden rib, or beam, who knows the little boy on the inside. She knows what he is really like, what his strengths and weaknesses are, and she is the hidden support of his life. Other than God himself, the woman is the most important thing in his life, or she should be. Without her, he is like a building without timbers to hold it up, and his life would collapse. I need you, Ffion. You are such a strength to me, and I can't imagine my life without you. I love you so much!"

"I love you too, my darling. Please continue sharing with me the things you have learned. I am learning so much."

"Thank you, Ffion. I will."

"It is very significant that God took Adam's rib to be fashioned into a woman," I said. "Without ribs, not only would the body collapse, but the heart would be vulnerable. The rib represents emotional support – the hidden, inward strength and encouragement without which a man would fall apart and not achieve his destiny.

I know this is true in my own life, Ffion, since I met you. Without your love and encouragement in helping me get through the last three years after losing Gay, I would have fallen apart and given up. You are the strong rib of my life!"

"And you are mine, my lovely man," she responded. I felt so encouraged by Ffion's response, and I continued to share with her.

"It is important to me, my love, that you understand that being my hidden support is a sacred trust. Your rib of strength covers and protects my heart."

More teaching from my friend the priest.

"The rib is positioned under a man's arm," I continued, "and it symbolizes the protection and provision a husband should give to his wife. God did not take a bone from Adam's foot, because Eve was not to be a slave, nor did he take a bone from his head, because she was not to rule over him. What I find so exciting here, is that God is beginning to reveal the unique roles of the man and the woman.

God took a rib from man's side, because the woman is to stand beside him as an equal. To love him, support him, work with him, counsel him, honour him as her protector and provider, and cherish him as her most intimate friend and lover."

"I hope I can live up to that, Kings…"

"You already are my darling, Ffion."

Ffion and I continued to talk and share until well into the night, and looking back, I felt that it was one of the most wonderful conversations in relation to our marriage relationship that we would ever have.

"Talking with you gives me intimacy," Ffion shared, and we drew closer and closer to one another, experiencing a 'oneness' that I believe was God's wedding gift to us.

We read the Bible verses, and studied them together, and learned so much more.

"When God brought Eve to Adam, it was a dramatic moment. Adam opened his eyes, saw this amazing creature standing before him, and immediately recognized her as part of himself! She was different from the animals of the garden.

Her bones were made of his bones; her spirit and her soul had been taken out of him."

In the morning we planned to hike up in the Preseli Hills and do some exploring, but tonight Ffion wanted to talk some more. So, we did. And we learned, in a deeper way, how "conversation" was one of our love languages.

There are many special events that happen in our lives, but some of them are so special that when they happen, we know that what we have experienced will always be a part of who we are, no matter how early or late in life that we experience them, we know they will always be part of what we choose to remember and celebrate through the years and seasons of our lives.

And tonight, Ffion and I experienced one of these special moments, as we understood scripture in relation to our marriage as husband and wife. And we made love with a knowledge and understanding that enriched our love and appreciation for one another – in a way that we had never experienced before, and it would be a part of our union for the rest of our lives.

As Ffion and I fell into each other's eyes, an almost violent, overpowering passion engulfed our beings, as we realized that we were right for one another, and that God had sovereignly and supernaturally brought us together. Suddenly we were in possession of one another, as one in spirit and soul, and consumed by thoughts of one another. I knew, loved, and had intimate knowledge of Ffion's spirit and soul, and she knew me in the same way. And we climaxed together, body and soul, moaning loudly in the celebration of our love. On this night, we became "one."

We made love all night and slept in until noon. And we woke to the cry of a jay bird outside our window.

"I hope he isn't a peeping tom," Ffion said jokingly.

"He is," I replied, "and he has told all his friends."

Ffion laughed again and kissed me, and it was time to rise and greet the day. We sure missed Innes bringing us our breakfast this morning, as we were not in the mood to cook breakfast.

"Let's eat out," I said. "We are still on our Honeymoon."

Yesterday had been our last full day at the caravan, and we packed the car, so we were ready to leave. It had been such a beautiful Honeymoon and we didn't want it to end. We still had most of the day, however, to do some exploring on the Preselies.

The caravan park is near a little village called Pentre Ifan, and Pentre Ifan has a little tea shop and eatery. We stopped and had breakfast there on our way to the hills. As we sat at the window, we could see the beautiful green hills in the distance, and we did not have to travel far to reach them. Once we had finished breakfast, we were on our way.

It only took us about ten minutes to get to the foothills of the Preseli's. We parked the car at the side of a narrow lane, and then walked up a rather steep sheep path into the hills. The sky was a deep blue, and the birds were in full song, no doubt excited about finding themselves a mate and making a nest in order to start their families.

"That is the case," a nearby magpie told me, as he bobbed from hedge to hedge carrying sticks to fortify his nest, the nest that he used from year to year with just a little touch-up. He was excited about all his plans for the spring.

And I was excited about mine. I had already found a mate, and we had a nest in Pennard Village, and we were bringing up our young.

"What a beautiful day!" Ffion echoed back to the birds and taking my hand as we traveled further up into the lonely heights. "It's so beautiful up here, and you can see for miles."

I smiled and nodded. The views were spectacular, and I breathed in the fresh spring air that danced over the hills to the sweet sound of the songbirds. All around us was a sea of rolling hills, and great empty stretches of heather, mountain grass, and bilberries, and occasional outcroppings of rock – which matched the grey clouds that waited on the distant peaks like actors about to make their entrance in a play. And it was our play, Ffion's and Kingsley's, and we welcome you to our special day!

We traveled about two miles from Pentre Ifan, and reached a Neolithic burial chamber, believed to be as old as 2000 BC! The burial chamber is on the Northern Edge of the Preselis, and it is one of the most spectacular cromlechs in all of Britain. And as spectacular as these ancient stones are, one feels pulled away from them by the view of the Irish Sea, which calls out even louder than the stones for one's undivided attention.

"Oh, it is so magic up here!" Ffion shouted out into the wind. And I held her in my arms as we surveyed our Garden of Eden like the very first man and woman that the Lord God had made. And that is what it feels like up here in these ancient hills. There is a barrenness that caresses the soul. It is not barren as in lonely, but its solitude and wide-open spaces awakens and delights the spirit.

As we continued to look out over the Irish Sea, white horses began to ride its emerald waves, telling stories of this wild highway that brought civilization to this place, with its knowledge of farming and thus the possibility of living a settled life – so different from those restless waves upon the wild sea, that shout and crash like Vikings against the rocks and never find land to rest upon. And today with my Ffion in my arms, I can build, and I can create a life in this land of the wild and the free.

Ffion and I turned our eyes away from the sea, and we stood in front of the Great Chamber. What a haunting site! A light mist shrouded the ancient stones, causing them to appear even more mysterious. Ffion was silent and stood in awe as she grasped my arm tightly. Was it a mist or was it low clouds that cloaked these rocks that seemed to have such a presence? "It feels like we are back in the past," Ffion whispered, as if scared that her voice would awaken the sleeping souls of the past.

The giant capstone looked to be about 18 to 20 feet tall and about 10 feet wide, and I wondered how the ancient people had managed to hoist it up and balance it upon the other rocks. It was indeed a mystery, not unlike how the ancients had somehow managed to transport the blue stones from these hills to Stonehenge over 200 miles away!

"Look! Look how perfectly positioned and balanced the capstone is on that one point!" Ffion pointed out excitedly.

The capstone rests on three high pillars, and as Ffion stated, one had pinpoint support. The fourth stone looks like a portal. And the cromlech stands towards the end of a long barrow, about 130 by 60 feet. I began to have the strongest desire to dig and see what I could find. I thought of Dad and my boys metal detecting on the Salisbury Plain. I wondered what artifacts they might have found by now.

I was sure that the ground here at Pentre Ifan Burial Chamber had been excavated many years ago, and that the experts had dug around in the stony ground for many hours looking for treasures.

"What I would not give to have my metal detector with me," I said. "You never know what someone might have missed, and it could be lying right under our feet! That is half the fun of archeology and digging around the ancient sites – you really have no idea what you might find."

"As long as you don't disturb some sacred remains, and bring a curse upon yourself," Ffion added, and her words were quite convincing.

"My dear woman, you have been reading too many books, or listening too much to my father!"

Ffion laughed. "You know what I mean," she said.

"Yes, I know what you mean," I echoed, "and I promise I won't allow anything to follow us home."

"Are you teasing me, caveman?"

"Maybe a little, cavewoman," I said with a smile.

But along with the laughter, I was haunted by the unpleasant thought that a phantom horse was having such an influence upon our lives. What could it all mean? And was that the spirit of my faithful friend, Great Thunder, who stood next to us on our wedding day? Or was it Nan's Nan who had come back to interfere in our lives again. I tried to reassure myself that it was Great Thunder who had come to our wedding, and not Nan's Nan. Thunder would never do me any harm – of that, I was sure!

Ffion, just like Gay, had as much interest in the pre-historic sites and the peoples of Wales as I did, and it enriched our relationship immensely. And today we made plans to explore more of the Preselis Hills another time.

We watched the sunset reflect its colours of yellow, purple and red upon the far hills. A mist was rising from the valley below now, as the evening air wrestled with the sun's last warmth, and it was time for us to go.

We held hands, and our hearts skipped with our feet as we rambled down the lonely hills that had become like friends.

The night clouds marched behind us, and a chill entered the air, and Ffion's hand felt warm and soft in mine, and I'd fallen in love all over again. We reached the car and kissed, and we were on our way home again, but after days like this, you are never the same. Your love is deeper and richer – goodbye, lonely hills, until we meet again.

⁓

We arrived home late, and the girls were already in bed. Jonathan and Benjamin were still away in Salisbury with Dad and Mary and would not be home until Friday night.

"I bet they are having a wonderful time exploring and metal detecting," I said to Ffion as we turned out the light.

Monday morning was busy as usual, with Samantha and Melody heading off to university and school. Ffion was going to do some gardening while I put in a full day's work at the church. I had not seen David since the wedding, and this morning was our weekly staff meeting.

David led the meeting as usual, and we discussed the

Sunday School, and a new teacher who was doing well in her teaching. I gave my report of the youth group and shared some of my plans for later in the spring and a camp I was organizing for the summer. David seemed happy with my work and my commitment to the youth, and he asked me to stay behind for a chat after the meeting. I thought he wanted to ask how Ffion and I had enjoyed our honeymoon, but that was not the reason.

David was upset about what had happened at the wedding. "I don't know what is going on in your family, Kingsley, but having that spirit being or horse, or whatever it was, come and interrupt your wedding is a serious concern to me! How long has this demonic entity been around, and what have you and Ffion been doing to attract such things?"

"Your guess is as good as mine, David," I said, feeling hurt by his words. "I don't understand what it is, other than feeling a presence of what I believe to be a horse, and then seeing it leave hoofprints as it made its way back to the sea."

"So, you have not been involved in any spiritualism, Kingsley? Because if you have, I cannot have you working here at the church. You know what we believe here – that contacting spirits is of the devil!"

"Now just a moment here, David, I do not appreciate the way you are talking to me in this accusing manner. I know what I believe, and what I teach to the youth here at the church, and it is good wholesome teaching from the Bible. Sometimes in life, things happen that we don't understand, and neither Ffion nor my family and I have ever been involved in anything cultic or satanic, if that is what you're asking. All I can tell you is what we know, and that is: we have seen what appears to be a spirit or phantom horse, and that is what I believe came to our wedding."

"So, do you believe this so-called phantom horse to be good or evil?"

"The horse that Gay disappeared on was a phantom or spirit horse, but the one that came to our wedding was different. I believe, it might have been my old friend, Great Thunder, but as you witnessed yourself, it was invisible, so I don't know for sure. But I don't think the horse that came to my wedding was evil, I believe it to be good."

"Is that so, Kingsley? Is that so.

I wanted to shout at David and tell him off, and certainly back up what Melody and I had seen. But just as Mrs. Pretty, the school counsellor, could not believe or understand what I was saying, neither could I expect David to. So, I just tried to reassure him that Ffion and I were not involved in anything that we shouldn't be involved in, and that what had happened at the wedding was something we did not understand.

"I hope so Kingsley," David answered. "Otherwise, we cannot have you teaching and ministering at the church."

I went home to Ffion quite upset and told her what David had said. Ffion encouraged me and said that I did the right thing in assuming that David could not understand, or even be open to what was going on with the phantom horse. Over the next few days, David did not say anything more, and things began to calm down at work.

Friday evening arrived, and Jonathan and Benjamin got back from their trip to Stonehenge and exploring the Salisbury Plain.

"It was fantastic, Dad," they said, bursting through the door. "Look! We found Roman coins and an old spearhead, which Grandpa thinks is from the Iron Age!"

"And I found part of a warrior's shield," Benjamin said, grinning from cheek to cheek.

"We all had a great time!" both Dad and Mary said, "and Stonehenge was magnificent!"

Ffion made some hot chocolate, and we sat in front of the fire and heard all about their expeditions. They had explored for miles on the Salisbury Plain, having learned how to use Dad's metal detectors, and then watched the sunset at Stonehenge. I felt happy as I heard Jonathan and Benjamin talk so excitedly about their adventures. Archaeology and metal detecting must run in the family, I thought.

Dad now talked a bit about the history of Stonehenge, and he was, as always, an encyclopedia of knowledge.

More than any other prehistoric site in western Europe, Stonehenge symbolizes the skill and ingenuity of prehistoric man. Dad and Mary had taken the boys to see Stonehenge early in the morning, and they had approached it from a northeast direction, so the great circle of stones rises ahead on the horizon and it looks grey and stark.

"It felt like we were creeping up on a lost civilization," Jonathan explained, "and we expected to see the ancient people come out to meet us at any time!"

"And we went in the evening too," Ben shared, just as excited as his brother. "The evening approach was even more spectacular! The sun was setting in the west behind the stones, and they illuminated orange and gold, like a lost city made of stone."

Ffion and I looked at each other, wishing we had seen it too. This was all so exciting!

Dad now explained the significance of the stones and how to approach them.

"On entering the enclosure, first walk around and circle the monument, and make for the Heel Stone, which is an isolated block of unshapen sarsen [hard sandstone] that rises 4.9 meters. This stone once had a partner on its western side, which was moved early in the site's history. These were probably the first stones erected. Then, with your back to the Heel Stone, face the main group of stones. You will notice a ditch and an internal bank that runs all round Stonehenge. When half of the circumference of the ditch was excavated in the early 1920's, it was found to be very irregular. Chalk was quarried from it, and was piled up to make the bank, which originally stood about 1.8 meters high. This is broken by an entrance gap on the north-east, opposite the Heel Stone, where two smaller stones once stood. One of them is known as the Slaughter Stone, which lies on the left, just inside the enclosure. Excavations between the north-east entrance gap and the Heel Stone have revealed a great number of stake holes that seem to mark many annual observations of northerly moonrise, together with the holes for five or six larger posts that marked the main stages in a nineteen-year lunar cycle. Just inside the bank is a ring of 56 evenly spaced Aubrey Holes, marked by white chalk. These pits vary from 0.6 to 1.2 meters deep and may originally have been dug to hold small stones or posts. Later, some of them were used as containers for cremation burials. It is quite likely that there was a ring of posts or a hut at the center of the monument, but hundreds of years of digging by treasure hunters has destroyed the most reliable information. All these features formed the First Stonehenge and can be dated between **3200** and **2500** B.C."

We were impressed as we listened to Dad recall from memory, and from his many expeditions exploring Stonehenge, his extensive understanding of its origin, design and history.

We all talked until about midnight, and then the girls headed off to bed. Dad and Mary were too tired to drive back to Swansea this late, so they decided to stay overnight. As the boys and I continued to talk with Dad, he shared the story of how he and I had buried some of the rare artifacts we had found in the back garden of where we used to live on Browns Drive here in Pennard.

"Are the artifacts still there?" the boys asked, still wide-eyed and bushy tailed.

"Yes," Dad replied, equally as excited as they were. "We buried some rare swords and daggers, and a bag of coins, didn't we, Kings, if I remember right?"

"Yes, we did, Dad, and I remember it like yesterday. I remember the police coming to the door and confiscating some of the artifacts that we had found. But we buried the good stuff in the back garden."

And just then, as I listened to what I was saying to my own sons, a desire was reborn within me, and I knew that I had to go and dig up our lost treasure.

"Let's go and dig it up," I said with deep conviction. "Those artifacts are ours, Dad! Part of our family heritage!"

At my words, a broad smile grew across my father's face, and I'd seen that look before, only not for a long time. And the look said, 'let's do it!' The boys looked back and forth at one another, and they were all in! All we needed to do now was plan it.

We put some more wood on the fire and began to plan.

"Now, you must realize, boys, that this is a risky business digging a hole in someone's back garden."

"Yes, Grandpa," the boys said, nodding their heads, and Jonathan looked across at me.

"How are we going to do this, Dad?"

"We are going to have to plan it very carefully, and we cannot get caught!" I said.

"We won't," Ben said, full of enthusiasm. "We can outrun anyone, and we can wear masks, so no one recognizes us."

Dad now looked across at me with a rather nervous look. And I had seen that look before too. And it translated into: "Are you serious about this? Are we really going to do this?"

And in my heart, the answer was a resounding 'yes'! It would be a fantastic adventure for the boys, re-capturing what was rightfully ours, and seeing the artifacts that Dad and I had found when I was a boy.

Just then, Ffion came into the room and asked, "Is everything alright? You boys are up late chatting tonight."

Her entry into the room had stopped our conversation in its tracks, and she quickly got the message that this was a boy's talk. "Goodnight," she said. "I look forward to seeing you all in the morning."

"We can't tell anyone about this," Dad stressed. "We could get in serious trouble if we get caught, and I am too old to be climbing over barbed wire fences and running away from perfect strangers."

He said it in a humorous way, but I knew he was serious. "No, we will do the hard work," I reassured him. "If you can drive the getaway car, the boys and I will do the rest."

"Yes!" the boys echoed, grinning like Cheshire cats. There was no turning back now.

We decided to go to the Plow and Harrow tomorrow night and plan our dastardly deed. There were too many ears here at the house, and we did not want any of the girls to know about it.

In the morning, Dad told Ffion and Mary that he was taking us boys to the pub for a meal in the evening. "I want to discuss some metal detecting," he said.

Mary said she wanted to take Samantha and Melody for a walk along Swansea Bay while us boys were at the pub. But as she was talking, Mary glanced across at me and gave me a discerning look, which said, 'I can smell a rat! I know you boys are up to no good!'

But regardless of Mary's insightful look, we were going to the pub, and I was looking forward to it.

The boys and I met Dad at the Plough and Harrow as planned. Old John Wheel was sitting at his table as usual, and after we had bought our drinks, Dad went over to talk to him.

"Does Grandpa know Old John?" Benjamin asked.

"Yes, they used to work together in Forestry," I replied, "and Grandpa told me that Old John was as strong as ten men when he was younger. He could cut a six-foot-wide tree trunk down, with a hand saw."

Jonathan looked him up and down and said, "Maybe he was as strong as five men, Dad, not ten."

"Anyway, he was very strong," I said, smiling.

Dad returned to our table and said to the boys, "No scrumpy cider tonight…" The boys laughed and said "No, that cider was so strong!"

"Well, let's plan this job of ours, shall we," Dad said.

So, with a beer in one hand and enthusiasm in the other, we planned our course to retrieve our treasure.

Dad would drive the getaway car and he would park on the road on the other side of the field, which was behind our old house. Jonathan, Ben and I would enter the backyard of number 23 from the field. That way, as soon as we were over the fence, we would already be in the backyard where the treasure was buried.

One of the things that we needed to remember was that all the houses on our old street are semi-detached, so even if we are not seen by the owner of the house, a neighbor could easily see us, if we are not careful. When we were kids, my brother Fraser and I used to go "Nobby Knocking," which is knocking on someone's door and then running away. Sometimes, if people's fences were low enough, we would run from one garden to the next, knocking on several doors. Then we would usually have two or three people running after us, which was a real rush! It was very much like a human steeplechase, jumping over fences until you crashed into one and you were caught to face the music.

It is different when you are in your fifties, however, and I did not want a chase on my hands while we were doing this particular job.

"You boys can run all day," I said, "but if push comes to shove, I have one good sprint to get away and that's it!"

Jonathan and Ben teased me: "Come on, old man!"

Dad drank his beer and seemed quite amused at our family debate.

"Right, let's get back to planning," he said, looking at me with that famous twinkle in his eye. "Now, every good robbery, I mean 'artifacts retrieval', needs to have a code name. How about 'Operation Brown 23'?"

"That's great, Dad," I said, "considering we used to live at number 23 Browns Drive."

"What about code name 'Artifacts Retrieval 23'?" Jonathan suggested with a big grin.

"How about ' Artifacts 23'?" Ben asked.

"Let's take a vote," Dad said. And we voted 3-to-1 in favor of 'Artifacts Retrieval 23'. The waitress came and asked if we wanted another drink, and we all ordered the same again, a pint of Speckled Hen, please. As she went to get our drinks, Dad said he was going back over to talk to Old John Wheel.

"I am going to ask him if he knows who lives in number 23 now – John might know."

And to the boys and my surprise, he did!

"How did he know, Dad? What were the chances of that?"

"The Gower is a close community," Dad answered, "and most of the old boys keep up with the news of who is moving in and out of different areas and houses. Now I have an idea…" Dad continued, "tell me what you think of this….According to Old John, the owners of the house are a retired couple, called Mr. and Mrs. Kent. Kings, why don't you knock on their door and explain that this was your childhood home, and that you have been away in Canada for 25 years. And ask them if you could see the house again and walk around the garden for memory's sake. That way you can check things out, see what sort of people they are, and then most importantly, check if the silver birch tree is still in the back garden. If it is, the artifacts are buried three feet beside it, on its right side as you are facing the tree looking out to the back field. If the tree is not there anymore, then you will need the metal detector to locate the artifacts."

"A great idea," we all agreed. I would go and knock Mr. and Mrs. Kent's door tomorrow evening and check things out.

We all enjoyed a nice evening at the pub, and the following evening, as planned, I went to talk to Mr. and Mrs. Kent.

The boys drove me out to number 23 and waited in the car while I rang the doorbell. We would phone Dad later and let him know how things went.

Things worked out far better than I had anticipated, and Mr. and Mrs. Kent were indeed nice people, and they invited me into the house. They showed me around, and I visited all the old familiar rooms on the ground floor that had once been a part of my everyday life. It was very much the way I remembered it, but what was amazing was that Mr. Kent, or Victor, as he asked me to call him, is a model railway enthusiast. And I told him about all the hours my father and brother and I had spent building and playing with our model railway layout in the attic.

"It was a wonderful surprise to find a full-scale model railway set-up already built in the attic," Victor said. "And your father built it?!"

"Yes!" I said proudly. "And I cannot tell you how many hours my brother and I spent enjoying the trains up there."

Victor excitedly told his wife about our railway connection, and they invited me to come and have tea with them next Friday evening. "That way you can see the garden," he said, "and I will show you what I have done with the layout in the attic."

As I returned to the boys who were still waiting in the car, I could hardly believe what had just happened! And I told the boys all about it.

⌒

When I got home, I called Dad immediately to tell him the good news! And I told him that Mr. and Mrs. Kent were a wonderful, kind couple. And both Dad and I felt guilty that we were planning to dig a hole in their back garden. "I think we need to call off our plan, Dad said. "Your visit with Mr. and Mrs. Kent has shown us the way to get our artifacts back!"

"How?" I replied, feeling disappointed.

"We will simply ask them if we can retrieve them from their back yard. I would put money down on them saying yes, given that they are a nice couple. And I think you would regret digging up their garden behind their backs, Kings."

"But what about having an adventure with the boys?!" I protested.

Dad, upon seeing my disappointment, and understanding that I wanted to do it to have an adventure with my boys, reluctantly agreed to carry on with our plans.

There was no turning back now, I told myself. Next Friday evening I would be inside number 23 Browns Drive, keeping Mr. and Mrs. Kent occupied while the boys dug up the artifacts, and Dad waited in the getaway car on the other side of the field! My conscience, however, was disagreeing with me, but I told it to go away!

"How are we going to know if the birch tree is still in the back garden?" Jonathan asked. "Shall we bring the metal detector in case it has been cut down?"

"Yes, great idea!" both Dad and I agreed, "That way, we can dig either way."

So, it was all planned for next Friday evening. Ladies and Gentlemen, I bring to you, operation code name "Artifacts Retrieval 23."

Next Friday could not come quick enough, and on Thursday evening, we went over our plan carefully.

Ben had bought two black balaclavas in the Swansea Market for him and Jonathan to wear. Dad had the car ready with the shovels and metal detector already in the boot, and Mary was none the wiser.

"After we have retrieved the artifacts, we will go over to your house, Kings, as the girls will have gone to Bristol for the weekend. This will give us time to inspect our treasures and decide what we are going to do with them."

"Aren't you going to keep them?" both Jonathan and Ben asked.

"It's not as easy as putting them on a shelf or a wall," Dad explained. "These artifacts are extremely rare, and they are very sought after by museums and collectors. I would like to keep some of them at my antique shop in Cardiff, and maybe sell one or two of them. But one must be careful, so as not to alert the authorities that artifacts are being collected or sold."

After our planning session, we all felt ready for tomorrow evening. Dad would meet us at our house at 6:30 and drop me off at the Kent's for 7:00 p.m.

"Bye, Dad, see you tomorrow."

"Bye, Kings, see you and the boys tomorrow, and remember – not a word to anyone."

When the boys and I arrived home in Pennard, the phone rang just as we were coming in the door, and it was Dad, who wanted to talk to me privately.

What could he want? I thought. We had just been together less than half an hour ago. I told the boys to go into the living room as I needed to talk to Dad alone.

"What is it, Dad?" "Is everything alright?"

"Not really, Old Son. My conscience is bothering me regarding our plans, and what we would be teaching the boys! Mr. and Mrs. Kent are obviously nice people, and I think we are going about this all wrong! I think if we go through with this, we will regret it, If not now, then in the future. You want to be a good role model for your boys, and I can see how they look up to you and idolize you. I know that you want to give them a fun and adventurous time while they are here, but you are already doing that. And you don't want to be teaching them anything that is out of integrity. They are wonderful boys, and fatherhood has given you a wonderful gift and a responsibility. Dad's words spoke to my heart, and I knew that he was right.

"I will tell the boys how you and I feel, Dad, and we will call things off. But of course, I would like the opportunity to get our artifacts back because they are part of our family heritage."

"I think there is a lesson for you to teach the boys in this, Kings. And what do you think the lesson is?"

"It's a lesson about not getting carried away with something that is not right, Dad."

"That is right, Son, and this is what I think you should do. Go and have supper with Mr. and Mrs. Kent, tomorrow night, as planned, and tell them about our family artifacts. Then ask them if they would allow you and your boys to dig up the artifacts in their back garden. They can only say yes or no, and from what you have told me about them, it is likely that they would agree to your request."

"You are right, Dad. I will ask them when I see them tomorrow night, and as soon as I get off the phone, I will go and talk with the boys."

"Well done, Kings, I'm proud of you. Now hang up the phone and go and talk to Jonathan and Ben."

"Okay, Dad, I will, and I will let you know how it goes tomorrow evening."

"Okay, Kings, bye for now."

"Bye Dad."

After speaking with Dad, I went and talked with my boys, and they were supportive of my decision. Ben even told me that he was relived we had changed course because he had felt that it was wrong. And the three of us had a wonderful conversation about various times in our lives when we had gotten carried away with things that we knew were wrong, and then afterwards were sorry we had done them.

"We are having a great time already Dad, and that time we had with the cows chasing us across the field is something we will never forget, we feel like we have lived part of your boyhood with you, Dad!" And we all had a good laugh and did not harm any one's property.

"I have decided to still go and have supper with Mr. and Mrs. Kent, tomorrow night," I continued, "and I am going to ask them if the three of us can go and see if we can find the artifacts in their back yard."

"Great Idea, Dad," they both said excitedly, "maybe they will let us, and we can still dig."

"I hope so I said, but it is getting late, I am off to bed, I will see you boy's tomorrow."

Chapter Seventeen

A Visit to the Kent's

Friday afternoon arrived, and Samantha and Melody arrived home from school. "Quick girls," Ffion said, "get your suitcases into the car. I want to get to Bristol before dark, and we are picking up Helen in Cardiff on our way."

And with a hug and kiss from each of my girls, they were on their way to visit Aunt Pearl. Meanwhile, the boys and I hung out at the house until it was time for me to go over to the Kent's for supper. I made tea for the boys, and then headed over to the Kent's.

"Don't get distracted by trains and forget to tell them about the artifacts," Jonathan shouted as I was pulling away, "and offer them a reward if they let us dig them up!" Ben shouted.

"I will," I shouted back, and I was on my way.

I arrived at the Kent's at 6:50 and rang the doorbell. Mrs. Kent arrived at the door with a barking dog behind her. That would have complicated things, I thought, if we had continued with our original plan. We had not anticipated a dog being in the house.

"I didn't know you had a dog," I said, trying to be friendly to the yappy little thing. Mrs. Kent led me into the living room.

"He is not our dog," she explained. "He belongs to my sister, who has gone away for a week. I hope you don't mind dogs?"

"No," I replied, lying through my teeth, "I like dogs."

'Hello boy, you little shit!' No, I didn't say that of course – I just thought about it, as I don't like yappy little ankle biters. Maybe he wasn't an ankle biter. I would have to wait and see about that. "Hello. Kingsley," Mr. Kent said. "It's good to see you again. Please sit down."

As I sat on the settee, I glanced out of the window to see if I could see the old silver birch tree. That is where dad and I buried the artifacts all those years ago. It was still there! Good, that would make it easy to locate our treasure if Mr. and Mrs. Kent agree to us digging it up in their garden.

"So, tell me, Kingsley, when did you first become interested in model railroading?"

"As long ago as I can remember, Victor. My father got me started when I was just a young boy."

"Well, it is a great hobby to have."

"How long will tea be, Adel?" Victor asked his wife.

"About half an hour," she replied.

Victor then asked me if I would like to see his railway layout in the attic. "Yes," I said excitedly!

As Victor and I climbed the familiar stairs up to the second-floor landing, I was being bombarded by memories of my childhood, and I wondered if the same old aluminum steps came down to the floor when the attic door was opened. And they did! And I just stood there watching as the years melted away instantaneously.

"Everything alright?" Victor asked.

"Yes, I'm just back in yesteryear – you still have the same old aluminum steps."

"Yes, I have never had to replace them."

As I looked down the hall, there was a doorway to the right. "That's my bedroom," I said. "I mean that used to be my bedroom."

"Would you like to see it, before we go up into the attic?"

"Oh, yes please," I said. "I lived in this house until I was 15 and a half years old." And as Victor led me into my old room, I became quite emotional. This was my room! The place where I had laughed and cried, slept and dreamed, and ran to when my world outside became too cold or harsh to bare.

And I had kissed my first girl, Elaine Thomas, in this room.

"I used to have a bunk bed in here," I said proudly. "My brother used to sleep on the top bunk, and I had the bottom one. We shared this room until I was 12 years old."

Victor looked at me almost sympathetically as he listened to my story.

"Let's go and look at your layout," I said, as I tried to get hold of my emotions. But I couldn't! And I wept openly as I saw the matchstick bridge that my father and I had made when I was a boy. And the tunnels and the station were still there too.

"You still have the bridge and the tunnels!" I exclaimed.

"Oh yes," Victor said, "they are so well made, and they look fantastic. I would never get rid of them."

As Victor talked about his trains and the various track layouts that he had built, I scarcely heard what he was saying. I was fully occupied conversing with my memories, and even talking out loud.

"What was that you said?" Victor asked.

"Oh, I was just saying what a great job you have done on the mountains and trees."

Although looking at them more closely, it seemed that they had not been touched since Dad and I had put them there. They were my dad's wonderful creations that Vince was taking credit for. And in these few minutes, in which lifetimes seemed to pass, I was reminded of what a wonderful father I had – and still have! A father who always spent time with his children, and who helped them to discover and build things. What a wonderful gift! Thank you, Dad, for what you gave me – I love you! Just then we heard Adel calling that dinner was ready, and we climbed back down the aluminum stairs to the landing. "Thanks for showing me the layout," I said, and we went back downstairs to the dining room.

"Come and sit down, you two," she said. "We don't want the dinner to get cold."

Adel had gone out of her way to make a lovely roast beef dinner with Yorkshire pudding and roast potatoes, and carrots and peas. And as we sat eating and talking together, I felt comfortable about asking them about the artifacts. "There is something I want to ask you, Mr. and Mrs. Kent."

"Oh, please call us Victor and Adel," they said together, smiling. "In fact, just call Victor, Vic, like all his friends do, now that we know you a little better there is no need for formality."

"I will," I said. "Thank you."

"I would like to ask both of you something," I continued. "When I was a boy, my father and I often went metal detecting together. In fact, we still do. It is a hobby for our whole family, and we love searching for artifacts from bygone days. "It sounds like fun!" said Vic with a smile.

"It is," I replied. "It's fun for all ages."

"Anyway, one day when I was eight or nine years old, my dad and I went treasure hunting, and we found some artifacts. And later we buried the treasures we had found in what is now your back garden, near the birch tree. And as far as we know, the artifacts are still there. We forgot about them for years and I had meanwhile moved away to Canada. Then a while ago, when I was still living in Canada, I thought that one day I would like to see if the artifacts were still there, and that it would be great to find them, because they are a family heirloom for my daughter and two sons who have recently come out from Canada. So, I want to ask you if my boys and I could come here and see if we could find the artifacts? I would make sure that we did not disturb the garden any more than we needed to, and I would certainly repair or replace anything that might be damaged, though of course we would be very careful."

Vic and Adel looked back and forth at one another, and then Vic said, "What do you think, Adel, if Kingsley and his sons dug in the back garden near the old birch tree?"

"It would be fine with me," Adel said, smiling at me.

Vic then stood up and looked out the window at his back garden. "How far from to the tree do you need to dig?" he asked. "I think the site is about three or four feet from the trunk of the tree," I replied, "and we have a metal detector to locate the artifacts."

"There is only a rough weedy lawn around the tree," Vic replied, "and if you put sod back over the hole, once you have finished, then I'm sure it would be alright."

"Oh, thank you!" I said excitedly. "It would be such a blessing for my family and me!"

Vic and Adel, seeing my excitement, smiled at one another, and then Vic asked when we would like to come and dig – and could he and Adel watch the treasure hunt?

"Of course you can watch!" I said, "and we can come anytime that is convenient for you."

"How about tomorrow night?" Vince suggested. "I don't think we have any plans tomorrow evening, do we Adel?"

"No, we don't. Tomorrow would be fine," she said, "and I'm looking forward to it."

"Thank you!" I replied happily. And I heard my dad's word's echoing in my heart. And I felt so glad that I had asked, and not gone ahead with our original plans!

"This is wonderful food!" I said, smelling the gravy as Adel poured it onto my Yorkshire pudding. "What a lovely supper!"

"I'm glad you're enjoying it, Kingsley," Adel replied. "Now, would you men like seconds?"

"Yes, please," both Vic and I said together. Once we had finished eating the delicious dinner, Adel said: "Can you eat a dessert, Kingsley, or are you too full?"

"Oh, I always have an extra tank for dessert!," I said, and both she and Vic laughed.

"Vic is the same, aren't you, my dear?"

Vic smiled and he winked at me. "Yes," he answered. "I like my dessert, just like Kingsley."

And as we sat and ate our dessert of rhubarb and custard, I celebrated in my heart, the two new friends I had made – in Victor and Adel.

Once we had finished our supper, the three of us sat in the living room and talked some more. They were interested in my life in Canada and the work I had done as a youth pastor. The three of us got on so well, and it was almost 9 p.m. when I left.

"We will see you tomorrow," they both said, as we stood at the door, "and don't forget to bring your boys. We look forward to meeting them. So, we will see you all about 6:00 p.pm."

"Thank you," I said, "and thanks for the lovely supper, Adel. And for showing me your model railway, Vic."

"You are welcome, Kingsley, see you tomorrow."

As soon as I got home, I told the boys the exciting news. "That is great!" they said. "We can go and dig up the artifacts tomorrow night! And we won't have to worry about getting in trouble!"

I laughed and I said, "Yes, and I think we have all learned a lesson from this!"

Meanwhile, Dad was excited that the boys and I could inspect the artifacts together as a right of passage into our heritage. "Now that they have agreed, I don't have to drive the getaway car and you can just come back to my place once you have the artifacts and we can examine them here."

"Thanks Dad, we will see you later tomorrow night."

"The boys and I stayed up until midnight. I told them stories about Dad's and my adventures metal detecting, and the things we had found. We slept in on Saturday morning and had breakfast across the road at the Heather Slade Café, as we felt too lazy to make breakfast. It was a great day for us boys to just hang out at home, as Ffion and the girls would not be home until tomorrow evening. Ffion rang mid-morning to see how we were doing, and it sounded like they were all having a fun girl's weekend in Bristol with Pearl.

In the afternoon, the boys and I went swimming at Pobbles Beach, and the sea felt wonderful. We had caught the tide about two hours before the high, and the breakers were rolling into the cove at the top of the bay. Several times we each caught a large breaker, and it was such a rush to feel like part of a crashing wave as we bodysurfed up the beach. The sun was hot up in the dunes, and we warmed up in the sand and watched the bikinis go by.

"What are you looking at, Dad?" the boys asked, laughing. And I replied, "What are *you* looking at?! And it was time to make a truce as we were suddenly surrounded by about 15 high school girls, as well as two mothers, who looked at me as if to say, "What are you looking at?" The boys and I had our tea at the café on our way home from Pobbles, and then we went home to change. We managed to find Melody's metal detector, which we took with us to the Kent's in order to find our treasure.

When we arrived, Mr. and Mrs. Kent gave the boys and I a good welcome, and we all felt comfortable right away! Adel had even made us sandwiches and then a nice apple pie and ice cream for dessert.

"I didn't know we were coming for supper," Jonathan said, enjoying his pie and ice cream. "This is delicious!"

"I am glad you like it," Victor said laughing, and we all had a second helping of pie. Then we headed into the back garden, and we took our measurements around the birch tree.

Dad had drawn us a map as to where to start looking, and Benjamin showed Mrs. Kent how to use the metal detector.

"This is fun!" she said, as he showed her what all the different beeps meant, and how to swing the detector from side to side over the ground. Then it was Vic's turn, and the beeper sounded loudly!

You must be right over it!" Jonathan said excitedly. And he and I began to dig. Fortunately, where we were digging was not part of the nice lawn. Rather, it was rough and sandy, and Vic said he did not mind us digging there at all.

Jonathan and I dug for about twenty minutes, and we were down about four feet!

"It has to be here somewhere!" I said, as everyone stared into the hole. "Run the detector over the top again," I said, and Ben turned it on and held it over the hole. It beeped loudly, and Ben said that it must be just another few inches – and it was!

There were two potato sacks with plastic wrapping taped around them to keep the moisture out, and the boys and I lifted them out of the hole and lay them on the lawn. The boys wanted to open the sacks right away, but I insisted that we shovel the earth back into the hole first, and smooth it out as best we could. And we did a good job of filling in the hole, according to Vic and Adel. If fact It looked better than when we started and Vic said to just leave the area and he could reseed it and a thank you for getting rid of the weeds! I did not feel like opening the sacks until we got them back to Dad's place, as planned, but I felt obligated to open at least one of the sacks to show Vic and Adel what was inside. So, I did.

Adel went into the kitchen and got a pair of scissors so

we could cut the plastic wrap that was over the sackcloth, and I pulled one of the artifacts out.

"It's a bag of coins!" I said, pouring them out onto the lawn.

"They're Roman coins!" both Jonathan and Benjamin exclaimed! And Vic and Adel were fascinated. We sat on the lawn and inspected them for almost half an hour, and then we said it was time to go, because Dad was waiting for us in Swansea. I felt a bit awkward not bringing anything else out for Vic and Adel to see, but they seemed to understand that this was a family activity that we wanted to do at home. And I gave them a Roman coin each before we left to thank them for allowing us to dig in their garden and retrieve our long-lost treasure. And after saying thank you and goodbye, we drove to Dad's house in Swansea.

The boys carried a sack of artifacts each, and one was bigger and heavier than the other.

"This one probably has a sword in it," Johnathan said, holding it up against the other. And we rang the doorbell.

"Come in!" Dad shouted from upstairs, "Come and show me what you've got!" Mary ushered us into the living room, where Dad was waiting with his eye glass to inspect our long-lost treasure.

"Okay, let's get the artifacts on the table and have a look, shall we," said Dad. And we cut open the sack and spread everything out on the table.

There were swords, a helmet, numerous pieces of jewelry and body attire, and several axes.

"Ah, I often wondered what had happened to these," Dad said, as he picked up an axe. "These are Bronze Age axes that I found up on Cefn Bryn. Bronze tools and weapons are found all over the country, and axes are likely the most common tool. Axes follow a dated sequence, starting with a flat type in the early Bronze Age that was hafted on the right-angled stick, split to embrace the axe, and bound with string. This developed flanges along the sides, so one could grip the haft more firmly."

"This one is a flat type," he said, and we each handled it as we passed it around the table. As I felt the axe in my hand, I imagined the person who had used it, and I thought of the Cave Family that lived in Bacon Hole. For me, holding an artifact in my hand is such a rush, and it gives me an instant desire to travel back in time and discover the history of the artifact. Gay's birthmother, Armes, claims that she can read an artifacts origin and history just by holding it in her hand. When she had made this claim, I had dismissed it as far-fetched, and not taken her seriously.

I would settle for a dig, I thought, as I ran my fingers over the blunt edge of the axe face.

"Careful, Kings," Dad said. "It might be sharper than you think." And I remembered a time when I had cut my hand rubbing the edge of a sword we had found, and Dad had to bind my hand with his scarf.

"The other axe is from the middle Bronze Age," Dad said, and we handed it around the table. "Look at the flanges along the side, different than the ones from the early Bronze Age." I held the axe in my hands and rolled it around, getting a feel for its weight and design. The defining characteristic on this middle Bronze Age axe was the 'palstav' the addition of a stop-ridge between the flanges to prevent the haft driving down too far and splitting.

"How much are these axes worth?" Ben asked.

"It depends on what you regard as worth," Dad answered.

"As far as money goes, a collector might pay anything from a few hundred to a few thousand pounds, depending on his or her particular interest."

"We could make some serious cash," Jonathan said.

"Indeed, we could," Dad said, "but the true value is the experience of them! Hearing the beeper go off on your metal detector, and kneeling to inspect the ground, and then starting to dig with your shovel or trowel. You never know what you are going to find! Is it a sword or a dagger? Maybe even a helmet or a shield from a warrior? A bag of coins, or a spearhead?"

At Dad's word's, we all got more excited!

"By the late Bronze Age, this type of axe had become a sturdy tool," Dad continued, "with a loop on one side of the stop-ridge, to attach a cord to for even better firmness."

As I looked at the expressions on my boys faces, I could see that they were enthralled by what they were learning. What a great heritage they were being given by my father! Archaeology can be a lifelong pursuit, and I know it has given me many hours of wondrous pleasure. And now my boys were starting their journeys of discovery.

"In the late Bronze Age, there were new types of axes introduced," Dad said. "For example, the Winged axe, in which the flanges were folded over as wings to grasp the haft; and the Socketed axe, where the whole axe was now a hollow container for a solid haft, tied to the head by a cord through the loop."

The boys were clearly as interested as I was, as Dad continued to share his knowledge with us.

There were also two daggers that Dad and I had found, and they were still in good condition. Dad had buried all the metal artifacts with a layer of grease and then wrapped them in cloth. Then they were put in three layers of sackcloth, and further wrapped in a plastic cling wrap to keep away the moisture. There were also two swords that were wrapped individually, and as the boys unwrapped one each, fond memories walked through the pages of my mind, as I recalled Dad and I metal detecting up on Rhossili Downs.

"Do you remember the day we found these two swords, Kings?" he asked, with tears in his eyes. "You were only eight years old. And when I showed you how to hold a sword, you swung one around and pretended to kill pirates."

"Yes, I remember that, Dad!" I said excitedly. "Do you remember, boys, when I told you that story?"

"Yeah, we remember," they both said, standing up and swinging the swords.

This is fantastic! I thought. My boys are getting to experience the very same artifacts that I did!

Once the boys had put down the swords, Dad explained what type they were. They were both from the mid to late Bronze Age, and they had long chaps of metal to protect the ends of the scabbards.

"This one is a leaf-shape type, made in the late Bronze Age," He said . He lifted it out of Ben's hands and waved it around the room. "This one widens out towards the end of the blade, and it has a tongue in one piece with the blade, to which a plate of bone has been fastened as a grip."

"What bone is it?" I asked, as I inspected it and then swung it around. Dad was unsure as to what animal the bone came from, but he was able to describe the different types of jewelry and their symbolism in great detail.

We spent over two hours inspecting our finds, or should I

say 'our retrieval' and I could see that a keen interest in archaeology had been born in both my boys over these last few weeks. They had heard my stories back in Canada, and now they had lived out adventures of their own in my beloved Britain.

We ended the evening by cleaning and identifying the various coins that Dad and the boys had found on the Salisbury Plain. We compared them with the bag of coins that we had retrieved from the Kent's Garden, and we all agreed that we could not put a price on these coins – they were priceless! Found by three generations of Hills! The boys were given several coins each to take back to Canada, and the rest of the artifacts we would take to Dad's antique store in Cardiff. Not to sell them, but to keep them safe.

Dad also suggested that we invite Mr. and Mrs. Kent over for supper at his place to thank them for their kindness. "Then they can see and share in the excitement of the artifacts, and Mr. Kent and I can talk about my old railway that I built in the attic." "A great Idea," we all said! And we invited Mr. and Mrs. Kent over to Dad's place the following Saturday evening.

Mary and Ffion made a lovely roast dinner, and Dad and I and the boys laid out all the artifacts that we had retrieved from the garden on the living room table. We all enjoyed a lovely supper, and then we retired to the living room to show Vic and Adel the artifacts. "We can see how important they are to you," they said. Dad and I told them about what we knew of the history of each item, and the boys passed them around the table so that the Kent's could hold them.

"This is such a wonderful experience for us," they both shared, as Vic held my old Viking sword in his hand, and Jonathan taught him how to swing it. Adel loved the jewelry that we had found, and especially an ancient Celtic necklace, and arm band, which had a picture engraved on the silver.

Dad also showed Vic his collection of steam locomotives which he had built from kits, around the same time as he had built the layout in the attic of the Kent's home. Vic and Dad got on like they were long lost friends, and Mary and Adel talked about Mary's collection of antique tea sets, as Adel had a collection herself. And I think we all learned something that evening. That life is meant to share! And especially our treasures!

"If we keep them to ourselves," Jonathan said, "then they are only alive to us. But if we share them with others, then they become even more valuable than just what they are worth in money, or something that came from the past."

"The past comes alive again when you share it," Benjamin said, "and we all share in that life as family and friends!" And that is what we did with our new friends, Vic and Adel, we shared life and heritage together!

⌘

Two weeks later, the boys returned to their university programs in Canada, and Ffion, Samantha, Melody and I got back to our usual routine of work and school. The boys had experienced such a wonderful time with us, and we looked forward to the next time when they would be able to take time off school and come back to Wales for more adventures.

♪❋

End of Part Four

www.ingramcontent.com/pod-product-compliance
Lightning Source LLC
Chambersburg PA
CBHW070052120726
47909CB00002B/368